MAST ISLAND

ANNE NICHOLS REYNOLDS

Copyright © Anne Nichols Reynolds, 2016

All rights reserved. Published by the Peppertree Press, LLC.
The Peppertree Press and associated logos are trademarks of
the Peppertree Press, LLC.

No part of this publication may be reproduced, stored in a retrieval system, transmitted in any form or by any means, electronic, mechanical, photocopying, recording, or otherwise, without prior written permission of the publisher and author/illustrator. Graphic design by Rebecca Barbier.

For information regarding permission,
call 941-922-2662 or contact us at our website:
www.peppertreepublishing.com or write to:
the Peppertree Press, LLC.
Attention: Publisher
1269 First Street, Suite 7
Sarasota, Florida 34236

ISBN: 978-1-61493-404-2

Library of Congress Number: 2015956275

Printed January 2016

DEDICATION

For Bill and Joyce Shriner, encouragers and fellow adventurers, who live life with passion. Whether serving your fellow man or the good of the community, you make a difference with your time, your smiles, and your support.

Over the decades, our families have enjoyed fun times together, canoeing, camping, traveling, marathons, running, lobstering, and making memories. Thank you for the uplifting fellowship, surprise trips, the laughs, and your love through joyful and tragic times. We are blessed to call you friends.

Also by Anne Nichols Reynolds—

Winter Harvest

A Will of Her Own

ACKNOWLEGMENTS

An author writing a novel relies on resources, written and oral, and life experiences to give the characters a rich and believable background. For me, fleshing out the characters and giving them life is the fun part of writing. When the reader becomes a participant in the lives you create, enjoys their stories, and learns something new, satisfaction is this author's reward. Thank you to my readers for your positive comments and eagerness for the next novel.

The writers of Avon Park Wordsmiths, a chapter of the Florida Writers Association, are truly writers helping writers. They encourage, give constructive critiques, and keep me accountable. Thank you for your positive feedback and your valuable suggestions. They make the finished product more powerful.

Thank you, my traveling companions and artist friends for the fun and laughter we've shared over the years. You have read parts of my novel to check for flow and consistency. A special thank you goes to Cathy Futral for her valuable comments and art expertise.

My deepest thanks go to all of the people who have enriched my life, shared my journey, and taught me life lessons. I have been blessed with a good family, a loving, supportive husband, children and grandchildren, special lifelong friends, and most importantly, a patient Lord.

Mast Island is a work of fiction, created in the author's mind. Any mistakes in this novel are the author's own.

CHAPTER ONE

Abigail Serena Parsons sat through the service numb with the shock of her grandmother's unexpected passing. The associate pastor, Cecil Baldwin, of Independence Methodist officiated. He spoke about a generous woman who gave her time and talents as a volunteer in the church and community.

Tears rolled down Abby's face at his words. Her grandmother, her friend, and sole relation was dead. The one who had changed her diapers, tied her shoelaces, took her to school every day, sewed her outfits, and made sure she received an education was gone. Snippets of her life rolled through Abby's mind like a film. If only she could rewind and go back to tell her gran how much she was loved and appreciated.

The last five years of Abby's life had been a roller coaster. Her mentor, Master Julian Tremayne, a retired professor of art from the Pennsylvania Academy of Fine Arts in Philadelphia, opened a school for gifted artists in his home. He restricted his registration to ten students over a four year period, and Abby was one of two females accepted. Julian Tremayne was an internationally renowned oil painter, whose art hung in museums around the world. He had been an exacting taskmaster. His tutelage in old masters traditional painting pushed Abby hard to develop the technical processes of the art.

Trained at the prestigious Royal Academy School of Arts in London, her mentor had no time for slackers, and he demanded one hundred percent from his students. Days and too many nights with little sleep kept Abby from visiting the woman who reared her.

Gran had not complained about her absence but encouraged her to follow her heart and to be the best in the field she had chosen. She took pride in Abby's successes and the awards she received in art show competitions. These awards and shows featuring A. S. Parsons added to a lengthy resume unusual for any artist of her age.

I'm sorry, Gran, for not being there for you. They lived in the same city, but Abby had been driven by her passion and her desire to succeed in a world dominated by men. They got together on special occasions, and Abby's guilt was compounded by the brief visits and the lack of meaningful exchanges and discussions.

Well-wishers came forward with their condolences before the service. Abby marveled at the number and diversity of her grandmother's friends and acquaintances.

Only a few people in Abby's new life were present. Mrs. Anthony, her landlady, sat beside her, patting her hand in support, making her feel less alone. The director and her assistant from Dove Creek Gallery, an art conservator from the Philadelphia Museum of Art, and a fellow student came.

Her grandmother's friends from the health department and church mixed with charity volunteers and the homeless as they filed forward to tell her what her gran had meant to them.

Mercifully, the service ended. Abby would accompany her gran on her final, earthly journey to the cemetery. She did not expect others to come out in the inclement weather. Tears fell like rain a she internalized her loss.

Abby pulled the *faux* fox collar tightly around her neck. The chill had more to do with her thoughts than the weather. She looked around to see if anyone watched her as she left the lawyer's office. Abby didn't know why she did it. She only knew a swelling panic and a metallic tasting fear had collided. Her life, as she knew it, shattered into a thousand shards of unidentified segments.

Naked trees lent a desolate, tragic air to the day. The gnarled limbs she had once enjoyed for their aesthetic beauty now appeared threatening and stark against the gunmetal sky. She filled her lungs with the crisp, cold air and released her breath quickly to dispel some of the tension building behind her eyes.

The park had always been her sanctuary, the womb that nourished her in good times and bad. She climbed many of these trees and read books in their leafy bowers, her hopes and dreams resting in the highest crannies she could reach. Nearby pines soughed in the wind. Their glossy needles once whispered encouragement. But now, the autumn death rattle of fallen oak and maple leaves rasped as they skidded across the asphalt to pile along its edge.

Abby struggled with the memories of the grandmother she had known and loved all her life and the person she had become in death, a stranger. Could a person maintain a life of deceit for twenty-seven years and not be moved to try and make amends? The letter written by her grandmother, Evelyn Marie Desmond, almost ten years ago and handed to her today by the executor, Mr. Mills, burned a hole in her heart.

She shook her head. *How long have I been looking at the pattern of tree limbs trying to make sense of my life?* Abby felt a creeping numbness spread throughout her body.

People hurried past, their heads down, oblivious to those nearby, forging onward to destinations unknown.

A man of ancient features and rheumy eyes saw her huddled in the corner of the bench. He was stooped, folded over in the middle and gripping a cane in an arthritic hand. The man stopped and glanced her way before muttering and shuffling onward.

I must look a mess, Abby thought, wiping the tears from windburned cheeks. She took a tissue from her pocket and noisily blew her nose.

It's not fair, God. I thought you loved me, wanted the best for me. Isn't it bad enough not to have parents? Now my grandmother isn't even related to me. Where are you when I need you?

A middle-aged woman passed not seeing or caring. Another couple followed, who must have been in their nineties. They held each other up as they made their way over to her.

"Are you all right, dear?" the woman asked sympathetically.

Abby nodded, not wanting company.

"May we rest here a few minutes?"

Abby nodded assent. *Guess this isn't my day.*

The man smiled benignly as he settled on the bench beside the woman.

Abby pulled her jacket taut, tucking herself securely in its shell. Only her eyes were visible behind the collar.

The man removed a glove and brought out a wrinkled paper bag from his coat pocket and dug around inside. He pulled out bread crusts and scattered them on the pavement, drawing several pigeons and a wary squirrel.

The woman clucked her tongue, chattering a secret language. The squirrel moved closer, ready to take off at the slightest provocation. He came within a foot of her shoe to get a morsel.

"Next week he'll be taking it from your hand, hon," the man told her in a gravelly voice.

The woman giggled delightedly like a pleased child.

He looked at her with eyes shining.

In that instant, Abby could see this couple was still very much in love. How rare a thing these days! Emotions welled unbidden as she wondered what it would be like to grow old with someone, to love someone so deeply it defied both time and circumstance. She had not met that special person yet, but there was still time. Abby knew she could never just settle. Her friends, most of whom had married, said she was too picky.

"Being single is not the worst thing that could happen to you," her grandmother had drilled into her. *No, Gran, you saved the worst for me to find out after you died.* The grandmother Abby thought she knew was not even a relation. Her first thought when the lawyer dropped the mantle of anonymity on her; *I've been abducted, kept from my family.* She didn't know who she was or where she came from.

Another squirrel joined the first, and for a few minutes, Abby was distracted by their antics.

The woman smiled and reminisced, "Those squirrels remind me of our sons, Benji and Robin. They were twins, always playing, teasing, or fighting each other." She turned toward Abby. "When they were taken from us, I thought I'd never be happy again. I can tell you from experience that happiness is a choice. I don't know what you're going through; it's none of my business. But I can see you're hurting, and I just want you to know; life goes on." She continued more forcefully, looking directly into Abby's eyes. "You have been given the precious gift of life. Only *you* can choose to live it."

Abby looked at the woman in amazement. *Does she read minds?*

"Well," the woman said, "come on, Henry, let's go home and start that fire. We've taken up enough of this young lady's time."

Henry's chin had rested on his gloved hands, holding the cane while she spoke, his silence and demeanor thoughtful. Now, he lifted his head, smiled, and said, "Em, you're a good woman. Whatever did I do to deserve you?"

"Why nothing, Henry, you just let me be myself and stayed with me in spite of it." She pushed herself off the bench, and taking Henry's arm, pulled him up beside her. She smiled back at him. "I sure was lucky the day you found me." They continued walking down the path, growing smaller and smaller until they were out of sight.

Abby realized she was gaping. She looked up and saw a spot of cerulean blue winking between parting clouds. This had to be a sign. *Choose to live life.* God's beauty surrounded her, and for half a day, she'd failed to notice. *Lord, how did I let myself become mired in self-pity?* That woman, Em, had suffered more than any woman should ever suffer in one lifetime. No one, not even the woman who had called herself "your grandmother" could steal her joy. She wouldn't let her.

Thank you, Lord. Abby wiped the tears and came off the bench with new purpose. She knew what she had to do.

Abby searched her grandmother's apartment for clues to her identity. The file cabinet gaped open, and papers lay strewn about her feet. She found folders with information she needed as the beneficiary but no photos or mention of her early life before her first birthday.

Mr. Mills, the executor, told Abby which government agencies and insurance companies would need to be contacted. He advised her to get multiple death certificates from the funeral home to corroborate her grandmother's death. Mr. Mills said he would put advertisements in the newspapers to announce the death to creditors.

Abby knew her grandmother didn't owe anyone money. She had paid her debts in cash. She didn't even have a credit card. Her gran didn't trust banks. The Social Security checks and a small pension she received from her years spent working in the local health department were cashed and the money hidden around the apartment.

Abby found cash in jacket pockets, in shoes, under sofa cushions, in books, and beneath her mattress. She found around nine hundred dollars and decided to search the apartment for more hiding places later. Most of her grandmother's cash paid off the car, which Abby now owned.

Her grandmother's important papers were not in a safety deposit box but in a cereal box bearing a note, "Save for Vacation Bible School." The insurance policy surprised Abby. She found her grandmother had been paying over the years for a policy worth a quarter of a million dollars, with Abby named as beneficiary. The attorney mentioned the policy in the list of assets, but she had not been listening. All she remembered were the words written about her non-relationship to the woman who reared her.

"Oh Gran, how could you do this to me?" Abby said aloud. She sat back on her heels and looked around the apartment, which had been her home for twenty-two years. Abby loved her life here and wanted for nothing, but her predicament left her desolate, her memories like dead ashes, belonging to someone else. She needed to get away after fulfilling her obligations. Should she rent the apartment or sell it? *Decide later.*

Her grandmother had shredded all correspondence. The only clutter, a pile of mail, mostly junk, she found on a table inside the door. The stuffed mailbox downstairs contained a note to pick up mail at the post office.

Notably missing from the paperwork was a birth certificate. Abby covered her face with her hands and massaged her temples. *How can I apply for a copy without knowing the details?* She had needed her birth certificate for school. *Where is it?*

She found one card in a book with a brief description of a painting Mary Adams had sold for seven hundred dollars to an ad agency. The name sounded familiar, and Abby remembered cards from her grandmother's mysterious friend, who lived in Towson, Maryland.

Abby found the address book and put it in her purse.

She returned to the bedroom. Everything had been neat, everything in place. The one extravagance, a fine sewing machine, was open with pattern pieces laid out to be sewn.

Abby smelled the sachet her grandmother hung in her closet and put into each dresser drawer. The lavender smell evoked memories of the woman she had loved and the stranger she had become.

Abby sat on the bed and reflected on her early life. *Who am I? How did you become my grandmother?* Her thoughts produced tears of longing, betrayal, and … fear.

Abby climbed the stairs to the entrance of the building where her small studio apartment had been home for the last five years. Her abode was in a decent, if not affluent, neighborhood of brownstones lined like sentinels along Philadelphia's Elm Street. She discovered the place after her first painting sold at Dove Creek Gallery. The gallery took most of her paintings now, and A.S. Parsons had become a recognized artist. The rent was not exorbitant, and Mrs. Anthony, her diligent landlady, kept an eye on things. Abby turned the key, entered the foyer, and crept up to the first landing.

Right on schedule, a door opened below, and a quivery voice drifted up the steps, a tentative call, "Hello?" A broad face topped with a profusion of bluish pin curls came into view.

Abby leaned over the railing to be seen. "It's me, Mrs. Anthony."

"Thought I heard someone. Thought I'd check. You have a package. I had to sign for it."

Abby retraced her steps.

Mrs. Anthony looked at her face as she handed over the small package. "What's wrong? Did that idiot, John, dump you?"

"No, Mrs. Anthony. I've had a rough day, and I'm not feeling well. And John is just a friend. I've told you that."

"Unh huh," she agreed without conviction. "He wants to be more if you'll let him," she said with a knowing wink and a nod. "Now you just go on up and take a nice, hot bath. And brew you some tea," she called out. "You'll feel better. I'll bring up some of my special pound cake when it comes out of the oven. It's even better when it's warm."

"Thanks, Mrs. Anthony. You're a gem," Abby replied, as she began her ascent, turning the box over in her hands. The label on the insured package said it was from a woman named Mina Kresge and postmarked in Baltimore. She didn't know a Mina Kresge from Baltimore or anywhere else. After putting the modified, skeleton key in the lock, she pulled on the door to open it, a tricky procedure.

The room greeted her with the latent smells of turpentine and linseed oil. Unused canvasses leaned against the walls, and a large easel stood by the window on a paint-spattered tarp. A side table held assorted brushes, rags, mediums, and squeezed tubes of paint. The colorful paintings which filled the wall space failed to cheer or give her satisfaction.

Abby placed the package on the kitchen table and put a kettle of water on the stove. Mrs. Anthony's suggestion of hot tea sounded good. She took off her jacket, wrapped it around the back of the chair, and searched for a teabag. *Orange Pekoe or Chamomile? Decisions. Decisions.* Her mind was definitely stripped.

Taking a knife from its holder, she opened the box. An envelope rested on top of a second box, her name scrawled across the surface. She opened it and took out the note.

Dear Abby,

I'm so sorry for your loss. Evie asked me to bring you this package after she passed, but my health is not so good. Please let me know that you received this to relieve my mind. Evie didn't trust that shyster lawyer to give it to you. My number is below. Know my prayers are with you now. Just remember Evie loved you, and she was so proud of you. She sent me photos of your artwork. What an interesting life you must lead! Hope you continue to be successful. I'm going to miss Evie. Let me hear from you soon.

Warmest regards,
Mina Kresge

Gran's friends called her Evie in school. She told Abby she had married young and that losing her husband in a boating accident two years later devastated her. They had a daughter, Serena Lucille Parsons ... *my mother*. Abby thought about the missing pictures; all of the ones that should have been there, but were supposedly lost in a fire. Gran had not remarried, and last week she died of a brain aneurysm at the age of seventy-two.

Abby opened the second box addressed to her in her grandmother's handwriting. A note was folded on top of the tissue that read,

My dearest Abby,

If you are reading this, I am no longer living on this earth but with your mother in a better place. Know that I have cherished our time together, and you are loved so very much. Please forgive me for not telling you everything, but I believe all I have done has kept you safe. These treasures belonged to your mother. I know she would have wanted you to have them.

Love Gran.

She reread the note and tried to relate to the woman who had reared her. *Kept me safe from what?*

Under the note was a birth certificate for Abigail Serena Parsons, born October 28, 1988, in Savannah, Georgia. No hospital name appeared, and in that space, Home Delivery was recorded. Abby's mother was listed as Serena Lucille Parsons, who died in childbirth. The father, Unknown. Evelyn Marie Desmond was listed as her grandmother. She refolded the Certificate of Birth and placed it on the note.

Abby separated the tissue, her hands shaking with anticipation. A gray velvet ring box identified as coming from Blackstock Jewelers, Atlanta, Georgia, held a gold ring with a five carat green gemstone suspended from a long, gold chain. She turned the ring over and inspected the surface. An inscription in longhand read, Together through eternity. The oval-shaped gem was open to the back and mounted on delicate gold filigree interwoven and interspersed with the Fleur de Lis. It looked more like an heirloom than a modern creation. Could this be an emerald? She slipped it on her right, ring finger, a perfect fit.

Another piece of tissue held a gold locket with "Bella" monogrammed on the outside. *Bella?* Abby opened the locket. Two color-tinted photographs revealed a man on the left and a woman on the right. The woman looked young; her silvery, blond hair pulled back with tendrils artfully falling about her face. The eyes were blue and mischievous. She had a pert nose, ivory skin, and lips that curved in a smile revealing a dimple in one cheek.

The man looked more familiar. His features were the masculine rendering of the face she saw in the mirror each day. He had auburn hair, high forehead and cheekbones, aquiline nose, wide mouth, and strong features. His eyes looked brown in the miniature, but they were probably a deep green like hers. They mesmerized Abby. *These must be photographs of my mother and father.* Tears filled her eyes and trickled down her cheeks. She was looking at her parents for the first time. She traced their features with her mind, each one leaving an indelible mark on her heart and memory.

Enclosed in a small envelope was a fragile gold chain which held a gold toe shoes charm. She took out other pieces of jewelry, of little value, but priceless because her mother had worn them, touched them. According to a fragile, brown newspaper clipping at the bottom of the box, an Isabella Claire Langford had been murdered. The article was more like a blurb than a news article, leaving out pertinent details of the case. *Murdered?* Abby's heart quickened. *Why? Who?* Questions rattled around in Abby's mind. *If this woman is my mother, who was Serena Lucille Parsons, the woman Gran said was my mother?* Chills raced over her skin, raising the hairs on her arms and neck. She shivered and focused on another clipping.

According to the second article and the obituary notice, Isabella was twenty-three when she died in Savannah, Georgia, in 1988. No family or next of kin were listed. Few facts were included in the pitifully short death notice. *Was Claire her maiden name and Langford her married name? Was the killer arrested?*

The empty box held no more clues.

Abby took the man's photograph out of the locket, but no name was written on the back. *Is he also dead, unnamed?* Abby's whole life had been a carefully fabricated lie.

Though no papers had been found in her gran's home which dealt with her history, Abby knew she had to find this Mina person, who had sent her the box, and ask her what she knew. The address book didn't have Mina Kresge's name in it, yet her grandmother entrusted her with Bella's treasures.

The only clues she had were the address on the box and a phone number.

Who is my father? Where is he?

CHAPTER TWO

Abby looked at the comfortable, little house with green shutters tucked well back from the quiet street. Two large maple trees flanked the open, wooden front porch, a sprinkling of red leaves still clinging to the ancient limbs crowding the house. White painted rockers were placed together on the porch and a variety of green ferns filled large, colorfully glazed pots and hanging baskets. Brightly colored artificial flowers were stuck randomly in the ferns, their spring-like appearance incongruous with approaching winter.

She walked up the empty driveway on a carpet of red leaves, climbed the green, painted concrete steps, and pressed the door bell. Abby heard a staccato series of notes inside. She waited a minute, and a face appeared, viewing her from behind a curtain in the side window.

"Mrs. Kresge, it's Abby Parsons," she called out. The lace curtain fell back into place, and a series of locks unlatched. Bells jingled as a tiny woman wrapped in a brilliant, sapphire and green kimono appeared in the doorway. Her dyed black hair, pulled back high on her head into a teased bun, leaned precariously over her right ear. The lively, black kohl-lined eyes were sunken behind heavily rouged cheeks. The woman did a quick assessment, checked to see if anyone else was outside, and then opened the door wide enough for Abby to enter. In a precise and efficient manner, she reclosed the series of locks.

"Oh dear, oh dear," a whispery voice repeated, as she shook her head, the bun sinking lower over her ear. "I didn't expect you to come all this way to tell me you received the package. I should have dressed this morning. Wasn't expecting company, so sorry, so sorry," she mumbled as she patted her bun back toward center and pointed to a red-striped wingback chair.

"I haven't been well," she added, "and call me Mina, a variant of Wilhelmina, my given name. I haven't been Mrs. Kresge for twenty-two years." Her mouth was a slash of red. Lipstick inundated the myriad lines surrounding her lips and tinted her teeth, giving her a garish look.

Don't stare, Abby thought as she looked around at an eclectic mix of furniture and art. Exotic, Victorian, and Oriental clashed and competed for prominence. *Amazing*! She knew she had never seen this woman, but her voice was familiar.

"I'm the one who should apologize," Abby stated. "I didn't call because I was afraid you might leave if you knew I was coming."

"Why ever would you think that?" Mina responded, her perfectly drawn-on black brows lifting in puzzlement. "Evie was my dearest friend. Why wouldn't I want to meet her granddaughter?"

She sounded sincere, but there was just enough reticence in her voice to give Abby pause.

"You tell me. Why haven't we met before now? Did you know she wasn't my real grandmother?" Abby asked pointedly.

Mina had the grace to look abashed. "So, you know." Mina's voice fell into a lower register. "Did Evie tell you, or did you search this out?" she inquired, her hands and thin arms rising with her voice, dramatically making circular motions in the air.

"She left me a letter. Naturally, it was a shock to discover her deceit and over so many years. I want to know why. Was I stolen, given away, adopted?" Abby again felt the stirring of anger coming to the surface and knew it was discernable in her voice. "Were you her accomplice? If you were her friend, why didn't I know about you? *And* my mother was murdered. What do you know about that?"

Mina drew herself up as if fortifying for the attack. Suddenly, she turned and walked briskly out of the room. "I'm making coffee," she called back. "You may come."

Abby blinked. *Who is this Bohemian woman?* She was having difficulty seeing common ground between the two women. Her grandmother had been conservative. Her most liberal act had been buying a Toyota Camry. Friends needled her about not buying American, but she laughed it off and said she was helping the economy by spending what she was saving in fuel.

Mina's strange dismissal, leaving her questions unanswered frayed what little was left of Abby's patience. She heard coffee beans being ground in the next room. Getting up, Abby moved cautiously to the doorway, not knowing what to expect.

Mina tapped the coffee into a filter. She took the carafe to the sink, measured the water, and added it to the coffee maker. Her actions appeared normal.

Abby looked around the kitchen, taking in the cramped space, the crowded counter and small square, red painted table strewn with books and paper clutter. Two chairs took most of the available space.

Mina didn't turn around. She reached for some delicate china cups and saucers on a shelf, her sleeves outspread like a psychedelic moth. "Don't mind the mess," she stated. "I'm totally right-brained."

That explains it, Abby thought. Drawings and Matisse-like paintings with glorious splashes of color adorned the stark, white walls. Posters of dancers and matadors filled the larger spaces. The artwork showed promise and indicated a creative bent. Florescent, sticky notes festooned the refrigerator, the walls, even the cabinets.

"I'm an artist. I can't organize. It destroys inspiration, you know. Yes," she sighed, "you *would* know." Mina opened the fridge and took out several individual creamers. She placed them on the only exposed spot on the table and busily removed the papers around them, clearing a larger space. "I'm not a housekeeper, never will be," she rambled on as she stacked, "and it's so hard to find and keep someone reliable these days." Her voice turned hard. "Sit down." It was an order.

Abby obeyed.

Mina had managed to keep her back turned and her head down. Now Abby saw the tracks of mascara that marked her cheeks and smeared as she dashed tears away. Mina began to shake as she pointed a bony finger at her.

"Your grandmother," she emphasized, her finger stabbing too close to Abby's face, "was the kindest, most wonderful, caring person in the world. I can't believe you would take that tone about her after all she did for you."

Abby shrank back, not believing Mina's vehemence.

"Without her," she accused, "you would probably be dead, or at least in an orphanage, or maybe shuttled around in foster homes." Her mouth worked furiously as she spat out the words. "You ungrateful ... ungrateful b ... girl!" At that, she flopped down and buried her head in her arms and sobbed.

Abby didn't know what to do. She was out of her element here. Obviously this woman and her grandmother had shared some unfathomable bond. There was a story here, her intuition on full alert.

Abby tentatively placed her hand on the woman's shoulder, and she didn't shake it off. "I'm sorry. I don't understand. I want to, but I don't. I didn't mean to sound ungrateful." Tears welled in her own eyes. "Please help me understand. I need answers, or I'll go crazy. And I'm a little scared," she admitted, realizing it was true.

Several minutes dragged by. Mina began to gain control, her sobs becoming loud snuffles, then quieter sniffles.

Abby got up and came back with a handful of paper towels. She blew her nose on one and tucked the rest under Mina's folded arms. She poured coffee, set the china on the table, and added a cream to hers. Abby blew into the cup before taking a sip. She waited.

"Evie and I were part of a dance troupe, *The Nonpareil Ballet Company*. We travelled around the country but performed mostly on the East Coast." Mina got up and added two teaspoons of sugar to her coffee. She blew her nose into a paper towel and dropped it in the trashcan before returning to the table.

"Your mother joined the troupe in Savannah. We spent several months there every year preparing for our new performances. Bella was beautiful and talented. Our choreographer, George Montbank, trained her to be a star in the production. George, Monsieur Montbank, as he wanted to be called, was a fussy little man, but he knew talent, and Bella had it in spades." She glanced at Abby and twisted a paper towel in her fingers. "Everyone loved Bella. She had a way about her that was naïve, endearing. Evie and I took her under our protection. There were men in our troupe, and some who came to the shows that didn't have her best interest at heart." She paused, shredding the paper towel.

"Did she tell you anything about herself?"

"Her name was Isabella Claire Langford, and she said she was from Charleston, South Carolina. She didn't talk about her past. She had big plans for the future. Her dream was to join the New York City Ballet. We gathered her family, or what was left of it, didn't share her dream and cut her off. She did some waitressing and saved enough money to get a train ticket to Savannah. She was nineteen." Mina raised the china cup and took several sips. She didn't say anything, just looked lost in thought.

Abby sat silent, willing her to speak.

"Bella met a man on the Riverwalk in Savannah. His name was Raphael, and he came from a fine family on one of the outer islands. Rafe, as she called him, was a bit older, in his early thirties we guessed."

"What was his surname?"

"We never knew. She was secretive about their relationship, and though he met her after practices and came to the shows, he just introduced himself as Rafe." She peered at Abby with tear-filled eyes. "You look like him." She dropped her eyes and continued. "They were very much in love. He took her to fine places and treated her like a princess. She said he was an artist, and his family owned an island. The family did not approve of Rafe's relationship with Bella. She was concerned about that, but he laughed and told her they could live anywhere, so she didn't have to worry about his family.

"One night, Bella came home hysterical and terrified, claiming two men with knives had jumped them several blocks from our boarding house. Rafe fought them and told her to run. Bella didn't want to leave him, but they had just found out she was pregnant, and she was afraid for the baby." She looked at Abby as if begging forgiveness. "We panicked. So many thoughts bombarded our heads and the questions. Was Rafe all right? What would Monsieur Montbank do if there was a scandal? What should we do?" She paused, and her tear-stained face revealed the horror of that night.

"We called the police, and they found blood on the sidewalk and on the curb, but Rafe was gone. They questioned Bella, of course, and Monsieur Montbank arrived when he heard the sirens and the commotion in the hallway. Members of the troupe lined the halls, wondering what had happened. It was a nightmare."

Mina stood and walked into the parlor where she had room to pace while she gathered her thoughts. "We never saw Rafe again, and as far as we knew, he was dead, and his body never discovered. The mind can imagine horrible scenarios when a body isn't found. Bella, bless her heart, went to her room and cried for days. She knew if Rafe lived, he would contact her.

"Then one day, she came to us and said, 'I'm through with crying. Rafe's baby is going to live, and I have to take care of myself.'"

"Monsieur Montbank wanted Bella to have an abortion, so she could go on with the show, but Bella refused, and he told her to get out. He would find another star."

Abby was stunned. *My father was also murdered?*

Mina pulled a chair to Abby's side and sat next to her. She took Abby's cold hand and held it in both of hers. She looked Abby in the eyes. "Bella told us Rafe had married her. When she said she was pregnant, we were shocked, but we didn't ask questions because we didn't want to upset her. Bella showed us the emerald ring Rafe had given her the day they married. He told her the ring had been handed down to the firstborn in his family since the French Revolution. The brides received the ring on the day they married. His family had escaped that horror and come to America to begin a new life." Mina wrung her hands as she moved. "Of course, we asked about his family, but Bella refused to tell us more. He had taken her to the island to meet his family. They didn't think she was good enough for Rafe, and she never wanted to see them again."

Abby drew the gold necklace out of her blouse. She had added the gold toe shoes and locket to the emerald ring chain. The ring looked valuable, and she didn't want it stolen.

Mina watched Abby examine the ring. "It's a family heirloom, and Bella said it represented the love Rafe had for her. He had a jeweler add the inscription, and he gave her the gold necklace with the toe shoes charm on her birthday. It was her prized possession, and she never took it off."

"What happened to my mother?"

"After the incident when Rafe disappeared, Bella was afraid to go out for a while. We took care of her. When I left with the troupe, Evie stayed. Evie had retired from dance several years before. She had then become the company's wardrobe seamstress."

"She wouldn't leave her alone. Bella was fragile, you see. They found a cheap room in a boarding house. Evie took in customers, who needed alterations or a new outfit, to make ends meet.

"We had a little savings, and I wired most of my paycheck to Evie. Some of the other women in the troupe took up a couple of collections, so Bella could see a doctor. Bella had helped several of the women, and they didn't like Monsieur Montbank, or agree with him when he told her to leave."

She nodded at Abby. "Evie later became a receptionist at the health department because of the benefits. A child is an added expense, and she didn't want you to lack the basics."

Abby bowed her head ashamed. She thought of the nights her grandmother stayed up late sewing after a day's work at the health department. She thought about the doctors and dentist appointments, the nutritious meals she prepared, and the smile that remained, even on the face of exhaustion. Her grandmother had loved and cared for her more than many children with parents. *Mina has every right to chastise me. I'm sorry, Gran.*

Mina looked at Abby, her face solemn. "The men, who probably made Rafe disappear, found Bella." Mina began to cry, her shoulders heaving with the force. "Oh, God, she was so sweet, why did they have to kill her? And they took the baby."

"What!" Abby sat up straight. "They took me?"

Mina swallowed. "No, they took your brother. You were a twin. There were two of you, a boy and a girl. You were about a week old. Bella was not well after the birth, and she wouldn't go to the hospital because she was afraid."

Abby sat spellbound, not believing she had a brother and didn't know. *Where is he now?*

Mina became agitated and shredded another paper towel in her hand. "Bella named your brother Rafe and you Rafaella, both after your daddy."

"But my name isn't Rafaella," Abby said perplexed.

"Evie and I changed your name. Give me a minute to explain."

Abby nodded. *Be patient.* "What happened? How did my mother die?" Abby closed her eyes, anguished by the thought of her mother's death and suffering. She had been so young, full of life, now gone.

"Evie was rocking you on the back porch when two men broke down the door to the room. Bella screamed. She had been nursing Rafe.

"A man grabbed the baby, and when Bella tried to get him back, he shot her.

"You were asleep, and Evie put you under the rocker wrapped in a baby blanket. She heard the men pulling out drawers and turning over furniture. She came inside and screamed.

" People were coming into the hallway, cautious because gun shots mean harm, curious to know what happened.

"One of the men shot Evie as they ran out the back door with the baby. Evie lost a lot of blood and played dead."

"They shot my grandmother?" Abby felt her life disintegrating around her.

"Yes." Tears rolled down Mina's face.

"Tell me the rest." Abby felt her body tighten with the shock. *My mother and grandmother shot. My father probably dead. I have a brother, Rafe.*

"Evie dragged herself to Bella's side, and when she saw no signs of life, she took the necklace from Bella's neck, and crawled outside to check on you.

"A neighbor, she and Bella befriended, saw her and tried to help her stem the blood from her side, but Evie would have none of it. She begged the neighbor to take you to her house.

"The woman was afraid, but Evie took her hand and placed it on your squirming body. She told the woman to take you to her house, quick. The men might return and kill you if she didn't.

"The two men had fled with little Rafe when they heard the sirens."

"Residents made their way into the room, the police behind, trying to get them to leave.

"Evie staggered back inside, giving the neighbor a chance to get away. She said it was a nightmare." Mina put her head down in her arms exhausted with the telling.

"What happened then?" Abby asked, her voice cracking, her throat dry.

"Evie told the police two men broke in and shot Bella and her. The men were looking for something, and they kidnapped the baby.

"The police believed it was a robbery gone bad, but they were in a quandary about why the baby was taken."

Mina took Abby's hand and looked at her with pain-filled eyes.

"Your brother is dead. They found little Rafe at a church. The coroner said he had been smothered."

Abby's eyes welled, and tears fell. "Why? Why would anyone kill a baby?" *My brother. Oh, God, my twin is dead.* She felt a wound deep in her chest. A wound she knew would fester and give her pain until the murderers were caught and punished. *Maybe this feeling of loss will never go away.*

"Evie saved your life. We figured the emerald and the baby were what the men came to get. Someone wanted Bella and her baby dead. Maybe family. Rafe might have had an inheritance someone didn't want him to have. That was our conclusion."

"Why Bella and the baby?" Abby murmured, numbness creeping over her.

"Loose ends. They weren't taking chances if Rafe married Bella and had a child. The murderers must have gotten wind of Bella's condition. They must have waited and watched."

"That's barbaric, sick. The article didn't mention a baby."

"Evie was in the hospital over a week. She lost a lot of blood. They removed her spleen and gave her transfusions. Her mental health was my biggest concern. Evie couldn't bear losing both Bella and the baby. She saved only the one article and obituary for you. She didn't want you to know about your brother."

"Why not?"

"She told me it would be hard enough on you when you found out your mother was murdered."

"So why did you tell me?"

"You are accusing Evie of heinous things, and you have no idea the depth of her love for you."

Abby frowned. She had betrayed the one person who had loved and nurtured her through sickness, adolescence, and hard times, always putting herself before her own needs. Abby felt sick, not only because of the revelation, but because of her own betrayal of that love.

"Evie decided moving away from Savannah and disappearing into a city would be safer. No one knew Bella had twins because she delivered at home.

"Evie made the neighbor swear on your life, she would remain silent, and she did when she found out Bella's other child had been killed."

Mina rose to her feet and poured a second cup of coffee. "Later, when my room was ransacked, Evie was afraid I'd been targeted, too. I left the troupe and moved to Baltimore where I married Paul Kresge, an old flame who wanted to help me. I thought we had a good marriage, but he left me because of my paranoia, and as you can see, I'm not much of a housekeeper."

"Did my grandmother marry, or was that also fiction?"

"No, your grandmother never married."

"How did I get the name, Parsons? Did she make that up, too?"

"Parsons was her mother's maiden name. Paul Desmond was her father. Evie gave you family names in case someone looked into your lineage. You were her main concern, and she desperately wanted you to survive and have protection. She loved you as if you were her own blood. How could you ever doubt it?"

Abby thought about the years of karate, kick-boxing, and other protection classes her grandmother insisted she take. Her words echoed in her mind. "We have gangs here, and people can take advantage of you or hurt you. I want to know you have the resources to save yourself if need be." Abby had earned a Black Belt by the time she was a junior in high school. She felt confident, safe, and until recently, she had not shared her grandmother's or Mina's paranoia.

"Evie and I corresponded by mail or spoke on the phone. I'm Mary Adams. I mailed all correspondence from Towson. You've seen and heard that name before. You've heard my voice."

Abby nodded, stunned by the revelation. Her mind went back to the cards, letters, and phone calls from Mary Adams, "a childhood friend" of her grandmother's. Mary Adams sent her a birthday card every year, and when she asked about this Mary, whom she had never met, she was told her friend worked in the intelligence field and led a solitary life.

"She spoke of you often and with fondness," Abby said. "She came to see you several times, always when I was away at camp or at school functions." Squiggles of paranoia wormed their way into Abby's psyche. These two friends, her benefactors, went to extraordinary lengths because of fear, a fear now settling into the marrow of her bones.

"We were afraid for you in case somehow we were watched. Now my best friend is gone, and I may not be long in this world."

Abbey stood and put her arms around the frail shoulders. "Are you sick?"

"My heart's giving out. I made arrangements for you to get the package if I passed first. You must keep the emerald safe. It's the only proof Bella and Rafe married."

"What about my birth certificate?"

"You were the only child listed. Your mother was listed as dying in childbirth, and your father unknown. Evie recorded herself as your grandmother and guardian. As far as I know, the information was never contested."

Mina stood and grabbed Abby's arms, her grip amazingly strong. "What are you going to do?" Her eyes were frantic as they searched Abby's for an answer.

"There must be a record of the marriage in Savannah. I'm going to look for it, and then I'm going to search for Bella's family and find Rafe's family."

"I was afraid you would say that. Please don't. I can't bear to think about you getting hurt or killed. You're successful and have a good life. Don't look for trouble." She laid her forehead on Abby's chest. "Please honor the sacrifices we made to keep you safe."

"What about my parents and brother? Does it honor them to let their murderers go free? I'm sorry, Mina. I promise to be careful."

CHAPTER THREE

Abby arrived in Savannah two weeks later and checked into a motel outside of town where the rooms were cheaper. She had some money saved, but it wouldn't last forever. Abby counted back nine months before her birthday and added three months, calculating probable marriage dates. She would search every church record for the months of probability until she found the marriage recorded.

Using the phone in her room, Abby ran down the names and numbers of churches in the phonebook, calling about marriage registrations. She gave her mother's name and Raphael, her father's name, his surname unknown. Most of the churches had computerized records easy to search, leaving smaller ones to physically check. The work was tedious, and for the most part, church secretaries were accommodating.

After compiling a list of churches she needed to visit, she set off on her quest. She lucked out with the fifth church on her two-page list, Trinity Reformed Lutheran.

As Abby leafed through the leather bound tome of marriages, an elderly man joined her.

"I'm Father Jon Ziegler, and I understand you're looking for evidence of a marriage. Maybe I can be of service. I performed most of the ceremonies during your period of search."

Abby stared at the stooped, saintly-looking man wearing a clerical collar and a well-worn suit. A nimbus of fine white hair framed his pale lined face like a halo. He had a British accent Abby found pleasing.

She stood and held out her hand. "I'm Abigail Parsons, and I'm searching for the marriage record of my mother, Isabella Claire Langford. I only have my father's first name, Raphael."

"A painter, yes," he murmured as he cast his mind back to another time.

Abby felt chills skate over her arms. Then she realized the reverend might be referring to the Renaissance painter.

"I remember," he said at last.

"What do you remember?" Abby leaned toward the man in anticipation.

He looked at her. "You're not the first to seek this information." He put his fingers on his forehead, deep in thought. "Something unfortunate happened," and his voice petered out.

"My mother and father were murdered," Abby said, bringing him back to the present.

"Your father, too? Yes, very unfortunate, a tragedy. Beautiful bride, so full of life, a tragedy," he repeated. "You look a bit like your father. The same hair and eyes. You say he was also murdered?"

"Yes," Abby said, and tears welled and fell at this man's remembrance.

"The ring I'll never forget. I had never seen an emerald of that size or quality and that setting. Oh yes, beautiful. A master's fine craftsmanship."

"Who was looking for the record of their marriage?"

"Let me see," he paused. "The man said he was an uncle of the bride, but I remember he looked more like the groom. That's why I remember, a mystery, that. I left him paging through the records."

"Do you remember my father's surname?"

"Of course, an old family, well-known." His fingers rubbed his forehead, and his face looked up, blank. "I had it a minute ago. Now, it's gone into the ether. The worst thing about age is forgetting even the most vivid recollections, especially names. Give me a minute," he stammered. "It's no use. The harder I think, the farther from my mind," he mumbled. "The name will come at the oddest moment.

"I counseled them about marriage and the vows. It takes a while to get a license here. You can't just come in off the street, you see. I remember they were very much in love, and they said no family would attend ... unusual ... most unusual.

"There's an index in the office. Your mother's name will be listed.

Let me check." He tottered off. "Langford, Langford," he repeated.

Abby's sighed in relief. He remembered. Then she shivered with the knowledge someone else, probably kin to her father, also looked. Maybe the murderer. The pages rustled as she turned them with trembling fingers.

Father Ziegler returned, shaking his head. "No, no, not possible," he mumbled as he approached. Moving her aside, he thumbed through the pages until he found what he was seeking.

"It's not here," he said, looking closely and showing her where the page had been cut out, probably with a razor. "The page is missing in the office, too." He looked at her, concern on his face. "Someone doesn't want this marriage revealed."

Abby raised her face, frightened by his speculation. This man was the only link to her parents. In fact, he was the only witness yet alive. She took both of his shaking hands in hers. "Please, you must help me. Would you write what you remember and have it notarized?"

He shook his head. "I don't know, I don't know," he said, apparently fretting over this discovery of sacrilege.

"Please, sir. You have a sacred obligation to help me. You're a man of the cloth, a servant of God. You know why this record is important to me."

"Murdered, murdered," he mumbled. "Both murdered."

Abby shook his shoulder to bring him back. "Father Ziegler, please, you must help me."

"How do I know you're a daughter of this union?" He said with a modicum of relief at maybe not having to help.

The emerald ring was pulled from where it nestled under her shirt.

He gasped and stepped back.

"Is this the ring you remember?"

The old man seemed to shrink inside himself. He covered his face with his hands and rocked on his feet.

"Yes," he said, "yes." He sat in the nearest chair, continuing to rock with the knowledge. "Forgive me," he mumbled. "Forgive me."

"Will you help me, now?" Abby asked, putting her hand on his shoulder.

He nodded and placed his hand over her own. "Yes, I'll help."

Abby sat with him until he composed himself. She decided not to leave him until the notarized account was in her hands.

Father Ziegler called an attorney he knew, filling him in, while Mrs. O'Neil, the church secretary, looked on with concern.

"Shona, I need some church stationery, if you please," he said when he hung up the phone.

Mrs. O'Neil handed him two sheets with the letterhead and a pen. He took them to an adjoining room, and Abby followed.

He began to write, his strokes large and scratchy. He looked up, eyes wide. "I remember. DuMond. Your father's name was Raphael Etienne DuMond. He had more names, but I remember Etienne because it's my uncle's name.

"The DuMond family has a history going back to the French Revolution and before. An ancestor of your family fled to the Americas. He survived a Creek uprising and settled on Mast Island. He named his plantation, Sologne, after his wife, who did not escape the guillotine."

Father Ziegler stopped writing to tell Abby how the first DuMond escaped France with enough wealth to build a plantation in the New World and perpetuate his way of life. "The money to run the place came from a lucrative rice operation and later timbering for shipbuilders. I've read he hated the slave trade, and he bought and freed slaves for heavy labor. They lived and worked on the island. I'm guessing he probably perpetuated a feudal way of life unfamiliar here. You will find the history in local bookstores and the library."

He returned to his writing, filling the two pages and requesting a third.

The door opened, and a man in his forties or fifties appeared. "Father Jon Ziegler, what a pleasant surprise!" He saw Abby and introduced himself. "Hello, I'm Pastor Foltz, and I see Father Jon is helping you. I'm the pastor here. Is there anything I can do to help?"

"Yes. Yes there is," Father Ziegler said, not looking up. "I want you to witness this, I'm almost finished."

While he wrote, Abby stood and introduced herself. "I'm so glad I met Father Ziegler. Without his help, I never would have accomplished my mission."

"That is indeed fortuitous because this is the first time I have seen Father Jon in about a year. He retired and attends another church near his home."

"Oh my," Abby said, realizing this meeting was not a coincidence. She had a brief thought of her parents interceding. *God's plan in motion.*

"Finished." Father Ziegler said, blowing on the ink before handing the pages to Abby.

She read through the detailed account from the time Father Ziegler met with, counseled, and married her parents. He also recorded finding the page cut from the registry and the office index. Because of the missing account, he guessed the approximate date was between the pages still bound.

Abby hugged the man with tear-filled eyes. "You're a lifesaver. Why did you come today?"

"I don't know. I planned to go to the market, and while I was compiling a mental list, my feet brought me here. God does work in mysterious ways." He took the pages and handed them to Pastor Foltz. "Please witness that I wrote this, and I was not under duress. Shona can also witness and notarize it."

Pastor Foltz took the pages, initialed each page, and wrote a brief statement followed by his signature.

Shona O'Neil added her signature and notarized the pages. She folded them and put them in an envelope.

Father Ziegler released a deep sigh of relief. "The deed is done," he remarked. He wrote a name and address on the envelope. "Please take this to my attorney. He will hold this in safekeeping for you." He looked her in the eyes. "I'd trust this man with my life. I've known Gordie since he was knee-high to a grasshopper. Surely, God is with you, Abigail."

She looked at the name on the envelope, Gordon Culpepper, Esq. Abby thanked them all again and began to leave.

"Wait." Father Ziegler said, and he left the office in a hurry. When he returned, he asked of Shona, "Do you have any thin paper, onion skin, or the like?"

Mrs. O'Neil rummaged through the drawer and took out some

photo-sized pages. "We use these for invitations. Will they do?"

Father Ziegler raised his arms and said, "Thank you, Lord. Now, I need a pencil."

Abby looked at him astonished.

"This is of the Lord. As sure as the bluebird's blue, this thought came from the Almighty. My feeble mind would not have made this connection."

Abby and Pastor Foltz followed the excited man back to the open ledger. He placed a thin sheet on the page and lightly ran the lead over the writing. The lead picked up indentations. He moved the thin paper down the page, stopping several times and getting another blank sheet.

Father Ziegler stood and beamed at Abby. "More information." He waved the last sheet aloft and presented it to Abby with a flourish.

She scanned the page, her excitement rising Some of the letters recorded did not show up on the rubbing, but her father's signature was boldly complete. Raphael Philippe Etienne Henri DuMond, and the date, January 15, 1988.

Abby flung her arms around the old man's neck. Thank you, thank you," she said, clasping the sheet to her chest. Tears fell freely, and Shona McNeil handed her the tissue box.

"You are most welcome, child."

The three signed and notarized the rubbing.

Father Ziegler laid his hand on her shoulder. "God be with you and keep you safe,"

CHAPTER FOUR

Gordon Culpepper's office was on the third floor of a bank building in downtown Savannah. His secretary said Abby was expected and showed her into his office.

Mr. Culpepper was tall and lanky, his thick, graying hair combed away from a high forehead. The piercing, dark eyes regarded her under bushy, wild eyebrows and registered surprise. A moment later, his eyes fell, his expression shuttered.

"Please have a seat. Father Jon was adamant I help you. He said you had something for me to keep safe."

Abby gave him a brief account of her story and handed him the affidavit and rubbing.

His eyes widened when he saw the name, and he dropped the sheets as if burned. "DuMond? You're the daughter of Rafe DuMond?" His face exposed an incredulous look. "Does the family know Rafe married and had a daughter?"

Her response was delayed, and when she shook her head in the negative, questions rattled through her mind. *Does he know the family? He must. He said "Rafe," not Raphael. How does he know them?*

"My god, Rafe was married, and by Father Jon, no less. He sat back in his chair deep in thought.

"Do you know the family?" Abby asked, wondering at the relationship.

"I do," he said and nodded.

"Mr. Culpepper, my parents were murdered. I'm not comfortable with the family knowing of my existence at this time." She left out the death of her brother.

He nodded sagely. "Yes, I quite understand." His brow furrowed in thought. *Murdered?*

"Well, I'm afraid I don't. How do you know the family?" Abby asked, her words blunt.

"I'm not one of the DuMond attorneys, so you can be sure this information will be confidential." He swallowed and looked uncomfortable. "My wife and I are members of the same yacht club, and we have stayed at Sologne on occasion. Our daughters are friends."

Abby noticed a dark-haired girl in a photo on his desk. She saw his dilemma.

"I'm sorry to put you in this position."

He waved his hand. "No, this is a surprise, nothing for you to worry about." He scrutinized her face for the first time. "You have the DuMond eyes and hair. What are your plans?"

"I don't know. Is there a place to stay on the island besides the plantation?"

"You don't know what happened to the island after Rafe's death." It was a statement.

"No, I don't."

"The south end of the ocean side was developed. Rafe wanted the island to be a refuge, a rookery. He was a scientist and an artist, against any development that would destroy the island's unique environment."

"That's a motive for murder." Abby said.

Mr. Culpepper grunted and said, "No," his voice adamant. "I'll never believe the family had Rafe murdered. They are close-knit, and though they disagreed with Rafe, they respected his stand. The family helped him with plans he had for the island, and they were devastated by his death."

"Someone was not happy with his plans."

"Yes, I take your point. Are you sure you want to meet the family? You must have some reservations."

"Actually, Mr. Culpepper, I'm scared. My mind says I should be safe. My family has no idea I exist. My heart says I need to meet them, learn something about them."

"I quite understand, but observant people familiar with the DuMonds, will conclude you must be a family member. Your heritage is stamped on your face."

After a brief silence he said, "There are some resorts on the island. You have to take the ferry or use a boat to get there."

"I guess arrangements can be made online. In the meantime, please keep these papers in safe-keeping. I may need you to draw up a Last Will and Testament."

Mr. Culpepper folded the papers and put them back in the envelope. "An important document you should have, but I hope a will won't be necessary at your age."

"I share that sentiment, Mr. Culpepper," Abby said as she rose from the chair. "Thank you for your time and your help."

Abby approached the dock where she would catch the ferry to Mast Island and spend the day. Her mind ran through the list of changes she had made. She opened an account at the bank after leaving Mr. Culpepper's office and acquired a safety deposit box. The contents of her grandmother's box would be safe. Abby felt a burgeoning sadness as she removed the necklace and ring. She fingered the charm and turned the ring over and over, memorizing the filigree design and endearment. She felt guilty taking the heirlooms off and putting them away. These items were all that remained of her past.

Noah watched the tall, young woman walk down the dock to the ferry landing. Her face, hidden in the shadow of a wide-brimmed straw hat, did not turn his way. She wore khaki overalls with numerous pockets and a tank top revealing wide shoulders and toned arms. The compact wooden easel she carried arrested his attention. *An artist. Interesting.*

Abby eased the heavy canvas bag from her shoulder and placed the easel on the bench next to the railing. The wind picked up, and she pulled out and donned a taupe, corduroy jacket. Her eyes searched the horizon across a sea of salt marsh for the barrier island bearing the name, Mast.

She glanced at her watch. The ferry wouldn't arrive for another half hour, so she looked at the fishing boats tied to several shorter docks. An antique-looking, wooden sailboat with teak trim and cabin was anchored apart from the other boats. The beautiful symmetry of the vessel had her bringing out her sketchpad and the tin box of charcoal from her bag. In minutes, the lines of the boat took shape. She measured the height of the two masts with her charcoal stick against the length of the boat. Abby's mind focused, her eyes guiding her hand over the paper. Using a little finger, she smoothed some of the lines, giving the sketch depth, perspective, and background.

"That's exceptional," a deep voice said at her shoulder.

Startled, Abby jumped. She hadn't heard the man approach, and turned to see he was probably in his thirties. A shock of windblown, sun-streaked blonde hair served as a contrast to his bronzed skin. The amazing blue-green eyes under darker brows took her breath. He was gorgeous, but not in a conventional way. A quick assessment of his features, taken separately, would not be considered handsome, but together, they gave his visage a masculine strength and interest. Reluctantly, her gaze returned to the drawing, her lips folding, embarrassed by her instant attraction. Abby was not a portrait painter, but this face prompted a vision of him painted with palette knives. "Thank you," she managed to say.

The man leaned on his arm, placed across the railing, and looked back at her. "Are you staying on one of the islands?" he asked.

The hair on his bare arm glinted in the sun, and a large, masculine hand draped over the rail, a hand that did manual labor. Abby swallowed and refused to look at his face again.

"Just a day trip."

"Where are you headed?"

Abby felt as if she were being interrogated and didn't respond.

"You've captured the character of *The Lady*," he said, changing tack.

"*The Lady*?"

"The sloop. She's a fine one, all grace and beauty catching wind and skimming the waves. There's not another like her on the East Coast."

Abby believed him. She heard love and something more in his voice. "Oh, that's her name."

"Yes." He said no more as he watched the drawing progress.

People began to stroll toward the end of the dock as the ferry came into view.

Abby felt uncomfortable with the nearness of the man. When several people came close and tried to view her work, she decided it was time to go. Abby replaced the charcoal in the tin, cleaned her hand, and closed the sketchbook.

"Can I buy the sketch?"

Abby looked up surprised. "It's not finished."

"I like it unfinished." He grinned, revealing white teeth, one a little crooked and overlapping an incisor. The beginning of a beard didn't hide the boyish look of laugh lines bracketing his eyes and mouth. The pock marks from earlier bouts of acne did not detract. They made him real, not a pretty boy. "Finished means the end. *The Lady*'s journey has no end."

Abby tasted his words, perceiving his appreciation of the boat. The words were almost poetic, and they touched a barren spot in her heart. She opened the sketchbook, carefully tore out the drawing, and handed it to him.

"How much?" he asked as he took the page.

"It's not for sale," she said, not looking at him. "My work is like a child to me. I can't sell a sketch loved by someone more than myself."

Abby turned away, gathered her belongings, and took her ticket from a pocket.

The ferry berthed, its bulk hitting the pilings, shaking the dock. She didn't look back.

When everyone came ashore, she followed the line of embarking passengers on board, moving to find a place near the front.

Noah watched the woman walk away, intrigued. He didn't know her name, and her lack of interest in him piqued his own.

He had studied her profile in the shadow beneath her hat. She had a prominent nose and a strong jaw, but the neck and fingers were long and feminine. Not beautiful by the world's standards, but she left him wanting to see more. What color were her hair and eyes? The woman's figure was lost in the shapeless overalls, but he suspected she had a body which matched her walk, erect, proud, and womanly.

Her lips had been well-defined and full, her voice warm honey, a voice one would never tire hearing.

Noah shook himself and moved down the dock to put the boxes of supplies on the dinghy. He didn't need to be thinking about women, and this one, he'd probably never see again.

CHAPTER FIVE

Abby contemplated her future as she looked over the railing to see how easily the ferry navigated the salt marsh at high tide. Stands of cord grass with tussocks of yellow-ocher seeds made islands in the waterways, crisscrossing the wet terrain which connected to creeks and rivers leading to the ocean. A sulfur smell emanated from the rotted vegetation, and she wrinkled her nose at the odor. She imagined the minutia of animal life and organisms which fed on the yellowing grasses after they decomposed and released the smelly gas. Her initial glimpse of a different world far removed from Philadelphia added to the sense of foreboding she harbored.

Mast Island was one of the smaller inhabited islands off the coast of Georgia. Her father's home loomed before her, looking wild and untouched. She gathered the development on the ocean side was hidden from view by the thick trees and vegetation. No tall buildings marred the view on the mainland side.

A Great Blue Heron took flight, majestic, its outline shining as the sun's rays bathed the bird in morning light.

They slid silently past a concrete landing dock. A crane, backed against the dark tree line, looked like a giant, metal praying mantis emerging from the woods. Buoy protectors were attached to each over-sized post. Abby assumed barges used this area to bring in larger equipment and supplies. Behind the structure was a bank covered with palmettos, shrubs, and a forest, which grew thick with oak, pine, and palm trees.

The ferry approached a wide, sturdy dock, the only other man-made structure she had seen. A couple of green shuttles came into view, and several men ran forward to secure the mooring lines. Two men with large, rectangular wheelbarrows strode over the wooden planks, the wheels singing, "clickety-clack, clickety-clack."

One of the deck hands extended the ramp, which clanked as the metal dropped and slid into position. Several people left the ferry ahead of Abby. Luggage was put into one carry-all, and various boxes, she guessed were supplies, filled the second. Another wheelbarrow appeared and awaited cargo.

Abbey stood on the dock and watched as more boxes, mail, and stacks of newspapers were passed into waiting hands. Looking into the tea-colored water, she saw small fish and shoals of oyster beds. Hermit crabs scuttled over the rocky seawall.

Other wheelbarrows arrived, carrying luggage, followed by those leaving the island.

One of the men said, "Better hurry if you want to catch the shuttle to your resort."

Abby walked briskly toward the tourists leaving the dock.

Mast Island Shuttle was emblazoned in metallic gold outlined in white on the dark green sides of the vehicles. Abby sat up front after the back filled with passengers, and her easel was loaded.

A truck lumbered onto the small lot to pick up the supplies.

"My name is Eddie, and I'll be driving you to your destination. Where's everyone going?" the driver asked, his smile wide and welcoming in his broad, black face.

"Silver Dunes" and "Sea Oat Inn" were mentioned. One said, "Sologne," and Abby turned to see the man who spoke. He wore a navy business suit, and his trimmed mustache turned up as he smiled back at her.

"Sologne" she told the driver who took the wheel and began his spiel.

"Mast Island is privately owned by the DuMond family. Phillipe DuMond escaped the French Revolution in 1789 and came to America to seek his fortune." He spoke the words she had memorized from the brochures and a tourist booklet with the history of the island.

Abby marveled at the huge oak trees, their crowns covering two and three times their height. Boughs arched outward and drooped to touch the ground in in places. Interspersed in the limbs were greyish green tufts of tightly curled Spanish moss, resembling beards. One mighty oak drew her attention, the girth marking its age in centuries. She composed a painting in her mind.

Goosebumps covered Abby's arms as she realized her father had been familiar with these same trees. He might have even climbed them to read as she had done in Philadelphia.

Palms, palmettos, and brush found in hardwood forests lined the packed marl road and thinned in areas impacted by fire. A tom and three turkey hens ran ahead of them, drawing excited comments.

"Wild animals live on the island. Please do not approach or feed them for your safety and theirs.

"Unlike Cumberland Island, we have no wild horses. They were moved to the mainland in the 1930s."

Several people groaned their disappointment.

"We have stables with horses you can ride, but unlike the bicycles provided by the resorts, horseback riding is an added expense.

"The DuMond family has the only vehicles on the island which cuts down on the traffic. If you want to explore the island, feel free to use the bicycles. Two Sologne vehicles give tours of the island twice a day. Sign up at your destination. If you aren't able to ride a bicycle or walk distances, the shuttles will carry you to the shops and restaurants. Twice a day, the shuttles meet the ferry. I suggest you check the times when you arrive at your resort. You will need to make a reservation."

He stopped at the Silver Dunes, a sprawling five story hotel painted white with aqua blue window and door trim. The hotel structure was curved away from the road, and Abby speculated the rooms had individual balcony patios facing the ocean. Colorful flowered vines climbed the walls, and in one area, reached the orange tiled roof. Several people left the shuttle, and they were met by men who handled their luggage.

Between the Silver Dunes and Sea Oat Inn, the next resort, white sand dunes with scattered palmettos, vines of pink wild bean, and a yellow aster-like flowered blanket of camphorweed wove through succulents, yucca, and bayberry. Golden sea oats swayed in the ocean breezes and adorned the tops of smaller dunes.

Sea Oat Inn had a simpler, less expensive looking décor and a Mediterranean feel. Terracotta stucco walls were five-story and also topped with a tile roof. If there were balconies, they would be on the far side. She and the male passenger going to Sologne were the only ones left on the shuttle.

"I see you're an artist. Have the DuMonds commissioned you to paint?" the man, who had moved up behind the driver asked.

"No, I'm just curious. I only have a day on the island, so I wanted to see the plantation first. The house was not pictured in any of the brochures. Are you staying there?"

"For a few days, yes."

Eddie turned and looked at her but didn't say anything.

The gates to the DuMond plantation were wrought iron with a fleur-de-lis design. The cream stone posts supported a sculptured stone arch. Wall posts were built with the same stone separated by wrought iron fencing with spear finials. A shiny brass plate bearing the name, Château Sologne and a crest, with the *Fleur-de-Lis*, was attached to one stone post. A plate which said PRIVATE, conspicuous in its simplicity was attached below.

The driver stopped at the gate, and a man came out of the guardhouse with a clipboard. "Names please," he asked.

The passenger said, "James Toomey."

"Abigail Parsons," Abby responded.

The guard looked at her. "You aren't on my list."

I'm not a guest; I'm family. She caught herself, and clamped the thought. "I'm sorry. I didn't know the house was off limits."

Mr. Toomey leaned forward. "The young lady is on the island for the day, Paul. She's just curious to see the house. Why not let her remain in the vehicle. Eddie will bring her right back out."

"I don't know," the guard said. "We have a policy."

"I'll vouch for her," Mr. Toomey said. "She'll be back in ten minutes, or you can call security."

"Yes, sir. Go ahead," he told the driver. "Just see she doesn't leave the vehicle."

Eddie nodded and drove through the gates and down a patterned brick drive, winding through Heritage oaks and tropical hardwoods. Abby gasped when she saw the house, or more accurately, the château named Sologne. The château was a mansion of finished cream stone, a wonder of symmetry and balance. The central, steeply pitched hipped roof with three dormers, and the roofs of the conical towers and turrets had metal shingles with the soft green patina of aged copper. A Roman arched entrance with wide, carved wooden doors and the copper-lined windows were recessed. The large, stone tiled courtyard circled around a box-hedged pool with a dolphin fountain.

The driver stopped at the entrance, got out, and opened the back to retrieve the luggage. A liveried doorman arrived and took Mr. Toomey's luggage and briefcase.

The guest came around and spoke to Abby. "She's a grand estate, the château, and a marvel of architectural achievement. I wish you could see the interior and magnificent grounds, but alas, not possible. This view is more than most tourists see."

"Thank you, Mr. Toomey, for the opportunity. I'll never forget my first sight of the château and grounds. I hope your visit is relaxing and productive."

"Thank you, and to you a safe journey."

The driver took his place, and they drove back to the gates where they both waved to Paul.

"Where do you want me to drop you off? Eddie asked.

"The Sea Oat Inn will be fine."

Abby thought about the name, Sologne. When she searched the Internet, Sologne was the name of a region in France. The ill-fated wife of the first American DuMond carried the name. She shivered with the thought of her ancestor's palpable terror at seeing the guillotine.

Shelving the morbid thought, Abby inquired about the château's inhabitants. "Are the owners of the château usually in residence, or is the place a seasonal home?"

"The DuMonds live at the château year round, with an occasional visit off the island. They're a secretive bunch, or maybe it's aristocracy that separates them from the common folk."

Abby read between the lines of dialogue. The DuMonds were not liked very much by the island people. "Do you live on the island, Eddie?"

"All my life and several generations before me. We were here purty much from the beginning."

"What did your family do on the island?"

"My great-great-grandparents were slaves, but they were freed to work the land. They worked the impoundments of the freshwater marshes for the rice fields the first DuMond planted."

"What's an impoundment?"

"Reservoirs built to contain the fresh water ... like dikes and such. They worked the rice fields. Then my grandfather and father worked at timbering the big trees for shipbuilding. The women worked on the château grounds or in the big house."

"You have quite a history here. Did any of your family leave the island?"

"Yes, ma'am. Most of them that left came back. It's a different world out there, and not so friendly."

They arrived at Sea Oat Inn, and Abby tipped Eddie when he retrieved her easel. "Maybe I'll see you this afternoon when I leave."

Eddie said, "I'll be here at four-thirty sharp."

Abby walked inside the lobby and looked around for a place to get a cold drink. One of the clerks pointed to the back and said she would find refreshment at the Tiki Hut.

The pristine, white sand dunes with sea oats waving in the breeze drew Abby toward the beach. She left her easel and tennis shoes at a table under a shady spot and took the wooden walkway through the dunes. Abby stepped onto the beach, her toes digging into the warm sand.

A man fished from the shore and a couple with several children had set up an umbrella. They played in the building waves. A woman with a bucket collected some of the bountiful shells left on the beach by the receding tide. A couple could be seen walking in the distance, but no others were present.

Abby dropped her canvas bag on one of the blue beach chairs and walked into the waves, folding over the shore. The water was warm and inviting, the sand racing back from whence it came, small shells somersaulting in the ebbing surf. She looked around, enjoying the many inspiring views. The Silver Dunes was not visible because the beach curved inland, but docks and boats could be seen. *The marina must go with the Silver Dunes.*

Abby watched a sailboat in the distance, and the man from the dock came to mind. *Does he work on "The Lady" or own the beautiful vessel?* She felt a degree of satisfaction, knowing he possessed her sketch.

Her face flushed, and she turned to walk back to the thatched-roofed Tiki Hut, putting him out of her mind. She needed to formulate a plan.

Abby took off her hat and sunglasses, laid them on the canvas bag, and shook out her curls.

A waitress, roses tattooed on her forearm, came and set a small napkin at her place. The name tag identified her as Gloria. "What's your poison?" she said good-naturedly, while chewing on a wad of gum.

"A water with lemon would be wonderful."

Gloria's face fell, and Abby asked for an island punch, also.

"Your hair is beautiful. I've always wanted to be a redhead, but the color makes me look yellow. I tried on a wig once," Gloria said as she put down a menu.

Abby looked at Gloria's brown pixie cut and dark eyes. "Your style suits your face and coloring."

She nodded. "Do you know what you want?" Gloria asked as she popped gum in her mouth.

"Let me think about it a few minutes."

The woman hurried off, and Abby fingered the menu, too excited to eat. She had brought her lunch for later. The prices here were astronomical. The price of the punch alone made her wince. One side of the menu had a few breakfast items and a list of appetizers. The other side offered salads and sandwiches for lunch or later. She decided to order a cup of fruit and looked for the waitress.

Gloria was studying her over the counter. When she saw Abby notice, she came back to the table. "Are you from around here? You look familiar."

"No, I'm from Philadelphia."
"Oh. So what have you decided?"

Back at the motel in Savannah, Abby packed her bags. She had made arrangements to stay at Sea Oat Inn for five nights, the closest hotel to Sologne, and the most reasonable of the five resorts listed on the island. The choice also gave her a sixth night free. She planned to tour the island, paint, and leave the rest of the plan in God's capable hands.

She called Mr. Culpepper and let him know where she would be staying. Abby felt better knowing someone had her itinerary. "I'll call you when I get back to the mainland."

"Please do. And thank you for letting me know your plans. Be careful."

Abby heard his voice catch, and knew at least one person had her interest at heart.

CHAPTER SIX

Abby followed behind the cart, which carried her easel, a folio of canvasses, and her grandmother's battered suitcase to the shuttles waiting on the dock. Eddie had the back open to load personal belongings into the farthest shuttle, and Abby slipped into that vehicle's front seat.

Eddie turned and stared at Abby when he got behind the wheel, delaying his spiel.

Abby had taken off her wide-brimmed hat and sunglasses to see his reaction. "Hello, Eddie. We met a few days ago. You told me about your ancestors on the trip back to the hotel from Sologne."

"I remember," he said hastily, his brow furrowed, his voice containing uncertainty. He turned and asked where everyone was going.

Two new hotels were mentioned by passengers, along with Sea Oat Inn.

Abby enjoyed the scenery as Eddie drove down the road and took a fork leading away from Sea Oat Inn. Five hotels were listed on the island, leaving Abby one to scout at another time. They passed a grassy open space surrounded by stately oaks, picnic tables, and a well-equipped playground. The name scrolled in gold on an elegant terracotta sign read, Loire Park. Abutting the acreage, a quaint restaurant had a patio and a good view of the park. A cluster of high-end shops wound through beautifully landscaped and manicured lawns. A parking lot for bikes looked almost empty.

"The businesses in Loire Park don't open until ten, and they close at seven. The dining areas close at eleven, so be sure you catch the last shuttle," Eddie said, answering a question from the back. Eddie talked about the island and its history as he stole glances at Abby.

Most of the passengers emptied at the Pink Conch, and one older couple got out at a rustic Sailor's Rest. Both hotels were not over five stories, so Abby guessed there was a building code or restriction.

Only one person, an older man who looked lost, was going to Sea Oat Inn. He spoke as they neared their destination. "My wife and I planned to stay here, but she died several months ago. She would have wanted me to come."

"I'm sorry to hear about your wife's passing," Eddie said. "I hope your visit will bring you peace."

Abby added her condolences and said, "I think you're going to like Sea Oat Inn."

The man lapsed into silence, but Eddie filled the gap. "How long are you staying on the island?" he asked Abby, followed by a second question. "Where did you say you were from?"

"About a week, and I don't believe I said, but my home is in Philadelphia."

"You're an artist," he stated. "Your easel made me think …" he said, his words ending, and his tone a tad more than curious inquiry.

"Yes, I am, and I can't wait to get started." Abby tried to make her comments upbeat and ingenuous even as her stomach churned with misgivings.

Eddie pulled in front of the hotel and hurried to the rear of the vehicle where he was met by men to take the luggage. Abby followed and handed Eddie a tip.

He placed a card in her hand. "Call this number if you need anything …" and his voice trailed off, "or help".

Abby looked at Eddie, puzzled. *Is this a warning?* His eyes regarded her, and she read concern on his features. He was beginning to connect the dots after her trip to Sologne several days ago. This man was smart, and so far, he was the only one who knew of her interest in the family. *I'm going to have to be careful.*

"Thank you, Eddie. I appreciate your offer. It's a comfort to know you care." She pocketed his card and walked inside to the registration desk.

A distinguished, older man with a high, balding forehead and shrewd, assessing eyes stood behind the counter and watched her as she gave the pertinent information to a young clerk. When she received her key cards, the man walked around the counter and approached. "Excuse me."

Abby looked up at him, noting his badge proclaimed him the manager. Not many men topped her five-foot-eleven. "Yes?" she responded, but he had already begun to speak.

"Have we met?" Then he held up his hand, an apologetic gesture, which matched his features. "I'm sorry, I don't mean to intrude. You look so much like someone I know, but now, I can see, you aren't the same person. Again, please forgive me."

"No problem," she said. "I'm frequently mistaken for a character actress." She gathered her things and left him trying to figure out which one.

Abby couldn't afford an ocean view room, but the one assigned was comfortable and clean. She washed her face and freshened up before putting on sunscreen.

Lifting the painting she had begun several days ago from her folio, she put it on the sofa to critique. Down the beach, not far from the hotel she had found an area of taller white dunes. Ghostly, scattered and whitened to silver driftwood littered the area, graceful and smooth, incongruous with their tortured features. A single dead tree, twisted and bent, displayed its years of struggle against the elements. *Perseverence.*

Abby used acrylics, water-based paints, which dried quickly when she traveled or did *plein air* paintings outside. The undercoat, a burnt sienna with a tiny amount of cobalt blue gave depth to the surface. Judging the work, she decided to take out the smaller pieces of driftwood. They made the painting look too busy. The tree was the focal point and occupied the space a little right of center, its torment and perseverance inspirational. Part of her identified with its lonely, stark presence. This painting would join a growing personal collection. Selling paintings was necessary. They were her main source of income, but parting with some of them still hurt.

She put the painting into a protective cloth bag and checked her canvas tote for the needed art supplies. Abby filled several water containers, adding weight. She gathered her hat and easel before leaving the room.

Downstairs, she found a vending machine and purchased peanut butter crackers along with two large bottles of drinking water from the Tiki Hut. Abby left the boardwalk, carrying her easel and supplies the quarter mile to the site.

The dunes looked like mountains when she arrived. Under the weight of her load and tired, Abby struggled upward and forward over several slopes. The footprints from her first visit, days ago, had been erased by the wind. She whooped when she reached the site, her mouth and throat dry from the effort. Several swigs of water and the dribble of wetness she dropped on her neck and down the front of her shirt revived her.

Because the sun had climbed high, Abby set up the easel facing east with the ocean's horizon in the distance. She would concentrate on the deletions and the details while she waited for the light to move behind her. The shadows were as important to the painting as the subject.

Abby worked until past midday. The sun broiled, and she felt its burn, though the air was cool. Rummaging in her bag, she found the sunscreen and reapplied a liberal amount over her exposed skin. Half her water was gone. She decided to walk and look for respite in the shade. But first, she secured her painting more firmly to the easel and turned it so the wind wouldn't make it into a sail. The legs were buried deep enough, the easel shouldn't move, and no one was anywhere around to disturb her work. Abby walked over several dunes interspersed with flattened areas containing low-growing vines, Marsh Elder, disintegrating coconuts, and other debris that had floated in from foreign places. At the crest of the next large dune, she saw the salt marsh and some wizened trees and brush along the bank by a small bay. Looking north, she saw the conical towers of Château Sologne barely topping the trees. A private landing area jutted out in the protected curve of land behind the estate, but no boat was docked. Abby realized she stood close to the southern end of the island.

Walking and sliding down the dune's slope, she stopped under one of the trees that had little underbrush. She basked in the welcome shade. Taking out a hotel towel, her crackers and water, she prepared to wait on the sun's movement while enjoying the view. White ibis, plovers, and terns walked along the shore, their beaks down as they foraged for food. Smaller birds she couldn't identify flitted from one limb to the next. A Great Blue Heron stood still like a statue. Lightning fast, the heron's sharp beak disappeared in the water and came up with a wriggling fish. The bird carried the morsel to shore, its bill maneuvering it into a head first position. In seconds the fish was swallowed. Abby watched fascinated. She remembered a heron the first day she arrived and wondered if it were the same bird.

Abby slowly munched her crackers and drank her water sparingly. She grew sleepy and started to nod. Her head jerked back as she caught herself. Hermit crabs came close and scuttled away when she moved. Yawning, she embraced her raised knees, rested her head on them, and thought about her next move.

Abby woke from an exhausted nap, shivering from the cold. The sun cast a three o'clock shadow. She hurried to put her things away, took a swig of water, and hurried back, not believing how long she slept.

She turned the easel and took out her supplies. Several minutes were spent organizing her work area and replenishing her colors. The advantage and disadvantage of using acrylics was how fast the paint dried.

Abby added texture to the tree and clouds using a palette knife. The strokes evoked a strong response to the wild and desolate scene. Her inner spirit responded with emotion as she added color. Satisfied with the work, she began to put in the lengthening shadows. Light crowned some of the branches, and she added small splashes of color to the trunk and shadows.

The wind picked up. When she looked around, she noticed a line of dark clouds to the north near the horizon and the shadow of rain falling from its eastern border.

Abby folded and locked her easel, emptied her water canteens, and threw supplies into her bag. She would be lucky to get back to the hotel without getting drenched. She slid down the dunes and headed for the hotel as fast as she could manage with a painting, catching the wind and holding her back. At least the weight had lessened with the empty water containers.

A low rumble of thunder sounded, and a lightning bolt slashed the purple darkness in the distance. Waves built and crashed on the shore ahead of the storm. Any other time, she would have enjoyed the sight and sounds.

The first raindrops fell as she approached the boardwalk. Exhausted, Abby dropped her burden under the Tiki Hut's roof and found a seat at the bar. She put her head down in her wet arms and waited for someone to take her order. Another woman worked at the bar today along with Gloria. She hadn't met this one, and Abby didn't miss her curious look.

As if summoned, Gloria appeared without the gum. "You okay, hon? You look a bit frazzled. What can I get you?"

"I'll take an unsweet tea and a chicken salad sandwich."

Thunder boomed and lightning streaked across the sky, lighting the grounds. They both jumped, and Gloria said, "Time to go inside for a while. I'll put in your order and have it delivered to your room. What's the number?"

Abby told her and gathered her things. When she got to the room, she wanted to shower and change, but she was afraid her meal would arrive. Looking over her painting, she checked it for damage. Everything had dried. If it had been an oil painting, the surface would have been pock-marked with sand or marred from disabuse.

She should have taken the shower. Her meal didn't come for another twenty minutes. She signed the bill, and left the meal untouched to take a hot shower and dispel the cold from the air conditioner.

Later, when she turned on the weather report, she learned tomorrow would be stormy with extensive rain. She chose Loire Park as her destination. She praised the Lord because she wouldn't have to carry anything heavier than her fanny pack.

CHAPTER SEVEN

The next morning, Abby woke after nine, an unusual occurrence. She rarely slept late at home in Philly. While she sipped hot tea, she had enjoyed watching the sun rise over brownstone rooftops across the street from her studio apartment. She missed her nest, the colors and smells different from the sterile room she now inhabited.

After a shower, she dressed in casual, tan slacks and a long-sleeved, amber flannel shirt. Looking in the mirror, she added a copper-toned lipstick and drew back her hair with barrettes on both sides.

Downstairs, she asked the clerk when the shuttle would be leaving for Loire Park. She had twenty minutes, so she took a complimentary cup of hot tea, croissant, and a small package of creamed cheese into the lobby to eat and wait. The hotel had an up-scale restaurant called Ballantine's, which served a breakfast buffet. All the items on the menu were steep, and Abby doubted she would ever take a meal in the place.

Abby watched the people coming down for breakfast. One family had twin boys around five or six years of age. They shoved each other as they tried to get the last pastry. She thought of the elderly couple she had met in the park, the ones who had lost twin boys. *Happiness is a choice.* Abby thought about her words. The woman told her that she had been given the precious gift of life. *Only you can choose to live it.* So much had happened since then. She thought of her mother, father, and brother. She sighed. *Their lives ruthlessly cut short. Why?*

The shuttle arrived, and half a dozen people went outside with her to board. The sky was overcast, and rain drizzled, keeping everything shiny and wet. Abby needed to buy an umbrella. Eddie was not the shuttle driver this time. The new driver introduced himself as Sam.

Abby patted her fanny pack where she had placed Eddie's card.

The more she thought about Eddie's concern, the more uneasy she became. Abby mentally shook herself. *You're making a mountain out of a mole hill.* She heard her gran's voice in her head as she had always said that when Abby was anxious about something. She felt guilt, too, that she hadn't thought about her grandmother in the last couple of days.

I miss you, Gran. I'm sorry I ever doubted you. Please watch over me. Abby felt better with the thought. She believed in the afterlife, and she could picture her grandmother telling God more angels needed to be sent to keep her granddaughter out of trouble.

The shuttle stopped at the entrance of Loire Park next to a covered shelter with wrought iron benches. The quaint water-slicked brick walkways which wound by the shops and the manicured landscaping must have cost a fortune.

One by one, the customers ran for the green and white striped awnings to protect themselves from the rain. Among the first shops were a bakery and candy shop. Abby stopped to watch women smooth fudge on a large marble slab. Later, the fudge would be cut into squares. The sweet, rich smell of chocolate permeated the air. A mini-addiction, chocolate made Abby's face break out, so she didn't go inside.

Next door, the aroma of freshly baked bread made Abby's mouth water and drew her into the bakery. She bought a crusty baguette, still warm, to take back to her room. Carrying the bread, she scuttled from awning to awning, window shopping while the rain continued to fall. One enterprising shop had set out a glazed pottery container full of umbrellas. Several people in front of her took one, and Abby decided having an umbrella beat the discomfort of staying wet. She chose one covered with colorful, geometric patterns and went inside.

The shop specialized in soaps, lotions, and candles, along with an amazing number of accessory items for the bath and bedroom. An aromatic potpourri of smells filled the room.

Abby wandered around until the checkout line shortened.

"Hello. Welcome to Daisy's Aromatherapy Emporium. I'm Daisy. Are you looking for a special scent?"

Abby turned and faced a young woman in her twenties with ash blond hair and sparkling brown eyes."

"Vanna?" The clerk looked momentarily perplexed. "Oh, I'm sorry; you look like someone I know."

"Someone local?"

"Yes, the resemblance is uncanny. Are you a DuMond? Sorry again," she said and smiled ruefully. "My mouth runs away, sometimes."

Abby laughed. "You mean the family who owns the island? I don't think so. I'm just visiting a few days." She picked up a candle marked *citrus* and smelled. "This one smells clean and fresh."

"We make all of our products on the island."

Abby heard pride in her voice and responded, "You're fortunate to have a business you enjoy and to have a part in its production."

"Yes, I know. My mother started the business, but she wanted to create, not get bogged down in sales. We have a mutually enjoyable working arrangement."

Abby picked up a candle and a lotion with the citrus scent. "I guess I'm ready."

They walked to the register, and Abby took money from her fanny pack.

Daisy cut the tag from the umbrella and folded each of Abby's scented purchases in plastic and pink tissue paper. She put them in a larger bag with handles. "Now you'll have room for the bread."

Abby thanked her and went outside. Opening the umbrella, she felt refreshed by the girl's smile and friendliness. *Someone here looks like me. Vanna. I wonder who she is?*

The rain stopped, and Abby enjoyed the clean freshness of her surroundings. The sun peeked through clouds and glistened on wet walkways. The shops ended next to Loire Park. A stucco wall enclosed an area, and an ornate wrought iron gate with a *fleur-de-lis* motif gave Abby enough of a view to see the flower gardens beyond. A PRIVATE plaque was placed by the gate. *Must be a DuMond family member.*

Abby walked back on the opposite walkway. Several clerks had stared at her but didn't mention her resemblance to anyone. People were curious, and she believed someone would say something to the DuMond family.

As she walked down the sidewalk, she passed a woman with an

Afghan hound. The tall, aristocratic dog, with long, silky hair, was the perfect accessory for the silver-haired woman on the other end of the leash. The owner had the same elegant, sleek look and a matching hairdo in the same color. This breed was not the kind of dog to be comfortable in a warm setting. Abby was musing about dogs and owners looking alike when a throaty voice spoke behind her.

"Vanna? Savannah Boucher, what have you done to your hair? You dare to walk by me and not speak?"

Abby turned and found herself confronted by the woman with the hound. "I'm sorry, were you speaking to me?" *Vanna again.* She looked around innocently and didn't see anyone else close by.

The woman stepped back, her hand at her throat. "You are not Vanna." Incredulity masked her face. "Who are you?" she demanded as though Abby were an imposter.

Abby also stepped back. "I'm not Vanna."

"I can see that," the woman ground out and repeated the question, "Who are you?"

Although Abby acted innocent, her voice contained an authentic quaver. "I'm … I'm a tourist from Philadelphia." She swallowed. "Why do you want to know?"

The woman relaxed. "You surprised me, that is all." She took Abby's arm, her grip like a vise. "You will forgive my rudeness." Imperious in tone, her eyes dark orbs, her mouth painted red and pulled into a straight line did not convey an apologetic expression.

Abby looked down at the jewels flashing on the hand that grasped her arm, fear clogging her throat. The woman seemed to come to her senses and let her go.

Backing away, her heart racing and surprised by the assault, Abby said, "I don't know you." She walked away, her steps brisk, leaving the crazy woman to come to her own conclusions.

Savannah Boucher. How are we related? Is Hound Lady a DuMond? She must be. If not, why would my presence elicit such a strong response?

Abby saw the man from the dock, who owned her sketch, enter the Tiki Hut and look around. She sat in a corner on the other side of the bar, reading the newspaper and watching people come and go. Abby couldn't explain how she knew he was looking for her, but she lowered her head behind the paper.

He didn't appear to see her and took the boardwalk to the beach.

Abby debated whether or not she should leave before he got back, but curiosity won. *You know what trouble curiosity brings.* She exhaled a pent up breath.

Gloria and the blond bartender looked after him as he left. Who couldn't help but notice this nice specimen of a man. Tall. Well-built. Khaki shorts. Navy polo shirt. Dockers. Clean shaven. Hair tamed. He cleaned up nice.

The man returned ten minutes later and stopped to talk to the blond.

Abby saw the bartender nod in her direction and quickly lowered her head.

He came to her table. "Hello. We meet again," he said as if this meeting weren't planned.

"I'm sorry?" Abby said, lowering the paper. "I had the feeling you were looking for me."

"That obvious?" He grinned, showing white teeth.

"I'm afraid so." She didn't return his smile.

He held out his hand. "You're right. Noah Hazzard."

Abby looked at the large, masculine hand but didn't take it. "Why are you looking for me?"

Without asking permission, he pulled out a chair and sat down next to her. Taking a menu, he held it up and said under his breath. "Cautious. That's good."

Gloria came over. "Noah, long time, no see. Where ya been, honey?"

"A man's got to work sometimes." He ordered water with lemon and the tuna salad plate.

"Need a refill?" Gloria asked Abby.

"No thanks. I'll be going in a minute."

"Please, don't let me run you off," the man said, eyeing the half sandwich left on Abby's plate.

Gloria handed Abby the bill and waited for her signature.

When she left, Abby repeated, "Why are you looking for me?"

"We have a mutual friend."

Abby hiked her eyebrows.

"Eddie." He looked her in the eyes, his serious and compelling. *Does this woman know how much trouble she's stirred up?*

Disconcerted, Abby thought, *He really is an attractive man in a rough sort of way.* He made her think, *uncivilized*, and she tried to refocus on the stilted conversation. "The shuttle driver?"

"Yes. He's worried. And when Eddie worries, I worry." He kept his voice low.

Abby didn't have to pretend her shock. "Worried about me?" she answered barely above a whisper.

Gloria returned with his water and handed her a small box for her sandwich.

"Thank you," Abby said, and turned her attention back to Noah Hazzard.

He smiled at her and looked innocuous. "Our waitresses are keeping an eye on us, so I suggest you loosen up a bit and look like you're enjoying my company." He nodded and leaned toward her. "Flirt with me. That's something Gloria and Una understand."

Temporarily lost for words, Abby's jaw locked.

Uh oh, not good, "You do know how to flirt, don't you?" he said in a teasing tone.

But it was what he said after the remark that chilled her to the bone. "Your life may depend on it," he said, still smiling.

Abby forced a laugh and said a little louder, "No, I'm from Philadelphia. This is my first trip to the South." Abby quaked inside with the effort to smile and look friendly. She hated the subterfuge.

"That's better," he said in a low tone and a bit louder. "What brings you to Georgia?"

"I've always thought of Savannah as being a romantic place. I'm an artist, and I find the area inspiring."

Gloria brought Noah his tuna salad plate. "Anything else I can get you?"

He said he was fine, and Gloria turned her attention to Abby.

"Change your mind? Do you need a refill?"

Abby looked at her and said pleasantly, "I think I'll have a Plantation Punch."

Gloria gave her a knowing look and sashayed away.

Abby's mind churned with questions. *Who is this man? How do I know he can be trusted? Why is Eddie worried? Am I already in someone's crosshairs?* Her common sense was telling her to leave Mast Island now and not look back. She felt guilty even thinking about leaving before finding out about the family. *My family.*

"Stop frowning," Noah said, leaning toward her. "Your questions will be answered soon enough. Act normal. We'll walk on the beach where prying eyes and ears can't interfere. Okay?"

Abby nodded. "I don't understand what's going on, and it's a bit overwhelming."

"Understandable," he responded and smiled up at Gloria who had returned with the punch.

"Thank you, Gloria, and put the punch on my tab," he said.

"You got it." She looked at Abby with raised eyebrows.

Abby sipped on her fruit-filled punch while Noah enjoyed his salad and its accompanying fresh fruit. She didn't speak, and again her thoughts centered on his mission and whether or not it coincided with her own. *How can his interference relate to my presence on the island? That didn't make sense?* "Do you live on the island?"

"No, but my work sometimes brings me here."

"What do you do?"

"I'm a biologist, free-lance photographer, and part-time detective."

Abby cocked her head, her curiosity aroused. "That seems a bit much. Who do you work for?"

"Biological Natural Resource Solutions, science magazines, and … Quantico." He continued to eat as if he had not said something astounding. Noah Hazzard had responded in a casual manner as if any of these professions were common.

"The FBI?" she whispered behind her napkin.

"Yes," he said in a low voice, his eyes holding hers, willing Abby to curb her questions. "Can we continue this discussion later? I'll answer your concerns in time." Then he put the napkin on his plate and laughed. "Yes, I'd love to see your paintings," he said as if responding to her remark. Noah sat back and watched emotion flit over her face.

He made the phrase sound like she had spoken the proverbial pick-up line, "Let me show you my etchings."

A red tide worked its way up her neck and flushed her cheeks. Abby was not amused.

CHAPTER EIGHT

Una scrutinized Abby's face as Noah paid the bill, but she said nothing about her resemblance to anyone. "Have a good day," she called after them.

Gloria, busy with another customer noticed, and Abby saw she watched them leave together.

Noah put his hand on the small of Abby's back as they walked toward the beach. The familiarity of his touch proclaimed his conquest, and she steamed, not wanting to seem easy to the two women.

When they were out of sight, she shook him off. "Did you have to make me look like ... like a woman desperate for a man ... *any* man?"

"I'm *not* 'any man'. Consider yourself a *femme fatale*. You're the first woman I've shown an interest in here."

Talk about arrogance. "Well, I don't like it." She stalked off, striding down the beach, leaving him behind. *Who does he think he is? God's gift to women?*

"That's beside the point," he said, catching up and putting a hand on her shoulder. Turning her around, he looked at her, his blue-green eyes a stormy sea. "What's your game, lady?" His voice was hard, not friendly. "Why did you come to Mast Island?"

"I came to paint. What's all this mysterious, 'Your life may depend on it,' garbage?"

He took hold of both upper arms, pulled her forward, and spoke with authority. "I'm investigating missing people, likely murdered, *dead* people, and you come here with a DuMond face, acting like an innocent, like nobody's going to notice. You're a time bomb." *Make that nuclear.*

Abby tried to pull back, but he held her fast.

"Listen to me. The DuMond family is living in the past. They still believe in sovereignty, *Le droit du Seigneur*, the absolute, divine right to govern. They believe they control all they survey." His voice lowered and had a cutting edge. "And they make sure they do."

He shook her when she tried to twist away. "Don't be a fool. You're an unknown with DuMond blood, a possible threat to their empire."

"How did I get DuMond blood? How could I be a threat? I'm an artist from Philadelphia, represented by a reputable gallery. I've lived there all my life, and I have no connection to this part of the world."

"You have a connection," he said, his voice implacable. "Now tell me what it is."

Abby looked at his hands still holding her and when she pulled back again, he let her go. She turned back to the hotel, rubbing her arms, walking away.

Two men jogged up the beach toward them, and Noah swore.

Swinging Abby around, he said, "I'm sorry," before his lips ground into hers. The kiss softened when she didn't resist. Her body leaned into him, pliant and willing, her hands clutching his arms. When he released her, she almost fell, and he hugged her to his chest, his heart beating double time. A wave of possessiveness overwhelmed him. He wanted to protect this prickly woman. She felt right in his arms, and he didn't want to let her go.

The two men stopped, for all the world like they went jogging every day in white, button-down shirts and suit pants.

"Hello, Mark, Paul," Noah nodded, his voice congenial. "Does the family know you're taking time off to exercise?"

"Very funny, Dr. Hazzard."

Abby tensed when she heard the title and tone of voice. She recognized the gate guard, Paul, but he probably didn't remember her because of the hat and sunglasses.

"What are you doing here?" the tall one demanded. "This end of the island isn't your workplace."

"I had to see my girl. She has an aversion to swamps."

Abby turned in his arms, giving them a brief look at her face before burying her nose in his chest.

The men stiffened, embarrassed. "Sorry," they muttered in unison and began to run back to the hotel.

"Now, I'm an adulterer," Noah said. "They thought you were Rouland Boucher's wife."

"Vanna?"

"So, you do know something. Yes, Mrs. Savannah DuMond Boucher. There's a striking resemblance. Let's get back to the hotel. I need to check your room."

As they walked by the Tiki Hut, Gloria joined them. "You must have scared the hell out of Mark and Paul. They asked for her," she said nodding at Abby. "I told them you were out there. They came back as white as the beach. Called us 'idiots', for not telling them the situation, so we didn't bother to tell them you weren't who they thought you were."

"Thanks. I owe you one," Noah said as he touched Abby's waist.

Gloria caught up with them. "Here, you forgot the rest of your meal." She handed Abby the box.

They thanked her, and Noah prodded Abby to get her moving.

She did not like the impression his physical touches were giving the staff. She thought about his kiss, the passionate scene he created for the two men on the beach. She saw the purposeful looks on the faces of the two men running towards them and went with the flow when Noah grabbed and kissed her. His arms were safe haven, and she enjoyed their warmth, his embrace, too much,

Abby's room had been invaded. "Someone's gone through my things."

"How can you tell? The maid's been here," Noah said as he wrote a quick note on the hotel's complimentary note pad, tore the sheet off, and then pocketed the pad.

Act confused. Don't know what's happening, the note read, and he began checking the room.

That won't be hard. "Maybe." she said, uncertainty in her voice. "What's going on? People stare at me, act like they know me, but I'm not whoever they think I am. I don't know anybody here."

"That part, I can clear up. You look like Vanna Boucher. She's the daughter of Jean-Jacques DuMond," Noah said, holding up a "bug" he found under the desk. He put it back and continued looking.

Abby cringed inside, her stomach tightening. Knowing she was being monitored added another dimension to her quest. "So what? People resemble other people all the time, and they don't make a big deal out of it. This whole thing is creeping me out." Abby rubbed her arms and shivered, acknowledging the truth. "I should have gone to Cumberland Island. They, at least, have wild horses." Abby paused as if thinking. "No, I think I'll go back to Philadelphia, by way of Charleston, and finish my vacation. There will be interesting places to paint in Charleston, and people might be friendlier."

Noah pointed to another "bug" in the towel cabinet and walked over to her. "You can't leave now. We just met again, and I want to get to know you better." His voice contained sincerity and interest. "Hey, you promised to show me your paintings," he said and laughed. "I don't want to hear any more talk about leaving."

"I only have one completed since I've been here. It rained yesterday, and I planned to go on the tour this afternoon to see about other locations to paint." She walked to her folio and took out her painting of the tree.

"You're good." He complimented her work like he hadn't expected her talent. "I mean, I know you're good at sketching. You gave me your sketch of *The Lady* the first time we met on the ferry dock. You captured her spirit. I didn't even get your name. But your painting … blows me away."

"Thank you." If you want to see more, you can go online to the Dove Creek Gallery site, in Philadelphia. They represent my work. I need a few more paintings for my December opening at the gallery. That's the reason for this trip."

"I'd like to come, especially if you have paintings of the island. Will you send me an invitation?"

"Are you serious? You'd come all the way to Philly for a black tie opening?"

"Of course. I said I wanted to get to know you." He looked at his watch. "How about an afternoon snack? We can get a gelato at

Summer's End. That's a restaurant bordering Loire Park."

"Not today. My tour leaves here at two, but I love gelato."

"A rain check then. What about tomorrow?" His voice was cheerful and hopeful.

Abby wished he were sincere and not pretending. "In the morning, I thought I'd go back to the ferry landing to paint. The shuttle will take me. A huge oak captured my attention."

"Maybe I'll join you. I have some lab work, but if I can get my results recorded, I'll stop by. We'll have a late lunch and some gelato."

He opened the door and pulled her into the hall, out of the planted bug's range. "I'm not sorry," he said, his eyes twinkling, voice low, promising. He fixed a light kiss on her forehead.

Abby colored, remembering the kiss on the beach. "Neither am I."

Noah grinned before turning to leave.

"Don't let it go to your head," she called after him, and he raised his hand to let her know he heard.

God, does that mean he's really interested in me? She watched him stride down the hallway, admiring his air of confidence. Abby welcomed Noah's interest and strength. She welcomed his protection. *FBI? Why is he really here?*

Her eyes surveyed the room as she closed the door. A sense of violation and disgust rippled through her at the thought of her every sound being recorded, someone rifling through her personal items. She wanted to crush and discard the listening devices, but she mentally filed the thought under things to do later.

Stripping down to bra and panties, Abby began the stretching exercises to prepare for the more strenuous martial arts moves. Bowing formally to her absent *sensai*, Manny Corolet, she began with basic stances and controlled moves before escalating into the katas. Maintaining balance, stepping, turning, and moving smoothly from one position to the next while trying to keep perfect form, required focus. Progressing into the more active moves, her arms flew as she used tension, flex, chop, thrust, and whip-like actions to defend, or to distract and strike an opponent. Abby found the moves easier when she had a partner to "read." Visualizing a scenario or an opponent was not as easy.

She followed the katas with self-defense kick-boxing strategies involving kicks, strikes, jabs, and punches. Abby liked the workout because it kept her in shape.

An hour later, as she stretched limber muscles, Abby realized the "bug" had been close. She smothered a laugh. Let her listeners try to decipher the grunts of exertion and heavy breathing. To make their plight even more unpleasant, she launched into loud renditions of praise songs and hymns, making a joyful noise in a tone deaf voice.

CHAPTER NINE

Abby walked through the lobby fifteen minutes before the tour bus arrived. She had turned up the volume on a television twenty-four hour news program. Maybe her listeners would catch up on current events. She entered the Tiki Hut to get a bottle of water and stopped at the vending machine for cheese crackers and a candy bar. She had eaten the whole loaf of bread yesterday with thick chunks of cheddar cheese she bought in the small market across from Loire Park. *I need more nutritious meals.*

Thinking about seeing the island, her father's home, filled her with excitement. Abby put on her hat and sunglasses, shouldered the canvas bag, and went outside.

An empty Mercedes truck pulled to the hotel entrance. The dark green, custom-built, convertible vehicle looked like it held a couple of dozen upholstered seats. Roll bars crossed the open top. They supported tarps during inclement weather and were now sandwiched alongside the seats, unneeded. The driver, a man whose shirt had a Sologne logo, checked off the names on his clipboard.

First in line, Abby took a place up front.

A woman with massive binoculars sat next to her. "I come to the barrier islands every year to bird watch during their migration. Birds have a refuge here at the northern end." The woman chattered on about the birds they would likely see. "Mast Island is not as big as some of the others, and it's easier to get around. Are you staying long?"

"Until Saturday," Abby said, looking around as they drove. All the trees bent toward the mainland, their resistance to high winds and hurricanes eliciting her admiration. The truck stopped at the Silver Dunes to collect more people.

The driver only talked when they stopped at scenic or historic areas to get off and photograph. He told them about the history of the island, pointed out the derelict rice impoundments and stopped at the remains of former, freed slave dwellings. Only a couple, in a deplorable state of disrepair, still stood with a couple of chimneys among the ruins.

A woman in the back called out a question. "Why did the first DuMond free the slaves? They were legal to have back then, weren't they?"

"During and after the Revolutionary War, slaves ran away, and the islands provided a harder-to-reach, safe environment rich with food resources.

"When *Comte* Phillipe DuMond bought the island, he found some of these run-aways. *Comte* is French for the English title, Count, he explained. The *comte* needed laborers, and he didn't have a militia to keep them here. They would run away again, so he offered to make them free men, and give them a place to live, where they could keep families together in exchange for their labor. They stayed, and when word got out, more slaves came to the island, until he had a considerable work force."

The guide made Phillipe DuMonde sound like one of the colony's first entrepreneurs.

Abby thought about the time when humans could be sold, families separated. The reality was more sobering. Slavery still existed in parts of the world today. Even in America, sex trafficking flourished. People were still bought and sold.

The cemetery looked desolate. Scattered tombstones, when visible, were small and inconspicuous, hidden by weeds. Abby thought it shameful not to keep the resting place of the laborers maintained. *Where are the DuMonds buried? Not here.* She was beginning to get an understanding of her DuMond ancestors, which did not put them in a favorable light.

Abby was careful not to ask about the family, in case someone was watching her. Whoever placed the "bug" knew she was on this tour. The thought sent squiggles of paranoia through her inner being. Abby let others ask the questions and forced herself to look at the scenery, not the people.

The driver stopped at the remains of an old saw mill. Logs and a century's worth of chips were piled nearby. "Timber from Mast Island was used to build ships, and the family specialized in making masts for the Clipper schooners and other sailing vessels plying these waters," the guide told the group.

Abby made a rough sketch of the building and equipment while others took pictures. She could have brought a camera, but she always felt her painting had more soul by catching the scene with her mind's eye. She then used colors which enhanced her setting, rather than leaving a stark, photographic image.

The refuge, the bird watcher mentioned, contained large marshy areas, with sloughs and creek tributaries leading to the impoundments, salt marsh, and the ocean. The tide was out, and birds raced back and forth, their beaks probing the mud for prey or skimming their meal from the shallows. The vehicle passed over two, sturdy wooden bridges. Numerous bird nests made island areas into rookeries, but only the hardy, native birds had not migrated farther south. Abby's seatmate checked each grouping to try and find one she hadn't recorded in her sighting log.

The bus parked on a shell lot, and everyone got off. One boardwalk with rails led into a swampy area, and another turned east to the ocean. The second bus was not present, and Abby thought its schedule must be different. They had thirty minutes to look around.

She stopped to take out her sketchbook. All but two men and the bird watcher stayed behind, trying to decide their choice. Abby followed the majority to the beach, and one of the men followed her. *Is he a watcher?* The hair at her nape stood on end at the thought. She didn't look at him until she moved into the first group of people and cast only a casual glance as her eyes took a panoramic view of the scenery.

The man, small and non-descript, good spy characteristics, stood out to Abby. When her eyes came to him, he bent and tied a shoe lace, paying no attention to her. *Maybe I'm wrong.*

Abby began drawing the larger pieces of driftwood with their lengthening afternoon shadows. She made a detailed sketch of a sea oat and looked around. Most of the people walked the beach to look over today's shell offerings. The man who followed her had taken off his shoes and walked into the water, never straying away. *Suspicious behavior for a man who just tied his laces.*

A horn blew, and everyone returned to the vehicle.

One of the women asked about the DuMond family and their plantation. "Will we be able to see their house?"

The driver said, "The DuMonds are private people. They don't allow visitors to tour the house or grounds on the southern end of the island. They live there."

One man guffawed, "They don't need our money now, but hard times are coming, and they'll lose more than their privacy."

The woman next to her nodded sagely, and told Abby, "You know, as many times as I've come here, I don't think I've ever seen a DuMond."

Abby smiled but didn't comment. She had been the last person on the bus before the driver, and she noticed the little man now sat behind her.

CHAPTER TEN

Abby took out the quick sketches that she made on the tour. She tried to decide which one would make a nice painting, but her thoughts kept returning to Noah Hazzard, FBI man and biologist. What was he studying? He had held her in his arms and kissed her. Noah said he wasn't sorry. He was a bit taller than she, and his height a nice change from some of the men she had dated in the past. An insistent rap startled her.

The door didn't have a peephole, and another knock sounded. "Who is it?" she called, feeling vulnerable. Abby wasn't expecting anyone.

"Vanna. Vanna Boucher," a voice said, and Abby's knees weakened. She was about to meet the woman who looked like her … maybe the first family member. Abby pulled open the door and stared at her twin. They both gaped and didn't speak for a space, just assessed what they saw.

"My god!" Vanna exclaimed, stepping back and speaking first. "I do not believe it."

Abby did a quick check of the hall, and seeing no one else, opened the door wider. "Now I understand all the attention I've been getting. Please come in." Abby felt shabby in her jeans next to this chic reflection of herself.

Vanna was dressed casually, but she had an aura of confidence and breeding, enabling her to hide the mask of incredulity quickly. She held out her hand. "I am Vanna, and I have heard so much about you, I feel like you are family already."

Vanna radiated friendly in her words, smile, and sparkling eyes. She was a little shorter, but not by much, and her hair was longer, smoother, and shone with obvious care. Abby noticed Vanna's speech lacked contractions, making her voice more formal.

Abby took her hand, "Abby Parsons." She gestured toward the upholstered chair and moved her painting aside, giving herself room to sit on the desk chair.

"I understand you are an artist from Philadelphia, visiting our area for the first time," Vanna said as she studied the sketches and painting before sitting down. "I know this tree well. You are talented. I can see why Dove Creek Gallery represents you." She explained. "I looked you up on the web."

"You seem to know a lot about me, and I know nothing about you, except we share a resemblance."

"You call *this* a resemblance?" she said and laughed while pointing at Abby's face and her own. "You are a DuMond, no doubt about that," her words adamant. "Whose you are is the question?"

Abby stiffened. Vanna insinuated her birth was illegitimate. She hoped she looked shocked. *This is dangerous ground.* Abby shook her head. "You're dreaming. I can assure you, I am not a member of your family." She felt a twinge of guilt at how easily the lie slipped through her lips. She guessed living life on the edge facilitated the fabrication. *Be careful. Think before you speak.* Vanna didn't feel like a threat, *but my life depends on not trusting anyone in the family.* "I'm sorry, but all I can offer you is bottled water for refreshment, and it isn't cold."

Vanna leaned forward. "I do not need anything except information about your background."

"My family doesn't come from noble stock. They were hardworking, honest, patriotic, and conservative." *I can't believe I said that with a straight face.*

"Were? You have no family living?"

Uh oh. Not a smart admission. This woman's intelligent. "No, just cousins, who live in various states. I lived with my grandmother, my mother's mother, until I left home. My gran died unexpectedly from an aneurism about a month ago. I had to get away and come to terms with her death." She paused, and Vanna didn't speak, so she continued. "Her name was Evelyn Desmond, and her husband, Paul, a fisherman, died when his boat capsized two years after they married. My grandmother never remarried. Their daughter was my mother, Serena Parsons. She died in childbirth. My father was unknown, and …

Vanna interrupted. "Your father was unknown?"

Abby could see the mystery ended here for Vanna. "I knew my grandmother, and I can tell you, if my father were of noble birth, she would have crowed the news to everyone she knew, and she would have sought child support. We lived from pension check to pension check. I received a full scholarship, or I wouldn't have been able to attend college." *I'm sorry, Gran.*

"Were you not curious? About your father, I mean?" Vanna looked like she had a hard time believing her, which meant others would also be suspicious. The "bugs" were still in place. Someone was hearing, maybe recording their conversation.

"I never knew either of my parents. My grandmother only talked about my mother, and when I was older and asked about my father, she told me to forget about him; he wasn't worth remembering. After that, when I asked, she clammed up. I assumed something dreadful had happened. I didn't want to know I was the daughter of a rapist, or murderer, or worse, so I stopped asking. I guess you don't understand, coming from a pedigree like your own. It's a fluke we resemble each other, but that's as far as the relationship goes."

Vanna sat still as if her mind reviewed all she had heard.

Abby felt uneasy in her silence. *Is my story believable, or not?*

"My father, Jean-Jacques DuMond, had four brothers and one sister, but the girl was stillborn.

"Uncle Guillaume went back to France years ago. Uncle Jules was killed when terrorists tried to blow up his ship in the Persian Gulf during the Iran-Iraq War. Uncle Henri sustained life-threatening injuries in a warehouse explosion.

"I never knew Uncle Rafe, the elder one. He disappeared before I was born. The family searched for him, but investigators came to a dead end. Years later, he was believed dead, and my father became head of the family." Vanna pursed her lips in thought. "Uncle Rafe did not marry or have children."

Abby tried not to show emotion at the mention of her father.

"Poor Uncle Henri was so traumatized and badly injured in the explosion, he requires round-the-clock care. He sired no children." Vanna chewed her bottom lip, her brow furrowed as if in deep thought.

"I cannot believe my father would abandon a baby. No," She said in a decisive voice, "my father would have acknowledged a child and brought him to Sologne to be educated and want for nothing." She waved a manicured hand. "My Uncle Jules, on the other hand, had a couple of children out of wedlock before he was killed, and they live at Sologne. I haven't heard anything about Uncle Guillaume. I guess he is still alive in France. No one speaks of him."

Abby was silent as Vanna ran through the family, verbalizing the possibilities.

"You can't be Uncle Jules's daughter. He had no qualms about foisting his children on the family. He was proud of his virility. Uncle Guillaume is a mystery. Why did he go back to France? Maybe everyone is wrong about Uncle Rafe."

"Again Vanna, your reasoning must be on the wrong track," Abby said.

"I believe in kismet. You were drawn to this island by blood. Now, we have to search out our relationship." She looked at Abby, excitement in her tone. "I have always wanted a sister, and you must be a cousin, which in our family, is almost as close." She stood. "You must come to Sologne. The family will want to meet you."

Abby's heart began a tattoo which drummed in her ears. "I appreciate the offer, and I'd love to see the plantation, but I'm leaving on Saturday. I don't want to encourage talk about a relationship with your family. That would be dishonest." *Forgive me, God. When did deceit become easy?*

"Nonsense. We know you are not here because of family. I want them to meet you. They will be astounded. What fun!"

"I can't," Abby said. "The dressiest outfit I have with me is slacks and a clean shirt."

"Do not worry. I will tell the family it is a casual affair. Some of them will appreciate the change."

Now that Abby had gotten further than she dreamed possible, she had reservations, serious life and death reservations. Noah's words filled her with dread. "May I bring a friend?" *a protector.*

"You would not happen to be speaking about that nice-looking Dr. Hazzard, now would you?" she asked with a mischievous smile. "Oh yes, news travels fast here. Besides, Rouland needs to see how Mark and Paul could have mistaken you for me. I can tell you my husband has a jealous streak, and I had a time convincing him I was not the woman in Dr. Hazzard's arms this morning."

"I got the feeling Noah isn't well-liked by your family."

"Most of us think he is here to work, but several think he is too nosy, maybe investigating the family."

"Why would a biologist do that?" Abby asked innocently.

Vanna frowned for the first time, her expression thoughtful. "I have no idea." She brightened. "Say you will come, and by all means, bring Dr. Hazzard. A car will pick you up here on Thursday at six."

Later, Abby called Room Service and ordered a bowl of New England clam chowder, a side salad, and a pot of hot tea. She didn't feel like talking to anyone else, and she was leery of exposing herself too much. She turned on the television and watched the news until her supper came.

Abby had no way of contacting Noah, so she hoped he would join her this morning. Her sleep had been fitful after the meeting with Vanna. The revelations and invitation shadowed her thoughts most of the night. Abby liked her and hoped Vanna was not part of a sinister plot.

She thought of Noah's words. Who was missing and probably murdered? *He can't be investigating my father's disappearance after all this time. Can he?* She had a lot of questions for him, and she wanted answers.

Abby walked to the Tiki Hut for a bottle of water. The widower she met on the shuttle sat alone, looking lost and despondent.

She checked her watch. Twenty-five minutes until the shuttle arrived. Abby walked to the man's table. "Hello again."

He looked up perplexed. Then a smile formed as he remembered. "May I sit down?"

He nodded, and she pulled out a chair.

"Have you been out on the tour yet?"

"No, I don't seem to have the energy," he said.

"It's a beautiful island. The shuttle takes you to an area where you can take a boardwalk into the swamp or go onto the beach to look for shells."

"Connie would have liked that."

"Your wife?"

He nodded.

"Tell me about Connie?"

"She liked to discover things. Her mother told me when Connie was a little girl, she had a metal Band-Aid box she used for her finds.

"The gravel parking lot held a multitude of treasures. She might find a button, paper clip, or penny. On a good day, she might find a dime. You could go to the movie for a dime." He looked at Abby, his eyes shining at the memory.

"Connie liked to quilt. She was in The Lord's Quilt Club at church. Her friends met two days a week to sew a quilt for someone in the community needing prayer. They added a pocket to each and put scriptures in them before handing them out. They told the person, they were added to their prayer chain."

"What a wonderful ministry!

"I lost my gran a little over a month ago. She was my only relation." Abby told him some of her story. "I guess if we live long enough, we will have special people leave our lives." She told him about the couple in the park and the words the woman said to her. Abby's ministry would be to pass along the wisdom when opportunity opened the door.

The man smiled. "Connie would agree. This is the first time anyone has asked me to talk about her. You understand," he said.

"There's still life in this old shell. I'm going to sign up for a tour."

"Good for you. Connie would be pleased. Think positive thoughts. Each day can be an adventure."

She checked her watch again. "I have to catch a shuttle."

CHAPTER ELEVEN

Abby stretched as she waited for the shuttle. "Spy Man," as she had dubbed her watcher, waited too, and he didn't carry luggage as did most of the visitors leaving the island. She smiled, thinking of him cooling his heels on the dock all day. If he followed her from there, he'd lose his cover.

The shuttle arrived, and Eddie moved to the back to load the luggage. "Spy Man" took the front seat, and Abby made her way toward the back. Eddie included her in his spiel after he picked up passengers from two other hotels. "I hope everyone enjoyed their stay on Mast Island. We hope you'll tell your friends and come back for another relaxing vacation."

Passengers talked among themselves during the ride, and most of their comments were positive. A couple said more entertainment was needed on the island.

Eddie didn't single Abby out before or after they arrived at the dock. Maybe he knew "Spy Man."

Noah Hazzard walked toward her from the dock when the shuttle stopped. He had dressed in khaki hiking cargo shorts with a canvas D-ring belt and a hunter green short-sleeved shirt with air vents.

Abby relaxed when she saw him and met him with a smile. "You came early."

"I worked late last night," he said, shouldering her load. He put his other hand on her back to propel her away from the dock area, which was filling with people. "If you want to paint here, we'll come back when the place is deserted."

They passed Eddie, but neither spoke to him as they walked up the road.

"I bet I can tell you which tree caught your attention the other day."

Abby stopped and leaned the large folio on Noah. She turned in a circle with her arms out as she soaked in the expansive view. "Spy Man" was almost out of sight. He watched them with a phone in his ear. "I have an update, and I have questions."

"Why am I not surprised?"

"You will be when I tell you who visited me last night." She took the folio and strode ahead as the massive tree came into view. A carpet of acorns covered the ground beneath the tree among newly fallen leaves.

"Whoa there, girl, don't just leave me hanging," he said as he reached her side. "Who came knocking?"

Abby ignored the question as she walked around the tree, looking for the best angle and stopped. She also considered the white spaces in and around her subject. "I'll set up here." She took the easel from his hand and in less than a minute had it open and ready for her supplies.

"How did you get here?" she asked taking in his tanned, battle scarred legs. Two fresh scratches marked his shins, and his all-weather hiking boots looked like they had piled on the mileage.

"Through the woods. I know a short cut that takes off a mile or two."

Abby noticed the sleeping bag attached to his backpack as he unhooked it.

"Are you planning to stay overnight?"

Noah laughed. "Not today. You sit on the ground here, and the chiggers make you pay an uncomfortable price. We'll be more protected with a buffer." He unzipped the bag and laid the sleeping bag flat over a white plastic tablecloth he placed on the ground.

Abby took out her canvas, paints, and water containers. "The little man in khakis with brown hair we left sitting on the post at the dock has been following me. Do you know him?"

"Marcel fits the bill. I saw him. He's one of the DuMond's loyal henchmen. Don't let his size fool you. He's a dangerous man. Who did you see last night?"

"Vanna DuMond Boucher." She took out her paint-spattered

coveralls and slipped them over her clothing.

"And?"

"And I need you to answer my questions? Who's missing, possibly murdered? Who's Eddie? What do you really do? Tell me about your doctorate and work."

"You don't want to know much, do you?" he said, amused by her caution. "Okay. This is need-to-know time, or you could get into some serious trouble. I've been thinking maybe you should leave the island for safety reasons. I can't be with you every minute."

Abby looked at him surprised. "Who asked you to? Be with me every minute, I mean? I'm not leaving." She turned the canvas, so the longest side was horizontal, and took out her wide, two-inch Hake brush to paint the undercoat. Mixing Ultramarine Blue, a touch of Alizarin Crimson, and a dab of Titanium White on her palette, she brushed the surface horizontally and then vertically with the color, giving texture to the background. She rinsed her brush, dried it on a swath of cloth, and sat beside him, wrapping her arms around her knees. "So talk."

"My doctorate is in Biology. I'm studying the bio geomorphology of the salt marsh, the sedimentary environment of the benthos and plankton organisms interacting with animal activity like shellfish filters. These interactions impact erosion, turbidity, and loss of habitat for the colonization of other organisms due to introduced toxins and human intervention. This causes a drastic change in the environment."

"Why not try to impress me with your knowledge," Abby said with a twinkle in her eye.

Noah looked at Abby, his mouth skewed to one side. This woman got under his skin and made him uncomfortable on some level he couldn't fathom. "The impoundments built by your ancestors shifted the saltwater marsh to a freshwater state which is now dominated by invasive species. The scientific community would like to see the salt marsh restored by tidal saltwater."

"That part I understand. Who's missing, possibly murdered?"

"My Uncle Max, my mother's brother."

Abby looked at him shocked by the revelation.

"Uncle Max was a detective in Savannah, opening a cold case

involving the DuMond family. He believed something nefarious was happening on Mast Island. A close associate helping him was killed in an accident after my uncle disappeared, and local police thought his death suspicious. The FBI got involved, and I volunteered because I had a personal stake in the case and a useful, professional cover. No one knew me in Savannah."

Abby listened to his account in silence.

"Eddie briefly became a source of information when he left his home to study. He knew my uncle, and they became drinking buddies in Savannah and on the island."

"That explains Eddie's interest."

"Eddie keeps his ears to the ground and hears things from people working at the château. Three days ago he contacted me in a panic. A woman looking like a DuMond had come to the island to paint. She stirred up the DuMond family to the point they practically had everyone on the island reporting your every move, including Eddie." Noah put his hand on Abby's knee and startled her. "Sorry," Noah said, and continued. "He didn't tell them he drove you onto the grounds of the château, and you asked about the family. Eddie worried James Toomey might have said something. Toomey's one of the DuMond attorneys. But then again, Mr. Toomey might not want to let the family know about his breach of protocol.

"Eddie said you had on a big hat and sunglasses. He didn't get a look at you until your second visit. When Eddie said, 'artist,' you instantly came to mind. My artist? Now," he paused, "your turn."

"Hummm," *my artist. Wishful thinking*, She sighed.

"Vanna knocked on the door, and when I opened it, my heart clogged my throat. I couldn't speak. Vanna regained her voice first. The resemblance is incredible. I like her. She seemed excited to have me as a member of the family."

"I met her once. She's a likable woman, but don't be naïve. You can't trust anyone in the family at this point. Are we clear on that?"

"Yes sir, Captain. I received the message loud and clear."

"This isn't a game, Abigail." He looked off, his mouth set in a straight line.

"Call me Abby. I understand your concern …."

"Do you?" he said, his anger barely under control. "Do you *really* understand?" He pulled her close and kissed her. Not a peck, but a full-blown, no-holds-barred, passionate kiss that rocked her all the way to her toes. He got up and walked away, leaving her in a melted puddle.

God, what a kiss! She realized this was really her first kiss worthy of being remembered. *Now, that's a sad commentary on your love life. What love life?* Abby's Amazonian size elicited unkind ridicule in school and intimidated most men. She remembered the embarrassment of having to sit or bend for kisses, and dancing with her partner's face plastered on her chest. The taller boys in school dated the petite girls, half their size. Who had confidence in themselves back then? She didn't.

Noah walked toward her, his hand massaging the back of his neck. "I'm sorry. That was an aberration. I apologize."

Abby stood. "I'm not sorry. Would you repeat, whatever you just said, to be sure I understand." She stood before him like a chastised schoolgirl, her eyes closed, her mouth lifted, waiting.

His eyes moved over her, memorizing her features, and not believing his ears. *What are you waiting for, you dope? The lady wants an encore.* He took her in his arms and repeated the lesson.

"Ahhh," Abby sighed, leaning into his strong chest, smelling his musky scent. "I got it. Thank you."

Noah grinned. He had never met a woman like this one. She rattled his cage and went off line, leaving him stranded and wondering how to handle the situation. Yet, her voice was warm honey that ran through him, soothing like a balm. He remembered liking her voice when they first met.

Abby opened her eyes, and matter-of-factly said, "That research was fun. Now, I have to paint."

She swayed as she walked to the easel and looked back to ask, "What are you doing Thursday night?"

"More research, I hope," he said and with cheer added, "Whatever you'd like to do."

"Good, you're my date for dinner at Château Sologne. We get picked up at my hotel at six. Casual attire. Be prompt."

"What! Haven't you understood anything I've tried to tell you?" *Is this woman looking for trouble?*

"Yes, but I'm willing to let you try again." She smiled mischievously at him and batted her eyelashes.

"You're a menace," he said. "You can't count on my being a gentleman when you act like a brazen ... brazen ..." Every word he thought had an inappropriate connotation.

"Promise?" she asked and laughed, a pleasing, uninhibited sound of joy.

Noah closed his eyes, gritted his teeth, and willed himself to return to a controlled state of mind. He never felt so out of his depth, even when he defended his dissertation. Noah never thought of himself as a ladies' man. He'd kept his nose to the grindstone, unwilling to forfeit his scholarships and grants for parties and dates.

Abby used a light blue to apply the outline of the trunk and limbs onto her canvas. She recounted the conversation with Vanna and about her attempt to find their family connection. She daubed in leaves, mixing colors and shading areas in darker hues. Her eyes automatically created light spaces which were as important to a painting as the painted images.

"Vanna described each of the brothers." Abby's voice quivered when she spoke of Vanna's missing Uncle Rafe. She believes I must be one of Uncle Guillaume's love children. He left and went to France, and she doesn't know why. Uncle Jules is dead. He has two love children living at the château. And she doesn't believe her father would have a love child without acknowledging him. Uncle Henri almost died in a warehouse explosion. He's unmarried and has no children they know about."

Noah listened as Abby related their conversation. "My notes say Jean-Jacques has three brothers, Raphael, Jules, and Guillaume. Who's Uncle Henri? He doesn't fit. And who are you? I think I deserve an explanation."

"Rafe ... Raphael is my father. He and my mother secretly wed because his family did not approve his choice for a DuMond bride. She was pregnant with me when they were attacked on the street in Savannah." Abby's voice wavered, "Rafe fought them, and my mother ran to get help. When she showed the police where the attack happened, they only found blood. My father was gone, never to be seen again.

"Vanna said the family searched for him to no avail, and he was later declared dead. Her father became head of the family."

Noah paced. He knew most of what she told him. Henri didn't fit the picture. *Who is he?* Something nagged his mind, but he couldn't get the thought to gel. "If your mother was pregnant when they were attacked, why doesn't the family know about you?"

Abby told him how her mother and her twin were killed, and about her gran, Evie, who was not her real grandmother, being shot, but surviving. She told him the story her gran and Mina Kresge concocted to keep her and her identity safe and about the kickboxing and karate her gran insisted she take.

Abby related the story about the box, its contents, the missing marriage page, Father Ziegler's help, and about the attorney, Gordon Culpepper. "I secured a safety deposit box to hold my treasures. The key is hidden in the gesso jar. I use gesso to prime my canvas." Abby showed him which jar and opened the lid, the key not visible in the goop.

Noah sat down, his hands scrubbing his face as he thought of Abby's plight, her dangerous mission, and his new feelings for this woman. *She's a legitimate DuMond heir.* He shook his head, realizing the danger had multiplied. And even more frightening, he might lose her if not to death, to her family position. *She's a DuMond, you sap. Stop thinking about yourself, and figure out a way to keep Abby alive.*

CHAPTER TWELVE

Abby looked at Noah sprawled under a sheltering limb of the mighty oak. He hadn't spoken since she revealed her identity. *What's he thinking?*

Noah leaned on an elbow, his head braced on his hand deep in thought. Filtered light and shadows moved over him in the cool breeze. Gain and loss, revelation and defeat scattered like the leaves, when no simple answers came to his mind.

Abby chose a smaller brush and outlined Noah's recumbent pose onto the canvas. His figure, dwarfed by the tree, gave her painting a focal interest that drew the eyes and Abby's heart. She sighed. This painting was destined to go into her personal collection. Abby needed paintings for her show. Paintings she could sell not hoard.

Noah looked her way and sat up clasping his knees. "I'm not comfortable with your insistence on going to the château."

"You'll be with me, and we'll make sure people know where we're going. We can't just disappear. People will talk."

"People have disappeared from the island without a trace. I'm afraid corruption is involved."

"Eddie's your friend. He would press for an investigation."

"Maybe," Noah answered. "He has family here. That makes him vulnerable."

Abby chewed the end of her brush. "I have to go. You don't have to get involved."

"Like hell I don't," Noah growled as he stood and approached her, eyes blazing.

Abby held up her brush, a feeble defense at his purposeful move. She swallowed, and hoping to deflect his intent said, "I hope you don't mind me adding you to my work." She backed away to give him a better view.

Noah glanced at the painting, but his progress was not deterred. He stood before her and kept his hands fisted at his sides. His stance, however, spoke volumes.

"Stop looking at me like that. I'm not stupid. I'll be careful, and I'm *not* helpless. My grandmother made sure I can protect myself."

"Against poison? A bullet? How will you protect yourself?" Noah's voice scalded her. "Here's a scenario to chew on. You get your belongings, check out, and leave the island. Two witnesses at the hotel, the shuttle driver, and a ferry hand corroborate the story. Your trail ends in in Savannah or another big city, and you become another cold case as investigators reach a dead end."

Abby lifted her hands in supplication before folding her arms across her chest. "Okay, your little tale scared me. Are you happy now? Is this what happened to your uncle? Are you implying my family is involved?" Her eyes misted. "All of them?"

"Abby, I'm sorry." Noah felt out of his element. He'd made her cry. He looked down and rubbed the back of his neck, signaling his impending defeat before this stubborn woman. He as good as accused her family of murder without a thread of evidence.

"I don't know what happened to my uncle. Investigator notes included witnesses telling that story. Eddie said a week after Uncle Max's disappearance; the shuttle driver supposedly left this island and never returned. His family hasn't heard from him. People here are scared. Ignorance is the inhabitant's only protection."

Abby swallowed her fear and felt acid burn through her body. "The DuMonds are my father's family. They are the only connection to my past. I have to meet them."

"Okay," Noah conceded. "Okay, I'll go with you, but I'm bringing in backup until you officially leave the island in one piece."

Thirty minutes before the ferry arrived, Noah and Abby walked back to the dock.

Abby asked, "Do you have siblings?"

"I have a younger brother who lives in San Francisco. Owen's married and has two girls, six and eight. He's in the import-export business.

"You said your mother came from Charleston."

"That's what she told my gran and Mina Kresge. I don't know if Isabella Claire Langford is even her real name. So many tales have been told, it's hard to separate fact from fiction.

"Would she have lied on a marriage certificate?"

"Are you going to look for your mother's family?" Noah asked.

"Yes, I'll go to Charleston after the show, probably in January. I never considered Bella's people a threat. Just nuts. I mean what kind of family disowns a daughter because she dreams of becoming a Prima Ballerina?"

"Your grandfather disowned your mother. He may have had a substantial estate, other children." Noah set her supplies on the dock nearest the shuttle stop. He sat down and dangled his legs over the edge.

Abby braced the painting against a post and held it in place as she joined him. She rubbed her fingers on the smoothed wood grain of the dock. "I'm looking for answers, closure, not new relatives or bank accounts. I haven't needed them for twenty-seven years, so I'm not planning to be part of anybody's annual family reunion. Is it so strange to want to meet my family, know my background, and have a medical history?"

"I guess not, but not everyone has murdered family members or risks his life to meet them. Do you think someone is going to confess to murder Thursday night?"

"That's unrealistic, but I'll have my antenna up, listening. Maybe I'll hire a detective." Her fingertips tapped the dock's surface. "You work with the FBI. You have resources. How is your investigation going?"

"I haven't had much time to do anything but lab work. Tomorrow will be the second time I've been to the château. Rouland invited me to lunch a couple of years ago, but I only met Vanna and Jean-Jacques at that time. Rouland, a decent fellow, and I enjoyed our conversation. He asked a lot of questions and appeared interested in my work and in the flora and fauna of the island.

"His wife, Vanna, livened the mix. She kind of bubbled, wanting the visit to go smoothly. You do share a remarkable resemblance to her. Jean-Jacques, her father, was more stand-offish, not as welcoming, clearly not happy about my presence."

Noah looked at Abby and wrinkled his nose. "I found their Old World domain stifling and a bit overwhelming. Your ancestors line the walls. Their portraits would fit nicely in a museum." Noah looked at her and tried to smile, but an ache tightened his chest. She was a DuMond and belonged to a rarified world which excluded him.

He took her hand and examined her palm. He ran a finger down one of the lines. "If this is the life line, you're going to live a long time."

"I'm certainly going to do my part to make that true," she said. Abby liked the warmth of Noah's hand as he held hers.

She laughed. "Let me see yours."

Noah opened his hand, palm up, and she traced the line with a finger. "Guess we're both going to live a long life."

"Don't go, Abby. Check out tomorrow morning, and don't look back. I have a bad feeling about you staying," Noah implored. "The DuMonds are being investigated. We can answer your questions in time. I promise to keep you in the loop. You can meet them later."

Abby dropped his hand and leaned away from him. Noah sensed her emotional withdrawal and changed the subject. "I lived in and around Charleston growing up. I don't remember any Claires or Langfords, but my family didn't socialize with the elite. My dad is retired military. My mom was a secretary in the school system. I'll see what I can find out after I leave here."

"Have you considered your life might be in danger?" Abby asked. "Vanna said most of the family believe you're here as a biologist, but some think you're too nosy. Sounds dangerous to me."

"I can protect myself."

"Against poison? A bullet? How will you protect yourself, Dr. Hazzard?"

He looked at her and grinned. "You're a fast learner. Just know I have my bases covered."

"Spy Man" sat on the ground leaning against a tree watching them, and Abby hoped the chiggers gave him a fit.

"Where is home now?" Abby asked.

"I have my parents' old house in the suburbs of Charleston. They moved to Mobile to be closer to my mother's family. Most times, I live on *The Lady*, wherever the job takes me. My grandfather and dad built her whenever they had time, over the course of six years. Some of my ancestors were shipwrights." Noah gave her a wide smile. "Would you like to tour my 'home away from home' and my lab?"

Abby chewed her lips, thinking. She wanted to see *The Lady*, but its size and locale away from shore might pose problems of intimacy she could not ignore. Not trusting her voice, she shook her head.

Believing he understood her hesitance, Noah said, "I promise not to take advantage of you. Like your room, 'bugs' are planted on board. My calls are strictly scientific in nature. Knowing someone is getting his jollies listening in on a sexual interlude would seriously hamper my performance."

Abby blushed. Noah didn't know how to use subtlety. He was plain speaking, not socially adept, and Abby liked that about him. "I'd love to see *The Lady*."

Noah nodded. "We'll go out first thing in the morning. I'll dock the dinghy at the marina, and we'll walk on the beach from the hotel. I'll have the coffee brewing for our return. Will pastry be all right for breakfast?"

"I'm not finicky. Anything will be fine."

"Bring your painting supplies. The dinghy will take us to some beautiful places tourists can't reach. I can take lab samples while you paint."

Abby grew excited at his plans. She was pleased with today's painting. Maybe tomorrow she could do two smaller ones.

"How did you get the scars on your legs?"

Noah kept his eyes on the water. "Shrapnel. I finished one tour in Iraq and was honorably discharged during the second. Unfortunately, not all scars are external."

"You have Post Traumatic Stress Disorder?"

"No, but I lost some buddies along the way. Meeting with their family members was traumatic."

"I'm sorry. War's hell. I pray for world peace and those in harm's way all the time."

Noah smiled and looked at her. "You're religious?"

"Born, raised, baptized, and saved. You?"

"I grew up attending church, but I found God the hard way … in the hot sands of Iraq. I believe He's still with me."

They watched hermit crabs scuttle over the rocks.

Abby saw the ferry approach and laughed when she saw "Spy Man" stand and scratch his rear end.

Noah searched her face for cause and Abby said, "Chiggers. I hope he gets a good case."

Noah nodded his understanding and rose to help her to her feet.

The first shuttle arrived, and people leaving the island stopped to look at her painting. She smiled at their compliments and handed out gallery cards she kept handy. A few sales had been made online.

Noah said, "We'll get off at Loire Park. A hot dog and gelato are calling my name."

"I think I'll stick to gelato and eat a more balanced meal tonight," Abby said.

"About tonight," Noah said, "don't open the door for anyone. Brace a chair under the door handle and scream as loud as you can if someone tries to get in."

"Is that a bedtime tonic guaranteeing a good night's sleep?"

"You know what they say about prevention."

Abby checked the window in her room. A straight drop from the third floor without a balcony should prevent entrance from that point.

She locked the door, put on the chain, and pulled a chair to the door. The chain had been loosened, which made her uneasy. Abby took out a palette knife and tightened the screws. Feeling safer, she turned up the television and made use of the facilities, the shower, and washed her hair.

Today's painting rested on the chair. She remembered Noah's comments when he saw the finished product. "Hey, you can tell it's me."

"That's the point," Abby had told him.

"Are you putting this one in the show?"

"Maybe." She didn't want to tell him about her private collection.

"Be sure the first SOLD sign goes on this one."

"My paintings are on the pricey side," she informed him. "I won't give this one away."

"I know. I checked the gallery site, and if this painting is in line with the others, I can afford it."

Abby admired the painting. Noah looked out of the canvas at her with blue-green eyes. She hated to part with this one, but a SOLD sticker early in the show was a good indication of success. And she would see him again after she left the island. All things considered, she decided putting the painting in the show would be the better choice.

Abby climbed into bed and turned the television off. She had left the bathroom light on, so she could better see the door. Paranoia kept her awake until after midnight, but she finally dozed.

A sound awakened her, and Abby struggled to open her eyes. The door handle moved, and adrenaline coursed through her body. Pressure budged the door a fraction. Abby held her breath. The handle stopped moving, and fingertips became visible in the opening. They disappeared, and the door was shoved inward. The chair held, and the door opened little more than a crack. The handle moved again, closing the door.

Abby's eyes fixed on the handle, but it remained still. *Did whoever tried to get in leave?* She realized fear stole her breath, and she force-fed her oxygen-starved lungs. Abby wanted to jump out of bed and confront the intruder, but caution kept her still. She should have gotten out her sharpest palette knife and cut his fingers. Or maybe a roundhouse kick might have crushed them. *Hindsight. Always too late.* Abby thought of Noah's directives and grimaced. She was not a screamer, but she was grateful for the chair idea.

CHAPTER THIRTEEN

Abby sat in the lobby and waited for Noah's arrival. He seemed surprised to see her. "You're an early bird."

Until this morning, Abby thought she wouldn't be in any real danger, and that Noah was an alarmist. "I'm sorry," she said, "for not taking you seriously." She told him about someone trying to get into her room. "I have to tell you, I'm not a screamer. The chair worked."

Noah looked grim as he reached for her easel and shouldered her canvas bag of supplies. As she recounted the night's events, they walked to the beach and turned toward the Silver Dunes.

Fingers of pink and gold stretched toward them across the horizon. Each dawn began with a different pattern of color and light, which streamed across the water and bathed the beach with a glow that took Abby's breath. No buildings impeded her view, and daybreak became a morning pilgrimage of delight.

Killdeer ran before them, racing back and forth to escape incoming waves, their plaintive cries piercing the silence.

Noah put his free arm around her shoulder and pulled her to his side. "Maybe you should stay with me tonight."

"No. I'm sure I'll be fine. They now know, they can't easily enter my room." Abby figured the temptation of spending a night together would be hard on both of them. *Face facts. I might lead him astray and scare him off. He's an academic, probably as inexperienced as I am.* Then she thought of his warrior status. *Innocent, my foot.*

Noah breathed a sigh of relief when she didn't take him up on his offer. *She'll be safer tonight away from me.* He didn't trust himself to keep his hands off her. *So much for control.*

He was sure a repeat performance on her room was out of the

question. The boldness of an attempt to reach her in a crowded hotel indicated desperation. *What do the DuMonds hope to gain? Do they want her out of the way before Thursday night's dinner? Why?*

They arrived at the marina and walked down the dock toward a lower landing, disturbing several sea gulls. Their raucous noise as they circled above had Abby dubbing them "ocean roosters" after a man emerged onto the deck of his boat and stretched. He looked toward the rising sun, now an orange blob floating on the horizon, saw them, and waved.

They both returned the friendly salute.

Noah and Abby reached the dinghy, and he held it steady for her. Before he untied the mooring, he put a finger to his lips and pointed under the seat, to remind her of listening ears.

She nodded and looked around the little boat. The bottom was wet and held several hand nets of varying sizes and a seining net. A tool chest, fishing tackle box, and two fishing poles were visible. Noah handed her a life jacket and told her to put it on. He donned a vest, pushed the boat away from the dock, and started the ten horsepower engine to carry them to *The Lady*.

Abby identified Loire Park as they passed. A sturdy dock with mooring spots, lights, and two lower landings projected a long way into the ocean. "Is that a public pier?"

"No, it's part of Jules DuMond's estate. Jules is deceased, and his widow, Cece, lives there."

She had a glimpse of a golden stucco building with ochre-colored columns before the house was lost in a tangle of brush and trees. Abby thought of Hound Lady, and wondered if the woman was Cece. She remembered the golden stucco wall and garden with a wrought iron gate that had a fleur-de-lis design.

Ten minutes later, they arrived at the side of *The Lady*, which was anchored about a hundred yards from shore

Noah secured the dinghy. "Leave your supplies on board."

The smell of brewed coffee lifted Abby's spirits, and she followed Noah into the cabin. Although she preferred tea, she never turned down a good cup of coffee.

The galley had room for one person to work on meals at a time. Beyond the little kitchen area, Noah had a lab table, with sides but without legs, chained to the wall. A laptop, an overhead light, and stereoscope shared the space. Beakers were stored behind a wooden rail. Labeled test tubes were lined up behind and secured in another wooden rack that had three levels. Instruments, graphs, plastic bags, and charts covered the area. The table could be lifted and secured to the wall. The chest below probably held his equipment. The place had a masculine feel and smell. He indicated wooden ladder steps near the center of the boat and on the right side of the aisle. He climbed them and opened a hatch.

She followed, her eyes enjoying his contracting calf muscles.

"This is the cockpit and the brains of the operation," he said, reaching down to help her.

Abby's hand circled a rail, and with his hand on her elbow, she emerged. A high, comfortable looking chair sat behind a large wooden wheel. Noah identified various navigational instruments, radar and gadgets, then swung down through the open hatch to help her descend.

"The head's back here." He opened a door and she saw a toilet and limited shower area. "My sleeping quarters," he said, stepping aside so she could see the built-in bed with a shelf of books overhead. A strip of wood crossed the area and held the books in place. A quilt was thrown haphazardly over the linens and pillow. Expensive looking cameras occupied the berth across the companionway. Her sketch of *The Lady* was taped to the wall. Two SCUBA tanks were secured in wooden holders, the BC's and regulators hung on the wall above them. "Not much room in here, but it's home." Every available space left was used for storage. They made their way back to the galley, and she sat at the small dining table to watch him.

Noah took containers of orange juice and milk from the fridge and produced two clear plastic cups. "I hope you like OJ with lots of pulp. It's the only way to start the day." He handed her a cup of cold juice and pulled down two stoneware mugs for the coffee.

From an elongated pantry, he extracted a box of cherry-filled pastries. He put four on a plate and popped it into the microwave. "I can cook you some scrambled eggs if you like."

"No thanks. I usually just have toast or a muffin for breakfast. The pastry's a real treat."

"You need a good breakfast to give you energy and build up your immunity."

Abby fiddled with the napkin he placed in front of her. "You sound like my gran." A picture of her formed in her mind. "She was always harping on a balanced diet."

Noah looked at her from below brows glinting in filtered sunlight. His eyes held her own. "I don't feel like your gran. Just thought you should know." He turned to pour the coffee, breaking the spell.

Abby mentally shook herself and drank the juice. The sweet citrus tantalized her taste buds, and she realized she was hungry.

Noah leaned into the counter and looked out the porthole at the wild vegetation and trees lining the beach and dunes. He shouldn't have brought Abby on board. The space was too intimate. Highlights of molten gold streaked her thick, auburn hair. His fingers itched to release the mass from the barrettes and let the locks run through his hands. She was Botticelli's "Venus Rising from The Sea," the temptation and the dream he would have to let go. *She's a DuMond.*

The microwave dinged, bringing him back to earth. Taking a mug of coffee to the table, Noah put out the sugar and milk and returned to slide the warm pastries onto white, plastic reusable plates. He added a fork to his offering, and Abby looked pleased. After getting his own mug and plate, he sat across from her.

She bowed her head to say a silent grace.

Noah said, "Thank you, Lord, for yesterday's rain, another beautiful day, this meal, your blessings, and letting me meet this stubborn woman."

Surprised, Abby looked at him and smiled in wonderment.

"What? You think I'm uncivilized? It's not every day I get out my fine china. The paper stuff is more convenient until you have to take it to the dump. And yes, I'm not ashamed to pray. So don't hide your faith on account of me."

Abby shook her head. "You're a complex man, Noah Hazzard. A scientist, believer, warrior," and she murmured under her breath, "Interesting, intelligent, real. I don't know anyone else like you."

"Hold onto those thoughts, sweet cakes. For the times I'm not so nice and cuddly."

Abby laughed. "Now that's a side of you I don't want to see."

They ate in silence, each tethered to his own musing.

Noah thought about future occasions when he might have a woman on board. *Maybe a colleague. Or a wife.* Everything would have to be rearranged to accommodate a woman. No, he'd have to have a larger vessel.

Abby looked around the confined cabin with every available space taken. There wasn't room for a woman to live on board. The thought was depressing. She wondered if he brought his women here. His bed was little more than a cot. *Probably not.* She visualized both of them sharing the bed and almost laughed at the vision of limbs tangled and hanging over the side. *He'd be better off sleeping on deck. Maybe he does.* Not liking her pattern of thoughts, she gathered the empty plates and stood to put them in the sink.

"I'll take care of these," Noah said, taking the dishes from her hands. "Why don't you go outside for some fresh air while I gather my equipment?"

Negotiating the nestled sails and rigging, she sat on the deck, her arms clasping her knees, thanking God for another beautiful day. Abby's eyes scanned the untouched beach and the wilderness beyond. The white dunes and sounds of gentle surf called to her inner being and stirred her creative juices. This new environment, so different from her ordinary fare, mesmerized her. She rubbed her arms as chill bumps, unrelated to the cool morning, skated over her. So many possibilities opened, and she comprehended a life-changing partnership with the ocean. She remembered the first line of a favorite John Masefield poem. "I must go down to the seas again, to the lonely sea and the sky." She quoted the words to Noah as he emerged from the cabin.

"And all I ask is a tall ship and a star to steer her by," Noah continued. "*Sea Fever* speaks to my heart." He flashed a wide smile.

Abby scrambled to her feet flustered at the brief, intimate connection to Noah's mind. A scientist acquainted with poetry, another unexpected dimension of him she itched to explore. He had donned a khaki photographer's vest with multiple pockets. She watched as he put a camera around his neck, lowered two canvas bags into the dinghy, and climbed aboard.

He reached up to help her, and his warm hand and steady grip gave her the confidence to trust Noah. She felt safe with him.

CHAPTER FOURTEEN

The dinghy neared the sandy beach, and Noah pulled up the motor to let a wave carry them inland. He hopped out into the shallow surf, unmindful of his hiking boots, and pulled the little boat farther up the shore, setting the anchor.

Abby waited until a wave receded before leaving the boat with Noah's help.

He retrieved the easel and their bags and dropped them higher up the beach.

Abby looked at the varied gifts the waves had deposited overnight, and for a moment, she longed to begin a sea shell collection from this paradise. Mentally shaking herself, she refocused on the paintings she needed to finish.

Noah opened a bag and took out sunscreen. "Put this on your exposed skin. The sun can be brutal on a fair complexion. My mom and dad see a dermatologist every six months, and it's cut or burn every time."

Abby admired his tanned complexion and appreciated his attention to detail. She had forgotten her own sunscreen in her hurry to pack following the foiled plot. She slathered the goop on her face, neck, and arms. Abby reached for her wide-brimmed hat. Like many redheads, freckles were her nemesis. Her long pants and tennis shoes covered the rest of her. Abby watched as Noah covered his exposed skin. A cold front had moved in after the rain, and the chill seeped through her jeans and long-sleeved shirt. Having wet feet didn't help. She pulled a jacket from her bag. The cold didn't seem to bother him.

Noah said, "How do you feel? Are you ready for an adventure?" He hoisted her easel.

"It depends on the adventure," Abby said as she picked up the remaining bag of supplies.

They trekked into a jungle of green crowding the landscape beyond the dunes. Noah held limbs for her to pass, stepped on vines, and looked for the easiest places to traverse. They came to a stand of ancient trees, their trunks and limbs twisted and bent inward, survivors marked by a century of damaging winds. Straggling palmettos became thick islands, barriers which blunted the wind's force.

Abby thought about the lone tree she painted on the other end of the island, and perseverance became ingrained in her psyche. *I will persevere.*

She stopped in a small clearing to look at the view. "I'm going to set up here," she told Noah, and he brought her the easel and the heaviest of her bags which contained the jugs of water.

"I need to go inland a bit," he told her. "There's a tributary I should finish testing. Call out when you want to move."

She set up her easel and retrieved her coveralls. She shivered as she donned the layers, putting her jacket on last. Weathermen were predicting snow in the western parts of Pennsylvania and New York. Maybe she'd see snow in Philly this Christmas. Today was the first day she felt cold, a harbinger of winter's arrival to the Deep South.

Abby had two medium-sized canvases with her. She put one on the easel and set up her palette. Several minutes were spent getting the right perspective. She painted the top third of the canvas in Cerulean Blue and the bottom two-thirds in Burnt Sienna with a touch of Magenta. She drew three lines on the canvas which intersected with the focal point in the bottom third, just left of center. Following one of the lines, she sketched in the three trees, each getting smaller as it melted into the background. Next she added palmettos following the last two lines with a small part of the clearing exposed in the left front.

As time passed, Abby stepped back to check her progress. The painting began to take on a life of its own. Abby added lighter colors over the dark areas which popped out the frond details. The closer ones were bright with light streaming across them, and as they receded, they became muted, more blue-gray in color. Three trees, their tortured limbs extended inland dominated the painting. The palmettos, a multicolored green foil to the starkness of the surroundings, gave her background life. Abby stepped back and admired the work. The painting displayed a passion rarely captured in a plein-air landscape. *I'll call this painting, Survivors.* This one would sell.

She collapsed her easel, cleaned her brushes, and repacked her bags, heaping them together. Abby had noted Noah's general direction when he left, and she called out to him twice. No response. She cupped her hands by her mouth to direct the sound and tried again, this time with a loud, "Whoo." Silence. Not a whisper of bird or bug song.

---※---

Noah headed west toward a tributary he began studying last spring. Sable Palms dotted the landscape and several large oaks, their limbs bearded with Spanish moss, hung over the muddy banks. Red Cedars grew in a raised shell-covered area, the reddish twigs and bark giving it its name. This salt marsh evergreen's rounded fleshy cones attracted the Cedar Waxwings, finches, mocking birds and tree swallows to a feast. The cedars were indicative of earlier Native American habitats, several of which could be found on the island. He thought this area a perfect spot for Abby to paint. He would bring her here next.

White egrets hunted for food on the edge of a stand of cord grass and sedge. A marsh hawk hovered overhead, looking for meadow voles or other furry prey. The hyena-like cackle of a hidden clapper rail sounded as it winged its way through the grass.

Noah hung his camera on a sturdy limb, and a canvas bag of labeled test tubes on a lower hanging limb. Each vial had a separate compartment. He selected six and distributed them in his pockets. The second canvas bag contained hand nets and cheesecloth to gather and store specimens in acid free plastic bags. He put the bag across his shoulders and waded into the tributary leading to an impoundment area.

A sturdy stick stripped of small branches served to check the solidity of the ground before him. Experience taught him to check for unseen holes and obstacles in his path. Noah lived for the fieldwork, loving the outdoors and the wet sites. He hired two eager graduate students to download and file the notes he sent from *The Lady*. They worked in a lab and recorded information on the specimens into a database. In return, he helped fund their studies at the Institute.

Noah worked a couple of hours, collecting specimens from the impoundment area. As he rounded a bend, he stopped to admire a majestic creature.

A great blue heron stood like a statue, waiting for prey to swim too close. Lightning fast, the bird caught a frog, and for a moment, Noah was mesmerized by the sight. As he stooped to take a sample, the bird let out a raucous cry and flew toward him, his dinner dropped.

Something wasn't right. Training took over. He ducked and melted behind an oak tree on the shore. Seconds later, a chunk of bark hit the side of his face. Noah knew a shooter with a suppressor had taken a shot at him.

Noah didn't have a gun on him. He had left his firearm on board in a hidden lockbox.

He looked around for camouflage. Noah had to make his way back to Abby. The shot came from across the tributary and a little to the right; the bullet's trajectory marked on the tree. The woods were thick on the shooter's side of the stream. Banks of palmettos hid his location.

The marsh circled behind Noah, leaving him exposed in open spaces, hard to traverse and keep under cover. He knew his vulnerability. The shooter had the upper hand. As his mind worked to extricate himself intact, Abby's voice called, "Noah," and again, "Noah." When he didn't respond, a loud "Whoo" was heard.

Noah knelt and looked around the trunk. He saw a man in the distance moving toward Abby's voice. The man's cap was pulled down over his face, but he had on a green jacket, the DuMond green. Keeping his eyes on the shooter, Noah backed away from the tree, crouching low. He circled around some dead cattails as silently as possible, his legs and boots coated with muck. When Noah reached the first bank of palmettos, he maneuvered through the fronds, his legs and arms scratched by their prickly teeth.

The shooter had focused on the direction of Abby's voice. Silence.

With danger imminent and no sound, Noah's forward movement seemed like wading in slow-motion.

Knowing the area where he left Abby worked to Noah's advantage. The shooter moved through the palmettos, pushing aside fronds south of the clearing. Noah hoped Abby would stay quiet. *Does she know danger is headed her way?* He wanted to warn her, but without a weapon, they would both be helpless. *Please don't make a sound, Abby.*

Noah saw the ancient oaks and risked sticking his head above the fronds to view the area. He saw Abby's painting and heaped belongings. Ducking, he peered through the fronds until he saw Abby crouching among the roots.

Abby's skin crawled as she looked around and realized she was alone in an unfamiliar place. *Am I being watched?* The hair on her nape and arms rose, and she ducked down and squatted behind some palmetto fronds, burrowing behind thick roots and hairy, orange-hued trunks undulating across the surface. The only sound she heard was the blood rushing in her ears. *Is Noah hurt? Maybe I'm being foolish. He's probably moved out of hearing. He'll find me.*

Instinct told her to be still. She waited, her muscles burning in their fixed position. Her straining ears caught a slight rustling sound of fronds being moved aside through a thick barrier of palmettos on the other side of the little clearing where she had painted. *Person or animal? Maybe it's a deer.* The human spirit still hoped when confronted with a dangerous situation. *Why didn't Noah answer me?*

Abby squeezed her eyes shut and prayed the intruder, who moved beyond her sight, wouldn't find her painting or pile of supplies. *Please God, let him pass and not see my things.* Moments ticked by. The intruder passed and headed toward the beach.

Just after she released a breath and started to ease her cramped muscles, the smell of rotted vegetation assailed her. A sound from behind startled her. Before she could turn, a hand covered her nose and mouth. She reached up and caught an arm, ready to do some serious damage and heard, "Shhh. It's me. Don't move."

Noah.

He removed his hand, and Abby collapsed into him, sighing her relief, ashamed she couldn't stop the involuntary movement or the tremors that shook her body. They remained still five, ten minutes.

They heard no returning sounds, and Noah helped Abby stand. "Stay low a few minutes," he whispered.

"I thought you might be hurt," she whispered back. Her eyes looked over his body for wounds. Blood trickled down the side of one cheek, narrowly missing his eye. She touched the side of his face. "What happened? These cuts need to be treated." Noah's hiking boots and legs were covered in foul-smelling muck, which now clung to her jeans.

"Someone using a suppressor took a shot at me. A chunk of bark took the brunt. I heard you call, and whoever it was, also heard and moved toward you. I didn't get a clear look at him. He was too far away, but he wore green, the DuMond shade."

"Oh, Noah," Abby said, grasping his arms. "You might have been killed. This is too dangerous."

He nodded. "I'm glad you're paying attention. Stay here. I'll be back, as soon as, I get a look at the bad guy." He began to move toward the beach.

Abby grabbed the back of his shirt. "No. You're not leaving me again." Her mind raced ahead, trying to make sense of what was happening. Why would the DuMonds want to kill them? She wasn't a threat. They had been careful, knowing someone listened. Now Noah was in danger because of her.

"You. Will. Not. Go," she ordered, each word separate, emphasized, her voice conveying her adamant "obey me or else" tone. Abby grasped more of his shirt to hamper movement.

Noah twisted around, a frown furrowing his brows, and his lips sucked in to hold back an inappropriate retort. Her wide, dilated eyes, trembling lips, and white face gave him pause. Abby feared for him. She didn't need more stress. "I'll stay. I won't leave you again," he said, his voice comforting, believable.

She released his shirt, and he hugged her quaking body close. Abby rested her forehead on his shoulder and tried to keep the tears at bay.

His other hand rubbed her back. "Shhh. It's okay. We're both safe. I'm thinking these are warnings. If the shooter wanted me dead, he was good enough to wait and make it happen. I was exposed. He didn't try again, and I think his miss was deliberate. Do you understand what I'm saying?"

Abby nodded. "It worked. I'm scared."

"Scared enough to leave the island in the morning, not go to the château tomorrow night?"

She looked up at him and shook her head. "Not until I meet my family." *Perseverance.* "Then I'll leave."

He heaved a sigh. "I was afraid you'd say that."

They waited a while before walking in silence to the beach. They reached the shore, and Noah swore. The dinghy had been cut loose and lay to one side scuttled in the water. Holes had been hacked in the bottom, and waves filled the little vessel. "We won't be getting back to *The Lady* in this." He checked the motor which was mostly underwater. He lifted out the toolbox and selected one of the tools to take the motor off. "It's probably ruined anyway. I'll get someone to work on it later." After taking it to the beach, above the wave action, he took off his hiking boots, rinsed them, and washed the muck from his legs.

Abby waded into the water, cleaning the muck off her pants and sneakers. She and Noah looked for footprints. Whoever the shooter was, he stayed on the hard-packed sand, the waves erasing signs of his presence. She saw no one in the distance, so he must have sprinted. *How far? Maybe he hid behind the dunes waiting. What is Noah thinking?* She rubbed her arms to quell her uneasiness. Noah's words returned when she remembered telling him she could protect herself. *I can't outrun a bullet.*

She hoped Noah was right. Her family wanted them to leave the island, not kill them.

They salvaged what they could from the boat and hauled the items farther up the beach.

Noah reached in a pocket and took out a phone. "Satellite," he said, as he punched in a number. "Eddie, Abby and I need a ride. My dinghy's out of commission." He paused to listen. "We should be at the swamp boardwalk in about an hour. Keep your eyes open, and let me know if you see anything unusual.

CHAPTER FIFTEEN

Noah and Abby arrived at the meeting place between touring groups. Eddie was waiting for them with cocked eyebrows and lips skewed to one side. "You're both a sight. You want to tell me what happened?"

Abby sat on the floor of the shuttle and tried to wipe the sand from her wet shoes.

Eddie handed her the whisk broom, and Noah took it and brushed off most of the sand. He remained barefoot, but his feet were dry, and not covered with the clinging grains. Noah filled him in on the events of the morning. "I'd appreciate it if you'd drop me by the marina on the way to the hotel. I need to rent a boat and go back for my things."

Abby was glad Noah had brought her bags with him. She had emptied the remaining jug of water to lighten his load on the long trek back. She stowed her painting, unused canvas, and bags in the back of the shuttle. Once they were inside the vehicle, they didn't discuss what happened. Abby wondered if the shuttle had a "bug" planted here, too. Nothing would surprise her anymore.

When they reached the marina, Noah opened the door and indicated she get out. He closed the door, and Eddie joined them. "I'm going to Savannah after I get everything stowed away on *The Lady*. I might not get back until tomorrow, but I'll be here before six to go with you to the château." His hands settled on her shoulders, and his eyes locked onto her own. "I want you to stay in your room tomorrow. Don't go off painting by yourself. Call Gloria for your meals, and don't open the door to anyone else. Understood?"

Abby didn't like it, but she nodded her assent.

"If anything happens that makes you uncomfortable, call Eddie. Do you still have his number?" When she nodded, he continued,

"Eddie will get hold of me. Promise me you'll do what I ask."

"Yes, I promise," she said exasperated that his tone smacked of speaking to a child. "I'll be careful. I don't want a repeat of today. Believe me."

He paid Eddie to take her to the hotel, nodded, and walked toward the marina's office.

When they reached the hotel, Abby went to the Tiki Hut and ordered lunch. She asked Gloria to bring it to her room.

Gloria looked at her disheveled appearance. "Sure, honey, anything you want."

Abby didn't wait for the meal this time. She took a hot shower, washed her hair, and put on clean clothes. After another ten minutes, Gloria arrived with her food. Abby signed the bill and asked her for her working hours. "I may need your help again." She added a generous tip, and Gloria left mystified but without comment.

Abby looked around her room, and tried to think of things she could do to make the place seem less like a prison until tomorrow evening. After eating, she placed Eddie's card by the phone and hoped she wouldn't need to call.

Gordon Culpepper entered her mind. She didn't have a will, and she wondered if a handwritten and signed letter would suffice. Abby couldn't call and ask. She took out the hotel stationery and began to write something that sounded legal.

Being of sound mind and body, I bequeath to Noah Hazzard, Ph. D., all of my assets, except those items belonging to my mother, Isabella Claire Langford, which may be sold and the money used to further Dr. Hazzard's research after paying Gordon Culpepper, Esq.'s fees.

Father Ziegler trusted the attorney, and she would have to trust he would do right by her.

My mother's assets found in Safety Box No. 2512 are to be given to Savannah DuMond Boucher, along with an explanation of why I had the ring.

She added the location of the safety deposit key. Abby looked out the window at the clouds scudding by. She couldn't believe Vanna had any part of what was happening. She seemed genuinely excited to have her as part of the family. The ring would have meaning to Vanna.

In the event Noah Hazzard, Ph. D., does not survive me, my assets are to be sold, and any monies after probate, are to be given to a charity that shelters women and children who need legal services. I appoint Mr. Gordon Culpepper, Esq., of Savannah, Georgia, to choose the right charity and use his discretion in the dispersal of funds. My possessions may not be of much value, but my grandmother, Evelyn Marie Desmond, bought the apartment on Archer, and she took out a life insurance policy on me worth a quarter of a million dollars today.

Abby wrote the names of the Insurance Company and the two banks where the Safety Deposit boxes were held, one in Philadelphia and the other in Savannah. Mr. Culpepper would know how to handle the details.

Abby read over the letter, signed, and dated it. She would need two witnesses. Gloria would be one, the other maybe a clerk downstairs. She would mail it to the attorney in the morning. Abby felt like a burden had been lifted. An envelope found in a drawer would serve. Abby began to address it and stopped. She would have to find the address in the Savannah phone book, downstairs. She knew the bank and street but not the numbers.

She enclosed a note to the attorney, telling him some mysterious happenings were taking place on the island, and about Dr. Hazzard, a biologist, who was helping her. She added,

I can't call you because my room is 'bugged,' and I don't want you to get into trouble with the family. We're having dinner at the château tomorrow evening to meet them. I've met Vanna, and she's sure I'm family, but she doesn't know where I fit. I'm sure I'll be fine, and the will unnecessary, but precautions never hurt. I will be leaving Mast Island on Saturday morning, and if it's possible, I'll try to meet with you on Monday morning. My flight to Philadelphia is at 5:10.

She signed the note and put it into the envelope.

Thinking she had covered her bases, Abby stripped down and stretched to limber her body before practicing her kick-boxing and her katas. The exercises drained the adrenaline from her system, and left a feeling of accomplishment, of self-control.

Abby took out her sketches and settled on the one of the sawmill. She set up her easel near the window after placing her coveralls on the carpet for protection. Her palette included Cerulean and Ultramarine blues, Burnt Sienna, and Raw Umber. She added Alizarin Crimson, Aurolean Yellow, and Titanium White. Her painting would be a contemporary rendering with looser strokes, using palette knives, unlike photographic realism.

Hours passed before Abby was satisfied with her work. She added the finishing touches and her signature. *Maybe I should have painted some beach scenes. Only someone acquainted with lumber yards will want this painting.*

She paced the floor wondering what Noah would be doing in Savannah. Her unease grew about meeting her family tomorrow. *Noah will be with me. Think positive.*

The digital clock by the bed proclaimed the time 6:05. Her watch read 6:11. Abby hadn't heard from Noah. The phone rang, startling her. *Noah.*

"Ms. Parsons, your ride is here," a man's voice, not Noah's.

"Do you know if Dr. Hazzard is in the lobby?" Abby asked.

"No ma'am, I haven't seen him today."

"I'll be down in a few minutes."

"Thank you," the man replied. "I'll let the driver know."

Abby walked to the mirror and rechecked her appearance. She wore tobacco-colored slacks and an amber turtleneck sweater. She tried to put her hair up, but locks escaped the pins, giving her a bedraggled look. Abby took her hair down and used reliable barrettes to pull her hair away from her face.

The weather report predicted temperatures in the 40s, so she donned her taupe corduroy jacket. Grabbing her purse, she opened the door and checked the hallway. Not a person in sight, so Abby double-timed it to the elevator. She met no one going to the lobby. No sign of Noah.

"Ms. Parsons," a clerk called as she emerged from the elevator, "Your ride is here."

Abby was escorted through the front door where Mark leaned against a black Mercedes Benz with his arms folded. She looked around but didn't see Noah. "I'm waiting for Dr. Hazzard. He isn't here yet."

"Probably detained, or maybe he took a nap," the driver said, his disdain obvious in his twisted lips. Mark didn't like Noah.

"We'll wait a few more minutes," Abby said.

Mark looked at his watch. "We're twenty minutes late. He'll catch up," he said as he opened the door for her.

Decision time. Her angst returned, wearing her down. *Maybe I should wait for Noah.* Abby realized her hands were shaking, and she clutched her purse, a tangible foil for her nervous thoughts. *Noah where are you? I need you.* Abby looked around, willing him to come, fretting when he didn't appear.

"Ms. Parsons?" Mark said, his arm gesturing toward the open door.

When she didn't immediately step off the curb, he said, "Do you want me to tell the family you have decided not to come?"

Abby forced a smile. "No, of course not. I'm just worried. Noah said he would be here before six." She ducked her head and entered the car.

"I'm sure he'll meet up with you later."

As the car moved away from the hotel, thoughts swept through Abby's mind. Thoughts of abandonment, danger, and excitement chased each other. She swallowed the fear which threatened to close her throat as she thought of meeting the family members Vanna had described. Her entire body vibrated with the anticipated meeting. Her existence was tied to this family.

CHAPTER SIXTEEN

The car passed through gates opened by a remote device. A man in the guardhouse waved as they passed. Mark wound down the drive, stopped at the massive carved portal, and came around to open her door. Abby stepped out onto the paving stones and looked around in wonder. The, trees, shrubbery, and dolphin fountain were lit by a myriad of white lights, enhancing the symmetrical beauty of the mansion and grounds.

The château door opened and a large man in liveried green and gold stepped out and spoke to her in a carefully modulated voice. "Welcome, Ms. Parsons, the family is expecting you. They are gathered in the salon. May I take your jacket and purse?" He eased both from her shoulders, and took them to a small room. When he returned, she saw in the light of the elegant chandelier DuMond features and coloring. *This is a family member?*

The man smiled, a sad-looking countenance in response to her look of shock. "Yes, Ms. Parsons, I'm one of the *lesser* members of the family. They call me Minneau." He led the way to a grand room containing the DuMond family, leaving her embarrassed by his plight.

Vanna, the first to reach her, smiled widely in welcome and held out her hand, pulling her into the room by her elbow. "This is Abby Parsons, who says she is *not* a DuMond." Her voice was cheerful and ripe with anticipation. She looked around. "And where is Dr. Hazzard? You did not bring him, after all."

"I'm sorry to be late. Noah must have been detained. Maybe he'll be here later." Abby saw varied responses in their faces. Shock. Hostility. Fear. Interest. Her eyes gravitated to an older woman of regal bearing dressed in black, who sat straight as a rail in an ornate Louis IV armchair, which easily passed as a throne. Her patrician features and dark, inset eyes looked her over with undisguised interest, her thin lips pursing in speculation. *The matriarch of the family?* One bejeweled hand covered the gold knob of a cane at her side.

Vanna recaptured Abby's attention. "This is my father, the *Comte* Jean-Jacques DuMond, and his wife, Collette." She did not introduce her as the *Comtesse* DuMond.

Jean-Jacques looked like the man pictured in Bella's locket, except the face was lined and his hair grayed at the temples. "*Bonsoir, mademoiselle.* Welcome to Sologne." He held out his hand, and when Abby took it, he clasped her hand with both of his. "We are honored to meet another DuMond branch of the family." He led her to the woman who dominated the room.

"*Ma maman,* my mother, the *Comtesse* DuMond."

Abby nodded in acknowledgment afraid to hold out her hand. She overcame the urge to bow in the woman's presence. The *comtesse* gave a faint nod in return and looked away. Abby was dismissed. *This is my grandmother? Oh Gran, how I miss you.*

Jean-Jacques's wife, Collette, a natural blond, didn't look much older than Vanna. She was slender with cool blue eyes that didn't warm at the introduction. She nodded in acknowledgment, a minimal response. Collette did her duty and asked Abby if she would like a drink. Holding up a cocktail and an eyebrow, she awaited her response.

Abby declined. An alcoholic drink with these people might be her last. *Would they dare poison me?* The unequivocal answer tightened her shoulders. *Yes.*

"Hound Lady" was present, her look hostile as her dark eyes bored into Abby.

"This is my *tante,* Aunt Cece, wife of my late Uncle Jules," Vanna said."

"Yes, I remember you. We met at Loire Park. You walked a beautiful silver Afghan Hound."

"The dog is named *Bijoux,* which means jewels in French. My aunt lives near the park," Vanna told her.

Aunt Cece's eyes shot darts at Abby.

My aunt. Abby shivered. *Not related, thank goodness. Cece's hounds's name means jewels, her husband's name, Jules. Interesting.*

"And this is my husband, Rouland Boucher." Vanna stopped before an older man who gazed at Abby beneath hooded eyes. The look detracted from his handsome face. Mr. Boucher stood apart from the others. "Yes, *ma cherie*, I see how the boys would have been confused." His countenance changed to one of welcome. "A pleasure to finally meet you. Welcome to Château Sologne." He held out his hand, and Abby took his warm offering.

Just as they all sat down, a man arrived, pushing a wheelchair. The occupant, with a mane of white hair and jade green eyes was swathed in a blue plaid comforter. His resemblance to Jean-Jacques was uncanny. Scars traced across his face. One arced up through an eyebrow, and another marked him from his right cheekbone to his chin.

Jean-Jacques stood. "This is my brother, Henri," he said to Abby, and to Henri, "I'm so glad you are feeling well enough to join us." He gestured to the accompanying male. "Tasse is Henri's personal assistant."

Tasse darted glances at Abby and said something in French.

Jean-Jacques said, "Speak English. We have a guest."

"*Monsieur* insisted we join you tonight. He wanted to see Ms. Parsons for himself." He wheeled her uncle across the room from Abby, so Henri sat facing her.

Abby stood and walked to him, sensing his presence was unexpected. "I'm so glad we were able to meet, Henri."

He looked into Abby's face, dropped his eyes, and rested his chin on his chest as if he could no longer hold it up. *Is he drugged?*

She turned to the others. "Thank you all for inviting me tonight. I feel like I've walked into a fairytale. How many visitors to the island get an opportunity like this?"

"You are the first," the raspy voice of Aunt Cece responded, her words and look toxic. "This woman may look like a DuMond, but it's obvious she is an imposter or a fluke of nature. I do not believe in coincidence." She paused and said, "I asked you once before, and now I want the truth. Who are you, and why did you come to Mast Island?"

Abby put her hand to her throat, trying to maintain some dignity in the face of this implacable woman. Fear battled with panic as she took in the stunned faces. "I'm Abby Parsons from Philadelphia. I came to paint. You can look me up online." She surveyed the disbelieving expressions. Even Vanna looked bewildered by the attack. "I'm sorry, I think I should leave."

Vanna and her father reached her side at the same time. "No. You must not leave because Cece has been rude. Apologize at once," Jean-Jacques demanded, looking at his sister-in-law, his eyes hard, his voice inflexible.

Cece stood rooted in place, her face once carved in stone, now crumpled under the fierce, unwavering gaze of Jean-Jacques. "I … I apologize," she said, swallowing, her voice quivering. Cece's eyelids drooped, her shoulders slumped, her submission complete.

Abby glanced at her grandmother. The old woman's eyes gleamed. A half smile lifted her lip on one side, her hand white-knuckled as she gripped the cane. She approved. Cece fought for her place in the family. Cold eyes caught Abby's, like a snake homing in on its prey. Abby turned from the malevolent visage, her heart beating a rapid tattoo. All eyes were on Cece, so Abby doubted anyone noticed.

Vanna put her hand on Abby's shoulder. "Please forgive *Tante* Cece. She's had a difficult time since her husband's death."

Abby moved away and thought about the scene. Her misgivings and fear notched up. Jean-Jacques, the head of the family, ruled with an iron fist. She remembered Noah's words, "They believe in the absolute, divine right to govern. *Le droit du Seigneur*." She had no problem believing her life could be snuffed out at any time. Did her father, Rafe, have the same iron will while he lived? No. If he had, Isabella's portrait would hang here. Abby's knees began to shake, and she worried about why Noah had not come. *Is he all right? What if he isn't?*

Collette looked as if she intuited her fear as only another woman could, and her mouth curled in a decided smirk. This wasn't Vanna's mother. *Her stepmother.*

Abby looked at the room for the first time, trying to distance herself from the fermenting enmity around her. Portraits of the DuMond female ancestors hung in spaces between ornate, gold and cream moldings, and gleaming sconces. She walked to the full-length portrait of a woman hanging over the mantel; feeling like all eyes in the room followed her.

An imposing noblewoman wearing a powdered wig, bejeweled gown, and a face displaying the confidence and bearing of station looked out over her subjects. Her eyes, small and dark above a long, pinched nose, and thin lips added little warmth to the image.

"Sologne Yvette Villaine, *Comtesse* du Montagne, who went to the guillotine during the Reign of Terror," Vanna said, her voice hushed. "She was the wife of the *Comte* Phillipe DuMond, who escaped France in 1794, and came to America. Phillipe named the château in her memory."

Abby looked at Sologne's long neck and shuddered. Her hands were folded in front, and Abby recognized the emerald ring.

Vanna walked around the room pointing to her line of ancestors. Most of the women wore the emerald ring.

A young woman in a 1940s ensemble with dark hair and chocolate eyes drew in the observer. Something about the softness of her expression appealed. She wore the emerald ring.

"This is Rachelle, my grandmother. She died before I was born."

Vanna moved on like she wanted to get away from the image.

The portrait of the grandmother she met tonight showed a younger woman with her wealth displayed in the emeralds and diamonds circling her neck, wrists, and fingers. Matching earrings hung from her earlobes like brilliant waterfalls, and she wore the emerald ring. Her pinched nose and severe features were evident even in her youth. She found nothing warm and cozy in her look and felt sorry for her grandfather. Abby knew nothing of him. He had to be dead. It was a credit to her acting that she didn't shrink or shiver from the coldness of the eyes which seemed to peer arrogantly down on her.

Abby stood before the last portrait of a lovely, blond young woman dressed in a hunter green gown and several strands of lustrous pearls..

"My mother, Juliet Beaumont DuMond," Vanna said, her voice wistful.

Abby admired the artist's rendering. "She's beautiful," and she noticed the emerald ring was missing. Trying not to be obvious, she walked back and looked at the portraits again. "Is the emerald ring an heirloom?"

She heard a gasp across the room, and Vanna looked at her. "You are very observant."

"I'm an artist. Attention to detail is a necessity in my profession. The emerald ring stands out."

"Yes, I see. The emerald is given to the bride of the DuMond heir on her wedding day."

Abby looked at Vanna's hand and the magnificent diamond cluster ring. Before she spoke, a groan coming from behind vibrated through her.

"Bel … lah," a deep voice called, then quieter, "Bella.". The tormented words came from Henri.

Abby froze, and chills marched up her spine in waves. *Bella, my mother?* She turned to the man in the wheelchair, who gazed somewhere in the distance. His shaking arm reached out, his face a mask of pain.

Abby sat in the nearest chair, her mind scrambling, her thoughts beyond belief. *The scars. Are they knife wounds? Wouldn't Henri have burn patches from an explosion? Could Henri be Rafe? My father? Alive?* She remembered Noah said Henri didn't fit. As tears gathered, a woman's voice, full of venom, saved her.

Collette's petulant cry, loud and bitter rang out. "The ring was stolen." Her arm up, her fist beat each word on her chest. "My ring was stolen. I should be wearing the ring for my portrait."

Tasse thumbed the brakes off and wheeled an agitated Henri from the room.

Beside her, Vanna stiffened, her hand tightened on Abby's shoulder, but she didn't voice her thoughts.

Jean-Jacques, the first to recover, said, "Bella means beautiful in English. Please forgive my brother's lapse. Henri's mind was damaged in an explosion."

Vanna and Rouland looked stunned, but other faces registered fear.

Her grandmother looked at Collette, her thin lips twisted in distaste. *The woman doesn't like her son's current wife.*

Jean-Jacques went to Collette and spoke to her in French. His gentle tone seemed to mollify her, and her hand dropped to her side. Tears of frustration coursed down her face.

He released a sigh, and walked to the corner of the room and pulled on a sash by the door. "I apologize for my family," he said to Abby. He looked down at her, his eyes leveled on hers and held, beseeching forgiveness. "You must have a poor conception of us. We will have to change that, in light of your probable connection to this family."

"A poor conception" didn't begin to describe Abby's feelings. Her growing belief that Henri was her father, Rafe, filled her with hope and despair. *How can I help him?* Jean-Jacques thought her connection illegitimate, and Minneau's position crossed her mind. *Does the comte think I'll live here as a servant, happy to be a DuMond in all but name?*

The man in her thoughts materialized, she supposed in response to an inaudible bell. "I am here. How may I be of service?" Minneau glanced at Abby, and she detected a flicker of fear in his eyes.

Jean-Jacques said, "Please let the staff know we will be going to the dining hall in a few minutes.

Abby's grandmother led the way, her arm supported by her son. Her other hand grasped the cane, its sharp tap resounding on the inlaid wood floor.

As they walked down the wide hallway, Abby saw a gallery of male ancestors lining the walls. Most of them carried the genes she and Vanna inherited.

"Sologne's husband, Phillipe," Vanna said, pointing to a man in 18th Century garb. She identified the others as they walked. She stopped as they neared the end of the line. "This is Gervaise, my grandfather," Vanna said. The man's expression exuded confidence. *Well, yes, he would have to be confident to marry my grandmother and not die by association.* Then she remembered she didn't know how he died. *Maybe poison.*

"How did your grandfather die?" Abby's curiosity got the best of her. She noticed her grandmother had stopped to watch her.

When Vanna said he died of consumption, Abby swallowed her

thoughts, not wanting them to show on her face. She walked to Rafe's portrait, a larger painting of the portrait in the locket. She didn't linger or show her interest as she passed on to look at the portrait of a younger Jean-Jacques. He looked dignified and so much like Rafe, they could have been twins. Noah was right. The portraits could have hung in a museum.

CHAPTER SEVENTEEN

The dining table was resplendent with lace, china, silver, and crystal. Three silver chased candlesticks with multiple arms of lit candles, flashed over the richly appointed settings. The dress might be casual, but the dinner was formal. *Do they eat like this every day?* She wondered if Rouland and Vanna lived at the château.

A man stood by her grandmother's chair to seat her. His covert glance at Abby was curious. The eyes proclaimed him a DuMond, but his complexion was several shades darker. *Another lesser DuMonde?*

Her seated grandmother spoke. "Roux, bring me a brandy."

The man, Roux, bowed and backed out of the room, his deference bordering on servitude.

Servants liveried in DuMond green and gold brought in the meal and served each of them, their work efficient, their eyes curious.

Abby couldn't eat or focus on everyone's conversations. Her mind kept returning to the possibility her father was still alive. Numbness spread through her body until her ears buzzed with the knowledge. She felt as if all her blood drained to her toes. Abby pushed her chair back and put her head on her knees embarrassed. She tasted bile. *I can't be sick.* Abby tried to regain her confidence, but her worry about Noah intruded. *Where is he? Oh God, Noah has to be all right. I must tell him Rafe might be alive. He'll know what to do.*

Vanna came to her and crouched beside her.

Abby noted her worried countenance. Humiliated by her weakness, Abby sought to refocus.

Vanna's voice, solicitous and concerned whispered, "Are you all right? Are you sick? You look pale. Can I get you anything?"

Abby regrouped. What could she say? "I ... I guess this whole visit is so overwhelming, unreal." She sat up, looked around, and saw everyone staring at her. She felt foolish and took a sip of water, willing herself not to faint or be sick.

The *comtesse's* eyes narrowed to slits, her lips flattening as if guessing the truth. This formidable woman was her grandmother. *I understand why my mother said she never wanted to return.*

John-Jacques frowned, and his sister-in-law, Cece, so recently subdued, seemed to rebound, her look as hateful as ever. *A nest of vipers if there ever was one. My family. I've seen enough. I have to get out of here.*

As Abby appeared to have recovered, Vanna returned to the seat by her husband, Rouland, who studied Abby beneath his hooded eyes, speculating, no doubt, about her heritage. "You must tell us about where you live and about your family."

Abby wanted to scream the truth. She wanted to demand to know if Henri was her father, Rafe. She wanted to know why Noah had not come tonight. Tension mounted as she swallowed and tried to string words together which made sense.

Vanna intervened. "Lighten up, everyone. Can you not see Abby feels unwelcome? I invited both Dr. Hazzard and her. You already know everything about her." She put her napkin on her lap. "You're going to do a DNA test to find out if she is a DuMond, but you already know she is. Why the third degree?"

Shocked by Vanna's words, Abby looked at Jean-Jacques. He met her eyes without a qualm. "We want to know your background. Is that disturbing to you, Abby? The softness of his voice mesmerized like a cobra swaying back and forth before striking.

Abby shook her head and pressed trembling lips together, praying for calm. She forced the words, her heart racing. "I'm just surprised you think my background is relevant. I'm sure Vanna told you what I know about my life. I'll be leaving Saturday and ..."

Jean-Jacques interrupted. "*Non*, you must stay here, with us, until we have our answers."

"I'm sorry, that's not possible," Abby began, fear rising to fever pitch. "I have a show coming up in December, and I have to get home to paint and make arrangements."

"You can paint here," Jean-Jacque said, his voice hardening, a command. "Vanna and Rouland can pick up your things at the hotel."

Abby looked around the table. Her grandmother stiffened, Collette frowned, and Aunt Cece glared at Jean-Jacques.

"*Oui.*" her grandmother said in unexpected acquiescence. Her imperious manner and speech grated on Abby, "Yes, we must learn about you and your place in the DuMond family. You cannot leave until we know."

Abby felt the coils of the snake tightening to hold her here.

Vanna's expression registered disbelief as did her husband's. They appeared to have no knowledge of what was happening. Relieved, she spoke to Vanna and Rouland.

"I really appreciate you and your family inviting me to Solonge, but I really must go." Abby wasn't sure if she should say anything about what happened yesterday, but if she didn't, and they had a hand in the shooting, wouldn't the family think it strange?

"Dr. Hazzard and I had an unsettling experience yesterday. He picked me up in his dinghy to show me *The Lady* and take me to paint in areas few tourists get to see. We had breakfast on board, and then we took his little boat to shore." Abby looked around at the family members gauging their reactions as her story unfolded. They had stopped eating, and all eyes focused on her.

Her voice shook as she relived the time. "I set up my easel and painted in a beautiful area while Noah went inland to another site. He was collecting samples for his work. Someone shot at him." Abby tried to capture each expression as she said the words. Fear was the most prevalent.

Vanna gasped. "What do you mean? Someone shot at him ... with a gun?"

"Yes," Abby said with trembling lips and chin, looking at the faces around the table, now immobile, closed to her. Only Roux's face registered shock, followed by fear.

Abby's grandmother followed her eyes and turned to see where she was looking. Roux lowered his eyes, and Abby continued, drawing attention back to her.

"Whoever it was, missed, but the shot came close enough, flying bark cut Noah's cheek."

"That's intolerable!" Jean-Jacques said, his voice hard. He stood and looked at Abby, his face a mask of outrage. "Are you okay? Did he report it?" Not awaiting her response, he threw his napkin on the table. "We must find this criminal who is shooting at people on our island and make sure it never happens again." He turned to the young man. "Roux, get Mark, at once."

Roux hurried from the room.

Jean-Jacques scowled toward his mother, his eyes flinty.

Her grandmother shrank back in her chair, eyes widening, lips white, tightening. Catching herself, she straightened and glared back.

Abby wasn't sure what she saw communicated. Seeing her grandmother shaken did little to quell her fear. Aunt Cece and Collette had a heated conversation going, their eyes watching her as they spoke.

Abby's lips trembled as she said, "Noah thought it was possibly a hunter, who mistook him for an animal, but we found that wasn't the case," Abby prevaricated. "Someone sabotaged his dinghy, and we had to walk back."

Aunt Cece and Collette both began speaking out, voicing concerns, mainly for the family and their reputation. "What if he reports this, and the police begin an investigation?" Aunt Cece said.

Collette added, "Our family name will be ruined. Visitors will be afraid and leave the island."

"How frightening," Vanna said, ignoring the two women and their fears. Standing and walking around to stand beside her father, she said, "Dr. Hazzard might have been killed," and her voice rose, "*You* might have been hurt."

"I know," Abby replied, her nails biting into her palms, wanting to flee. "Noah found me, and we stayed low until the danger passed. I can tell you, I was plenty scared. That's why I'm worrying about Noah not showing up tonight. Someone doesn't like him or want him here. This is personal." Abby's hands twisted together in agitation, and Vanna came to her. She crouched, placed her arm around her shoulder, and hugged comfort.

Vanna looked at her father. "We must check on Noah, now." Her words were not a request. She looked at Abby with concern. "Oh, Abby, you should have told us this right away. No wonder, you have been so uptight and distracted."

Rouland stood and walked to his wife, his voice soothing as he supported her statement. "You are right, Vanna." He looked at Jean-Jacques. "We must make sure Dr. Hazzard is all right."

Footsteps were heard approaching in the hallway, and Jean-Jacques left the room. They heard irate voices, and as the tenor in tone increased in volume, they walked farther down the hall, their words indecipherable.

Cece and Collette were silent, and Rouland left the room, following Vanna's father.

Her grandmother's hand worked the knob of the cane, her face set, her eyes staring at Abby as if she could will her to disappear.

Jean-Jacques returned. "Mark and Rouland are driving to the marina. They will take the boat out and check on Dr. Hazzard." He turned to Abby. "I believe in light of recent events, you must stay with us tonight. Vanna will have everything you need until tomorrow."

"Yes," Vanna said. "You must stay. I insist."

Roux returned and asked in his lilting voice if anyone wanted dessert.

Jean-Jacques dismissed him with a curt, "No. We are retiring to the parlor for a drink. You may assist us there."

The telephone rang, and Jean-Jacques answered the call. Someone spoke on the other end.

"What happened?" Jean-Jacques barked, and listened. "Why was I not notified immediately?" He looked at everyone, but his eyes settled on Abby. "Stay at the dock. I'm on my way."

Jean-Jacques's face held a worried look. He walked to Abby and took her hand. "I am sorry, Abby. There has been an explosion. The marina manager, Doc Ellis, confirmed it was *The Lady*."

Abby clutched her throat. *No. No. No. This can't be happening. Noah has to be all right.*

"Why did we not hear about this?" Vanna's voice rose as she stood by Abby's side.

"Everyone thought a jet broke the sound barrier. People returning to the marina from Charleston saw fire on the water and scattered debris."

"What about Noah?" Abby cried.

"I'm sorry, Abby. They are searching for him now."

"No" Abby shouted. "I'm going with you."

"There is nothing you can do. I am sorry." Jean-Jacques walked from the room, his step brisk. Everyone, including her grandmother, looked shocked. Abby clutched Vanna's arms, shaking her, tears welling in her eyes. "I have to go. I have to."

"Yes, I know," Vanna said, concern and worry evident. "I will bring a car around. We can at least go to the marina and wait until he is found."

CHAPTER EIGHTEEN

Vanna parked by the side of a boat dock near the marina office. People milled around under the night lights, and boat lights could be seen on the water in the distance.

Rouland saw Vanna drive up and met her at the car. "You should not have come. Your father will not be happy." He glanced at Abby.

"We could not stay home while Dr. Hazzard is missing. He is Abby's friend, and I understand why she is upset."

"The Coast Guard is here and *others*" he said in an undertone, "asking questions. You should leave now."

Abby opened the door and ran toward the office. She needed answers.

Rouland and Vanna caught up with her as a man with a white beard, cap pulled down over his curly hair, and a worried face emerged from the building.

"Mr. Boucher, the *comte* wants to see you inside." He looked at Vanna and Abby under the bill of the cap, a question in his faded blue eyes.

"Doc Ellis, this is Abby Parsons. She is a friend of Dr. Hazzard."

"I'm sorry, Ms. Parsons," the man said, looking at her. "They're talking about giving up the search until morning. Thinks there's not much to see out there right now." He looked at Vanna and said curtly, "I don't agree."

Abby crumpled inside at his words. Somehow, they made this awful scene real.

Vanna took Abby's hand and pulled her into the office. She confronted her father. "The search cannot be called off."

Her father drew up, his face compelling in its display of anger and spoke rapidly to her in French.

"We are not leaving," Vanna answered in English. Her voice, though shaky, was adamant.

Jean-Jacque's face reddened at her obstinacy. He turned furious eyes on Abby. "Dr. Hazzard went to Savannah yesterday and reported what happened." His voice rose an octave. "The FBI was there on another case, and now they are involved with the local authorities. Our visitors are upset. Questions are being asked." He hit his hand with his fist. "*Mon Dieu*, What happens now?"

Abby found her backbone. "I'm glad he reported it. Someone could have been killed. And now, Noah might have been murdered." She covered her mouth to keep from saying what she thought.

"*Non!*" Jean-Jacques raised his hand in a threatening manner, and Rouland stepped in front of Abby.

"Please, let us calm down. We do not want more publicity," Rouland said. He looked around. "Where is Mark?"

"I sent him out to help with the search," Jean-Jacques said in a lowered tone, his teeth set in frustration. "Someone had to stay and field questions."

"Why did he not wait for me? I should have gone with him," Rouland said, his voice questioning, not understanding.

Abby noticed other people near the front desk watching them, their avid expressions showing interest at the exchange.

Vanna held her husband's arm. "Please Papa. Do not call off the search."

Jean-Jacques looked at her, his face still flushed with anger. "The authorities are now in control. They will decide what happens."

A uniformed police officer and another man walked inside, showing identification, and began to question Doc Ellis. Two people in casual clothing came forward, the man holding a notebook in his hand. "I need to speak with Abby Parsons." He looked around, his eyes moving from Vanna to Abby and back.

"I'm Abby."

"This is Special Agent Jenna Mackey, and I'm Special Agent Kent Helms with the Federal Bureau of Investigation. We'd like to ask you some questions."

The two original officers looked their way, and the stout one, wearing slacks and a jacket, joined them. He identified himself as Detective Sgt. Abel Norris with the Savannah Police Department.

Abby looked at the other two in their casual clothing. "FBI?" They didn't look like FBI agents.

Noting her hesitance, they produced wallets with badges from their sweat jackets. They held them out for her to see.

"Okay," Abby said.

The three authorities looked around the office which had a desk, a captain's chair, and four folded chairs leaning against one wall. They asked everyone else to leave the room.

Jean-Jacques's stance showed his displeasure at this dismissal, and his eyes bored into Abby's as he walked to the door.

She lifted her chin and returned his stare. *You aren't in control now.* For the moment, she felt safe, and some of the tension left her body, leaving her close to giddy.

Special Agent Helms closed the door and fixed a chair for her.

He said as he took a chair for himself, "I understand you were with Dr. Hazzard yesterday when a shot was fired. Is that correct?"

"Yes."

Det. Norris began to write notes in his notebook. "Please tell us what happened, Ms. Parsons."

Abby told them about her morning with Noah.

Det. Norris then asked questions about Noah's actions. Notes were taken.

Agent Mackey, a woman who looked to be in her thirties or early forties leaned forward and said, "We want you to tell us why you came to Mast Island, and what has happened since you arrived … from the beginning."

They know. Noah must have told them. "Was Noah … " *No, he is not dead.* "Is Noah a Special Agent with the FBI?"

The two agents exchanged glances, and Det. Norris looked interested, his eyebrows raised.

"Noah is a support professional with the FBI, working legitimately as a scientist while investigating a crime," Agent Helms said.

Abby was relieved they didn't use past tense. "Are you friends of his? Do you work with him?"

Again they exchanged glances. Agent Helms said, "We've worked with Noah on several assignments. Who else knows Noah is working with the FBI on Mast Island?"

"Noah told me Eddie, a shuttle driver, knows. Noah suspected the DuMonds might know. Someone 'bugged' his boat."

"And your room," Agent Mackey stated.

"Yes, Noah showed the 'bugs' to me. Did he tell you yesterday?" She looked at the window and saw the DuMonds watching from outside.

Agent Helms noticed and pulled the shade down.

Det. Norris had listened at first, but now he asked questions about how long she had been on the island, and how well she knew Dr. Hazzard. "Are you in a relationship?"

"Good heavens, no. We've met and talked. Mostly about my family. He tried to persuade me to leave. Now, I wish I'd listened."

Thinking about Noah injured or suffering because of her added to the guilt. Her mouth dried, and she crossed her arms over her chest and looked at Agent Mackey. "Do you think Noah is dead?" Abby's voice shook and her breathing escalated, but she had to ask.

Agent Helms answered. "If he isn't, he's going to be livid about his boat being destroyed."

Agent Mackey glanced at her partner before adding, "Noah is strong and intelligent. He's a survivor. I will believe he's alive until proved otherwise. "Now, please start at the beginning, and don't skip any details," Agent Mackey said, her voice coaxing her to begin again.

Abby began with her grandmother's death and her discovery of a fictional relationship. She told about receiving the package, the note, and details of her search for family.

Abby walked outside accompanied by the two agents. She felt wrung out. They had asked her to repeat parts of her story over and over. When they asked about her family on Mast Island and if she felt she was in any danger, she answered, "Yes."

Vanna hurried to Abby's side. "Are you all right?" She looked at the agents. "What have you done? She looks whipped."

"And you are ...?" Agent Helms asked.

"Vanna Boucher, and this is my husband, Rouland, and my father, Le *Comte* Jean-Jacques DuMond."

Special Agent Helms did not offer his hand. He nodded slightly to indicate a certain deference and said, "I'm glad we've met. Expect us to stop by the château tomorrow. We have a few questions for you."

Jean Jacques spoke, his voice autocratic. "I have no idea why you should need to interrogate us. We hardly knew Dr. Hazzard, and no one left the château during the time of the accident."

Putting his hands in his pockets, Jean-Jacques looked at Abby and continued. "Miss Parsons is a guest at the château. We will see she gets home."

Agent Helms raised an eyebrow and looked at the *Comte* Jean-Jacques DuMond unintimidated by his title or haughty demeanor. "That won't be necessary, Mr. DuMond. Miss Parsons has indicated she would be more comfortable in her own room. We'll see she gets back safely."

Jean-Jacques's back straightened and his hands fisted. He looked offended by the tone of the agent's address and angry at his will thwarted. Visibly upset he stalked outside. Vanna and Rouland followed.

CHAPTER NINETEEN

Abby sat in the chair by the window of her room. She looked beyond the night lights on the grounds below, her fears haunted by the black edges of the wilderness beyond. *Is Noah out there somewhere injured and helpless? Did he make it to shore?*

Jean-Jacques sent Mark to look for him, and Abby didn't trust anyone in her family. Even Vanna and Rouland might be involved. Jean-Jacques was Vanna's father. Her loyalty belonged to him.

Abby bowed her head and prayed as she had never prayed before. *Please let him be alive, God.* She pleaded for Noah's life but she felt her prayers fell on deaf ears because of her willfulness. *I should have prayed before making my decision.* Why did she insist on coming to Mast Island? If she had stayed away, Noah would be alive. *No! Don't think negative thoughts. Noah's alive. He has to be.*

Special Agent Mackey said she would call if they received any news. She looked at the phone and jumped when it rang. She put her fist to her mouth, dread slowing her movement to take the call.

"This is Abby. What's happening?"

"Abby, it is Vanna. Are you all right? Do you want me to come and stay with you?"

"Vanna," she said, and tears formed in relief. "I'm okay, just shaken by what's happening. I didn't expect the FBI to be here, or to be questioned."

"We did not expect them either. My father is worried they might think the family had something to do with the accident."

"Why would they think that?"

"It is a long story. I am worried about you. Are you sure you are all right? I can pack a few things and stay with you tonight in case there is news."

"No, please," she responded, her voice firm. "I'll be all right." She didn't want company, especially a member of the DuMond family.

"What did they ask you?" A pause followed. "What did you tell them?"

A chill iced Abby's blood. Vanna sounded anxious. Were her father and husband or the rest of the family listening? She assumed the "bugs" were still in place.

"I told them the truth." Abby's answer was met with silence, a silence that stretched her nerves.

"And *what is* the truth, Abby?" Vanna's voice had hardened. She sounded ... what? Like the princess that didn't get her way? No. Her voice conveyed a touch of malevolence, underscoring her words. Vanna was no longer the excited, light-hearted, welcoming cousin. She was her father's daughter, the daughter of *Comte* Jean-Jacques DuMond, head of the DuMond Dynasty, owner and ruler of Mast Island.

As if sensing Abby's withdrawal, Vanna changed her tone. "I will come, and we will talk," her voice once again conveying care.

"No. Don't come," Abby's words abrupt. "I'm sorry, but I want to be alone right now." She hung up, and hoped Vanna didn't show up. *What if she does?*

Don't open the door.

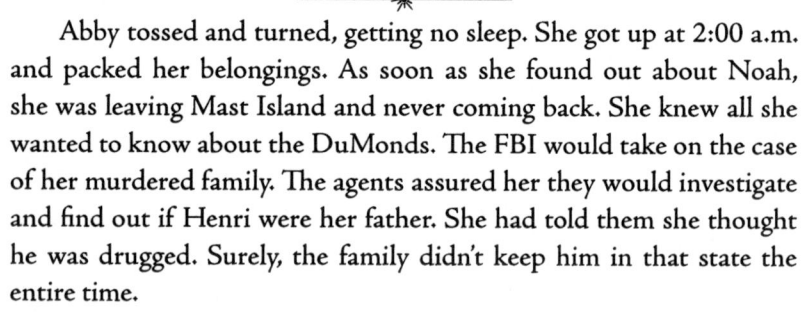

---✳---

Abby tossed and turned, getting no sleep. She got up at 2:00 a.m. and packed her belongings. As soon as she found out about Noah, she was leaving Mast Island and never coming back. She knew all she wanted to know about the DuMonds. The FBI would take on the case of her murdered family. The agents assured her they would investigate and find out if Henri were her father. She had told them she thought he was drugged. Surely, the family didn't keep him in that state the entire time.

She thought of the man in the wheelchair. She felt guilty about leaving, but she couldn't help him if she were dead. *Is Henri, Rafe? Could he be my father? Is it possible?* Noah had said Henri didn't fit, but he hadn't elaborated. Noah. Morbid thoughts of Noah torn apart and eaten by fish and crabs knocked on the door of her mind. She tried to shut them out, but they came back. Not knowing Noah's condition hurt. She felt empathy for all people with missing children or loved ones, so she prayed they would know the peace that passes understanding; the closure she needed now.

———✳———

Abby looked at the clock. The hands were at 9:10. She had missed breakfast, and her stomach rumbled. She couldn't just stay here. Her nerves jangled, and she couldn't sit still.

She called Eddie. He didn't immediately answer, and her mind began to work overtime. *Is Eddie alive? Was he with Noah?* Abby touched her mouth with a fist and bit her knuckle.

"Good morning, Ms. Parsons." His voice cracked. "I'm sorry about Dr. Hazzard."

Abby released a breath of relief when she heard his voice. "Did they find him?"

"I haven't heard." Eddie sounded shaken. "Did you need a ride?"

"Yes. I want to go to the marina." She knew the place was about a twenty minute walk on the beach, but she didn't want to take chances.

"I'll be there in fifteen minutes."

Grabbing her purse, she removed the chair from the door, and cautiously looked down the hall in both directions. No one was in sight, so she made a dash for the elevator, keeping alert, ready to do battle if necessary. Feeling foolish.

The lobby was mostly empty, so she made her way to the Tiki Hut.

Gloria looked like she hadn't gotten any sleep either. "What a tragedy! Dr. Hazzard, such a nice man. It's not right he's gone." Her eyes welled.

"Have you heard anything?"

Gloria shook her head. "He loved that boat. Both gone." She shook her head again. "I couldn't believe it when I heard about the explosion last night."

"There's still hope. He has to be alive."

"Oh, honey, I hope you're right." She mopped her eyes. "What can I get you?"

Eddie picked Abby up, and she sat up front as they drove to the marina. "Can't believe what happened yesterday. Dr. Hazzard was a good man," he said, shaking his head. "We'll miss seeing him on the island."

"What do you know, Eddie?" She remembered the shuttle was probably "bugged", and didn't expect him to answer.

"I know his boat exploded. I was out looking last night and heard some talk. The explosion blew the stern to smithereens, and *The Lady* sank. There are some FBI people here with local authorities, asking questions, and everyone's nervous."

"Is there any way Noah could have survived the explosion?"

Eddie looked at her. "There's always a chance. Depends on where he was at the time, and if the blast didn't knock him out. I believe in miracles, Ms. Parsons."

"I do, too, but I'm scared. Why haven't they found him?"

"Maybe we'll get some answers soon." He drove to a space near the marina office.

A few people loitered around, giving their stories about where they were when the blast happened. A boat had pulled in, and a man tied the vessel to the dock.

"Have they found anything?" one of the men on the dock asked.

"Don't know. They've got divers in the water, checking around what's left of the boat. They don't talk much, just telling us to leave. There's people on shore walking the area. I heard a dog. Could be a tracker." He scratched his head, and took a couple of fishing rigs and an igloo off his boat. "Someone found one of those fancy vests with lots of pockets on the beach, but it was tattered. If the fella made it to shore injured, they should've found him by now."

"Are you going back out?' another man asked the boater.

"Nah, I was out most of last night, and there's really nothing to see. The authorities don't want people on the beach because gawkers churned up whatever evidence was there, walking around. They're keeping boats well away from shore."

They went into the office. Doc Ellis sat on a stool by the window, looking out.

Abby walked to a map of the island on the wall. "Do you know where Noah had his boat anchored?"

"Yep," Doc Ellis said, leaving his perch. "Those FBI people asked that, too." He got up and ran a calloused finger along the shore and stopped. "I reckon this is the last place I saw him anchored."

Abby looked inland. She saw the tributary on the other side of the island, and figured Doc Ellis had pinpointed the right spot. Memories flooded back as she looked around the site. Two days had passed since she felt the security of Noah's arms around her in this place. Two days, a lifetime. "What's around this area?" she asked the harbormaster.

"Nothing but marsh, swamp, and palmettos."

"Where do people live who work on the island?" She looked at Eddie.

"Most live on the mainland and commute by boat or ferry each day. Some, like me, have places scattered near the swamp north and east of Loire Park. My house is here." He pointed to an area near where the tour shuttle stopped to look at the sawmill.

"I didn't see any houses."

Eddie looked down. "The area is hidden from the tourist's view. You aren't supposed to see where we live." His voice took on a sarcastic tone. "We wouldn't want anybody's sensibilities to be bothered by poverty."

Abby touched Eddie's arm. "I'm sorry."

Eddie seemed to shrink inside himself as he moved away.

Doc Ellis frowned and spoke in soft undertones. "Be careful Eddie. The walls have ears," he said and walked back behind the counter, taking himself out of the conversation.

Eddie grimaced. "I need to learn to keep my big mouth shut." He turned and looked out the window toward the blast scene, leaving Abby to think about the conversation. She didn't know anything about Eddie. He wore a wedding ring, so she assumed he was married. Did his wife work at the château? *So poverty exists beyond the rich trappings of the château and upscale resorts.*

Eddie's phone vibrated, and he looked to see who called. His face fell, and he hurried outside to his vehicle, leaving Abby alone with her thoughts. *I should have listened to Mina and Noah. I should have never come here.* The guilt she felt was overwhelming. How would she ever forgive herself if Noah were dead?

CHAPTER TWENTY

Eddie had been gone about a half hour when they heard the loud "whomph whomph" sound of an approaching helicopter. Abby ran outside onto the dock and shaded her eyes to see the low-flying aircraft heading toward the prohibited area.

Did they find him? Abby's body began to shake, her thoughts unbearable, her prayers for Noah's safety fervent.

Doc Ellis joined her on the dock. He put a hand on her shoulder and squeezed a message of support. "We'll know something soon, one way or the other."

Special Agents Mackey and Helms guided their boat to the pier. In the distance, a helicopter was heard leaving the island.

Abby ran down the dock to meet them. "Did you find him? Is he okay?" *He has to be alive. He has to be.*

Agent Mackey looked down, her lower lip trembling. "I'm sorry, Abby."

"Nooooo," Abby cried and fell to her knees, hugging herself in denial. *No, no, no, he can't be dead.*

The female agent left the boat and knelt to embrace Abby. "I'm so sorry."

Doc Ellis arrived to hear the bad news. "Where did you find him?" His voice caught, his curiosity overriding any hesitance. "What do you think happened?"

"Quite a way from the site," Agent Helms said, ignoring the last question and keeping his voice even as he secured the vessel. "The blast must have disoriented him, and the current carried him quite a way. We're amazed with his injuries, he made it so far."

Doc Ellis left them and walked to the office at a brisk pace, shaking his head and mumbling under his breath.

Abby stumbled down the dock, held up by Agent Mackey. She felt numb, empty. Cold. So cold. She hugged herself and doubled over with the pain. Noah had died alone. In the place he studied, in the wilderness he loved. Alone. *Had he felt pain? Did he know he wasn't going to make it?* Abby's held breath escaped, an audible sound of distress as she stood.

Agent Mackey hugged her closer, not allowing her to fall.

Noah's gone. No, no, he can't be dead. He was special. Abby had never met anyone like Noah. He was so alive, warm, and intelligent, with a future ahead of him. Gone. Just like that, in an instant, erased from her life, removed from all he might have been, might have achieved. *Why God? He survived the war. Why did You allow it?* And just like that, anger flared, and a hatred for her family took root. The unfamiliar sensation ignited a desire to see the DuMond family pay and pay dearly. Her tears dried as revenge turned her thoughts away from God and into a realm she had never entered.

Doc Ellis got off the phone when they arrived. He went to the next room and came back with a chair for Abby. "Is there anything I can do?"

Agent Helms said, "You could call us a shuttle. We'll see Ms. Parsons gets back to the hotel."

"Are you leaving the island now?" Doc asked the agent.

"When we wrap up a few details." The agent didn't offer any more information.

A shuttle arrived, and the driver wasn't Eddie.

Where is Eddie? Abby wondered if Eddie knew. *Did someone tell him? Was that why he left in such a hurry?*

The agents went with her to the hotel, both silent.

The driver watched them in the rear view mirror, but he didn't say anything.

At the hotel, everyone stared at Abby like they knew what had happened. She went to the front desk and put in her morning ferry reservation. The clerk looked at her and stammered. "I liked ... Dr. Hazzard. I'm ... I'm ... sorry." He looked past her to watch the agents leave.

Tomorrow can't come soon enough. She would plot the demise of the DuMond's aristocratic hold on Mast Island when she was on firmer ground.

Abby took the painting of Noah reclining under the mighty oak from her folio. She set it on the chair, remembering his words. He had wanted her to put SOLD on this one at the opening in December because he wanted it for himself. Abby decided to put the painting into the show, and maybe someone would buy it. She didn't need a constant reminder of what might have been, what she had lost. Noah's memory would be fresh in her mind a long time.

The digital numbers on the clock showed twenty minutes had passed since she looked last. The time was a little after ten. She paced the room. A long night stretched ahead.

Abby sat on the bed, and the phone rang. She looked at the blinking light as it rang again. *Who would call at this hour?* She picked up the receiver. "Yes."

Eddie's voice said, "I need to see you. It's urgent."

Abby listened to his tone. He sounded upset. *What happened?* "Are you all right, Eddie?"

"No." His answer short. "Please come. I have to talk to you."

"I'll meet you in the lobby."

"No. I can't be seen. Come outside. I'll be parked just down the pavement out of the light. No one must know."

Abby replaced the receiver. Trepidation rooted her in place for several seconds. *Can I trust Eddie? Yes. Noah had trusted him.*

She pulled on her jacket and left the sanctuary of her room to meet the man, who might know more about what had happened to Noah. Eddie had left abruptly after a phone call at the marina. *Why?*

No one noticed in the lobby when Abby walked outside. She felt like she stepped out of her skin as she walked to the car barely visible in the shadows. Eddie got out, came around the car to open the door. This wasn't the shuttle she expected.

Abby looked at him, wondering why he came in a car, a DuMond car.

Eddie hung his head, and apprehension raced through her. Seized by fear, Abby turned to flee, and the back door opened.

An unfamiliar, high-pitched voice, spiced with malice, stopped her. "Take another step, and Eddie dies."

Abby pivoted to see who threatened harm.

Marcel, "Spy Man", held a gun with a suppressor pointed at Eddie. He opened the front passenger door, moved away from the vehicle, and motioned with the gun. "Get in the car, Ms. Parsons. You too, Eddie."

"Why are you doing this?" Abby said. She stopped, and a "pfft" spit from the gun.

Eddie grabbed his left shoulder and spun around, gasping in pain.

"Get in the car, now," the deadly voice commanded, his gun trained on her.

Abby walked toward the car, dread leaching the blood from her head. *I can't faint.* "Eddie?" She watched him while she moved. He stumbled around the car, clutching his shoulder.

"Up front, and close the door," Marcel told Abby.

Abby complied, her movement slow. Questions rattled in her brain as she tried to make sense of what had happened. No answers presented themselves. She closed the door.

Marcel slid in behind her. She assumed he kept the gun leveled at Eddie. She thought about moves she could use to escape, but her captor stayed well out of range, and she had Eddie to consider. Whatever happened, Abby knew she wouldn't die without a fight.

"Lock the doors," Marcel ordered, and the locks engaged.

Abby looked at Eddie. Tears slid down his face. *From pain? Fear? Betrayal?* She asked, "Why Eddie?"

"They have my granddaughter." A sob escaped as he said the words. "I'm sorry."

"Shut up and drive." Marcel said.

Abby crossed her arms over her stomach, bent over, and tasted bile. She internalized Eddie's fear and pain. And the pain of family betrayal. *My flesh and blood, murderers. Oh, Gran, forgive me.* Then with eyes squeezed shut, *Help us.* Was she appealing to her grandmother or God? *Will God abandon me now?* Her thirst for revenge was not

God's way. Not the way Jesus taught in the New Testament. *No. He won't forsake me for human weakness.* Abby's mind sought the words to restore her faith. *"I will never leave you or forsake you. Lo, I will be with you always."* A calm which passed understanding mantled her spirit.

She thought of the sacrifices Gran and Mina had made to keep her safe, and how her willfulness put other lives in jeopardy. Noah. Eddie. A granddaughter.

Eddie listened to Marcel's directions, turned from the main road, and drove toward the sawmill. Abby saw the sweat beaded on his brow and his eyes wide with terror. Eddie's fear transferred and brought a chill. The reality of their situation embedded. *Did Noah feel this way when he knew he was dying?*

"I have her," Marcel said, and Abby guessed he spoke to someone on a phone.

Who would meet them? Who wanted her dead? Noah dead? She thought she felt a light touch on her shoulder, but when she reached to touch it, nothing was there. *I am here.*

She was not abandoned.

You are not alone.

Her strength returned as they drove into the lumber yard.

CHAPTER TWENTY-ONE

Eddie parked by a pile of logs and waited for instruction. "Get out of the car and walk toward the entrance. Slow. No heroics. Running will only shorten your life." His snort of pleasure and the high pitch of Marcel's voice grated eerily on Abby.

Mark came outside, gun in hand. Abby gauged her distance from the men, and Mark stepped aside for them to enter. *Too far. Do they know about my training? No.*

The muted voice inside her head came back. *Do as they say.*

Eddie and Abby walked inside, their eyes adjusting to the dark interior. A dim lightbulb did little to facilitate sight.

Abby's eyes searched the dark places until they found her grandmother in the shadows. She straightened, pulling her shoulders back as she confronted the elder woman. "So, Grandmother, what now? Do you kill the legitimate granddaughter of your own flesh, in cold blood?" Her words meant to shock the *comtesse* did not have the desired effect.

Her grandmother stepped forward until her razor-sharp eyes and distorted features became visible. "I am *not* your grandmother," the old woman sneered and forced a laugh, maniacal in tone. "I *never* whelped weaklings. Mercifully, Rachelle did not survive the birth of Jean-Jacques." She circled Abby, her breathing loud, nostrils flaring, her body stiff with indignation. "*You* think you have all the answers." She tapped her chest with her fingers, her words loud, almost a shout, reverberated around the room. "I *know* who you are."

Her laugh, short and scornful, scratched Abby's mind.

"I have known from your birth, just as I have known you would come here one day to destroy us." Her voice lowered, her cold black eyes mesmerizing, the snake of legend, a basilisk, homing in on its prey.

"I *know* who you are." The gun in her hand followed Abby and did not waver.

Shocked by the old woman's words, Abby stepped back, her knees buckled, and she almost fell, her fear replaced by a relief so great, she trembled with the knowledge. *She's not my grandmother. Oh God, she's not my grandmother. Thank you, God. Thank you. Thank you. Thank you.* An adrenalin rush followed. "You killed my mother, my brother, my father. Why?"

"*Non.*" The old woman struck the concrete surface with her cane, the sound echoing her strong denial. "Imbeciles! They were not to kill, to scare only. Jules did not order their deaths. Raphael almost died. Later, they were to bring us the child. Idiots! They smothered him to keep from being found by the police. Your mother, nothing but a showgirl, got in the way," her voice, one of distain. The dowager smiled, amused. "The miscreants paid for their incompetence."

"Don't speak about my mother that way. My parents were in love," Abby retorted, her indignation threatening, inciting a desire to physically take the woman apart.

The old woman made a sound of disgust. "Love. Pah. DuMonds do not marry for love. Gervaise learned with Rachelle, and Jean-Jacques's Juliet was weak. Love made them weak."

"Henri is my father, Rafe," Abby said, reverence and awe swelling her voice. *My father is alive. Gran. Rafe is alive.*

A tear fell, and she swiped the evidence of weakness away. *Have I found my father, only to lose him again?*

"You knew last night" the *comtesse* said as if speaking in a rational conversation. "I saw the knowledge dawn in your eyes. Everything we worked to achieve, to put behind us, crumbled because I let you live." Her voice lost some of its haughtiness when she spoke the words of regret, then hardened. "Where is the ring?"

"My mother's ring? Rafe and Bella were married. But you know that. The church record was removed, but I have witnesses. They won't stay silent if I disappear."

Abby had to know. "Why did you kill Noah? He was a good man, a scientist."

Marcel snickered, and the sound iced her veins.

"He was a detective," she said, her words scathing. "He snooped in our mausoleum. He wanted to destroy our family. Where is the ring?"

"Did you kill Noah's Uncle Max, too?" she said, ignoring the imperious demand. "Are you the murderer with blood on your hands?"

This information stunned the *comtesse*. "His uncle?" She appeared to draw back. "His death was an accident. Mark found him trespassing, and they fought. He fell and hit his head."

"Why didn't you report it? Call the authorities?"

"Enough," her grandmother said, holding up her hand, the gun trained on Abby. "I will find the ring, and I will start with that puling woman who raised you." For the first time, Abby was glad her gran was dead, and she and this madwoman would never meet.

The *comtesse's* eyes found Eddie. He still held his shoulder, his face slick with perspiration. "Eddie, you must prove your loyalty to the family."

Eddie cringed. "I did what I was told. You said my granddaughter would be released."

"And she was left at your house when Marcel called. I keep my promises, Eddie." The calm chill of her voice resonated as madness. Her tone softened, coaxed. "Now, I need your help, proof of loyalty. Your family will be handsomely compensated."

"No." Eddie shook his head. "No. Not that ... Please."

"You need medical help, Eddie. You will dispatch this meddler and live, or ..." she shrugged one shoulder, "medical attention will not be necessary."

The madwoman walked to Eddie and handed him the gun. Her face radiated the confidence he would do her bidding. Mark and Marcel gave her that confidence.

Eddie held the gun in a shaking hand. He looked from her to Abby and back to his tormentor. "You're evil." He pointed the gun at the *comtesse* and pulled the trigger. The gun clicked but did not fire. He pulled the trigger again and again in rapid succession. Nothing. He threw the weapon at the old woman's head, but she stepped aside, and smiled.

They watched Eddie sink to his knees in defeat. "God have mercy," he mumbled.

The *comtesse* picked up her gun and very deliberately took bullets from her pocket and reloaded. "Marcel, you know what to do."

Marcel moved closer to Eddie, licking his lips in pleasure at the summons, his smile feral, forgetting Abby. As his gun hand began to move upward, she struck, surprise her advantage.

"No," Abby yelled. She stepped in, her energy marshalled, and as he turned toward her, an opening appeared. She threw a swift straight leg and foot push kick to his solar plexus. Abby followed through with a rear leg push kick hitting his upper thigh, missing her target, the groin.

He reeled backward off balance, his gun arm flung outward. Marcel landed on his back. The gun discharged as his head and hand hit the floor with force, the bullet striking the concrete and ricocheting harmlessly into the black void.

Abby landed a powerful kick to the dazed man's wrist as he brought his arm up, and the gun skittered past the still kneeling Eddie.

Marcel rolled away and leapt to his feet, head shaking, legs planted in a combative stance. He rushed forward, closing the space. Abby grabbed his injured wrist, using his momentum to spin him around.

He grabbed for her neck and tried to sweep Abby's feet from under her. She reversed, spun toward him and slung her forehead into his nose, shattering it. Her knee forcefully struck his groin this time, and he doubled over, retching.

Abby moved in. A flat kick to the side of his knee cracked bone, and effectively immobilized him.

Marcel howled as he balled into a fetal position, writhing and cursing, blood streaming from his nose and mouth.

Seconds ticked by. Mark and *Grand-Maman* stood paralyzed in place, mouths open.

Abby bent at the waist nauseated, waiting for the bullet that would end her life, and yet feeling an unexpected euphoria that she had created havoc with the madwoman's plans.

Outside a car door slammed, and running footsteps resounded.

Mark left to check, his gun out, ready to use.

Jean-Jacques appeared, with Paul at his heels, the *comtes's* eyes finding Abby.

"*Non, Maman*. This ends now. Jules is dead." Jean-Jacques pointed to Abby. "She is a DuMond. Family."

Abby watched in horror as the old woman's eyes glittered with hatred and became steel.

"Yes," she said. "Family. She will rest in the family crypt with her ancestors." Her eyes followed Jean-Jacques as he walked to stand at Abby's side.

"I'm Rafe's legitimate daughter." She wanted him to know before she died.

"Yes," Jean-Jacques said, not looking shocked or turning in her direction. "More killing will only compound our problem with the authorities. Please *Maman*, give me the gun." He walked toward his mother slowly, Jean-Jacques's eyes never leaving her own, his empty hands raised chest high. His voice low, soft, like he would talk to a child he loved but who had disappointed him. "Please *Maman*. Jules no longer needs your help."

"You are weak," she said, her words bitter, dismissive, "You have always been weak. Jules should have succeeded, not you."

Her gun swung in Abby's direction and fired.

Jean-Jacques stumbled and fell, holding his chest. He had stepped in front of Abby when he saw his mother's intent.

The weapon dangled in her hand as she rushed to Jean-Jacques's side. "*Non*, this cannot be. *Non*," she cried as she reached him. "I did not mean it. I did not mean it," his mother repeated, crying and clutching his arms, broken.

Eddie stretched for the gun near him, and Mark raised his own.

"No," Abby shouted. "Help the *comte*. He needs you." Mark looked conflicted.

Another car arrived, and Mark ran toward the open door.

A voice ordered. "FBI. Drop the gun and move away." Mark did as he was told. The gun clattered to the floor, and he raised his hands. Eddie raised his one good arm and remained on the floor.

Agent Mackey patted Mark and Paul down and used plastic ties on their arms while Agent Helms kept his gun ready.

Abby released a sob of relief and knelt by Jean-Jacques. "Thank you, God, thank you," she said, checking for a pulse in the man's neck. He was alive but unresponsive.

The *comtesse* bent over Jean-Jacques's body and sobbed, her keening words in French muffled in his bloodied shirt.

Help me," Marcel squealed. "You have to help me." His good hand clutched his broken knee as he writhed on the floor.

Both agents walked to him, their looks scornful. "I don't think you're walking anytime soon," Agent Helms said, looking at the unnatural placement of his lower leg. He patted the man down, removed a knife from his boot, and pulled his arms back to secure the ties. Marcel screamed when they moved him and shouted a stream of invectives before passing out.

Another vehicle arrived. A man entered, preceded by his weapon. He took stock of the situation and replaced the gun in a shoulder holster. "John's checking the area. The hotel got us a shuttle." He raised his phone and made a call.

The second agent came inside. "Perimeter's safe. Nothing but crickets and a cat out there."

Behind them, one of the new agents barked, "Put the gun down!"

But it was too late. The *comtesse* had turned the gun on herself and fired, the bullet entering her chest. Her body convulsed and covered her son.

Abby fell away from Jean-Jacques as the gun exploded. Blood spattered her clothing and face. The nausea returned, and she swallowed bile, trying not to be sick.

Agent Helms bent at Abby's side and lifted the lifeless body of the *comtesse* away from Jean-Jacques to check the damage.

Blood covered the comte's chest.

The agent searched for the bullet's entry. He found the area and put his hand under the victim. "The bullet is still in him, but it missed his heart. I don't believe his wound is life-threatening. Blood bubbled from the site of entry." He pulled off his jacket and rolled it up, placing it over the wound and directed Abby to use it as a compress.

"He saved my life," Abby said, her voice trembling, her body shaking as reaction set in.

"He's my uncle ... family." Tears began to well at the words.

"Eddie needs help," she said, looking at the man sitting on the floor, no longer kneeling.

Agent Helms nodded and moved to Eddie, easing his jacket off to better see his wound. When Eddie saw the blood soaking his shirt, he too, passed out.

Agent Mackey cut the undamaged sleeve from Eddie's other arm and wrapped his wounded shoulder. "The bullet went through."

"I'm calling for a chopper," Agent Helms said, and walked outside.

Agent Mackey squatted beside Abby. "Are you injured? We got here as fast as we could."

Abby shook her head, still not believing the danger had passed.

Agent Mackey took tissues from her pocket and wiped blood from her face.

Jean-Jacques stirred and groaned. "*Maman? Maman?*"

"I'm sorry. She's dead," Abby told him.

Jean-Jacques closed his eyes and sighed. "It is best."

CHAPTER TWENTY-TWO

Abby walked outside into the cool night and tried to put what happened into perspective.

Eddie followed her out, his head down, silent.

My father is alive. Jean-Jacques saved my life. The woman I thought my grandmother is not my grandmother. My God, she's dead. Oh, Gran, how I miss you.

Another memory intruded. *Noah. Dead. So much death because I came to Mast Island.* She kicked a piece of wood across the pavement, watching the fragment spin, like her life.

Jean-Jacques had recognized her as family. He tried, in his own way, to make amends. His mother, the woman who reared him, was dead by her own hand. What fueled the *comtesse's* hatred? Jules, her son killed in the war, must have created the monster she became. What happened? What did Jean-Jacques mean by Jules didn't need her help anymore? Guillaume, the youngest, must also have been her son. Why did he go back to France? Did madness run in her family? So many questions needed answers. She hugged herself and tried to be content with the answers she knew.

Above her, stars twinkled, millions scattered across the inky universe, a lit pathway to other worlds. *Noah will never see these marvels of creation ever again. Not from earth* she reminded herself. *Maybe now, his view is far better than my own. Why don't I feel better?* She needed to rid herself of the negative thoughts, or she would spiral into depression.

Gran, my father is alive. Rafe is alive. She closed her eyes and savored the thought. She wanted to see him as soon as possible. She realized others also needed to know what happened. Vanna and Collette. She needed to talk with them. Tonight.

Abby heard the familiar "Whomph, Whomph" of the helicopter's rotating blades. This was their second visit today. The sound reminded her of the last time she heard them, and a wave of sadness swamped her.

Abby guessed Noah's parents knew by now he had died in the explosion. Would he be buried in Charleston or Mobile? Should she make an attempt to see his family? What could she say? *I'm the woman he died trying to save.* No, at least not now, she told herself. Their loss would be raw. *Maybe later. Much later.*

Agent Helms had placed the three vehicles at triangular points, their lights, beacons displaying a landing spot for the approaching aircraft.

Abby breathed the night air. The smell of rotting wood awakened her senses. She was alive. Eddie and Jean-Jacques were alive. Eddie's granddaughter was alive. She turned to Eddie, who was slumped over, one hand over his face. "Thank you for trying to help. I'm glad your granddaughter's all right." She added, "I understand."

Eddie tried to speak, but his voice became garbled, lost in the heaving sobs at her words. She knew his guilt would haunt him as she herself was haunted. She patted his good shoulder, trying to console. "We're alive, Eddie. Be grateful."

The agent, named John, came to get Eddie, and they walked to the helicopter.

Only Noah had perished. *Noah.* She missed his quirky smile, his blue green eyes searching her own for answers, appreciating her, looking to the future. *To what? A relationship on a deeper level?* After the revelations under the oak, he had withdrawn, said little. *Why?* She closed her eyes. *Because I'm a DuMond? Don't go there.*

The helicopter lifted off with the three injured men and one of the agents, Agent Mackey walked with Abby to a car. Abby wanted to go to the château to see her father, Vanna, and Collette. "The family needs to be told."

"I'll go with you. I have questions."

Agent Helms stayed behind with the authorities that arrived on the helicopter. They and another agent would be with the body to fill in notes while waiting for the coroner's investigation and the forensic evidence to be collected.

Surprised, Abby saw Roux sitting in the car, one wrist manacled to the wheel.

Agent Mackey handed Roux the keys. "Take us back to the château." The agent explained as they got into the car. "Noah contacted us while he was in Savannah. He knew something like this might happen, and he wanted us to keep an eye on you. He wanted to be sure you safely left the island. You *know* he planned to be with you at the château."

Abby twisted her hands in her lap, remembering his words, knowing he would have been there for her if not …

"Two agents were stationed at the hotel." Agent Mackey continued. "When you left in the car, they called us. Their main concern, your safety. The subject was aiming his gun at you. He had shot the driver without much provocation, and they didn't want to give him a reason to pull the trigger again.

"Agent Helms and I were on the grounds of the château when we received the call. They didn't have transportation at the hotel, so we moved to commandeer one of the DuMond vehicles when Jean-Jacques barreled out of the garage and sped past us. This man followed. He gave us the keys to the last vehicle. We couldn't leave him behind to warn the others."

Minneau opened the door as the car drove to Château Sologne's entrance. A man watched from the gate house, and he probably called to warn the rest of the family.

Behind Minneau, Vanna appeared, her features distraught, followed by Collette and Cece. When Vanna saw Abby and the blood on her, she cried, "You are hurt."

"It's not my blood," Abby said.

"You are all right." Vanna's face crumpled and she hugged Abby tightly, sobbing, unmindful of the mess. "You are all right. We have been so worried." Vanna's body shook, and Abby believed she cared.

Vanna lifted her tear-stained face, looking behind her and only seeing the agent. "Where is Papa? He left to find you. He was frantic when he did not find *Grand-Maman*."

Collette stepped in front of Abby. "My husband. I must know if he is alive." Her mouth twitched nervously, and she looked on the verge of collapse.

Abby nodded and stepped aside.

Rouland came to support Vanna. "Please come in." He saw Agent Mackey. "We must talk. We learned astounding news tonight. You will want to know."

They were escorted to the salon, and Vanna took Abby's hand and tried to smile through her tears and snuffling. "My father. You have seen him?" Her eyes hopeful, pleading.

"Yes," Abby said, "Your father is alive. He saved my life." Seeing hope dawn in Vanna's face gave her the strength to continue, "He's been shot and is now being taken to the hospital in Savannah by helicopter. The agents believe the wound is not life-threatening."

Collette cried out, and Cece held her. Collette wailed and caught herself. Her eyes became lasers finding Agent Mackey. "Why did you shoot him? Why? What did he do?" she demanded.

Vanna folded inward, her hands covered her face.

Rouland's arms surrounded her and held her to his chest.

Abby continued, ignoring Collette's diatribe and addressing Vanna. "I'm sorry, your grandmother is dead."

Cece pushed forward. "The *comtesse* is dead? How? Tell me." She could not hide her delight at the news. Cece's smile and relief were palpable. The woman made Abby's skin crawl.

Vanna looked shocked by the news and grasped her arm. "Tell me what happened. Please, I have to know."

"First, tell me about Henri," Abby said.

"That was the news," Rouland said, stepping forward, his voice raised, excited. "When we returned home, Jean-Jacques told us an incredible story. The *comtesse* was angry and tried to stop him, but he said he would no longer live with secrets. The death of Dr. Hazzard shocked him, and Jean-Jacques said he wanted no part of murder."

Agent Mackey opened her notebook and began writing.

Vanna continued the tale. "My father said Henri was his brother, Raphael. Even Collette did not know. He told us the circumstance that left Rafe injured. He believed you were Rafe's daughter, and the *comtesse* corroborated the fact. She told us you were a surviving twin intent on ruining the family, and she should not have let you live.

"We were stunned at the change in her and frightened for you," Vanna continued. "My father blamed his brother, Jules, and *Grand-Maman*, who had tried to save her favorite son by covering his crimes. Papa will have to tell you what happened. He told us Jules did not die honorably in the war. He was killed by gun dealers in Yemen."

Cece bristled at the words, her demeanor combative, but she remained silent.

Rouland spoke. "Jean-Jacques was frantic when he found the *comtesse* left the château and a car had been taken. I would have gone with him, but he told me to stay, and if the *comtesse* returned alone, to get away somehow. He said she was mad. If he did not return, we were to call the authorities in Savannah."

Abby stayed silent. Her recent thoughts about destroying her family gave her pause. Some family members appeared innocent, and Abby felt relief. Evidently, Vanna, Rouland, and Collette were not involved. She looked at Cece, whose countenance had become somber. As Jules's wife, what part did she play? And Minneau, who hovered in doorway? He and Roux were sons of Jules.

"Please," Vanna implored, tightening her hold on Abby's arm. "Tell us what happened tonight."

Abby returned to her room at Sea Oat Inn after a harrowing night and startling confessions. She had seen her father sleeping peacefully in his room and decided not to waken him. Tomorrow would be soon enough for them to speak. *What will I say? Will he understand?*

Removing the "bugs" and stepping on them gave Abby a sense of satisfaction. She discarded them in the wastebasket and felt free.

She lay on the bed still clothed, sleep eluding her, and pondered possibilities.

Her first thought to take her father home with her did not make sense. She lived upstairs, and the building did not have an elevator. Her grandmother's apartment had front steps. *I'll have to find an apartment with an elevator. What if he doesn't want to leave?*

She had to assess the extent of his injuries. Could he walk? Did he require a male nurse or assistant like Tasse?

She thought about the DuMonds. Criminal intent, harboring a known felon, lying about Rafe's disappearance, and maybe unsolved murders crossed her mind. Would DuMonds be prosecuted, go to prison, lose their way of life? Had she ruined them? Who engineered the explosion? So many questions unanswered.

---✴---

Dawn's light filtered through the window too early.

Abby rose from the bed feeling heavy. Sleep never came, and she knew without looking in the mirror, her eyes were red-rimmed and blood shot. Then she remembered today she would meet her father, and with the thought, excitement boiled up and motivated her. A hot shower and clean clothes worked wonders.

She was too nervous to eat, but she went to the lobby for complimentary hot tea and to wait for the car being sent from the château. Clerks looked her way, their eyes curious, pitying, but no one approached or spoke to her, even when she cancelled her shuttle reservation. Coming to the lobby might not have been a good idea. She checked her watch for the tenth time. Fifteen minutes dragged by, before Roux entered the lobby.

"Ms. Parsons," Roux said in his lilting voice, "Ms. Boucher asked me to bring you to Château Sologne." Roux's eyes were downcast, avoiding contact. The last time she saw him, he had been shackled to the steering wheel. His subdued voice hinted the discomfort of his mission.

Abby felt his pain. "I'm sorry about your grandmother, Roux."

He nodded and walked outside to open the car door. Roux didn't speak as he drove, and Abby didn't ask questions. She wondered about his position in the household and if the death of his grandmother made a difference in his situation. How did Cece view Roux and Minneau, her husband's illegitimate children? Were they tolerated because of the *comtesse*? Would they continue to stay at the château?

A man waved them through the gate, and Minneau met them at the entrance.

Abby repeated her condolences to Minneau, the other grandson.

"It is best," he said, repeating the same words Jean-Jacques had used. "The *Comtesse* DuMond would not have survived an interrogation. She was too proud." His voice lowered. "She rarely left the château. Her heart was failing, so we were surprised by her sudden departure."

Vanna met Abby at the door, surprising her, since Abby figured Vanna would be at the hospital in Savannah first thing this morning. "I thought you and Rouland would be gone."

"I wanted to see you first," Vanna said, hugging her. "I spoke with Papa on the phone, and he understood. Collette is at the hospital with him.

"I have to tell you, Rouland had breakfast with Uncle Henri ... I mean Uncle Rafe. I'm sorry, Henri is the only name I've ever known. Rouland told my uncle what he knew and what had happened. He told Uncle Rafe his daughter was alive and coming to see him this morning. We thought it best to warn him and allow him time to think upon it, instead of springing you full-grown into his life unannounced." Her arms lifted as if to invite cheer into the conversation. "The news filled him with joy, and he is anxious to meet you. I am truly happy for you both."

"Thank you, Vanna. I've been nervous about meeting him as his daughter for the first time, not knowing how to begin." Abby's anxiety eased. Vanna and Rouland appeared to care about her and her feelings, like family.

"Tasse has taken Uncle ... Rafe to the garden, his sanctuary. Rouland and I are leaving for the marina in a few minutes."

"You and Rouland have my deepest gratitude. I'll come by the hospital later to see the *comte*. What's his prognosis?"

"He told me the bullet glanced off a rib and pierced his lung, which collapsed. They removed the bullet. His pain is being monitored, and he is out of ICU."

"I hope he recuperates quickly."

They arrived at a side door which opened into a glorious garden.

Abby's father sat on a patio chair in the sun, his wheelchair on the flagstones nearby. His eyes were closed, his face raised to catch the morning light. Tasse sat on a stone bench, facing him.

Surrounding them were hibiscus, pinks, anemones, nasturtiums, roses, and a variety of other colorful flowers and greenery. A spicy fragrance filled the air, and bees buzzed as they collected pollen. Several arbors covered in vines surrounded the area.

Vanna walked to her uncle and gave him a hug. "Uncle, I have someone here, who wants very much to meet you. This is Abby."

Rafe opened his jade green eyes and stared at Abby, mouth agape, arms outstretched. "Bella, my Bella." His voice caught, and red-rimmed eyes filled with tears. When Abby took his hands, he lowered his head and wept into them. "Bella," he said, his voice broken, the hot tears covering her hands.

Abby lowered her head next to his own. "Papa," Abby said, using the word Vanna called her father. She choked on the words she wanted to say as her own tears flowed.

Vanna and Tasse left them, and Abby sat on the bench, not letting go of her father's hands. "My name is Abby."

Tasse returned with a box of tissues and left without speaking.

They both reached for the tissues at the same time, and Abby snuffled. "We have a lot of catching up to do."

He nodded, blew his nose, and looked at Abby with wonder-filled eyes. "I have a daughter." His eyes looked clear, his voice lucid. "Abby."

"Yes. And I have a father. This is the best day of my life!"

They sat in silence, eyes drinking in features, thoughts swirling.

Have the worst days of my life been just weeks old, days old? In so short a time, I lost my identity, my history, and Noah. Now, I understand the depth of your love, Gran, and your precautions. I've disrupted the lives of another family and gained a father. Miracles still happen.

"Vanna told me you can walk but not great distances." She looked at her father's legs. He had on boots and corduroy pants. They were not covered by a blanket.

He cleared his throat. "Tasse's mission is to keep me mobile. He makes sure I exercise. One leg is damaged, not as strong as the other."

His eyes traveled over her, noting every feature. "You are a DuMond. My daughter, Abby." He paused. "You know, Bella and I wed." His voice began to waver as he said the words, and then became adamant. "We wed." He watched for her reaction as if he needed her to believe his words.

"Yes, Father Ziegler married you and Bella. He remembers."

Her father was silent as he searched for words. "Tell me about your life. Where have you been?"

Abby began at the beginning. She told him about her life with Gran, her love of art, and receiving the box of mementos after her gran's death. She left out her feelings of abandonment, devastation, and depression.

His eyes welled again when she mentioned the emerald ring, the necklace with toe shoes, and hearing Mina's story. Her father's eyes fell as he slipped into the past. "We were wed. I loved you, Bella. We would have been happy together."

CHAPTER TWENTY-THREE

Abby decided to delay leaving the island until Monday. The first day with her father and her disclosures exhausted him. She had told him to get some rest. He wanted her to stay, but she said they'd speak in the morning. Resolving issues assured a good night's sleep, and the time passed quickly. Today she would learn more about her father.

Minneau opened the door to the garden, and Abby saw her father in the same place, but Tasse was not present.

Rafe was dressed warmly and held a red rose in his hand. He handed her the flower after she kissed his cheek and sat down on the bench which still felt a little warm. *So Tasse must have left when he heard me arrive.* A box of tissues was left on the bench. Abby had been happy to find her father lucid and not drugged continually. Tasse told her he gave Rafe something to calm him when they first met. Rafe didn't appear to be under the influence of a drug today.

Rafe began by saying, "I want to stay here where I grew up, where I am comfortable. I have Tasse to help me." This information offered at the beginning of their conversation seemed to relax him, and he eased back in the wheelchair.

"I want to paint again, take part in the community." His hands and features were animated as his passion returned, his desire to participate in life evidenced by his tone of voice.

Abby nodded. She understood his attachment to his home, to those memories he still retained. She also felt relieved her own life wouldn't be disrupted by moving and finding a place for him in her daily life.

"I have a daughter, Abby. You can live here with us on my island."

Abby thought how easily he said, "my island." Would he reestablish himself as the head of the family?

She took his hands into her own, fingers connecting with flesh shared by birth. His hands were smooth, stronger than she imagined. Not Noah's hands, Noah's touch. Sadness swept over her.

Her father noticed, and his hands began to shake, so she let them drop back in his lap.

"I understand your connection to the island, your home," Abby said, bringing herself back to the present. "I also have a home where I'm comfortable, where I work. I need to get back." She told him about the opening in December.

"I need to know more about you, your life here, and ... the subterfuge." She hesitated saying the word, but she had questions which needed to be answered.

"Why did you live with the DuMonds as Henri instead of Rafe?"

He nodded. "I was almost dead when the men who attacked us brought me home. I had lost a lot of blood. I had no memory. I was told I was Henri. Authorities believed *Maman* while they searched for me.

"Amnesia from the traumatic experience kept me in the dark several years, or so I was told by psychiatrists who saw me. My family tried everything, including hypnosis, which didn't work. I fought losing myself. Everyone called me Henri, and I accepted the name because it is also my name. I am Raphael Philippe Etienne Henri DuMond.

"I began to recover bits and pieces of my memory, and ..." Her father's hands clasped, twisted, and then smoothed down his pants' legs in agitation. "I wanted Bella with me." He sat in silence, swallowed, and tried to speak. His lips trembled, and his eyes welled again. "*Maman* told me Bella was dead as was the child. I did not want to live without Bella. I told them we were married. *Maman* said we were not married. No record existed of our marriage. But I knew.

"Jean-Jacques goaded me to live when I wanted desperately to die and be with Bella. He is my brother. Now he needs me."

"What about your brothers, Jules and Guilliame?"

Rafe looked away from Abby. "*Maman* loved only Jules. He was her first child, her bright star, so confident, and mean." He shook his head and tried to find the words. So … so consumed by greed. He always wanted more … more development, more money. We fought over the future of Mast Island. He was a demon. I was not sorry when he was killed in Yemen, but *Maman* never recovered from his death."

Several minutes passed. "*Maman* was demented, a wild woman. She screamed. For days she would not dress or eat. Then she became angry, angry because Jules, her son, was buried across the ocean in heathen ground." His chin dropped to his chest, not wanting to continue. His words, barely audible came out in a groan. "He killed Bella and the baby."

Abby gasped, and Rafe looked at her. "*Non*, his men killed them, but he sent them. To me, the same thing."

Jules must have been the person who removed the evidence of marriage from the church.

"Now I find I want to live. I have a daughter … Abby, who paints. I paint, but it has been a long time. Come, I want to show you my work. I have seen yours online" He unlatched the brakes and turned the wheelchair toward the door.

"Tasse showed me the gallery site. I am so proud to have a daughter who sees the inner beauty of nature and not just the outside trappings. You have the sight of a true artist."

Abby felt tears gathering again. She thought she had cried them out. Her father understood her like no other person in the world. He voiced the feelings just beginning to bud in her being. He said the words so beautifully; she felt she was an extension of this man, a stranger separated by time but not by genes. She stood and hugged him. "Thank you for your vision. I very much want to see your work."

A whistle blew as the ferry approached the dock. People gathered belongings. Bits of their chatter reminded Abby that each passenger had a story. Her own story had progressed in a matter of weeks.

The thought of separation had tormented Abby and her father, but she knew they connected and would see one another again.

The ferry ride back to the mainland was anticlimactic. Memories of her arrival, seeing the salt marsh for the first time, and meeting Noah intruded. These memories would be part of her life forever.

Abby waffled about wanting to have anything to do with her father's family. She liked Vanna and her husband, but any relationship took time, one commodity she didn't have at the moment. Her opening, advertised by the gallery, was a month and a half away. Abby knew she had work piled ahead of her. Distance might help her decide how to view the family.

She remembered her father's words, his insight and felt the warmth of knowing her father would be part of her life. His paintings were magnificent. They had painted some of the same subjects, but his paintings had a passion which sprang from the dark field of his upbringing, his tragic circumstances. Some had violent backgrounds that stirred emotions almost to a fever pitch. The wildness of the ocean, the dunes and trees assaulted by winds, turbulence that was easier to imagine, harder to capture on canvas.

The paintings of his family had a tortured appearance, his inner conflict depicted on canvas for the observer to interpret. *Had family members seen his view of them?*

His paintings of Bella left her breathless. Rafe's view of life calmed with Bella as his muse. He had painted her sewing, dancing, and nude, her hand bearing the emerald ring protectively across her abdomen. The casual portraits shouted love, and she knew he had defended those paintings, saving them from his mother, who no doubt wanted to destroy them. She imagined her father's ultimatum. "Destroy the paintings, and I will destroy you." Yes, he had strength when it mattered.

The hospital loomed before her. The imposing walls of Memorial Health Hospital proclaimed a sterile environment lay within. Abby didn't want to enter, but she had told Vanna she would visit her father, Jean-Jacques, Abby's newfound uncle. He had saved her life and lost the only mother he knew. She had to see him.

The information desk gave her the room number, and she stepped into the gift shop to buy a card and flowers. She chose a small, silvered vase holding several red roses, white baby's breath, and greenery. She signed the get well card and walked to his room.

Vanna sat in the chair by her father's bed. Rouland and Collette were not present.

Jean-Jacques opened his eyes when Vanna's chair scraped the floor. His gray face was etched with lines of pain probably caused by family revelations and devastation.

"Abby, you came," Vanna said, her voice hushed.

Abby nodded and looked at Jean-Jacques. An oxygen tube was attached to his nose. Several other tubes led to a colostomy bag and an IV, his vitals constantly monitored.

Abby set the flowers and card on the mobile tray. Her small offering appeared lost among several larger bouquets in the room. "I came to tell you I'm sorry you were shot, and sorry for the trouble I've caused. I only wanted to meet my family, not take anything from you. I didn't know my father was alive."

Her mouth dried as she thought of the circumstances which brought him here. "Thank you for saving my life."

"You have seen Rafe?" Jean-Jacques asked, dismissing her thanks, his words raspy from anesthesia.

"Yes, we've talked the past two days. He wants to stay at the château where he is comfortable and Tasse can help him."

"Yes" he said, a thoughtful look on his face. "This is as it should be. The château is Rafe's by right. I took his place because he no longer had an interest in day-to-day decisions. Now, he knows he has a daughter, and his time has come, his interest will surely return."

Abby did not hear animosity in his voice or even regret. She believed he would be all right with the decision. Hadn't she seen Rafe's renewed interest herself?

"You may be right. He showed me his paintings, and they were impressive. He wants to paint again."

"I am glad to hear of his desire to paint," Vanna said, her face lighting up. "And I am overjoyed to hear about Noah. You must be so happy."

"Noah?" Abby felt the blood draining from her head and sat down on the chair Vanna had vacated, her head down, feeling faint. She had seen the glance between father and daughter, a questioning glance as if maybe Vanna misspoke.

Silence followed, and when Abby looked at Vanna, she noted her pallid face.

Vanna hesitated, looked at her, and said, "I thought you knew. We only just found out … by accident. Noah, too, was in ICU, but I have to tell you, Abby, the outlook is not good." Her saddened voice spurred action.

Abby ran from the room, down the hall, and asked for directions to ICU from a nurse rolling a medicine tray. She didn't bother to use the elevator and took the stairs down two floors.

At the nurse's station, a young woman working on a computer looked at her distraught face and stood. "Are you all right?"

"I have to see Noah Hazzard. He's in ICU."

"What's your name? Are you related? Only family members can see him," she said, her voice caring, but adamant.

"Abby Parsons, and I'm," she swallowed and said, forcing the words, "his sister."

An older woman standing nearby, holding a chart said, "I heard him say your name. Your family …," but she didn't have a chance to finish.

A tall woman rushed to her, put her arms around her, and squeezed tightly. She said, "Sweetheart, we didn't expect you so soon. Your dad is in the waiting room. We must let him know you're here." She took a dazed Abby's arm and drew her down the hall into a nearby room.

A man was sitting with his elbows on his knees and his face in his hands.

"Look who's here," she said to the man. "Abby. It's Abby, the artist who drew *The Lady*."

The man rose to his feet, his face lined with grief. "Abby?" He walked to her and took her hand. "Noah said you were special. We didn't expect to meet you like this." He stopped talking as if to find words.

This must be Noah's father. He, too, was fair, his brown hair liberally sprinkled with gray. He stood erect, his military bearing evident.

Abby looked at his wife. She was tall and had freckles sprinkled on her face. She too, displayed evidence of grief around her eyes and mouth, her blue-green eyes red from crying. *Noah's eyes.*

"Please stay and talk with us," she said. "My name is Jane, and I'm sorry I startled you. You ran past me, and I couldn't help overhearing your conversation with the nurse at the desk. Noah is our son. As Dave said, he has spoken of you."

Abby stood across from them, and Noah's mother held her husband's arm. "We arrived this morning, and we were only allowed to see Noah for a few minutes."

"I thought he was dead." As Abby said the words, anger took hold. "They told me he was dead." She brought a fist to her mouth to stifle the sob, which threatened to cave her.

"I'm sorry. Do you mean his colleagues, the agents who worked with him?"

"Yes. How could they do that?" Abby rubbed her arms, wanting to punch something. *How could they let me believe he was dead?* She closed her eyes and willed herself to calm down.

"They said what he wanted said," his mother told her quietly. "His friends told us he didn't want you to see him die. In fact, they had to tell him they were calling us, despite his wishes to wait."

"Tell me," Abby pleaded, "what is his condition?"

His mother bit her lip. "He's critical." Tears welled in her eyes.

Noah's father put his arm around his wife's shoulders and said, "He has numerous broken bones. Doctors removed one kidney and part of his intestine two days ago. They wanted to postpone surgery because of swelling, but they had to operate. He was bleeding internally."

"One side of his face will need reconstructive surgery, and he may lose his eye," his mother said, and began to weep, turning her head into her husband's chest.

His father continued Noah's list of injuries. "He has first and second degree burns over twenty per cent of his body, and his hair and eyebrows were singed. They shaved his head. He was lucky the water put the flames out quickly. The doctors claimed Noah had a hard head because they didn't find any skull fractures, other than the orbital bone which protects the eye."

A semblance of a smile appeared before his mother said, "We could have told them that." She shuddered with emotion and reached for the tissue box on a nearby table. "Doctors said he would probably lose some of his hearing."

"The good thing is Noah's alive," his father said. "We have to stay positive. We have a prayer chain back home praying for him, for us."

"Yes," Abby said. "Attitude is everything when it comes to healing. Will I be able to see him?"

Noah's mother turned to Abby and looked her in the eyes. "I think if he's going to get better, he has to see you. Noah has to know you are not put off by his appearance. That will be hard for you, but I think part of him doesn't want to survive like he is now. This is different from his war injuries." She closed her eyes and leaned on her husband.

Abby sat in the nearest chair and thought about what she had been told. Noah was alive but in critical condition. She bowed her head and prayed, *Surround Noah with Your presence, Lord, Your assurance, and be merciful. You are the divine physician. Nothing is impossible with You. Nothing. Thank You, Lord, for hearing our prayers.*

Abby's mind repeated the thought, *Noah is not dead.* The wonder at thinking those words ministered to her. *He's not dead. Dear God, he is not dead.* Beautiful words. Words of hope.

Noah's father cleared his throat, and regained Abby's attention. He was tall and nice looking, but his clothing was rumpled as if worn several days. "Noah scanned the sketch you made of *The Lady* and sent it to us. You have a gift." He stopped talking, and they sat in silence, each with his own thoughts.

Jane murmured, "They put temporary metal plates and screws in his arm, hip, and leg yesterday, instead of casts because of the burns. A pin will stay in his hip. A hip replacement may be required. The surgeons worked on him most of the day. We were told infection is the enemy. The next seventy-two hours are crucial."

Abby pondered their words. *What will I say to him?*

CHAPTER TWENTY-FOUR

Dave and Jane Hazzard insisted Abby should see him next. She tiptoed into the room, stood by the bed, and looked at Noah without speaking. An oxygen tent covered his head, but she could see his face was swollen and purple with bruising. His head and eye were swathed in bandages, his nose taped as if it had been broken, and stitches ran from the corner of his mouth to his ear and down his neck. A cold pack lay over his eye. Wet gauze wrappings covered an arm and a leg, which were suspended in traction. She assumed the box-like structure under the sheet covered his hip. She wondered at the extent of the damage. She tried to wipe the horror and evidence of fear from her face, before she sat by the bed, touching an exposed hand covered with cuts and bruises.

"Noah, if you can hear me, you *have* to fight," she demanded, her voice raised because of the tent separating them, "You *have* to live."

Noah groaned and moved his head. A grimace followed the effort. "Abby," he said, the word slurred, barely audible. He opened his eye and looked at her. Then he closed it and tried to turn away.

"Noah Hazzard," she said forcefully, "Don't you wimp out on me. I still need your help. You survived the war, and you can survive this. Do you hear me, you ornery man?" She put her hands on her hips and gave him her best shot. "I thought you had a warrior's heart."

A grunt or grumble was heard as if he wanted to laugh in a cynical manner. "Sure thing, sweet cakes … got … duty."

"Don't you laugh at me. I'm alive because of you, and if you insist on dying, I'll … I'll just have to fade away and die, too. It's my fault you got hurt."

Noah's one good eye opened to stare at her. "Pisshed are we?"

"Darn right, I'm pissed. How could you feel sorry for yourself when so many people love you and need you?"

He looked steadily at her. "You … you … love … me, Abby?" his voice, though hesitant, seemed stronger.

"How would I know? We haven't had a chance to get that far."

A monitor began to beep, and a nurse came into the room. "You have to leave now," she said as she checked the machine.

"He's okay, isn't he?" Abby's worried expression got her attention.

"He's okay. His pulse rate and blood pressure picked up."

Abby returned to her motel room and contacted the attorney, Gordon Culpepper, Esq. and set up an appointment to see him on Tuesday afternoon. Her flight back to Philly had been changed to the following morning. The new flight reservation strained her budget. Staying in Savannah to be with Noah wasn't practical. His parents were with him, and she was beginning to stress over the planned gallery opening.

Before returning to the hospital, she called Father Ziegler to tell him her father was alive, and she had met him for the first time. She did not tell him about her brush with death.

Father Ziegler said, "I'm truly happy to hear the news and to know you have met your family at last. I will pray the Lord blesses your reunion and future visits."

Mina was more astute when Abby called and told her the news. The questions flew not waiting to be answered. "What happened? Are you all right? How did the family react to finding out about you? Who did you see? What is your father like now?"

Abby knew Mina's fear for her had been real, and she gave a brief answer to each of her questions. She ended her conversation with, "I don't know if I'll pursue a relationship with the family, at this point, but my father and I will spend time together after my December art opening."

"Oh, my dear, I've been so worried you'd get yourself killed by trying to locate your family. Please come and see me when you have time, so you can tell me everything."

Abby promised she would see her in January. She replaced the phone and sat on the bed thinking about Noah.

He's alive. Thank you, God. Forgive me for not trusting you. Please give Noah the will to live and get better, without complications. She would see him again. How would he react after a night of thinking about their previous conversation? He had asked her if she loved him.

I could love him, she thought. He was unlike any man she had ever known. Now, his injuries complicated things. *Be positive.*

That evening, Abby met Noah's mother and father, Jane and Dave, in the waiting room. They had both changed and looked refreshed.

"Noah's breathing better," his mother said. "I think he's fighting to live. I don't know what you said to get him back on track, but it's what he needed."

Abby blushed and nodded as she sat in the chair next to her. "He needs to be challenged."

"Please tell us how you became involved with Noah. He told us you're a good artist, and you came to Mast Island to paint."

This was the last thing she wanted to tell Noah's parents. How could she tell them Noah would be fine if he hadn't tried to help her? She stayed silent and fidgeted with her hands.

"We don't mean to pry," Jane said. "Noah told us he invited you onboard *The Lady*. He seemed happy, and for the first time he mentioned he might need more space. In fact, he told Dave he might take on another person, and for that, he needed a larger boat."

The comment brought a blush to Abby's face. She answered an earlier question. "Yes, I came to Mast Island to paint. I have an art show scheduled at Dove Creek Gallery in Philadelphia next month." She changed the subject.

"Were you able to see Noah this afternoon? How is he?"

"We only got a brief glimpse of him." Dave said. "They've been removing splinters and changing dressings. He's sedated. The nurses said it would be better to let him rest. We're staying in case … well, in case we're needed."

"And we don't want to miss any doctor's report," Jane added.

"Have you eaten?" Dave asked Abby. He sounded concerned about her.

"Yes, I ate a sandwich before coming here."

"I should have arranged for you to have dinner with us. Jane and I didn't think about eating until after you left. There's a diner around the corner. Maybe you can have lunch with us tomorrow."

"Thank you. I'd like that." As soon as she said the words, Abby realized meeting with Noah's parents might mean uncomfortable disclosures. She had not told Noah her father was alive, or that her uncle, Jean-Jacques, had taken a bullet meant for her.

Dave Hazzard stood when Abby arrived the next morning. "Noah seems better. The doctors are optimistic. It's still early days, but his numbers have improved, and he asked when he could eat real food, which is encouraging."

"Unfortunately," his mother added, "solid food won't be in his future for a while. I promised him his favorite meal when he heals enough to eat it."

"Will I be able to see him again today? I have to return home tomorrow." She reminded them about her show opening in December, and they understood.

While they were talking, the eye surgeon, Dr. Freeman, came to give the Hazzards an update. "The CT scan on Noah's eye shows orbital blowout fractures." He explained the orbital bone is strong and protects the eyeball. A hard blow can break small bones, and the result can break the orbital floor which is thin and not as strong." Dr. Freeman used his hands to show the damaged area while talking. "The break in the lower orbital floor caused blood and fluid to seep into the maxillary sinus cavity causing swelling in the tissue."

"Will Noah be able to see out of the damaged eye?" his father asked.

"He will need surgery. Ice packs are placed over the area to bring down the swelling. He will be advised not to blow his nose for several weeks after surgery, and he will need to see an ophthalmologist or optometrist later to see if he has any other damage to his eye. They can better determine his scope of sight."

Noah's mother squeezed Dave's hand and asked the doctor, "When will you do the surgery?"

"We'll know by tomorrow if the surgery can be scheduled. The burn treatments are a priority because of infection, so we need to have the antibiotics working in his system before we begin treatment."

Abby offered to pray with the Hazzards after the doctor left, and they stood, holding one another while Abby prayed for every person who had contact with Noah. She prayed for the surgeons, Noah's healing, and the intervention and mercy of the Divine Physician. She ended with a prayer of reassurance for Noah's family and for peace that all would go well.

His parents hugged her and thanked her for the prayers.

Abby was amazed the prayer she offered covered more territory than her normal, short prayers. Somehow, she felt calm and hopeful. "I'm sure God will hear us and intercede on Noah's behalf." *I have to believe that.*

CHAPTER TWENTY-FIVE

Abby walked up the stairs to see Jean-Jacques while Noah's parents took turns visiting their son. She would see Noah after them.

Agent Mackey was sitting on a chair in the hallway outside of Jean-Jacques's room. She stood as soon as she saw Abby enter the hall.

Abby approached Jenna Mackey, her hands fisted at her sides. Anger flared, flushing her face. "How could you do that to me. Tell me Noah was dead!" she shouted, getting the attention of people at the nurse's station.

The sound of her loud voice attracted the attention of an orderly, who approached them.

Agent Mackey held up her hand as if to fend off a physical attack. "Hold on," she said, her voice calm. "I never said Noah was dead. I said, 'I'm sorry,' and you made the assumption. We didn't correct you because Noah didn't want you to know how badly he was injured. He believed he was dying and wanted to spare you."

Abby wasn't ready to concede. "You both let me believe he was dead." Her body shook with the betrayal.

"Yes. We couldn't lie to you about his condition. It was easier to let you assume the worst." She appealed to Abby's logic. "We thought Noah might be safer 'dead' because we didn't know what had happened, and who was responsible for the explosion."

Abby recognized the truth of the last statement, and she relaxed her stance. She remembered Doc Ellis walking to the office and phoning someone after the agents arrived at the dock.

"Why are you here?" Abby asked Agent Mackey.

The hovering orderly turned back when Agent Mackey told him everything was okay.

"We have an ongoing investigation, and we don't want a suspect, man of interest, or witness to disappear. We also don't know his connection or involvement in alleged crimes."

"Jean-Jacques saved my life. Would he have done that if he were involved?" Abby didn't want her uncle to be charged for Vanna's sake, and her own if she were honest.

"Time will tell. Until we have indictments …," Agent Mackey hesitated and said emphatically, "You should not speak with anyone about this. If allegations lead to a court trial, we will be sure our man doesn't leave the country. Witnesses have been separated and are being questioned. Most of those retained have lawyered up, including your uncle, Jean-Jacques."

Abby hadn't thought about a trial or being asked to stay as a witness. "Will I be able to go home? I have a lot of work ahead of me."

"Yes, I'm sure you can leave, but you'll have to return when you're subpoenaed. This may be weeks or months from now."

"May I see Jean-Jacques?"

"Only if you refrain from discussing the case."

Abby nodded, and Agent Mackey opened the door and allowed her entrance.

The room, filled with bouquets of flowers, smelled like a funeral home. The back of Jean-Jacques's bed was elevated, so he could partially sit up. Collette sat on a chair with a newspaper in her hands. She looked up and smiled as if all were forgiven. Abby couldn't fathom the woman's strange behavior or change of mind.

Jean-Jacques held out his hand. "So, *ma fille*, have you seen Noah?"

Abby took his cold hand into her warm one. "I saw him a short time yesterday, and I'll see him later today." She noted his improved color, the pink in his cheeks.

"How is he?" His hand continued to hold hers as if he needed the connection.

"Critical but holding his own. The next forty-eight hours are crucial."

"I will pray for his recovery." He dropped her hand. "Tell me about his injuries."

Abby told him what she knew and winced at the telling.

He nodded and grimaced at some of her descriptions. "Have they found out what happened? What caused the explosion?"

Collette spoke in a tight voice, "My husband had nothing to do with the explosion." Her eyes teared. "Nothing. That blood-sucking vampire is responsible for everything that has happened. My husband is only guilty of allowing her to live with us."

Jean-Jacques sighed as if weary of the subject. "I had no choice, Collette. You know her position precluded her dismissal."

Blood-sucking vampire. Leave it to Collette to come up with a colorful description of the comtesse. Abby squelched a smile at the apt designation.

"Guilt will be determined by a jury if a trial is scheduled," Abby said. "I've been told not to comment on any part of the case, and I think that's a good idea."

"Do not worry, little one. A trial will exonerate me," Jean-Jacques told his wife.

Turning his attention to Abby, he said, "We heard the altercation in the hall a few minutes ago. I have been told I am a suspect, and someone will be outside my room until I leave the hospital."

"Yes. You must be truthful, and tell authorities everything you know," Abby said.

"Do you question my integrity?" Jean-Jacques said, his arrogant demeanor returning, his jade eyes probing her own.

"No, just stating a fact. The FBI has spent years compiling background files and notes on the DuMond family." She thought about her talk with the agents in the marina office. "Hiding information will make you appear guilty. That's all I'm saying on the subject."

Jean-Jacques nodded, looking somewhat appeased, and Collette kept mercifully silent as she kept her eyes on her husband.

"I'll fly home tomorrow, but I'll be back before Christmas to see my father."

"You will stay with us ... I hope," Jean-Jacques added. This time, his invitation was hesitant, not a demand. "I, too, would like to know more about your life, Abby. We are related by a history we cannot escape. Beyond blood, Vanna likes you. She has always wanted a sister."

Abby smiled but did not commit. "I've grown fond of Vanna." Her feelings about the rest of the family and their relationship with those living and working on the island needed thought.

Collette looked at Abby. "The *comtesse* said you came to Mast Island to ruin the family. Was that your plan?"

"No," Abby said. "When my gran died, I found out she was not a relation. My life was a lie fabricated by two women who wanted to save me from whoever killed my mother, father, and twin brother. You can't begin to imagine my feelings."

Abby paced the room as she spoke. Her anger resurfaced as the indelible memory of that day played in her mind. "I received in the mail a box of mementos belonging to my mother, with an article about her murder and the obituary notice. They spurred me to investigate." I met the woman, who mailed the box. Mina was my gran's friend and mentor, and she filled in some of my early history." Her body began to tremble.

After stopping a minute to gain control, Abby continued. "I found the church where my parents were wed and the man who married them. Someone, who looked like me, removed the evidence from the index and register.

"My attorney has a notarized affidavit, signed by the pastor, who married them, proving the marriage took place."

Abby looked at Jean-Jacques. "I came to Mast Island to find out about my father's side of the family, *not* to become part of the family," she stressed and faltered. "I didn't like what I found."

Jean-Jacques looked stunned, and Abby waved off the comment he started to make. "The hidden poverty, the reality of listening devices, paranoia, and fear among those living on Mast Island were not what I expected. And I certainly never seriously contemplated an attempt would be made on my life."

She interrupted Jean-Jacques's effort to speak. "Noah is in critical condition because of my family, because of me. How do you think I feel about the DuMonds? I found my father alive. I'm grateful you cared for him. His life is what is important to me."

She walked to the door and opened it.

Jean-Jacques spoke to her departing back. "You are a DuMond. Family," he emphasized. You can be part of the change on Mast Island."

Abby turned to look at him. "What do you mean by change?"

"The reign of *Maman* is over."

"Vampire," Collette said under her breath.

Jean-Jacques shook his head at her and continued. "Rafe will have his way. Changes will come to Mast Island, and we will all be part of its future. Hopefully, you will see family in a different light."

"Maybe." *Don't hold your breath.* "We'll see how everything works out."

Agent Mackey stood as Abby closed the door. "Family bonding?"

"Whatever will be, won't happen overnight."

"You'll be wise not to get involved, until we understand what has happened," Jenna said.

"Do you know what caused the explosion on Noah's boat?"

"Divers are collecting the pieces. We'll know the findings when they become available."

Abby entered Noah's room and found him awake but surly.

"You. Again? Why don't you go home and get your life in order." The words were less slurred, and the bruising had taken on a yellow tinge. She noted the morphine drip he regulated in his hand.

"Funny you should mention that. I'm leaving for home tomorrow." Abby tried to keep the words upbeat. She felt guilty for going so soon. She felt worse when Noah's countenance fell. *He really doesn't want me to leave.*

Noah's eye focused and bore down on her as he studied her face. "You don't have any reason to feel guilty. I'll get through this. Don't worry."

"I know you will. You're a strong man, Noah Hazzard, with a warrior's heart, don't forget."

He harrumphed. "You live in a fantasy world." He was quiet a moment. "So, do you have a new title?" His tone held a modicum of sarcasm, and it took her a space to figure out what he was asking. Family, of course. *Someone must have told him my father is alive.*

Without thinking, she blurted, "The title is still Miss, but I'll be on the lookout for a Mrs. in the future."

Noah closed his eye and sighed. *Don't look at me. I won't be the same man you knew.* "Well, sweet cakes, I'm sure there is some lucky man out there searching for you." He turned his head away.

"That's a mealy-mouthed thing to say. And here I was thinking how much I'd miss seeing you and learning more about the estuary and wildlife on Mast Island in the future."

"The future?" He turned back, his blue-green eye searching her face. "You're going back to Mast Island?"

"Yes. I'm spending Christmas with my father.

---✳---

Abby thought about her visit with Noah while she walked to join the Hazzards for lunch. Noah's color was better, the swelling down in his face. His attitude needed an adjustment. One minute he wanted her to leave, and the next, she was sure he wanted her to stay. He oozed unspoken bitterness, and she remembered him calling her "sweet cakes" and telling her to hold on to her kind thoughts of him during times he wasn't so "nice and cuddly." *Like now.*

That's guilt you're feeling. Abby knew Noah had a long, painful road to recovery ahead. Scheduled surgeries would take their toll. *Please, Lord, keep Noah infection and complication free. Increase his faith and give him reasons to be optimistic.*

Her thoughts turned to the visit. *Noah knows my father is alive. Does he know everything that happened?*

The knowledge Noah wouldn't be able to come to the gallery opening next month saddened her. She would put a SOLD sticker on the painting he wanted and buy it back if he changed his mind. Abby sighed. She wanted to see him again. *What if he doesn't want to see me?* The coils of insecurity she felt as a teenager tightened.

Noah's question about her title threw her at first. He referred to her family title, which added a touch of acid to the conversation.

I'm an idiot. What I said sounded like I was fishing to become a wife. She closed her eyes and leaned into the cold, sterile hospital wall. *Sweet cakes? An endearment? Yeah, Noah, I'm sure men will be falling all over themselves wanting to marry me.* "Ha!" she said aloud and straightened. She made a decision to stay in touch with him by phone or through the mail if he wouldn't speak with her. She refused to let him dismiss her from his life, especially after the mind-blowing kiss.

The Hazzards stood when she arrived in the waiting room. Jane was what Abby considered a handsome woman. Her toned physique matched that of her husband in height. Noah inherited her features and coloring. This morning her blue-green eyes were red-rimmed and bruised circles lay beneath as if she didn't get enough sleep.

Also tall, Dave looked solid and fit, his brown and gray sprinkled buzz cut and military bearing were stamped on his stance and features.

"How did you find Noah?" Dave asked.

"He looked a little better, but I can't say his attitude has improved."

Jane smiled and said, "We took your advice and challenged him. Dave and I won't allow him to feel sorry for himself. After his initial surgeries are complete, we're moving Noah home to Alabama for rehab."

"Let's get lunch. I could eat a bear," Noah's dad said, gesturing toward the door.

After the waitress took their lunch orders, Jane said, "We've learned some things about your visit to Mast Island and Noah's involvement."

Abby looked down at the colorful placemat stamped with a map of Savannah and its landmarks. *How much do they know?*

Dave leaned forward. "I can understand why you don't want to speak with us about your family. Jenna Mackey told us what happened."

Abby's eyes welled as she looked at Noah's parents. "I'm sorry Noah got involved."

"Surely, you don't think any of this is your fault," Jane said, patting the hand Abby had used to crumple the corner of the placemat. Her eyes, Noah's eyes, were disconcerting. "Noah's job and legitimate research took him to Mast Island to find out what happened to my brother. When he saw your resemblance to the DuMonds, he worried your presence on the island might be dangerous for you, and he was right."

"Then you know it was because of me, the explosion happened." Abby's voice faltered, and she picked up the napkin and blew her nose.

Dave's brow furrowed. "No. We don't know that. Noah took his work with the FBI and the company where he was employed seriously. He would continue to investigate Max's disappearance even if you weren't there. We don't blame you for what happened.

"Noah's concern was well-founded, but he doesn't blame you. I think he's most disturbed by your position as a DuMond. He told me your father was alive, and your nobility, a barrier …"

"I think that's why Noah's hurting," Jane said, cutting in. "He likes you, and for the first time …," She left the words dangling. "Well, he'll have to take whatever he feels for you from here.

"Agent Mackey, Jenna, told us their search of the château uncovered Max's grave. He was buried in a family sarcophagus with two other people, one recent, the other ancient. The investigation, forensics will take time. We presumed Max was dead, so this discovery, though it saddened us, did not come as a shock."

Abby nodded. She told Jane about the revelation by the *comtesse* in the sawmill. "She said Max's death was an accident, but I don't know what to believe. My family appears to have a dark side."

The waitress arrived with their drinks, and Abby sank back in the booth, her thoughts in turmoil. *Jenna must have told Noah what happened at the sawmill and about my father, Rafe, being alive.*

Abby shivered at the thought of Max being found in a sarcophagus on the château grounds. *If Noah hadn't sent his friends to watch over me, I might also have been interred there. Life is tenuous, a thread that can be broken at any moment.* She thought about Noah on the dock and how they looked at the life lines on their hands. Both were supposed to be long-lived.

Jane's words invaded her thoughts. "Noah grew up in military housing. A lot of children lived around us, and Noah enjoyed the outdoors. He chose to climb trees to read books and to build a lab in our garage instead of playing football or building forts with neighborhood kids."

Abby thought about reading books in trees and smiled. She thought about trees in the park back home, and the days she spent reading in their leafy bowers.

"In high school he chose academia instead of athletics, much to the chagrin of coaches and classmates. His size alone was their incentive to recruit him. So, he wasn't part of a popular clique, which didn't seem to bother him. He had a few friends, who shared his vision of making the world a better place but no girlfriends."

Dave spoke. "I'm sorry to say, I was one of the ones who pushed him to get on a team in school. He worked out at the gym, watched what he ate, and kept in good physical shape. I knew he would be good at anything he set his mind to ... and I thought he might even get an athletic scholarship. Instead, he received scholarships because of his GPA and high test scores. He made us proud." Dave sighed.

Jane watched her husband as he put his thoughts about Noah into words.

"I think Noah enlisted after college and chose the Army Rangers to prove his manhood to me and maybe to himself," he said. "The training was rigorous, and he survived both the training and the war. He was wounded and received a Purple Heart. Noah was honorably discharged before his second tour ended."

Abby nodded. Noah had mentioned his service when she asked about his scarred legs.

"Noah used the G.I. Bill to return to the university and get his Ph.D.," Dave continued. "Since he took a position with BNRS, a biologic resource firm, he's received several grants, and up to now, I thought *The Lady* and work were his life.

"We called Noah's colleagues at the lab to let them know the circumstance of his absence. Noah said they have enough work to keep them busy until he gets back on his feet. They can use his research findings to write papers."

"We had no idea he was a support professional with the FBI until we met his friends, the agents, Jenna Mackey and Kent Helms," Jane said. "I gather he met Kent at university and his partner, Jenna, later. They are both so nice and concerned about Noah."

Abby squelched her ire over the agents allowing her to believe Noah had died. "I understand Noah called them in to help. He told me he couldn't watch over me every minute, and that made me mad. I mean, I didn't expect Noah to be my protector," Abby said. "But I'm so glad his friends were there, or my plight might have had a different outcome."

The waitress arrived with their meal, and revelations ceased.

CHAPTER TWENTY-SIX

Abby climbed the steps of the brownstone in Philadelphia. The events over of the last several weeks drained her energy, and for the first time, she felt disconnected from her loft. The ocean's song and its salty tang scenting the air tugged at her inner being. They seemed as far away as the panoply of stars she had enjoyed viewing away from the city lights.

She cocooned herself in what she called a "blue funk," or pity party mode.

The front door creaked. As she mentally added to her "I miss" list of her time on the island, Mrs. Anthony's door opened.

"Oh, my dear, you're back. I'm so glad you're here." The little woman fussed over Abby, her riot of blued curls tamed by a red and black paisley scarf. "I've been so worried." She leaned in and whispered. "A man has been here." Her eyes moved about as if he were nearby, "Looking for you," she said, her head down but looking up at her from under raised brows and biting her lower lip.

Abby straightened. "What man?" A chill worked its way up her back to her nape, raising her hair. Paranoia returned with a bang.

"I don't know." She whispered. "He didn't give a name. He put his finger to his lips and said, 'Shhh. This is a surprise.' His face gave me goosebumps. She placed her fingers while she spoke over Abby's lips. "Then he put his fingers on my lips like this and said, 'You won't tell her, now will you?' I took his tone as a warning. I've been so frightened for you."

Alarm bells rang in Abby's mind. "What did he look like? Have you seen him before?"

"No. The strange thing about him is he kind of looks like you. But I know you don't have any family. I've kept an eye out, and he stood across the street a couple of times, looking up." She shook her head. "I haven't gotten much sleep, I can tell you."

Abby patted Mrs. Anthony's shoulder, trying to think of something to allay her fears. "I found some of my family near Savannah, the reason I left. Maybe, he's a distant cousin, who heard of my existence and wanted to surprise me. I'm sure it's nothing to worry about. I'll see him if he comes by again."

Mrs. Anthony released a deep breath and with her hand over her chest said, "You won't tell him I told you. Please. It's supposed to be a surprise, and I don't want him upset with me. You won't tell," she repeated, her words laced with uncertainty.

"No, Mrs. Anthony, I won't tell."

Abby's heart pounded as she carried her load up the steps to her loft. *Who looks like me? Minneau?* Jean-Jacques was still in the hospital. Roux's skin color would have been mentioned. Who else looked like her? Why did Mrs. Anthony feel threatened? *Why do I?*

Abby opened the door of her apartment and looked around to see if anything had been disturbed. The room looked like she had left it. She dropped her load and went to the window to check the street. Only a woman pulling a shopping cart was visible.

She began to pace as she tried to make sense of what was happening. The mystery man had to be Minneau. How did he get here? What did he want?

Should I call Jenna Mackey? Did she know Minneau had left the island? Abby found her card in the fanny pack along with Eddie's. She set them by the phone. *Should I call Eddie to check on him?"*

Abby phoned her father, and Tasse answered.

"This is Abby. How is my father doing today?"

A pause. "Henri is … Rafe is most active. He is ordering new paints and canvasses, changing the menu, and adding gardeners. He is walking short distances with a cane. I have never seen him this happy. He speaks of you no end."

Abby smiled at Tasse's exuberance and wording. "May I talk with him?"

"*Oui, mademoiselle.* Yes, I will put him on."

Abby heard voices and a door closing.

"Abby? Is this you?" Her father's voice sounded strong.

"Papa. I called to let you know I'm home and to see if everything is all right. Jean-Jacques said you would make changes."

"Yes, I have. I am. You have seen Jean-Jacques?" His voice held excitement. "I will go tomorrow to see my brother. You are all right?"

"Yes, Papa." *Should I mention Noah? Does he know about him?* "Papa, will you check on Noah for me?" She bit her bottom lip, waiting for his response.

Several seconds passed. "Noah? Who is this I should check on? A man?"

"Yes, Noah Hazzard. He's in the hospital, too. Vanna or Jean-Jacques will tell you. He is a special person to me." Her words were followed by silence.

"Special? How may I ask?" His words had an edge.

Maybe I shouldn't have mentioned Noah. "Um, he's a biologist I met on Mast Island." She straightened as if the move gave her backbone. "He helped me stay alive. I'm in debt to him."

A long silence followed.

"Papa, are you there?"

"Yes. I am thinking." A pause. "I must check on this person who is special to you."

"Thank you, Papa. You'll like him. His parents, Dave and Jane Hazzard, are at the hospital with him. He survived an explosion. His condition was stable but not good when I left."

"I will see him," her father said, his words decisive.

Abby changed the subject. "What will happen to Minneau and Roux now *Grand-Maman* is dead?"

"We will speak of this later. I have not decided …" He stopped abruptly. "Cece wants them to live with her."

"Are they still at the château?"

"Yes. Why do you ask?" A pause. "No. Minneau travelled to see his mother."

"Oh. Where does she live?" Abby held her breath.

"Why do you ask, daughter? What is this matter to you?" His tone had an imperious ring which grated Abby's nerves.

"No reason. I saw them and knew they were family. I'm curious."

"They are not your concern."

"I understand. Well, I must get my paintings ready for the show. I'll see you for Christmas."

They said their farewells, and Abby's heart ached. Her father sounded almost a stranger. She had enjoyed getting to know him, but he sounded like the lord of the manor, imperious, not the man she had met, not her father.

Abby's phone rang. She did not have Caller ID.

"Abby?" Mrs. Anthony's voice.

"Yes, Mrs. Anthony. "It's me."

"I just wanted to check to make sure everything is kosher."

"Everything is fine. Please don't worry. I think the man was my cousin, Minneau."

"Oh, good. I'm glad you have an inkling. Sorry I disturbed you."

"No problem, Mrs. Anthony. You're a good woman. I appreciate your concern."

"Well, dearie, you know how it is in the city. We've got to watch each other's backs."

"So right," Abby murmured. "Thank you."

Abby sorted through her paintings. She took out her latest Mast Island works and a few she hoarded in her private collection. Her eyes went to the painting of Noah sprawled beneath the oak. His eyes seemed to contemplate the future. She wanted to believe he included her in his vision. *Don't be silly. Only you would hope that.* She touched his face, the face that would need plastic surgery. She prayed for a good outcome.

She walked to the window for the umpteenth time and saw Minneau looking up at her. Abby jerked back but then leaned forward to peer down. She knew he had seen her.

Minneau raised his hands, palm outward, and turned in a slow circle. He appeared to want her to believe he was harmless.

Hand to her chest, Abby swallowed and tried to make sense of his presence. His facial features and eyes pleaded what? *Sorrow?*

Abby jumped when the buzzer rang. She made the decision to see Minneau, but she didn't buzz him through. *I can handle him. I can,* she told herself. *What could he want?*

Curiosity won.

Reaching the ground floor, she knocked on Mrs. Anthony's door before proceeding to the front door. Behind her, she heard her landlord's door open. "I want you to meet my cousin," she said loudly over her shoulder.

Minneau stepped through the portal after she hit the enter button.

They looked at one another, Minneau speaking first. "I wanted to surprise you, *cousin.*" He emphasized the word after hearing her voice earlier. His eyes went to Mrs. Anthony's partially ajar door, and Abby turned to see her landlord's wide eyes watching through the crack.

"Mrs. Anthony, this is Minneau … DuMond, a cousin from Mast Island. You remember me telling you about finding family?'

The older woman looked at Minneau and nodded. "I hope you enjoy your visit," she said and closed the door, the sound of the lock, a loud click.

"Well, Minneau, this is a surprise. Totally unexpected." Abby turned and walked up the steps. "You may as well come up, now you're here."

He followed her up the stairs, and as soon as her door closed, she confronted him.

"Why did you threaten Mrs. Anthony? You nearly scared the life out of her."

Minneau smiled. "I am sorry, but I was afraid you would be frightened and run if you knew I had come or call the police. So, the woman told you. She is strong like you."

"Why are you here and not at your mother's?"

Alarm masked his face. "Who knows I'm here?" His voice was hushed, anxious.

"Everyone knows," she said and smiled at his obvious fear. "You deserve to sweat after scaring us half to death. Only two of us know, for now," she added.

"I am sorry." Minneau's face fell, his eyes downcast, subservient.

"Sit down, Minneau." Abby gestured to a chair at the table. "I'll fix us some tea, and you'll explain." She filled the teakettle with water and turned on the burner. The cups and saucers rattled her nervousness as she took the china from the cabinet. "How did you get here?"

"By bus," Minneau answered. He sat at the table, his size making everything seem miniature. He looked about at the array of paintings and her studio set-up. "I know that tree," he said, looking at the twisted tree on the south end of the island, the one she had named *Perseverance*.

"So do I. Now tell me why you're here," Abby said her voice impatient.

"I am the son of Jules DuMond and Marie Dessler, who was once a servant of *Grand-Maman*. My name is Minneau Dessler, not DuMond."

Abby nodded. "I'm sorry if I embarrassed you."

"*Non*, Miss Abby, you are nice, accepting, not like others.

"Roux's mother was Jamaican, a woman my father met on his journeys. He was brought to Mast Island as a child. We received the same education as Vanna in school. But we did not go to college. This was our choice. Our home is at the château. We have separate quarters from the family. We are happy there, and our station in life is accepted by most."

"Does Tante Cece want the same for you?"

Minneau vigorously shook his head. "*Non*, Miss Abby. She is not nice. She is a bad woman, very bad." The kettle whistled and startled Abby. She rose to fix the tea, her mind in turmoil at Minneau's words.

"She did not have children and has much bitterness. She will get us in trouble or killed," Minneau continued. "She will make us do bad things."

"What do you mean?" Abby didn't understand.

"Guns," Minneau said, getting Abby's attention. "My father ran guns, and that woman helped him. She will want us to help her, to stay alive or to die. Our lives are nothing to her. We do not want to help her.

"Jean-Jacques took care of us. Please Miss Abby, you must speak to your father. We must stay at the château. He can protect us."

Abby returned to the table, the tea forgotten. "Cece, a gun-runner?" She had a hard time wrapping her mind around this revelation. "Is everyone in the family involved?"

"Non. The *comte*, Jean-Jacques, he learned of this and stopped it years ago. The *comte* is a good man. When I was eighteen, he found guns stored in a tomb and broke them to pieces. We took them out and dumped them in the ocean. He said, 'This madness is finished. We will not speak of it again.' They fought. My father, Jules, and the *comte*. Jean-Jacques told him to leave the island and not come back.

Grand-Maman denied my father's guilt or any crime happened. Jules did not deliver the guns, and he was killed. *Grand-Maman* and Cece were filled with hatred for each other and Jean-Jacques."

"But Cece is accepted at the château," Abby said.

"She cowered, cried, pled for her life, her home. Said she did not know, and she hated Jules for doing this thing to her, to the family. Jean-Jacques believed her, but *Grand-Maman* did not. *Grand-Maman* and Cece were at the *comte's* mercy. He could turn them out."

Abby covered her face with her hands to hide her dismay. She thought about the conversation with her father. How could she intervene? How could she not? "Does my father know any of this?"

"I can say he heard the arguments, saw the fight, and said nothing, did nothing. He has lived in another world so long; it is hard to know his awareness. I would say he knew and did not want being involved. He became like a turtle, his head tucked inside. Only Tasse, Pepe, the gardener, Vanna, Rouland, and Jean-Jacques spoke with him for any time."

"Do you know who put listening devices in my hotel room?"

"Agents looked but did not find equipment at the château" Minneau answered. "They were thorough."

"You suspect Cece was involved?"

"Yes. I do not know if her house was checked. Information to the agents was little."

"Why don't you leave the château? You aren't a slave. My father can't make you do something you don't want to do."

Minneau shrugged his shoulders and lifted his hands in supplication. "Where would we go? What would we do? We work but have little pay, nothing except the good life given to us. I worry about Roux. He can have a hot head. He will leave and get in trouble."

Abby told him about calling her father and feeling her father had changed.

"This is true. When you left, he ordered everyone to the salon. 'I am *Comte* Raphael Henri DuMond. My place is head of the family. You will bring concerns to me'.

"Everyone was surprised. We believed he was Henri, and Raphael was dead. Only Jean-Jacques, Cece, and *Grand-Maman* knew the truth. This is now the talk of the household. What changes are coming?" He hesitated before saying, "I think Tasse knew. I do not trust him."

Abby was shocked. Minneau didn't trust the man who took care of her father? She wanted to stop him but decided to let him continue.

"The *comte* is angry with the agents, who came to the château with warrants. They turned everything inside-out and they have found bodies that should not be there. Everyone was questioned."

"Have they arrested anyone?" Abby's heart raced at Minneau's words.

"*Grand-Maman*, their main suspect, is dead. I have heard Marcel, Mark, and Paul are in custody of officials.

"Eddie is free. He told all he knows, and authorities had notes.

"Cece hopes Jean-Jacques will be arrested. She thinks she can handle Raphael, but she does not know the different man."

"How do you know this, Minneau? Why do you distrust Tasse?"

"Gina, Cece's *femme de chambre*, lady's maid," he translated when Abby raised her eyebrows, questioning. "She is my special friend." He put his head down and appeared embarrassed.

"Your girlfriend?"

Minneau looked at her, his jade eyes, DuMond eyes, narrowed. "No one must know she tells me things."

"Does she tell you Cece is going back into the gun-running business?"

"Gina says men come to the house in the night from the dock. They are not good men, and she is afraid. They have guns, but she does not know about business.

"She tells me Cece has much hatred for you. This is why I am here. Gina says you are in danger. She wants you warned. Gina has a good soul. She hurts to hear bad talk. You will be careful."

"And Tasse?"

"Gina says Tasse meets with Cece and is too familiar. They are close. Not lovers. With Gina, I do not like this." Minneau sat back in the chair with a labored sigh. "Now you know," he said. "You will be careful?"

CHAPTER TWENTY-SEVEN

Abby sat at the window looking out at the gray tableau. The weatherman predicted a light snowfall that would not stick. After turning her life upside-down by warning her of danger, Minneau had left.

She had advised Minneau to meet with her father and tell him his concerns about leaving and about Cece's dislike of Roux and of him. She thought Minneau needed to warn her father of danger from Cece and her quest for power and money illegally. In the event they were turned out by her father, he and Roux should come to Philadelphia, where she would help them find employment. Gran's apartment was empty. Abby planned to rent it after December, but she didn't tell Minneau about the possibility.

Oh Gran, I wish things were different. I shouldn't have tried to find my family. I should have listened to Mina. Abby agonized over the imminent ruin she might cause, and her heart ached for Noah and his family. *No, everything is worth finding my father alive and meeting Noah. Will I ever rid myself of the guilt? What will happen to my father? What if I don't pursue a relationship with him? I don't really know him.*

Her cell phone rang. Mobile, Alabama. Abby accepted the call from Noah's parents.

"Hello Abby," Jane said. "Dave and I just wanted to check to see if you returned home okay. We enjoyed getting to know you."

"Likewise. How is Noah?" Abby asked.

"He's improving. Noah's not the best patient because he wants to get out soon. They say that's a good sign. The plastic surgeon repaired his face. The doctor said the scars will almost be invisible except for the zee the surgeon had to make to close one of the cuts on Noah's cheek.

"Dr. Freeman operated on his eye this morning. He believes with care, the orbital fractures will heal, maybe stronger than before. He didn't see any fragments in the eye which gives us hope he will be able to see."

"That is good news. What else is happening?"

"The two baths a day, sloughing off old skin and changing the burn dressings are difficult for Noah. They had to debride a couple of areas and used skin grafts from the back of his good leg.

"Now tell me how you're doing. Have you begun planning for your show? I'm sorry Dave and I will be unable to come. We hope Noah will be home by then."

Abby thought about how little she had accomplished since being home. She didn't want to worry Noah's parents about recent activities. "I'm really just getting started. I've decided to write Noah, whether he wants to hear from me or not. Please keep in touch."

"Thank you, Abby. We appreciate your help. Dave is talking to Noah about helping him design a new boat, and he's seen a spark of interest. Dave told him to think about the floor plan and how *The Lady* might be improved upon."

Abby thought about the idea and decided being involved with designing a new boat would be a positive start. "I'm glad Noah is showing some interest in living."

"Noah's brother, Owen, is flying here soon. He'll be here a week while Dave and I check on things at home and look at rehab facilities in our area."

"I'm glad to hear Noah's improving. Thank you for the update."

"You have our address and phone number in Mobile. Don't hesitate to use them."

Abby sorted through her paintings, but her mind kept wandering to Minneau's new disclosures. He didn't trust Tasse. She walked to the phone and picked up Jenna Mackey's number. Turning the card over and over in her fingers, she contemplated the advisability of calling the agent. The information Minneau shared was mostly hearsay. Would the new information count or just open up another can of worms? The angst rippling through her body didn't feel like hearsay. She returned the card to the table and grabbed her purse and keys.

She drove to a card and gift shop where she spent half an hour choosing a dozen Get Well cards, a mixture of meaningful and funny. She also purchased a writing tablet with an outdoorsy, masculine motif and envelopes. Her writing campaign moved into high gear.

Not wanting to return to her studio apartment, Abby drove to Dove Creek Gallery on Broad Street, also known as the "Avenue of The Arts." The gallery, situated in an area which promoted the performing and cultural arts, catered to a high end clientele, seeking new and upcoming artists. The high foot traffic area was dotted with restaurants, shops, and hotels.

The gallery had black-tinted windows, a black and white striped awning, and gold metallic script letters proclaiming fine art could be found inside.

Claudia Chadwick, the gallery director, met Abby with a huge, relieved smile. The tall, angular woman with a finely sculptured face and intelligent, piercing eyes always looked chic. A royal blue sheath hugged her figure, and her black hair pulled back in a modest chignon gave her a sophisticated, cosmopolitan look.

"Mieka and I were just discussing you." A perfectly manicured hand fiddled with the rows of silver beads wreathing her long neck, the only indication she was unhappy. "That's a polite description of our conversation. I don't like waiting until the last minute." Her voice raised an octave to a more strident tone. "Really, *caro*, you might have kept us abreast of your plans. The brochures have gone to print without adding a single photo of any new works." Her black eyes raked Abby's casually clad figure. "The clientle list is waiting for approval and updates. The invitations must go out this week." We've been scratching the walls in frustration here, and Mr. Mobley is due tomorrow."

Mr. Thomas Q. Mobley, Esq. was the owner of Dove Creek Gallery and a newer gallery, The Persephone, located several blocks down the street, near the Kimmel Center. His new mini-museum promoted *avant garde* art.

Mieka, a slender, petite woman of Eurasian background, came out of the back room. "Abby!" she screamed with delight. Claudia's assistant and gallery designer wore leotard-fitting black pants and knee high boots. She wore a wool mini dress, the design an abstract work of art in bold colors. Her teal and magenta hair was bobbed in the latest, sleek style. "Have you brought your new work?" She clapped her hands. We can't wait to see."

"I have a confession. My grandmother's death and finding my family …" Her voice trailed. They had no idea the tsunami that had awaited her on Mast Island. This wasn't their fault.

Claudia and Mieka looked at her with raised eyebrows. "Could you elaborate," Claudia said, her voice taking on a caustic tone. "Are you trying to say we won't be ready for opening night?"

Abby thought fast. This was a huge break for her, and she didn't want to ruin her opportunity. She thought of her private collection and knew the paintings had to go. No one had seen the works she hoarded. "Oh, no, no, not that," Abby said, her hand at her throat, her stomach in a knot. "I won't have forty paintings, only thirty-five, but some of them are quite large. The problem is that I haven't had time to get some of them framed."

Claudia sighed her relief and Mieka said, "No problem. I'll give them to George, and he'll have them ready in a couple of weeks. How many are we talking about?"

Abby gave them her best guess. "Maybe twenty," she said and winced at the number.

"Twenty?" Mieka responded. "George is good, but we aren't his only customers."

Claudia appeared to be adding the time left on her fingers. "I'll contact Sergei. Maybe he can take ten of them," she said. "This is coming out of your pocket, young lady. Their work isn't cheap."

"Yes, I know." Abby tried to think of someone else who could frame her five Mast Island paintings in record time. She'd check with people she knew at several galleries.

"I'll send the truck tomorrow morning. Please have your paintings ready," Claudia said and stalked to the office.

"I'm sorry to cause you trouble," Abby said to Mieka.

"Don't worry. Everything will go well. It always does. Claudia's uptight because Mr. Mobley is expected tomorrow."

Abby nodded. "Thank you for your optimism. I need it today."

Abby called several galleries until she found the name of a man, who had time to frame her work within the time constraint. She took the Mast Island paintings to his shop on Market Street.

John Vincent, the owner, inspected her canvasses. "Nice," he commented. "Are all of these from the same area?"

"Yes. Mast Island, off the coast of Georgia."

"May I make a suggestion?" His kind blue eyes were the first thing she noted when she met him.

"Of course. You're the expert."

"These are acrylics, your strokes minimal, capturing untamed nature, and stirring the inner emotion." He brought closed hands to his chest as he said the words. "I think frames of weathered wood will enhance the settings of your work. I can make subtle changes, so the frames will not be all alike. For instance, the sawmill calls for color on the frame. I can pick up the rust and greens and add those colors. Let me show you what I mean."

He took her into a work room and sorted through framed paintings. He took out one of a covered bridge. The weathered frame had a few, dry brush strokes of color on the wood. The red, green and white marks were subtle, and they added interest.

Abby loved the idea. These paintings would have a different look from her oils. "Thank you for introducing me to your work. I like your frames and the concept." She visualized all of these paintings exhibited on one wall.

Abby spent more time deciding which frames to order. She knew Mieka would like the framing, but Claudia would balk. Would she allow these paintings to be hung?

After sending her paintings to the gallery and taking the last five to John to be framed, Abby fell into an exhausted sleep. She woke with the remnant of a dream about *The Lady* edging her consciousness.

Fully awake, she recalled her visit to the schooner and the look Noah gave her when he said, "I don't feel like your gran. Just thought you should know." His hair had glinted gold in the sunlight and those incredible eyes held hers spellbound. She knew he was the man for her when he quoted poetry. Yes, Noah was a complex enigma. *Lord, he has to be okay.*

Another card addressed to Noah in the hospital lay in front of the door, so she wouldn't forget to mail it later. Nine days had passed. Maybe the time had come to call him.

After breakfast, Abby found the hospital phone number online and had the call transferred to his room.

A man answered, but he didn't sound like Noah.

"Um, is Noah there?"

"I don't know. Depends on who's calling. Are you in Noah's little black book?"

The man's question startled her. "This is Abby," she blurted.

The man said, "Do you know an Abby?"

"Give me the phone, you troll, and see if you can find me a doughnut."

A man laughed in the background. "Sure bro. I'll give you some privacy, but donuts aren't on your menu yet."

She heard footsteps, and "He's all yours, Abby," before a door closed.

"Abby?" Noah's voice sounded stronger, more receptive.

"Yes. Just checking to see how you're doing?" She worried her bottom lip. "Am I in your little black book?" She chewed on her knuckle while she waited. *He has a little black book?*

"You're the only woman listed," Noah said and then added, "after I tore the other pages out."

Abby laughed. "Was that Owen?"

"Yep. I'll be glad when he goes home. He's worse than the nurses about getting me up to walk."

"You're walking? That's great."

"I'm using a walker and taking baby steps. Nothing to get excited about. Rehab stretching reduces scar tissue build up. It's a pain, literally."

"I'm sorry you have to go through this."

Noah was silent a moment. "I have it better than some of the kids in here. Breaks my heart to see little ones hurting so badly. Especially when a parent has hurt them. Some people don't deserve to live, and they shouldn't have children." He changed the subject.

"I've enjoyed your cards, especially the funny ones. I'm glad you're getting done what needs doing for the opening. Whoa, that sounds like a bad sentence. Must be the morphine.

"Do you have that SOLD sign for my painting?"

"You sure you still want it?" Abby asked.

"You'd better not sell that painting to anyone else."

"I wouldn't think of it. Claudia, the gallery director, will be over the moon."

"You'll never guess who visited me a couple of days ago."

"My father..."

"How did you know? Surprised the hell out of me."

So Rafe looked up Noah. "I hope he was nice." The silence that followed stretched Abby's nerves.

"He told me he had a long talk with his brother. Jean-Jacques filled him in on the explosion and the bullet he took for you. Your father asked me to tell him how I saved your life. I figured you put him up to the visit."

Now Abby was silent. Her father had been direct. "I may have said something to him."

"Hmmm," was his only response.

The door opened, and a female voice said, "Bath time, your favorite time of day."

Noah groaned. "They have a torture chamber here. Gotta go. It's good to hear your voice" then softer, "I've missed it."

"I've missed you, too," she said and hung up.

Abby marked off the days until the show on her calendar. Five days left. She had to find the right outfit. Shopping for clothes was on her list of least favorite pastimes.

MAST ISLAND

For two weeks following Minneau's visit, Abby had kept an eye on the sidewalk outside. She played the "lose someone game" she read about in thrillers, even though she didn't think she was being followed. Her cat and mouse ploys seemed silly now, and she stopped checking.

Did Minneau speak to my father? She and her father had not spoken since his visit to the hospital. They might as well be on different planets. These thoughts had her rethinking her Christmas trip.

As Abby suspected, Claudia did not like the frames on her Mast Island paintings, but five days before the show was too late to make changes. Her island paintings were relegated to an inconspicuous back wall away from her oils. Abby's *plein air* paintings were looser and had an untamed look, while the oils had layers of paint reminiscent of the great masters.

A price of five thousand dollars was put on the painting which included Noah. Claudia didn't price the acrylics as high as the oils. She grumbled about loss of revenue because the framing did not meet the standards of what she considered museum quality.

Claudia's attitude improved when Abby told her the painting had sold. These shows were not just to introduce new artists or to display a well-known painter's works but to make a profit. Any sale was a *coup* in Claudia's book.

Abby thanked her lucky stars her mentor, Master Tremayne, had business in Spain and would miss the show. She knew he would not approve of her Mast Island paintings and might even insist she remove them. He had sent her an encouraging note along with his regrets which said he knew her show would be a success.

Mieka thought the framing perfect for the Mast Island paintings, and she wanted John Vincent's contact information. She thought she knew all of the framers in and around Philadelphia. Mieka's reputation and clout in the art world assured John Vincent's business would flourish.

CHAPTER TWENTY-EIGHT

The night of A. S. Parsons's December Opening finally arrived. Abby was so nervous, she scarcely ate. She wore a dark green silk jumpsuit with a full-length, filmy jacquard patterned silk jacket in gold, green, garnet, and sienna. Her filigreed gold and garnet dangling earrings matched the choker necklace she wore, and the three-inch heels gave her enough height, she towered over most of the women and some of the men present.

Claudia complimented Abby on her outfit but said her hair, which she had pulled back with a bow and left loose around her shoulders, too casual. Nonetheless, she squired her around the room introducing her to clientele and extolling Abby's masterful use of shadow and light to prospective buyers.

Abby noticed a young man escorting an attractive woman as soon as they arrived. They were appropriately dressed for the black tie affair, but he looked familiar. They walked around the gallery and ended up at the Mast Island exhibit. She watched as the man caught Mieka's eye and pointed to the painting of the solitary tree, *Perseverance*.

Mieka beamed and placed a discreet red sticker in the corner of the painting to indicate a sale. Seven thousand dollars. Abby was thrilled and saddened at the same time. This painting was one of the cherished canvasses she wanted for her private collection.

Abby walked over, and Mieka proudly introduced the artist to the buyers.

"Owen and Rachel Hazzard," the man said, holding out his hand. "We finally meet. Have you forgiven me for the 'little black book' remark?" he said, his voice teasing, his eyes friendly. "Noah hasn't."

Mieka looked at Abby in surprise, and Rachel's face held a quizzical expression.

Owen told his wife he'd fill her in later. He inherited his brown eyes, hair, and genes from his father, Dave, and stood almost as tall as Noah. His features were less rugged, less weathered.

Abby shook his proffered hand stunned. *Owen and his wife came to my opening.* "I can't believe you came from San Francisco for tonight's showing."

"Noah said he'd forgive me only if I bought this painting for him. Besides, Rachel and I want to soak up some of our country's history. We'll tour Independence Hall on Monday."

"Yes," Rachel said, "I'm less enthused about visiting the battlegrounds, but Owen insists we see everything while we're here."

"I'm going with you to the antique shops and museums," he reminded his wife.

Rachel was of medium height, with chestnut hair and hazel eyes. She wore a floor-length black sheath which hugged her figure, and she carried an original-looking ebony, appliqued stole in emerald and sapphire.

Abby found her voice. "Noah told me he wanted this one," she said pointing to the huge oak that included him.

"Yes, I know. He wants both. I have a blank, signed check for the two paintings," Owen told her.

Mieka, who had discreetly backed away, grinned as she moved forward and placed a red sticker on the second painting. "I love decisive men, don't you, *caro*?" Her smile had a wicked tilt as she left them.

"But they're too much," Abby said in a small voice. "He wanted to encourage me, but he didn't need to buy both."

"My little brother has a mind of his own. You can take it up with him." He took Rachel's arm. "We'll let you mingle with your adoring public for now and talk with you later."

As they walked away, Jean-Jacques, Vanna, her father, and Tasse arrived. Abby had sent them an invitation but didn't expect them.

Claudia greeted Abby's family at the door, and appeared overwhelmed when Jean-Jacques introduced the *Comte* Raphael DuMond.

Her father looked handsome as he left the wheelchair to take Claudia's hand. The ornate cane in his other hand gave him balance. "Are you responsible for this showing?"

Claudia started to answer when Vanna rushed by her to meet Abby. "This is exciting," she said. "We are so proud of you."

Abby arrived to greet the others, and her father said, "Well, daughter, show me what you have accomplished." His deep voice and its ring of authority were only tempered by the pride shining in his eyes.

Claudia's face registered astonishment. "This … is your father?" She looked at Abby as if she didn't know her.

Abby nodded and looked at Rafe. *I know why my mother fell in love with you.* His white mane, once auburn as her own, was brushed back, his wide forehead, jade eyes, and chiseled features, though marred by the scars, gave his face interest. A scarlet-lined, black cloak fixed at his neck by a magnificent, gold heraldry brooch set with a fleur-de-lis in magnificent rubies, drew attention. His height and swashbuckling appearance would make any feminine heart beat faster. Abby noticed he captured the eyes of nearby ladies and the interest of the men.

Even Abby stared up at him in awe. *My father. A lion among men.* She blushed at the euphemistic comparison and swallowed, her heart full. He was not the man she remembered in the salon, the garden, or the man who showed her his paintings. This man exuded power, and Abby wasn't sure she could handle his elevated position or find a place in his life. She had a brief thought of Minneau and Roux, wondering how they fared.

"Come," he said, taking Abby's arm. "I want to see your work."

Jean-Jacques took Vanna's arm and smiled widely at Abby. He appeared to be enjoying himself.

Abby slowly walked her father by her oil paintings, and Tasse kept the chair away from the crowd, discreetly following.

Her father stopped to make comments about her use of colors, perspective, and her motivation to paint the subjects. He asked the location of each painting, and he particularly liked the ones she pulled from her private collection. He understood, without being told, which paintings spoke to her heart.

They came to the Mast Island paintings. Her father said, "You have sold two, or did you keep these for yourself?" Raphael searched her face as he awaited the answer. He must have guessed she had a private collection.

"These have been sold." Abby noticed Owen and Rachel in the vicinity, listening. When she looked at Noah's brother, he winked and took out his phone. Holding the device up, he shot a surreptitious photo of the group.

"Who bought these?" her father inquired.

"Um, Noah Hazzard," she said, looking in Owen's direction.

Her father looked around. "Noah is not here, and I think it will be a long while before he travels."

"Noah told me you visited him," she said, adding cheer to her voice.

Undeterred, her father pursued the answer to his question. "How did he buy these paintings?"

"Well, he told me on Mast Island to put SOLD on this one for him, and his brother, Owen, brought Noah's check for both. Noah also wanted this one," she said, pointing to her tree, *Perseverance*.

"I, too, would like this painting. I will have to see if he will part with it."

Abby looked over at Owen, and smiling, he shook his head in the negative.

Jean-Jacques inspected the price on *Island Sawmill*. He caught Abby's attention and said, "I must have this one."

Abby's surprise must have shown.

"The painting represents my freedom. I shall never forget stepping into danger and making the most momentous decision of my life." He took Abby's hand and lifted it to his lips. "Thank you, Abby."

She looked at Vanna, who had tears in her eyes. Vanna smiled and appeared to accept the change. *I wonder how Collette has handled her position of no longer being the comtesse?*

Mieka returned and hovered around them with sale stickers in her hands. Abby introduced her to the family.

"Have you decided to buy this one?" she asked Jean-Jacques, indicating the sawmill painting.

"Of course," he said. "I thought you heard me say I wanted it."

Mieka put on a red sticker and faded back into the crowd.

Claudia came to Abby. "You are making some sales, and you need to meet the clientele, answer their questions, and find out what they like." She looked at her family and said, "This is an important night for an artist. Abby will have to visit with you later. I hope you understand."

"Of course," her father said. "Run along and meet your admirers. We will talk later."

As they walked away, Claudia said, "I must say your family is impressive." She moved Abby toward the entrance. "Your show is going very well for a first time. Mr. Mobley is impressed."

"Mr. Mobley's here?" Abby looked around.

"I'll introduce you," she said, and walked toward a stout man with receding hair and impressive jowls. He was speaking with a bejeweled woman, with upswept white hair and wearing an art deco style purple gown. Abby had noticed the woman watching her earlier. The second man standing in the group had a notebook in his hand.

Claudia whispered, "That's Adam Crump, the art critic. We hope he has good reviews for you."

"Ms. Pierelli, Mr. Mobley, Mr. Crump, may I introduce the artist, A.S. Parsons." She beamed at them and nudged Abby forward.

Mr. Mobley scrutinized Abby's face. "You're young to reach this stratum in the art world. I'm impressed with your work, and tonight, you are collecting patrons. Congratulations." He bowed his head to acknowledge his respect. "It's been a while since we've promoted a popular artist of your caliber."

Abby noticed Mr. Crump scribbling in his notebook. "Thank you for your representation, Mr. Mobley. I appreciate you taking a chance on me."

Ms. Pierelli said, "Oh, my dear, your work is splendid." She had tears in her eyes as she looked at Abby. "Your passion is evident in every stroke. I wanted that tree back there, the one entitled, *Perseverance*, but it had already sold." She held out her hand, "I'm so glad we've had the opportunity to meet." Her refined features quivered, her lips tightened, and a tear escaped.

MAST ISLAND

Abby wasn't the only one who thought this woman's tears and accolades over the top. Claudia's open mouth was an anomaly, and the art critic's raised eyebrow made a statement.

"Thank you, Ms. Pierelli, for your kind words. You humble me."

The elegant woman patted her hand. "I adore your work. I'm sure we'll meet again."

Claudia walked to the table where champagne was being served along with delicious looking hors d'oeuvres, petite fours, nuts, and mints. She raised a stemmed glass over her head and asked for everyone's attention. "I would like to introduce our artist, A.S. Parsons. You are among the first to meet this rising star in the art world. Thank you for coming tonight, and thank you for making this night a success. I toast Abigail Parsons."

Everyone holding a champagne flute raised it to the artist.

Claudia turned to Abby and whispered, "Your turn."

For a moment, Abby didn't know what to say. "I, too, would like to thank all of you for coming tonight. I'm ... I'm overwhelmed ... grateful ... and humbled by your acceptance of my work. Thank you."

"Good," Claudia said after a smattering of applause. "Now go meet your buyers."

Abby walked around the gallery amazed at the number of red stickers. When she stood by a sale, she noted the buyer would come to meet her and talk about his painting. Abby noticed her father had returned to the wheelchair. He looked tired.

Owen and Rachel came to say their farewells. "I don't know what your plans are for tomorrow. Ms. Chadwick said I could pick up the paintings then, but I've asked her to have them shipped. After seeing the prices, I don't want the responsibility."

Rachel said, "I'm so glad we came. This is a first for us. And we're so happy for your success."

"If you give me your number," Owen said, "I'll call tomorrow to see if we can meet for a meal before we leave."

"I'd like that." She gave him her number, and he wrote it on his hand.

Rachel rolled her eyes. "Why do men do that?"

"Haven't a clue." Abby looked at Owen. "Thank you for coming and for helping Noah."

He looked behind her, and Abby turned and saw Tasse pushing her father toward them.

"Well, goodnight," he said, taking Rachel's arm.

"Hold on. I want you to meet my father."

"Papa, this is Noah's brother, Owen, and his wife, Rachel. They came all the way from San Francisco."

Raphael held out his hand but did not try to stand. He smiled at the couple. "I met your brother in the hospital. I pray he continues to heal without complications."

"Thank you, sir. I spent a week with him, and he's making progress. I appreciate you asking about him."

Raphael nodded. "Abby said you bought two paintings on Noah's behalf. He must be successful in his field."

"He is," Owen said. "Noah is frugal, and like a Scot not one to splurge. He has a discerning eye for art and appreciates quality over quantity. In this case, his opinion of the artist is a bonus."

Abby blushed at his words, and Rachel grinned.

"Do you think I could get him to part with *Perseverance* if I made it worth his while?"

"I'm sure he won't part with either painting," Owen told him unequivocally.

"Then I will defer to your judgement and not harass him. I am glad we had the opportunity to meet. If you are ever on Mast Island with your brother, please come by the château. I will add your names to the guest list at the gate when I get home."

Surprised, Owen looked first at Abby to gauge her reaction and then at his wife. "Thank you, sir. We might take you up on the invitation."

"I am counting on it," the comte said, looking at Abby. "We are making a few changes at the château and in the community. I hope our plans will meet with my daughter's approval."

After the Hazzards left, Abby's father looked up at her, his eyes searching her face. "I understand you learned some unsettling things about your family on the island. If we continue a familial relationship, change is inevitable but comes slowly. I hope you will be patient."

Abby perused her father's earnest expression, and her eyes misted. "Thank you, Papa," she said, kissing him on the cheek. "I look forward to Christmas with my family."

CHAPTER TWENTY-NINE

After the gallery closed, Abby and Mieka met in Claudia's office, where the director raised a flute of champagne to celebrate their success. All of Abby's Mast Island paintings sold, much to Claudia's amazement, and twenty-three of the thirty oils were taken off the market.

"Almost two hundred thousand dollars," Claudia enthused after tabulating sales. "Mr. Mobley will be pleased."

"And so he should," Mieka interjected. "This is the best night he's had for a newcomer, since I began working with him nine years ago." She turned to Abby. "I'm not surprised. You have a good eye and command of your art." Touching Abby's arm, she said, "I also appreciate your discovery of John Vincent. The Mast Island paintings sold quickly, and taking nothing from your talent, I believe the frames enhanced your subjects."

Claudia did not comment but continued to look at sales. "Ms. Pierelli bought three paintings. I thought her tears unusual, but she really liked your paintings to the tune of $32,000. plus tax."

"Who is she?" Abby asked, her curiosity piqued by the woman.

"I'd never met her, but Mr. Mobley added her to the invitation list at the last minute. The names on the check read Clayton and Olga Pierelli. The address is in Charleston, South Carolina."

The color drained from Abby's face. Mieka noticed and grabbed a nearby chair. "Are you all right, girlfriend?"

Abby nodded. *Charleston, South Carolina, my mother's home. Coincidence? Yes. I'm making too much of this. Lots of people live in Charleston. My mother's family may not even live there now.*

"I'm fine. The excitement must be getting to me. I need to eat." She walked into the kitchenette and snacked on leftover hors d'oeuvres and sipped punch, her mind in turmoil.

The next morning, Claudia called Abby to congratulate her. "Your show was a 'smashing success,' according to Mr. Crump's review in The Philadelphia Inquirer.

"Mr. Mobley called to say he is willing to up your commission fifteen per cent if you will give his galleries exclusive rights to sell your work for the next ten years." She explained Mr. Mobley had two galleries in Philadelphia, one in New York City, and one in Chicago. He would be opening another gallery in Los Angeles next year, so her paintings would have a home in these galleries and promotional exposure in the art media world.

Abby received a forty percent commission from the gallery. A new contract would give her fifty-five percent, which sounded like a good deal. Not ready to commit, she told Claudia she would have to give it some thought.

Abby ate breakfast with her father in his suite at the Ritz Carlton. Tasse served their plates and poured the orange juice and coffee.

"Last night you made me proud. You are a DuMond, Bella's daughter." His look turned wistful as he spoke his wife's name. "She, too, would be proud of your success." His voice lowered, "I miss her." His chin fell to his chest, and his lips trembled with emotion.

"Thank you, Papa. Your presence last night was more than I dreamed possible." Many thoughts whirled through her mind concerning Ms. Pierelli, Minneau, and Roux. Did he know yet of Cece's perfidy, her desire to destroy family? How could she begin the subject?

In the end, Abby said, "Tell me about my mother."

Raphael DuMond lifted his head, his eyes fixed upon her own. For a moment, he was silent, and Abby thought he wouldn't speak.

"Bella was my life … my muse … my lover." His eyes closed. "How do I describe a sprite with golden hair and sparkling eyes the hue of sapphires? A girl who captured me with her youth, laughter, and grace?" He opened jade eyes and studied her. His hand moved in concert with his words. "Bella lifted me with her kindness and brought me to my knees with the depth of her love." His voice deepened. "For her, I would move the moon and the stars. For her, nothing would be denied. His eyes questioned as he grieved. "How could I lose so great a gift? How could her life and the life of my son end in fear and treachery?"

Tears welled in her eyes. Abby's heart ached that she would never know the woman who gave her life or held her father's heart. She would never hear her voice or feel a mother's embrace. A void yawned in her chest, a space no other could fill. "I'm sorry if speaking of her brings you pain. You have given me a vision I will always cherish."

"You are my future, Abby, my inducement to take the reins of family once more. Together we will move Mast Island into a future that will lay waste the past. We move in another direction, one that will make my daughter proud to be a DuMond. You will live at Sologne, and together, we will work for the greater good."

Abby dropped her fork, and embarrassed lifted the napkin to cover her shocked countenance. "Papa, I can't live at Sologne. I need space. I need the freedom to be me. Sologne is beautiful but not my home. The château, the history will sap my energy, kill the inspiration I need to paint. Surely, you know this future can never be mine."

Raphael set the utensils carefully across his plate. His eyes and mood darkened as he faced his daughter. "I know nothing of the sort. You will inherit my estate and my island. You must be ready. I will not live forever." His voice became that of Jean-Jacques when he demanded she stay at the château weeks ago.

Abby worried her lips at his words. She didn't want the future her father thrust upon her.

Raphael put his elbows on the table, clasped his hands, and leaned forward. "I never thought I would have a child, and one born of my Bella did not enter the realm of possibility. Yet, you are not a mirage. You are real. You carry the genes, the blood of nobility in your veins. From this you cannot escape." He sat back in the chair, his arms resting on its sides.

"I see you are not happy with my words. My intent is not to

smother you or enslave your future. My desire is to know you. To experience together the bonds of a familial relationship. We share interests I want to explore. Is that so abhorrent to you?"

"No, Papa. I, too, want these things, but I can't live at the château and be happy. My gran said you were prepared to go away with Bella if she did't want to live on Mast Island."

"Is this what you ask of me? To leave Mast Island? Is this the price you want of me, to prove my devotion?"

Abby shook her head. "No, I would never ask this of you or expect it. I want the same freedom you had when you decided what you wanted. Mast Island is your home. You and your family belong there. I have other plans."

Raphael's lips pursed before he spoke. "Do these plans concern Noah Hazzard?"

Shocked, Abby straightened. "Noah's a friend. He showed me the natural beauty of the island, places to paint, and he saved my life. I don't know his plans now, but I did briefly think about a future with him." She fidgeted with the memory of him saying, "So, do you have a new title?" Abby looked at her father. "I don't think Noah believes he is noble enough for the daughter of a *comte*."

"What do you believe, Abby?" Her father's eyes held her own, their intensity not wavering.

Abby straightened to meet his challenge. "I believe any woman Noah chooses to share his life will be loved and appreciated on her own merits." She bowed her head and murmured. "She'll be a lucky woman."

Rafe studied her, his thoughts at once gratified for her seeming interest in Noah, a man he came to admire, and saddened to think he might lose Abby. "Am I to believe you have given up hope for a future with this man?" He paused. "I think not."

Abby spoke plainly. "Noah's in the hospital with injuries that would kill a lesser man. The sloop he loved, lived, and worked on lies in pieces at the bottom of the ocean. He helped build *The Lady* with his father and grandfather. My family is responsible for his losses."

Raphael appeared to know the story. He nodded but did not show shock at this revelation.

"You think he blames you for these misfortunes?"

"I wouldn't call destroying property and someone trying to kill you misfortunes. They were criminal acts. And no, he doesn't blame me," Abby shifted uneasily in the chair. "I blame myself. If I had not come to Mast Island, had not needed his protection, Noah would have his life back."

Raphael placed his hand over her own. The warmth of this gesture settled emotions threatening to unravel. "You do not know this as fact, daughter. Noah is an agent of the Federal Bureau of Investigation. His presence on the island and his mission were enough to endanger his life. He told me this himself." He looked at Tasse and asked him to bring fresh coffee.

Abby didn't want to think about Noah and her family's involvement. As long as Cece was not considered a suspect, her father's life and the lives of others were in danger. She had to say something. *Why the reluctance?*

"Has Minneau spoken with you?" Abby's voice was tentative.

Tasse looked her way, curious and maybe shocked.

Raphael's brow furrowed at her question, and his eyes bored into her own. "Why is Minneau your concern?"

Noting her discomfort, he asked Tasse to take their tickets to the concierge and confirm their return flight.

Tasse's instantaneous frown and reluctance to leave caught Abby's attention. When he noted Abby's interest, he grabbed the tickets from a side table and exited in a hurry.

After the door closed, her father restated the question.

Abby parsed her words. "Minneau and Roux are family." She saw a slight softening in her father's eyes and demeanor.

"You think of them as family?"

"Yes, of course. They're not responsible for their situation. I was fairly sure when we met, Jean-Jacques didn't know I was legitimate. When he insisted I was a DuMond, and my place was to stay in the château, it crossed my mind, my place might be as a servant."

"A servant? He intimated this to you?"

'Not at all. Jean-Jacques made me feel welcome. I assumed after meeting 'one of the lesser members of the family' as Minneau introduced himself, this would be my future if I had indeed been illegitimate and stayed."

"Minneau said these words to you?" Her father leaned forward, his hands moving across the tabletop as if smoothing a cover.

"Yes, and I felt compassion for him. Minneau was one of the first family members I met at the château. He and Roux shared DuMond genes, and they were servants."

Abby's father did not speak right away. "You asked if he had spoken with me. Why?"

"I talked with Minneau after the explosion, and the FBI became involved. He hoped to stay at the château with Roux and continue to live and work where he grew up. He probably felt insecure after his grandmother's death." Abby had not lied yet, and she thought it best to drop the subject. She needed to call Jenna Mackey as soon as possible.

"Cece wants Minneau and Roux to live with her. She has asked this," he informed her.

"Have you asked them what they want? How does Cece regard her husband's illegitimate sons? She does not strike me as a person to treat them kindly. I told Minneau to speak to you. He is not a slave to be handed over." Taking a deep breath, she continued, "I told him if they lost their home at the château, to come here, and I would give them a place to stay and help them find jobs."

Her father drew back as if struck by a blow.

Abby swallowed and lowered her eyes. "I'm sorry if I misspoke. I have not grown up with nobility nor have knowledge of their ways. My gran taught me to treat everyone as an equal, and no one is insignificant in God's eyes. I believe this."

She looked up and saw her father relax and lean back, his face changed by a smile which tugged at the scar on his face. He regarded her with an expression she intuited as pride.

"I would have liked this gran of yours. She was a wise woman."

CHAPTER THIRTY

Abby had a healthy bank balance after receiving a check from the gallery. She twirled around the apartment, singing *Top of The World* along with Karen Carpenter from an old album she had saved. The record player and her collection of albums and LP favorites were some of the items she had removed from her grandmother's apartment. Her spirits soared with the song.

"Thank you, God, for Your many blessings." Abby felt blessed and happy. As the woman in the park told her, "Happiness is a choice." *Oh, Gran, I wish you were here to share my journey.*

The conversation with her father gave her new insight into the man her mother had loved. This same man his stepmother considered weak, grew in Abby's estimation. He exercised the strength of his convictions yet displayed a sensitivity which gave Abby hope for future changes on Mast Island. Her father accepted her views without condescension.

After she left the Ritz Carlton, she had returned to her apartment to retrieve Jenna Mackey's card. Finding a pay phone in a nearby hotel, she called the agent and relayed Minneau's fears. One weight was lifted off her chest, even though a residual paranoia she hadn't been able to shake remained.

Abby called the gallery and asked Mieka for Olga Pierelli's address and phone number. She sat by the window of her studio, thinking about what she would say. What if she were wrong about the woman being related to her mother? *Well, then I'll know.*

She picked up the phone and punched in the numbers.

"Pierelli residence," a pleasant woman's voice answered.

"May I speak with Mrs. Pierelli?"

"Who shall I say is calling?"

"Abigail Parsons, the artist." She watched the mailman go into the building across the street. Few people were outside because of the wind chill.

She heard a man's voice in the background say, "Who is it, Millie?"

The woman put a hand over the mouthpiece to answer, and a man took the phone. "Ms. Parsons?"

"Yes. May I speak with Mrs. Pierelli?"

The man waited a beat before answering. "This is her husband. May I ask why you are calling?"

The man did not sound friendly, and Abby was unsure what to say. "Mrs. Pierelli bought several of my paintings, and she spoke of meeting again."

"Yes, the paintings arrived this morning. They are very nice, but my wife has a tendency to be overzealous in choosing art. I was not present to curb her spending. We will not need additional paintings. I hope you understand." He hung up the phone before Abby could speak.

She sat by the window several more minutes, trying to make sense of the aborted call.

Is he really upset about his wife's purchases, or does he not want me to speak with her? One way to find out. I'll call again later.

Abby walked into the storage room and rearranged her earlier paintings in their niches. They did not have the professional quality needed to hang in a gallery, but Abby couldn't bear to throw them out. *Maybe I can donate them to a nursing home or the thrift shop.* No, her mentor, Master Tremayne, would never forgive her if these paintings ever saw the light of day.

She held up a tempera rendering of her grandmother. She had painted her in ninth grade, and the signature was large and amateurish. She took the work into the kitchen and hung it on a nail. Her portrait had the primitive simplicity of something Grandma Moses would paint. Gran loved her likeness and had it framed.

I like it, too, Gran. You look good. A keeper in my book. Satisfied with her choice, she returned to clean and organize her paints, brushes, and jars of mixes.

Abby checked the time. An hour and a half had passed. She sat down and let the phone redial the Charleston number. The same woman answered the phone, and when she said she would get Mr. Pierelli, Abby told her not to bother. *I guess I'll just have to go to Charleston, Mr. Pierelli, to find the answers I need.*

Abby looked up the travel schedules on her computer to see if a train stopped in Charleston. One did, and she purchased a ticket.

She would be going to Mast Island the following week for Christmas, so she made arrangements to get transportation to Savannah also. Abby wanted to get her mother's box of treasures out of the safety deposit vault and carry it to the château.

Packing to be away several weeks took up the rest of Abby's day, and that night she wrote a note to Noah in a funny card. She would call him from Charleston to let him know what happened.

———※———

Charleston, the quintessential gem of the South, evokes memories of Southern belles, mint juleps, Crepe Myrtle, Honeysuckle, Magnolias, and genteel manners. Situated on a point at the confluence of two rivers, Charles Towne became a major port and a hub of trade during Colonial times.

Attacked by Native Americans, the French, and Spanish, the town was once fortified by walls. Now, The Battery, a historic defensive seawall and promenade was listed as a place to visit. One colorful note in Charleston's history included the pirate, Blackbeard, who besieged the city for a time, disrupting commerce. The Grand Old Dame of the South survived the Revolutionary and Civil Wars but not unscathed.

Reading the rich history of Charleston on the train, Abby was surprised to discover the town was almost destroyed by an earthquake in 1886. She had not thought about faults on the East Coast. Over the years, the city's growing population tolerated a melting pot of military personnel, multiple religions, and diverse ethnic groups.

When Abby arrived at her destination and drove through the historical section, horses and carriages were lined up by the curb. She determined to take a tour on one before she left the city.

Christmas wreaths decorated the doors of Charleston's architectural wonders. Homes from the Federal, Georgian, Victorian, and Colonial eras were resplendent with decorations to celebrate the season. The streets and trees were lined with lights. She noted a Holiday Festival of Lights was held in a park each year.

Abby's heart swelled as she sensed the nostalgia of being part of the surrounding history. Noah would be familiar with these sights. She wished he were here to share the wonder with her. This was where Bella grew up. She looked at the city through her mother's eyes, knowing many of these same buildings stood here while she lived.

The Pierelli house was in the next block. She had taken a taxi to their address and walked around the area until dark. The houses which lined their street in rows were elegant, two to four stories, narrow in front and longer in depth. The Pierelli's house had a side portico with an impressive entrance and a balcony above. The cream, cut-stone façade had three windows embraced by black shutters across each of four stories. Red tiles covered the roof, and round medallions indicated where iron bars were added through the house to protect it from another earthquake.

She turned a corner in the neighborhood where the Pierelli's had a home. Abby smelled gingerbread, and her mouth watered. A bakery, still open on this frosty evening, beckoned with aromas she couldn't resist.

An older gentleman smiled and held the door for her as she entered. People in the South moved at a slower pace, not the frenetic activity found in some big cities. They took time to open doors for you, speak, and smile at strangers. She liked the difference.

Inside, Abby looked at the array of sweet offerings. She ordered two soft gingerbread cookies still warm from the oven and a cup of coffee.

The amiable woman behind the counter said, "You're new around here. Are you staying at a Bed and Breakfast?"

"No, my motel is out of town. This area is too rich for me."

The woman laughed. "Well, you just have a seat and soak up the warmth and enjoy the sights."

Abby sat at a table by the window, thinking about what she would say when she made an attempt to see her patroness tomorrow. Would she gain entrance?

A horse and decorated carriage passed, its occupants laughing she guessed at something said. Christmas music was heard outside when someone entered the bakery.

The gingerbread melted in her mouth, and Abby closed her eyes and savored the taste of sweet molasses and ginger. She remembered the last time she had gingerbread. One Christmas when she was around ten or twelve years old, she and Gran made a gingerbread house. The smell and taste took her back to those days when she made construction paper chains and strung cranberries and popcorn to decorate their tree. One year, they made and pulled taffy, making a mess and laughing until their sides hurt.

Her quest for her biological family did not erase those special times she shared with the woman who reared her. She viewed her gran as her real grandmother. No one could take her place in Abby's life.

Taking her phone from her purse, Abby called the taxi driver, who had given her his card. He said he would be at the bakery in ten minutes.

CHAPTER THIRTY-ONE

The next morning, Abby sat on a park bench across from the Pierelli's house, eating a warm cherry pastry from the bakery and sipping from a cup of hot coffee. She had watched a uniformed woman enter earlier in the morning, and she assumed this was the housekeeper. A second woman similarly attired followed. The maid? Maybe she was the cook. Abby wondered how many people worked there.

Around nine o'clock, a man left the house. He was tall and distinguished, suavely handsome and impeccably dressed in a grey suit. He got in the black Jaguar out front and drove away.

Abby gathered her trash and put it in a nearby receptacle. Smoothing her outfit and hair, she crossed the street and rang the bell. A magnificent wreath of blue spruce decorated the black, painted wooden door. Its branches held pears, pomegranates, apples, red berries, and golden ornaments held in place by ribbons and a large red bow.

The door was opened by the first woman who had entered.

She took in Abby's appearance and said in a formal voice, "May I help you?" Her voice matched the person who had answered the phone.

"Yes, I would like to see Mrs. Pierelli."

The woman stiffened slightly and sucked in her upper lip. "I'm sorry; Mrs. Pierelli is unavailable at the moment." She moved to close the door.

Abby said, "Unavailable or under house arrest?"

The woman, who looked to be in her late fifties or early sixties, straightened and replied, "I'm sure, I don't what you mean." Her shocked expression lasted two seconds, and the door snapped shut, the lock engaged.

Abby rang the bell again. And again. *I can do this all day, lady, until I get answers to my questions.*

After the third ring, Mrs. Pierelli opened the door, her face lighting in welcome when she saw Abby. "Come in child, come in. Oh my." She put a hand over her mouth, her eyes welling. She released a sigh as she looked at Abby. "I wish I had known you were coming," she fussed. "Please follow me. The door led through a piazza and to another portal. They entered a large, spacious room, and Abby noticed the three windows facing the street. The house was only one room wide.

"Millie," Mrs. Pierelli called, and the woman who answered the phone and the door came into the room, her face implacable.

Abby smiled satisfaction and knew the woman gritted her teeth.

"Millie, why didn't you answer the door?"

The woman had the grace to look abashed. "I'm sorry, ma'am. I was coming," she lied.

"Never mind." Olga Pierelli turned to Abby. "You're really here. Please have a seat." She waved toward a rose, damask-covered wing chair. "Would you like some refreshment? Yes. Of course," she answered herself. "Millie, please brew us a tea. Oh my. You're really here," she repeated.

Abby felt the hair on her arms stand up at Olga's reaction to her presence.

The abbreviated expressions of welcome proclaimed Olga's excitement. She sat on the edge of a loveseat, her eyes traveling over Abby in wonder. "I know you must think me a dimwit." She swallowed and took a deep breath. "My maiden name was Langston, and Isabella, your mother, was my sister." She put a fist to her mouth and stifled a sob.

Abby sat stunned, and then moved to take her hands. Tears rolled down her own cheeks. Suspecting a relationship didn't prepare her for the power of the revelation.

Olga Pierelli clasped Abby's arms tightly, her face burrowing into her shoulder. "I wanted to tell you at the opening, but I didn't want to become emotional and spoil your special evening. As it was, I almost lost it." She pulled back and called Millie.

When the housekeeper arrived, Olga sent her for tissues.

Millie took in the scene of two crying women, her expression befuddled, not knowing what brought on their tears.

"This is my niece, my sister's daughter. Izzy's daughter. This is a happy day, one I will treasure always."

Millie hurried from the room and returned with the tissues. She looked at Abby, her lips folded inward, her face one of regret. "I'm glad you've come," Millie said and sounded sincere. Abby smiled her forgiveness as she took the box of tissues. Olga's husband was another matter to be tackled.

They sat and faced one another, aunt and niece.

Olga began the conversation. "When Noah Hazzard contacted me, he told me about you. What a shock! Izzy's daughter." She shook her head. "I didn't know you existed."

My mother, Isabella, is called Izzy by her sister. Rafe called her Bella.

"He sounded like such a nice young man, and Noah told me his mother had found the connection through a genealogist at the library." She wiped her eyes and blew into a tissue.

Noah. Abby closed her eyes at the sound of his name. *Noah didn't forget. He had asked his mother to help.*

"Such a tragedy. Izzy left to follow her dream of being a ballerina in New York. Daddy tried to talk her out of leaving, and when she didn't listen, he became angry and told her not to come back, begging to return to the fold.

"Our older brother, Jeremy, and I were crushed. Izzy was like sunshine in the family. A light went out when she left. Jeremy searched for Izzy in New York, without success, after he left home,

"When we received word that Izzy had been murdered in Savannah, along with her child, Daddy suffered a physical setback. His heart was broken, and he lingered several years, blaming himself."

Olga sighed deeply. "Jeremy passed away last year." She looked at Abby and said, "If only he had known of your existence.

"You don't look like Izzy, but twins run in the family. Our grandfather was a twin."

"I look like my father's side of the family," Abby replied.

Millie returned to say the tea was ready in the dining room, and they followed her into a beautiful formal room, with cherry furniture, and an Aubusson rug. One of Abby's landscapes hung on a traditional Colonial wall-papered panel between arched crown moldings and bronze sconces. Several other high-end art works graced the walls and pedestals.

"Your paintings are beautiful," Olga said. "You capture the light." Her words trailed off as they sat at the table for Millie to pour the tea. Olga added milk to hers. "Please tell me about your life. Noah told me nothing about your past. He informed me that you were having an opening this month for your work, and friends helped me finagle an invitation. I was bursting to grab you and not let go, but of course, it wouldn't have done to make a scene."

Abby liked this woman. Olga's refined features glowed, and Abby basked in her acceptance. She told her aunt about her gran and how she saved her life and reared her as family. Abby spoke about Gran's unexpected death and finding herself without a past. She shared how she began her search, about the box of her mother's treasures, finding the marriage record, and going to the DuMond château on Mast Island.

"Izzy married," Olga cried. "We didn't know. Did you find your father? Is he still alive?"

"Yes and yes. He, too, came to the opening."

Olga put her hand to her chest. "He was there? My Izzy's husband was at your showing?"

"Yes, I'm sure you noticed. His presence would be hard to miss."

"Oh my! The tall man in the black cape with the ruby heraldry brooch. The man with a head of white hair and an impressive bearing. That man?"

"The very one." Abby responded. Her father exuded authority and an air of mystery.

"Oh my, oh my, Izzy!" Her hand lifted as she studied Abby. "Of course, you have the same look. The people with him … were they also family?"

Abby told her about each member and about Mast Island. She told Olga the DuMonds didn't know of her existence when she met them. Abby didn't tell about her brush with death or about still feeling threatened.

"Izzy married a French count, and we didn't know?" Olga shook her head. "Oh my."

They exchanged stories, and Olga left to retrieve some early pictures she collected of Isabella and their family for a future meeting.

The morning flew by, and Olga had the cook make club sandwiches for lunch.

"You are an amazing young woman." The words were barely spoken when her husband arrived.

Abby straightened in her chair and readied for a confrontation.

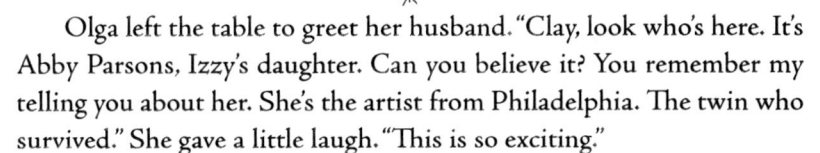

Olga left the table to greet her husband. "Clay, look who's here. It's Abby Parsons, Izzy's daughter. Can you believe it? You remember my telling you about her. She's the artist from Philadelphia. The twin who survived." She gave a little laugh. "This is so exciting."

Clayton Pierelli was younger than he appeared at a distance. *Maybe twenty years younger than Olga.* His jacket had been removed and a cream tie hung untied down his blue silk shirt. He shone from the tips of his Belvedere black lizard-wingtips to his gold Rolex watch.

"Ms. Parsons." His head tilted to the side, his neck cricked as if he had pain. "This is a pleasant surprise." His words sounded friendly, but they didn't match his frosty gaze. "My wife has spoken of little else since she returned from your show. How long have you been here?"

"I arrived a little after nine." She saw by his narrowed eyes, he calculated and knew she waited until he left the house. "We've had a wonderful time catching up after all these years. *My aunt* has been sharing pictures of my mother's early life." Her hand waved over the table filled with framed pictures and albums. "She's welcomed me into the family. I hope we'll be friends, and we'll be able to keep in touch by phone," she said, daring him to deny her future access.

"Lovely," he said, placing a light kiss on his wife's temple. "I hope you saved me some lunch," he said to her.

"Of course, dear. I'll tell Millie you're here." Olga left the room.

For a minute Clayton was silent, sizing Abby up. "You're a fast worker," he finally said.

"Not nearly as fast as you," she replied with a satisfied smile.

He looked taken aback, and walked from the room, following his wife.

Abby stayed in the motel two nights instead of the Pierelli's house. She told her aunt she needed time alone to sort out her new families, and Olga didn't press her to stay.

Back at the motel, she had called Noah to thank him and update her progress.

He sounded happier with this call than any of the others.

"Olga Pierelli, my mother's sister, lives in Charleston. She was very nice and excited to see me. We've talked two days, and I'll see her tomorrow. She hoped we'd keep in touch."

"I'm happy for you, Abby. You've found family in record time."

"Yes, and you had something to do with the discovery. I can't thank you enough."

"So, tell me, where are you now?" Noah asked.

"On the way to Mast Island for Christmas with my father." Silence on his end had Abby chewing her bottom lip.

Noah finally spoke. "You shouldn't be going. Jenna told me danger still exists."

"How much has she told you?"

"I'm not at liberty to say," he explained. "We have an ongoing investigation."

"Can you tell me about the explosives that were used?"

"That's confidential. You'll know when the time is right."

"Well, what do you know that *you can* disclose?"

"I miss seeing you, hearing your voice."

Abby blushed and shuffled her feet nervously. She wasn't used to men saying words like these.

"You know I'm a little deaf, right? I didn't hear whatever you just said," Noah told her. "Could you repeat it, a little louder?"

"I was thinking. You couldn't hear me think even with one hundred per cent hearing."

"Good thoughts, I hope," he said.

"I like hearing your voice, too."

She changed the subject. "How are you doing with rehab?"

"I'm getting my strength back, walking with a cane." He filled her in on his progress and on the plans for building *The Lady II*.

Abby looked through the genealogical papers Olga had printed out and given her before she left. She marveled as she ran her fingers down through the centuries of forefathers. Their names blurred as her eyes welled. She read the births, deaths, and places her ancestors had lived. Notes had been written in the margins, stories of events, personal milestones, or tragedies which breathed life into the recorded names. Some of the writing had faded, and some had been written in Old English and had to be studied. Her finger stopped on some of the entries.

"*A grat comit passes ovr us. Londin 1664. Fathr feers eval coms.*" An inch below this message read, "*1665 Bertie 2y., Sulie, 6y, Georg 11 y and Mothr dide wif plag. My lif spard. Fathr als. Wy me? Sarah 14y.*" Abby traced Sarah. The girl was in her direct line. Life is tenuous. Abby existed today because a miracle saved Sarah from the plague in 1665.

More deaths were recorded. "*Danny lost at sea, Sep. 1774.*" Abby found Danny in the record. He had been 16 yrs., 5 mo. Another family grieved.

"*Sylvie died. Baby Teddy born dead 21 July 1820. angels in his kingdom. Lord help us.*"

Abby had roots, deep roots in England, Scotland, Germany, and France.

Cope, Gobbel, Hawthorne, Tanner, Gluck, Foster, Hepburn, Gordon, and Cooper were among family surnames.

The Claire line, on her grandmother's side of the family, came into Charles Town in 1821 from the Alsace Lorraine region of France.

Tomorrow would be Abby's last day in Charleston. She wanted Olga to know how much she appreciated the treasure she had been given.

CHAPTER THIRTY-TWO

A cold, stiff wind blew as the ferry negotiated the ribbons of water channeling through the salt marsh. Abby felt the burn on her cheeks, and the chill in the marrow of her bones. Abby was returning to Mast Island for the third time.

Her mind drifted to the visits with her aunt, Olga Pierelli. She thought about the copy of her lineage Olga had given her. The Langford genealogical records went back to thirteenth century England. She had spent several hours going over the pages in her motel room. Olga had spoken of more recent Langfords.

Jeremy Langford, Abby's deceased uncle, had two children, a son and a daughter, now in their thirties and living in Charleston and Gooseneck, South Carolina. Both were married, and each had two children.

Olga had a daughter, Lauren, with her first husband, Buford "Sonny" Waite. "She lives in Rhode Island and is still unmarried at thirty-one," her aunt told Abby, "She's been living with a philosophy professor for three years. I don't understand young people today. I hope they marry soon. I pray for grandchildren."

Abby had asked how Olga met Clayton, and learned Clay worked in Sonny's real estate firm seven years. "When Sonny passed away, Clay helped me sort out the financial records, and made sure I didn't 'vegetate' at home. He squired me to performances, parties, and dinners. We share similar interests and tastes." She hesitated and then continued.

"I know he's a lot younger," Olga said, "and people talk, but Clay has been a charming and faithful husband. He's more mature than he looks, and I dismiss any gossip as jealousy. You might have noticed he's also a good-looking man."

Abby agreed, and Olga said, "He's so caring and solicitous of me."

Maybe Clayton has been good to her, but he's over-solicitous. Stop it. It's none of my business who she loves.

Clayton Pierelli now ran the firm, and according to Olga, under his leadership, Waite Real Estate and Properties had grown and prospered.

Olga said a tearful farewell at their last meeting. She hugged Abby and made her promise to stay in touch.

The château was quiet as Abby slipped out for her morning walk.

Jean-Jacques came outside and briskly walked to catch up with her. "I must speak with you," he said, catching his breath from exertion.

Abby worried his healing lung might cause trouble. They were almost to the gate. She pulled her jacket closer and braced herself for this talk. She turned to retrace her steps, shortening the distance to give his damaged lung some relief.

"I apologize for any discomfort I have caused you. Please forgive me. My anger should not have been directed at you. My ire stemmed from years of discontent with the history thrust upon us. *Maman* never let Rafe or me forget our shortcomings. She said weakness would be the undoing of the DuMond Dynasty, a dynasty Rafe and I did not want to perpetuate."

Abby turned his words over in her mind. His statement gave credence to her father's conflict. *He's taking on the reins of the family for me? I have to make him understand we live in a modern world. He must follow the path he wants for his life as I must follow mine.*

She stopped and looked at Jean-Jacques. One thing haunted her, and she wanted an answer. "Did you have my room and Noah's boat bugged?"

"Bugged?" he said, looking shocked. "A listening device?"

"Yes, I had two in my hotel room. Noah showed them to me."

Abby's eyes widened when several expletives were loosed. Jean-Jacques reddened and looked apoplectic. *What if he has a stroke?*

"You think *I* would do this abhorrent thing? To a guest? To a DuMond? Am I this monster? *Non!* I did no such thing."

Abby believed his denial real. "Someone did, and they tried to get in my room in the middle of the night. If you didn't do it, who would have the means, the knowledge? Your mother? Cece?"

"*Non*, Even *Maman*, with her deranged mind, would not stoop to this level." He seemed to retract his statement. "*Maman* tried to kill you. The family is not perfect, but this goes beyond the pale. Maybe the FBI did this."

"No. They knew about it, though. I'm sorry I thought you were involved."

Jean-Jacques rested his hands on her shoulders and looked into her eyes. "*Non*, I am sorry you were so abused. I would not do this thing, Abby." His eyes pleaded for her to believe him. "I would not condone nefarious behavior. I will speak with people and find out what they know."

Jean-Jacques released her and began to walk, shaking his head. His warm breath sent out puffs of vapor in the chilled morning. "You said you did not like what you found on Mast Island. Now, I understand. I will speak with Rafe. He will not be happy. We will search out this ... this culprit, together."

Abby considered Jean-Jacques's determined expression. He was a man with a mission.

Abruptly, his tone changed as he glanced her way. "You must understand, Rafe is not weak. He has always been sensitive but in control of his emotions and beliefs. He did not want Mast Island developed. His vision as an artist and biologist was to leave everything in its natural state, to be a rookery and a destination for naturalists. This did not meet with the family's approval or expectations. Insufficient income had left us without any other option but development or sale. We have properties in France. Some came to the family through *Maman's* inheritance and some have belonged to the DuMonds for centuries. As comte, Rafe also owns a magnificent collection of family jewels. While *Maman* lived, we would not think to put our heritage on the block."

"Haven't you wanted to live in France or return to your roots? How do you manage properties so far away?"

"We have property managers, consultants, and stewards who

manage. Sheep and fly-fishing keep the bills paid, but the estates need upgrades we can't afford. I doubt the family will keep them long term.

"One of the properties in Alsace Lorraine contains a profitable vineyard. Several years ago, it became a valuable asset.

"We stay here because we are Americans."

They walked in silence. Abby thought about what he said. *Did the development begin after my father was injured? Did Jules plan for Rafe to die? We'll never know. Noah and my father have a love of nature in common.*

"When I arrived on Mast Island, I noticed none of the resorts is over five stories? Do you have building restrictions?"

"We compromised and limited development to five hotels and one marina with restrictions. We do not have vehicles clogging the island. Walking and biking do not cause undue stress on the native flora and fauna. We have tried to keep visitors away from the upper half of the island, so rookeries will be undisturbed. I am proud of our efforts to keep some of Rafe's vision for the island intact."

"What about Loire Park? Do you have plans for expansion?" She thought about Daisy's Aromatherapy Emporium. "Are the shops privately owned?"

"No, we built the village, and business owners rent the spaces. This assures consistent architecture and upkeep of the buildings. The bank branch and food pharmacy complex across the street are privately owned The post office is attached to the market."

"So, has the development been sustainable?"

Jean-Jacques nodded. "After twenty-four years of taking out loans and putting money back into business, we are seeing a nice profit. We burned the mortgages one-by-one, until the last, five years ago."

They walked around the château into the garden. Frost had killed or wilted the most fragile of the landscape's offerings, lending sadness to the overcast day. Abby wondered if the damage to the garden would reignite her father's depression.

Jean-Jacques led her through another gate, and a cemetery came into view. A marble mausoleum surrounded by a wrought iron fence was the centerpiece.

Abby held back when Jean-Jacques opened the gate to go inside.

"You have nothing to fear from the dead. Our ancestors rest here," he said.

Abby wasn't thinking about harm from the dead. She was remembering the words spoken in the sawmill, and she wasn't ready to be interred in this place. Abby remained outside, and Jean-Jacques did not press her to enter.

Jean-Jacques lips moved as if he tasted something unpleasant. "Our father, Gervaise, was not a businessman. His interest lay in maintaining an opulent lifestyle. His first wife, Rachelle, the woman he loved, gave him Raphael and myself. She took little interest in our history and died when I was born. Rafe was three years old.

"*Maman*, Gervaise's second wife, came with enough money to maintain our lifestyle. She came from nobility and believed the DuMond Dynasty had to be protected. As far as I'm concerned, *Maman*'s unhinged behavior has put our family's future in jeopardy." For a moment he was quiet.

Is he wondering about the trial? Is he worrying about his family? I may have misjudged this man's intentions. He did welcome me into the family.

Jean-Jacques continued. "Jules and Guillaume were *Maman*'s sons. Jules shared her Machiavellian philosophy and delved into illegal activities to bolster his bank account. I was forced to deal harshly with him, and he was killed. *Maman* never forgave me."

Abby scuffed bits of gravel on the paving stones as she listened. His words painted the picture of a dysfunctional family. Thinking about the dowager *comtesse* brought back unpleasant memories of her venom and evil actions at the sawmill. *Thank you, Lord. We aren't related.* She bowed her head. *Thank you, thank you.*

"I believe your mother loved you more than you knew. Maybe she was not aware of it, until you were shot." Abby remembered the old woman's distress when she realized Jean-Jacques took her bullet. "She thought she killed you and shot herself."

Jean-Jacques nodded. "Madness ran in *Maman*'s family. She denied Guillaume's existence and sent him to an institution for the mentally ill in France. He tried to burn the château to the ground, and we had to make extensive renovations in the back quarters where Rafe now lives.

"Our father, Gervaise, was adamant about sending him away, and he swore Guillaume was his last child with *Maman*. She did not take his physical estrangement well."

Abby wanted to change the subject. "Tell me more about my father. He is still a mystery to me."

"Your father and I have always been close though separated by three years. He did not want his entailed inheritance. He told me he might leave the island and the title to follow his muse, his love." Jean-Jacques began to walk again, taking a trail through an open gate and around the château walls down to the protected landing she had seen on the edge of the salt marsh. Abby followed his steps.

Jean Jacques continued. "I understood Rafe's yearning for freedom. I was finishing my MBA when Rafe brought Bella here. She was everything he described and more. I, too, fell under her spell of beauty and spontaneity.

"Like my brother, I wanted to be as other young men, unencumbered, with choices. I wanted a life of opportunities, a life not strangled by my heritage."

Yes, Abby understood his position. Her father, while incapacitated, placed the yoke of authority on Jean-Jacques's neck. As Rafe recovered, he didn't seek the responsibility of his position.

"*Maman* had a fit of epic proportions. She frightened Bella, who insisted Rafe take her back to the mainland.

"Rafe demanded an apology, and *Maman* gave a laudable performance of a heart attack. The doctor was called, and he corroborated to everyone's surprise, *Maman* had heart irregularities, which later developed into heart failure.

"Bella left Sologne never to return except in Rafe's delusional imagination."

Abby let him continue to talk. She knew how important making a clean breast of things could be. He had apologized for his abrasive behavior, and Abby understood how his words and demeanor could stem from discontent. She was beginning to feel strangled herself.

Jean-Jacques fidgeted as he buttoned and unbuttoned his jacket at the neck. "*Maman* was the only mother I ever knew. And yes, I believe she loved Rafe and me in her own way, despite her belief we shared Rachelle's defective genes." He kicked a palm frond to the side of the trail and became silent as if pondering his next words.

"Rafe came home after the attack, lame and without memory. As he recovered, he kept to his room or the gardens, not wanting to participate in family or life. He surrounded himself with his portraits of Bella and his memories of a happier time.

"*Maman* called him Henri, to deflect the authorities' interest in the family or any connection to Rafe's disappearance, which might lead them to the murders in Savannah.

"Rafe chose to remain Henri, nonexistent. I encouraged him to paint, but he balked. I believe from his ramblings, this was a self-imposed sentence to assuage his guilt for not protecting Bella." He leaned on the landing rail, looking out over the salt marsh, his eyes following a flock of white birds flying across a deep lavender sky.

Abby's eyes also followed the path of the birds. A few streaks of pink and gold appeared as the sun rose behind them. She remained silent, wondering if he would continue.

"We nurtured Rafe's growing passion with gardening to bring him back into the world he abandoned. He blamed *Maman* for Bella's death and the death of his son because she enabled Jules to continue his criminal activities. We did not know of your existence."

Abby tried to understand the convoluted machinations of her family. "You allowed your mother to make decisions even when she showed her mental instability."

"Yes, I took the easier path, and I regret not taking the upper hand. We may all pay for my lapse."

Collette was not at the château when Abby arrived. Jean-Jacques told Abby that Collette had left him after he got out of the hospital. She went back to live with her parents for a while. He didn't know if she would return.

"How did you meet Collette?"

"Collette," he repeated. "I met her at the Yacht Club. She reminded me a little of Bella. I think it was her blondness that attracted me first. She was young and popular in the jet set. I was flattered by her interest. What middle-aged man wouldn't have succumbed? She was an heiress, and her family let me know they would exchange a large portion of their assets for their daughter to have a title. I should have known better, remembered my father's plight, but I did not heed past mistakes. So, we are married for the present. I am not sure for how long. I tried to keep my part of the bargain, but as you know, my position has changed." He was silent a moment. "She is two years older than Vanna. My marriage alienated me from my daughter for a time, but Rouland talked Vanna into returning home." He sighed. "Collette wants children. My reluctance has caused friction. I look forward to being a grandfather, not starting over."

Abby nodded her understanding.

CHAPTER THIRTY-THREE

Abby was to meet with her father in the salon. He had not arrived. Her eyes traveled the room as she remembered what had occurred on her last visit to Sologne. She shivered. The fear, not knowing what had happened to Noah, and the horror of the *comtesse's* intent and subsequent death slammed through her. Rubbing her arms vigorously, Abby hoped the friction would alleviate the chill.

She focused on the ten-foot Christmas tree in one corner, elaborately decorated with gold and crystal ornaments. Presents, artfully wrapped, lay below.

Roux entered the room and started a fire. The flames leapt to consume the logs. "You should be warm in a few minutes," he told her.

He lingered and spoke. "Thank you for speaking to your father about Minneau and me staying at the château. And for offering to help us find jobs in the city. I am glad we will not have to leave the island. This is our home." He looked relieved and grateful.

"I'm happy for you, Roux. Maybe sometime we can discuss what you want to do on the island."

Roux's expression showed shock or maybe disbelief. "Do you mean work somewhere else?"

"If that's what you want. Do you dream of doing something different?"

Rafe arrived without his wheelchair, and Roux walked to the door. "May I bring you anything before I check on dinner?"

Both said they didn't need anything.

"So, daughter, how have you been entertaining yourself?" Rafe inquired as he sat on a straight-backed arm chair. He avoided the "throne" vacated by his mother.

Abby also sat, describing part of her conversation with Jean-Jacques that morning. She told him she had explored the château and its environs. There was a lull in the conversation, and Abby decided now was the time to mention Olga Pierelli.

"Did you know my mother had a sister and a brother?"

Rafe's eyes narrowed. "I knew about them, though we never met."

"Bella's sister, Olga Pierelli, attended my opening and bought three of my paintings."

Rafe's eyes widened. "She was in the gallery that night?"

"Yes. Olga was the attractive lady in the purple gown and white upswept hair. I met with her at her home in Charleston a few days ago." Abby imagined gears turning in his mind while he absorbed this information.

Olga and Jeramy, Bella's siblings, he thought. *She missed them and wanted them present at our wedding, but I wanted to marry as soon as possible. Bella did not know the family pressure. Our marriage had to remain secret until she became pregnant.*

Rafe was silent, and when several minutes passed without a word, Abby told him what she had learned about Bella's family.

Rafe studied her face while she spoke, so Abby tamped down her excitement, not wanting to hurt him. She had no idea how he would take her findings.

"How did you get this information?"

"Noah asked me if I would try to find my mother's family. I told him I'd go to Charleston and investigate after the exhibition. He was going to help me, but his mother found a genealogist to help. Noah told Olga about my scheduled opening at the gallery before … She stopped, not wanting to bring up the night their world changed forever.

"Olga didn't tell me she was my aunt when we met. She wanted me to have a successful night and not be emotionally distracted. When I told her you were also present, she remembered seeing you."

"Noah," Rafe said, changing the subject. "Have you spoken with him? Do you know how he is progressing?"

"Yes, we talked yesterday. He says he looks less alien with his hair and brows growing back. Rehab is going well. His bones are healing, and soon all the metal holding them together will be removed. That is, all but the pin in his hip, which is permanent. His eye has healed, but he lost some hearing in one ear."

"Rafe listened, his attention mining her words for personal feelings. At least, that's what she suspected from previous conversations.

"The good news is he and his father along with friends who work at a shipyard are helping to build a new boat, *The Lady II*. I believe this project has given him the incentive to live. He has research projects to complete."

When her father didn't speak, Abby continued. "I guess you could say he's better than expected. The main thing he is, he survived."

Rafe looked down for the first time, his expression hooded.

Is he wondering if the family will survive a court case?

"I have been thinking on our conversation in Philadelphia," he finally said. "I have plans for Mast Island, and I would like to have you at my side to see them realized. Although you do not want to live here, will you visit several weeks at a time to help me with my work?"

"What are your plans?"

"I want to build an institute, a place of learning and for researching the flora and fauna of the island, of other islands also. We will need labs, computers, special equipment, and housing for visiting scientists, maybe invite students to intern here.

"Rouland told me Dr. Hazzard spoke to him about opening the impoundments. I think allowing tidal water to get rid of invasive species makes sense. All invasive plants should be removed from the island."

Abby felt excitement rising. "Your plans sound ambitious. Can you afford a project of this magnitude?"

"We will begin small and grow when there is a demand for our work. Research will be published. Grants may be pursued. What do you think?"

Abby loved the idea. Then she thought about the poverty on the island, the disparity of the native population and the resort guests. She told her father her feelings on seeing the local cemetery and hearing about poor housing on the island. "Do your plans include working on these problems?"

Rafe nodded sagely. "You will be in charge of these changes. The projects require ordering everything from the mainland and managing or hiring someone to oversee the work. I have already begun looking into the permitting process for the institute. I will have the information available when we bid out and hire a firm to do the work."

Abby knew her father thought of a way to tie her to the island by giving her the job of fixing those things which made her uncomfortable. She thought about Noah. *Is this his way to bring Noah here also?* "Are you doing this, Papa, to bring Noah back to the island? For me?"

Her father shook his head. "No, I am doing this for me. For the dream I had thirty years ago. I am not a matchmaker, Abby. I would welcome Dr. Hazzard's expertise, but you must find your own happiness when the time is right."

Thoughts ran through her head, chasing each other across a panoramic screen as she visualized the future. *Maybe a future on the island.* The idea did not seem as distant as before. Abby did not want to commit without reviewing what needed to be done. She wanted to paint, her passion, her profession. Two weeks had passed without picking up a brush or even making a sketch. The edginess she felt was akin to withdrawal symptoms. *Can I do both and find inspiration?* "I will think on these things, Papa. Your plans intrigue me."

Rafe smiled, and she knew he thought the deal done.

A thought popped into her head. "How did you meet Tasse, Papa?"

The smile was wiped from his face, and his brow furrowed. He had no time to bask in his success. "Why do you question me about Tasse?"

"I'm curious. Tasse has become a necessity in your life. How did you find him?"

"He was here when I came out of the coma. I believe Jean-Jacques told me Cece found him."

"Do you trust him?"

The blunt question was unwelcome. Rafe appeared lost in thought. Then he said, "I guess I trust him as much as anyone. He serves me well." *How does Abby know my unsettled feelings about Tasse?*

He looked at her, his expression guarded.

Abby dropped the subject. *He will think on my words and wonder. Maybe he will be more alert.*

She reached into her shirt and pulled out the necklace with the toe shoes charm and the emerald ring. As Abby pulled the necklace over her head, she told him about the necessity of her temporary will and the plans she had made for the ring.

He reached for the jewelry, his large hands carefully removing the ring from the gold chain. He enfolded the heirloom and brought it to his chest. "Your mother ... my heart. We were wed," he said, the timbre of his voice reverent. "I slipped this ring on her finger when we married. She looked at me and laughed." He smiled as he put the memory into words. "The ceremony was one of commitment, not a formal affair, and I laughed with her at the words she spoke. She said, 'Good Lord, Rafe, do you expect me to wear this heavy thing? I can feel the centuries weighing me down,' and the pastor looked stunned. I don't think he saw the humor in her words."

No, but he remembered the ring.

Cece joined the family in the salon before Christmas dinner. She perched on a straight-backed chair in one corner. Feathers of silver hair sleeked back and hugged her face like a helmet. Her head followed the conversations, but she didn't contribute. Cece resembled a bird of prey, waiting for a live morsel to present itself for her delectation.

Abby tried to shake off the morbid thought and looked around the room at the portraits of her ancestors, the DuMond women. Her eyes gravitated to a younger *Grand-Maman*, whose dark orbs peered from her portrait and accused Abby of destruction and death. She felt cold seep through her body. Vignettes of the night at the sawmill passed through her mind, leaving vestiges of fear. Tension roiled inside, and she looked at her father. Rafe sat to Cece's right.

Tasse stood behind him, the faithful companion ready to serve. His innocuous appearance and manner did not seem dangerous, yet the seed of distrust had been planted.

"How long have you known Tasse, Cece?" her father inquired.

Abby noticed Tasse's brief start at the question and Cece's sharp look at Rafe.

Conversation around the room lulled to hear her answer.

"I knew him in Lyon. He helped my father after his stroke. I thought of him when you returned to Sologne. Why do you ask?"

"Are you related?"

Cece bristled. "Whatever gave you that impression?"

"His name is Bernard Sevier, and I believe Sevier is your family name. Am I mistaken?"

Cece stood. "What is this interrogation? Are you trying to humiliate me?" She looked at Rafe with scathing eyes. Her voice rose in anger. "Do I look like I grew up in a hovel, a barnyard?"

Tasse's eyes widened at her malicious remark.

Abby saw the hurt he could not conceal.

"If you had, there is no shame in it. You have made a successful life for yourself."

"I do not have to listen to this … this rubbish. You know nothing. Sevier is a common name in France." She swept from the room, her chin leading.

The room was silent. Five, ten, twenty seconds passed, and Vanna cleared her throat. "I have news," she said, her voice subdued.

Rouland stepped forward and took her hand. "We both have wonderful news." He looked at his wife with adoration. "We are going to be parents."

Abby whooped and went to hug Vanna. "What a beautiful Christmas present! I'm so happy for you both."

Jean-Jacques's somber expression brightened as he embraced his daughter and shook Rouland's hand. "This is indeed wonderful news. I am looking forward to being a *grand pere*."

Vanna had tears in her eyes as she returned her father's embrace. Was she concerned about her father's depression after Collette left him?

Roux appeared and announced dinner would be served.

They walked to the dining hall, the incident with Cece forgotten.

Minneau entered the dining hall as everyone sat. He whispered something to Jean-Jacques, who immediately left the table.

The table resplendent for the Christmas meal was set with candles, silver serving vessels, delicate china, and fine crystal goblets. A dinner featuring standing rib roasts had been served and half-eaten when Jean-Jacques returned. A smile lit his face as he entered with Collette on his arm. "Collette loves me," he announced. "She wants to remain in our family."

Vanna rose from the table and went to Collette. "We have missed you." She hugged her step-mother, whose eyes flooded with tears.

Others rose from their seats with words of welcome, Rafe among them, and Jean-Jacques was visibly shaken by everyone's acceptance. Abby moved down, so a place could be set for Collette next to Jean-Jacques.

The conversation was stilted, until Collette leaned forward and said to Vanna, "I have just heard the news, and I'm truly happy for you."

At this, the conversation livened, and the Christmas spirit returned.

Rafe sat in the salon watching Christmas presents being distributed by Minneau. He saw Minneau's face when he found the rectangular packets at the bottom of the pile with his and Roux's names on them. Minneau looked at him startled, and Rafe nodded. He hoped he did the right thing. Inside the packets were deeds to property on the island in the names of Minneau Dessler DuMond and Roux Lubiere DuMond. Minneau hurried from the room, the packets unopened.

Rafe stood. "I have an announcement. No, I have several. First, I have acknowledged Minneau and Roux as DuMonds. They are family and free to pursue their dreams." He paused to look at their responses and continued. "They have been deeded property near the dock where they may build their homes and rear their families bearing the DuMond name."

Abby had never been prouder to have Rafe as her father. She must tell him later how much his attention to her thoughts meant to her.

A stunned silence met his announcement, and Abby stole a look at Tasse. He didn't bother to mask his anger.

The clatter of shoes rapidly approaching the salon was heard. Minneau and Roux entered and knelt at Rafe's feet, their faces at once excited and tearful.

Rafe appeared to be at a loss. "Get up. Stand up straight," he said, his voice rasped by emotion. "You carry a proud name. Now you must be mindful to use it for good, to make the family proud." He looked around the room. "I expect the same from everyone in the family."

Abby spoke first. "I'm happy for you."

The others nodded their acknowledgement of Rafe's directive without complaint.

Minneu spoke. "We would like to continue our work here for the time being. We do not know what the future holds. But we want you to know, we will never betray your trust or the honor you have given us."

"Your loyalty is gratefully accepted. You may as well remain for my other announcements because they affect everyone in this room."

Abby looked at each face. With the exception of Tasse, no one appeared to harbor ill feelings toward Minneau and Roux. They only gaped in surprise.

Tasse shook with the effort to control his anger and remained in the room.

Abby wished she could hear Tasse tell Cece what had occurred in her absence. She thought of the "bugs." *Maybe she already knows.*

"I have never been comfortable with the idea of inheriting a title or an island," Rafe continued. "Forgive me, Jean-Jacques, for thrusting my responsibilities onto your shoulders, for I knew full well you shared my sentiments.

"Now, I have a daughter, who has opened my eyes to some truths I preferred to forget."

He looked at Abby and smiled. "As far as I am concerned, Jean-Jacques earned the title, *Comte*. As Americans, we will share the title, legal or not, and share the decisions made for this island and for our families from this moment forward. The winds of change are hard to battle, and we have a history that has run afoul of the law. We must face whatever comes from our failings and support one another through these hard times."

Collette grabbed her husband's arm for support when she heard Rafe's words.

Jean-Jacques started to speak, but Rafe delayed him with an upraised hand. "I am almost finished. My last announcement concerns plans I have discussed with Abby, and these plans I place before you now."

Rafe outlined what he hoped to accomplish on the island with Abby's help. "I hope you will consider and share my dream for Mast Island."

Vanna spoke up, her voice excited. "I want to help Abby with the renovations. This has been my dream for a long time, but I didn't know how to see it accomplished."

Collette hugged Jean-Jacques. She was still a *comtesse*.

Rafe looked at Collette. "I believe I have something of yours." He reached into his pocket and removed the emerald ring. "You will need this for your portrait." He gave the ring to Jean-Jacques. "You should do the honors."

Collette's hands covered her mouth as she squelched a sob.

Everyone looked at Abby, who smiled.

Rafe may have been drugged in the salon that first night he was introduced to her as Henri, but he remembered the ring meant something to his brother's wife.

"But …" Jean-Jacques began.

Rafe cut him off. "I have it on the best authority, some traditions need to be broken. For me, the ring is a beautiful memory. Abby sees it as a bauble to pass down to Vanna when it has served its purpose. I believe she told me Vanna would be more appreciative of the family heirloom."

Everyone looked around, taking stock of each family member in the room. This Christmas Day would be marked as a milestone in the DuMond history.

CHAPTER THIRTY-FOUR

The New Year came and went with Abby still at the château. Her desire to paint and to return to Philadelphia was tempered by her need to begin renovations on the island.

She and Vanna took a car and drove through the area where Eddie had indicated poverty existed. A few structures looked in fair shape, but most were shacks in various stages of disrepair. All were weathered and needed pressure cleaning along with several coats of paint. Lumber for railings, steps, and missing or damaged pieces would be ordered.

Chickens ran free, and an occasional cat was seen curled in the sun on the steps of a house. A dog barked as they approached, but he was chained.

Writing on a yellow pad, Abby mapped each house and made notes on outside structural needs. Missing shingles and tarps indicated some roofs needed replacement. Abby said, "I think tin roofs would be safer in case of fire," and Vanna agreed.

The DuMond car generated attention. Curious eyes watched them from porches and windows, but no one came out to greet them.

A network of clotheslines zigzagged through the yards, their colorful, pegged offerings flapping in the cold breeze. They saw a couple of ancient washing machines with rollers to squeeze out water on porches. All of the homes were elevated and mostly protected from the elements by trees and high dunes.

"Have you ever been here?" Abby asked Vanna.

"I drove through with Rouland several years ago. Papa said this area was off limits because he didn't think it was safe. He forbade me to come."

The surprise was finding a wooden church building at the end of the road built on a rise and flanked on one side by a well-kept cemetery. The building had been painted white, its spire topped with a cross.

Vanna stopped the car when Abby said she wanted to see the inside.

They walked to the door and tried the handle. The sanctuary was unlocked, and they stepped inside.

Straight-backed wooden pews and chairs were assembled in rows. An altar adorned by a hand-carved cross was floor level, and a large Bible on top was opened to the Book of Ecclesiastes.

Two steps led up to a choir loft. Abby counted nine chairs. She didn't see a piano or an organ.

Everything looked clean and in good condition. The rectangular windows contained old and new glass panes. Shutters bracketed them inside and out. An unused gas heater sat toward the back.

Abby sank down on a pew and looked at the cross. How long had it been since she sat in a church? She went to church for Gran's funeral, but before that, her visits had been sporadic, even non-existent for months at a time.

After the explosion, she had prayed fervently for Noah to be alive and prayed for his recovery without complications. God answered those prayers. Now, Christmas had passed without celebrating the true meaning of the season. Abby felt separated from God, and emptiness yawned in her spirit. Leaning forward on the wooden back before her, she bowed her head and prayed for forgiveness.

Vanna also sat and bowed her head.

They turned and stood when the door opened.

Eddie entered. He had lost weight, but his smile was the same. "I should have guessed it was you, Miss Abby. You have caused quite a stir." The smile vanished and was replaced by a guilty expression as the past intruded.

Abby had not seen him since the night at the sawmill. His betrayal still hurt, though she understood his conflict. He, too, appeared to still have misgivings.

"Hello Eddie." She walked toward him, her hand out to put him at ease. Eddie had worried about her and brought her to Noah's attention. He had tried to save her, putting his own life in danger. She would stand up for him in court.

He grasped her hand. "I'm so sorry for what happened." He looked down, "and for Noah."

"I know. We need to look to the future. Noah is going to be fine."

"I heard. I'm glad. He's a good man. God still works miracles."

"Yes, miracles happen. How is your granddaughter?"

Eddie frowned. "Livy still has nightmares and fears the man with the gun will come back. We tell her the bad man is in jail and can't hurt her now or ever."

"I'm sorry. Hopefully, time and love will heal." She turned to include Vanna. "I believe you've met."

"Eddie inclined his head, acknowledging her presence. "Yes, but I have not seen you around here, Miss Vanna."

She smiled at Eddie. "Well, that is about to change. You will be seeing a good deal of us this year."

When he looked askance at Abby, she told him their plans.

"First, we need to find someone with construction expertise to evaluate and order materials."

"Yes," Vanna said. "And he will need a team of workers to help him. Maybe some of the people who live here will work. They will be paid, of course," she added.

Eddie grinned. "You can count on it. Another miracle. Praise the Lord! God is good."

"All the time," Abby said, and Eddie looked at her anew, his eyes filled with admiration.

"We think a community laundry building should be built with updated appliances. What do you think, Eddie?"

"I think I have died and gone to heaven."

That evening, Abby and Vanna met the others in the salon. They were excited about their plans. Roux and Minneau were asked to join them. They stood stiffly to one side, not quite believing they were included.

Rafe poured them a glass of wine, and they relaxed. When he gestured to two chairs, they sat.

Jean-Jacques said, "James Toomey is coming tomorrow to finalize the legal paperwork. Our financial advisors will give us an updated report and an architect will be sought to draw plans for a rudimentary science building and lodge. Permits will have to be drawn. When the time comes, we will put the construction up for bids."

Abby remembered Mr. Toomey, the attorney had vouched for her the first day she saw the château. Their meeting seemed to be years ago instead of months. Did he know about her? Of course, but he probably didn't know she was the person he befriended.

Her father wanted Abby to legally carry the DuMond name. They had argued and then compromised. She would keep her professional name, A.S. Parsons, for her artwork, but she would add DuMond on other correspondence and official documents. She did not need to wear the emerald ring to feel the weight of her family's history mantling her shoulders.

When Abby retired for the night, she sat and wrote Noah about their plans. She told him Vanna's news and about their trip and seeing Eddie at the church.

Noah mostly called instead of wrote. She enjoyed hearing his confident voice, his updated assessment of rehab, and their plans for building *The Lady II*. She worried the calls were shorter and less frequent. Abby vowed to persist and keep the connection, however tentative.

She looked at the floorplan of *The Lady II* taped to her mirror. The plans had stimulated Noah's recovery, and he was anxious to work. Several of his father's friends at the shipyard had offered to help, and they ordered necessary materials.

Unable to sleep, Abby took out her floor mat and began her nightly kick-boxing exercises and katas.

After a shower, she lay awake several hours as she reviewed the day and more critically her life separated from God. Her gran had been a pillar in the church, and until she left home, Abby's faith played a major role in her development. That she didn't have time was no longer a credible excuse. Her prayer life consisted of what she needed in the moment. *How shallow!*

Noah had told her he was unashamed of his belief and not to hide hers.

What of my family? What do they believe?

Only after speaking her heart and mind to the Lord was she able to sleep.

Two days later, James Toomey arrived at Sologne. He spent an hour with Jean-Jacques and Rafe before the others were called to meet in the library.

"Mr. Toomey," said Abby as they were introduced. "I must thank you for letting a visitor get her first glimpse of Sologne. You are a gentleman, and I'll always think kindly of you for your help." She told the rest of the family about her first day on the island. Everyone looked surprised.

They settled into chairs around the library while James Toomey explained the legalities of name changes, IRS, revising a Birth Certificate, and Social Security information.

Cece entered the library and addressed them in her usual abrasive manner. She saw Roux and Minneau seated in the room, and spewed her rage at Rafe, "What do you think you are doing? Are you mad? You can't just make these changes. You are tearing apart the DuMond legacy. Our heritage," her voice rose and her hand slapped the desk for emphasis.

That had to smart. Abby hid her smile as Cece cradled her hand to her chest.

Rafe stood and towered over her, his face set, his anger barely leashed. "I have the power to do as I see fit. Jean-Jacques and I share authority for the plans and maintenance of Mast Island. You will abide by our decisions, or you will leave."

"Why wasn't I told?" She rounded on Jean-Jacques, who stood by Rafe.

"You left our Christmas dinner early. Your feigned ignorance of matters at Sologne is not credible."

Cece drew her shoulders back, her eyes black coals burning contempt. "What are you implying?"

Rafe and Jean-Jacques stood as one, tall and formidable.

Jean-Jacques answered. "Make of it what you will, Cece. If you want to stay, sit and be quiet."

She swallowed her next words at the order and sat, her cheeks sucked in, mouth pursed, and her expression dark.

Everyone took a breath and focused on James Toomey, who spread papers across the desk for them to sign. He didn't dignify the harsh words spoken but continued his part in a professional manner.

He held out a checkbook to Abby along with a specified draft for renovation materials. "You and Vanna will be authorized to sign after your signatures are recorded at the bank."

Cece squirmed in her seat. "Where are you getting the money?"

Rafe answered. "We have found a better use for the DuMond jewels. They will be removed from the bank vault and put to work."

"They belonged to *Grand-Maman* and to Jules."

"The gems and lands we still have in Loire were her dowry and came to my father by right of marriage. We know *they* have no further use for them."

"As the widow, I have rights. They belong to me." Cece set her teeth and looked like she wouldn't let go.

"Jules forfeited your rights when he involved the family in criminal activity." Jean-Jacques said, and his next words delivered the death blow. "Roux and Minneau have more rights than you. They believe in what we are doing and have given their blessings."

Abby looked around the room at family faces.

Confident they were protected, Roux and Minneau stared at Cece without looking down. Abby saw pride shining in their eyes, pride Cece couldn't take away.

Vanna, Collette, and Rouland took in the scene without comment, and as if, nothing were new.

Abby bowed her head and thanked God one more time for the years of love and encouragement she had spent with her gran.

The insurance policy came to mind, and she knew Gran would

approve her intent to use the money for good causes locally. *I'll speak with Mr. Toomey later.*

Cece looked like a dog shaking off water as she struggled with her pride. She glued herself to the seat, her mouth set in a straight line.

---※---

Abby stopped by the bank in Savannah to sign paperwork. She also found a garage where she could store her car when she drove it back from Philadelphia.

The Christmas trip to see her father had lasted longer than Abby expected. She hadn't brought painting supplies. She planned to pack them in her car and drive back. On the way, she would fulfil her promise to Mina Kresge and tell her what happened.

The flight took almost two hours, time for Abby to think about her future. She was becoming entrenched in family emotionally and financially. Her father's vision for the island excited her, and she visualized a different place a few years from now.

The wheels of the plane dropped and locked into place, scattering her thoughts. She looked out the window at streams of cars crossing the Schuylkill River and the concrete, steel, and glass jungle beyond. The city couldn't compete with the wild beauty of Mast Island.

CHAPTER THIRTY-FIVE

Cold, March winds whipped Abby's hair and scraped her face as she stood at the bow of the ferry taking her back to Mast Island. She gloried in the reminder of life, one she had taken for granted. A reminder that each day was numbered, each breath, a gift. More than a month had passed since she left.

The time had been spent in Philadelphia, making arrangements to move from her apartment studio. She couldn't bring herself to fully commit to a permanent change of address. Abby found climate controlled storage for her paintings and furniture. She then arranged with a real estate agent to lease her gran's brownstone apartment on a year-to-year basis. Her home would always be there if she needed to return.

"I'm going to miss you, dearie," Mrs. Anthony said to Abby when she handed the landlady her studio key.

"You've been so good to me, Mrs. Anthony. Believe me. I'm going to miss you, too." She hugged the lady with bluish pin curls and lively eyes. The woman had no children, so she kept tabs on Abby, her youngest tenant. Like a mother, she encouraged and fussed over her.

When Abby spent days in her room painting, Mrs. Anthony brought up homemade soups, Italian dishes, or baked goods, clucking Abby needed to eat better.

"I'll miss your cooking, too."

"You sure there's not a man involved?" Mrs. Anthony cocked her head and looked her over. "Don't wait too long, or you'll end up a spinster like me." She nodded her head as she pointed out, "You should have been nicer to John. He would have made you a fine husband."

"Yes, Mrs. Anthony, I'm sure John will make someone a fine husband. The only man in my life right now is my father. I'll be staying with him."

She thought briefly about Noah and driving to Mobile, but she nixed the thought as being too forward. Phone calls and writing would have to do for now.

"You'll write and let me know how you're doing?"

"Of course. And I'll visit when I come back to Philly." She saw tears forming in Mrs. Anthony's eyes and quickly opened the door. Abby hurried down the steps to her gran's car, not looking back to see if her landlady watched. Farewells were difficult.

The studio easel divided the car in half, and her bags were packed around it. Her travel easel, new canvases, and paint supplies filled the trunk.

───────❋───────

Abby drove to Baltimore to visit Mina Kresge. She thought back to their first meeting, and knew she had to alleviate Mina's fear for her.

The woman, who begged her not to begin the journey to find her family, broke down when she saw Abby. Time had not been kind to her, since they last met. She appeared frail and drawn, despite the theatrical make-up. One arm, encased in a cast, hung in a sling. "My bones are brittle. So glad my hip didn't break when I fell. Got rid of that pesky rug."

Mina made coffee, and they sat in the little kitchen while Abby updated her findings. She told her about the family on Mast Island and meeting Bella's sister, Olga, in Charleston. She did not tell her about Noah, the attempt on her life, or her paranoia. Mina didn't need more worries.

The woman wasn't satisfied with a condensed version. She plied Abby for details, descriptions, words spoken.

They moved to the parlor when the hard chairs became uncomfortable for Mina.

Rafe and Olga garnered the most questions.

Mina finally relaxed and sat back, looking like a doll swallowed up by the larger wing-backed chair. She sighed. "Bella and Evie would be so proud of you. Look what you've accomplished. You found Rafe alive, and you know what happened to her family in Charleston. I wish Bella had known."

Hours passed before Abby could comfortably leave. Mina insisted she stay the night, but Abby wanted to get to Savannah before noon. Her family expected her on the afternoon ferry, and timing would be close. Abby promised Mina she'd keep in touch when she finally settled.

Abby arrived in Savannah tired but within her time frame. She had stopped many times to stretch her legs when drowsiness threatened.

She parked near the ferry landing, put the front seat down, and wrestled the large easel out onto the dock. She left it there and drove the car to the storage garage, hoping the easel would be there when she returned.

Abby carried four bags with her in the taxi. One bag held her paints. She couldn't afford to have them dry out. The rest of her art supplies were left stored in the trunk of the car. Another trip to get her things would have to be made. Maybe Rouland would help.

The ferry bumped the dock as it berthed. Her father stood at the end, leaning on his cane, waiting for her. His clothing was casual, khaki pants, flannel shirt, down jacket, and laced work boots. Tasse was nowhere in sight.

Her father had been self-conscious, at first, about making appearances in public. Abby was proud of his effort to change the perception of her family on the island. She remembered the birdwatcher's words about never seeing a DuMond. Now, they became familiar persons, making their presence known. Some of the plans for restoration leaked out before Abby left, and an air of excited anticipation had permeated the island.

"Well, daughter, you took your time getting back. We have made progress in your absence."

She did not hear reproach in his voice. "I had business, Papa, and came as quickly as I could."

One of the ferrymen lifted her easel onto the dock along with her bags. Rafe signaled for Eddie to come and help.

Construction materials were piled on the concrete dock and lined the ferry landing. Abby sighted a forklift in the parking area.

Eddie's smile widened as he neared. "Welcome home, Miss

Abby." He passed by to get her easel. The rest of her bags were loaded onto a cart.

Home. Abby loved the island, but Sologne would never feel like home.

"Welcome home, Abby," her father said, repeating Eddie's greeting, putting a hand on her shoulder. He leaned in and placed a kiss on each cheek.

Abby's chest tightened. The changes in her life became a runaway train she felt powerless to control. She needed space.

The route to the château was studded with work vehicles. Abby gaped when they passed a cement truck, churning its load. She turned to her father, and he answered before she asked.

"Barges. Very expensive, but necessary. The concrete landing had to be built before supplies could be brought to build the resorts and village."

The immensity of the project awed her. Viewing the plans on paper and seeing them implemented was like leaping from one to eight on a scale of ten. Her father didn't waste time.

Tasse drove the car, and Abby saw him watching them in the rear view mirror. *Friend or foe?* He didn't appear threatening.

Vanna met them at the door. "Welcome home," she said, hugging her, and a knot formed in Abby's stomach.

"I cannot wait to show you what has been accomplished. You will be so proud."

She rattled on about supplies and the man, Harvey Olsen, hired to oversee the work. "I am finally over the morning sickness, so I can come with you without embarrassing myself."

Abby smiled at her enthusiasm and itched to get out and see the project.

CHAPTER THIRTY-SIX

Weeks passed, and Abby had not retrieved her painting supplies from her car in Savannah. Feelings of anxiousness pressed on her spirit. Never in the last five years had she gone so long without painting.

Abby approved the choice of Harvey Olsen, who oversaw the structural changes, plumbing, electrical, and roof replacements. He agreed tin roofs would be safer, and his easygoing manner and attention to detail and safety were pluses.

Eddie helped Olsen supervise and acted as a liaison when his shuttle duties permitted. "You know, Miss Abby, I never would have believed the changes you have made. My head can hardly contain the thought of the *comte* working with the islanders. We are in awe just seeing him."

"I've noticed." Abby had watched faces change when Jean-Jacques or Rafe made an appearance. Expressions of fear and avoidance of eye contact gradually changed to curiosity and acceptance. As time passed, the islanders became more receptive, less cautious, and the atmosphere of distrust diminished.

A number of residents pitched in to help, especially painting outdoors, their smiles and laughter heart-warming. They brought drinks to workers and shared what little food they had for snacks.

Vanna made sure the market delivered bags of fruit or sandwiches for laborers. Oranges and tangerines were favorites.

At times, spontaneous voices lifted in song. Some of the lyrics, passed down from their ancestors, filled the air, their cadence matching the music of hammers and saws at work.

Building repairs on homes took a lot of Abby's time. She and Vanna spent their days working with families. Abby helped paint inside walls, and measured spaces for appliances needing to be added or replaced.

The islanders chose bright colors for rooms and the exterior walls. Abby's shoulders hurt and her arms ached at the end of the day, but she slept soundly at night satisfied with her work.

Vanna ordered necessary items for the homes. She knew every thrift shop, used furniture outlet, and Salvation Army store in Savannah. Nothing was elaborate, but every addition was a necessity and appreciated.

Bunk beds were popular items. Children had slept on floors or on sofas.

"I am running out of places to get good, used refrigerators," Vanna told Abby. "I have to find two more. I cannot believe some people do not have refrigeration in their houses."

"Are you serious? How are they preserving their food?"

"They collect ice from family members who have refrigerators and use a cooler. I also found a couple of young families who did not have an oven, just a one or two coil electric top. Mama or grandma does the baking or roasting," she added, "when they have meat. Chickens and goats are saved for special occasions." The islanders did have small plots of vegetables. Potatoes and beans were staples. One yard was decorated with collard green plants that lined the walkway and surrounded the base of a tree.

Abby thought about how some people barely got by at the poverty level. The construction provided jobs, and she saw personal improvement in dress and in pride.

She wondered if Vanna thought about the disparity of life in The Project, as they now called the community, and her life at Sologne. Abby found the contrast less jarring as the community took shape. The colorful houses brought smiles to their faces each day.

"We need to get help with education for the younger children, who don't yet go to school on the mainland," Abby said.

"Maybe we can find a new intern, in the Public School System, who will help," Vanna responded. "You are right. Education is the key. Island children attend high school on the mainland. A number of them drop out and don't graduate."

"Eddie told me most people who left the island returned because life off the island was hard and not friendly," Abby said.

Roux spent his mornings working in The Project, his afternoons planning meals and overseeing the kitchen at Sologne. He quickly became a favorite of the island children and blossomed with their attention and comradery. Whenever he was first sighted, the cry went out, "Roux's here," and all of the children ran to meet him. He usually had cookies or some treat the kitchen staff at Sologne made to share.

Before the youngsters let him work, he had to play ball with them. Sometimes they shot baskets into a bare hoop, minus the net, or he showed them soccer moves to practice. Roux had enjoyed soccer in high school, and Abby found out he had been a good player.

Roux asked Vanna and Abby about a budget for athletic equipment. "We can use a few hoops for shooting practice in the neighborhood, but soccer takes more room. Can we get some soccer goals, so we can play in Loire Park? And a couple of footballs would be good."

Vanna loved seeing the children outside playing. "Physical activity is healthy."

Abby saw Vanna put her hand protectively over the slight baby bump. *Is she thinking about her child's future?*

"Maybe later we can build a basketball court," Vanna said with enthusiasm. "We have to concentrate on basic needs first."

Roux nodded. He understood.

Vanna ordered two hoops, soccer goals, and the balls to play in Loire Park.

Abby noticed Roux was beginning to own the family relationship and the responsibility his part entailed.

Vanna watched Roux toss a plastic ball to the younger children and saw over the days and weeks, his sullen attitude toward his station change. He was a handsome young man when he laughed and played with the children. She no longer took his presence at Sologne for granted. They began to bond. He was family.

Minneau came out a couple of hours, several afternoons a week, but his interest lay in the new science building being erected. He told Abby, "I want to go back to school and learn enough to help with research at the institute one day. Math and science were my best subjects.

"Will Dr. Hazzard be coming back to work here?" he asked Abby.

She hadn't thought about Noah returning to the island to finish his research. He was immersed in his work on *The Lady II*.

"I don't know, Minneau. When Noah finishes rehab, and he's ready to go back to work, he'll probably want to see how the institute is progressing."

The criminal case on the island would one day close. She thought briefly of Cece and Tasse, Minneau's concerns. She'd let the FBI handle them.

"I am sorry for what happened to Dr. Hazzard and his boat. Everyone says he is a good man. I am glad he is alive."

Do he and Roux think about their grandmother's involvement or the circumstances of her death?

"Thank you, Minneau. We are all grateful for God's blessings." Abby had not heard from Noah for several weeks. She didn't communicate with him, feeling he was getting on with a life which didn't include her. She didn't want to be pushy. Noah had to make the first move. *Maybe I should call. No, out of the question. Don't think about Noah.*

Dove Creek Gallery sold one of Abby's oil paintings, and Claudia asked when another would be ready to take its place.

Mr. Mobley was prepared to sign the new contact, and the director asked if she should mail the contract to her Mast Island address for a signature.

Abby was conflicted. Her mentor, Master Tremayne, told her that she had an opportunity few artists would ever have. She pressed her temples, a headache beginning to nag her.

She made a note to get her supplies from the car. Her art must be a priority. She would think about the contract later.

CHAPTER THIRTY-SEVEN

Rafe woke from a dream. Light flickered on the wall and ceiling. He blinked several times. The unfamiliar sound of exertion and ripping brought him fully awake and sitting up. Someone was in his room.

Metal glinted in the candlelight, and a knife slashed through a portrait of Bella.

"No!" Rafe screamed. The destruction of Bella's painting squeezed his heart, impelling him to the side of the bed, his breathing tortured by rage.

"Tasse, get in here!" he yelled. "Tasse!"

Cece turned, her distorted face aglow in the dim light. Eyes burned as lit coals in her maddened face.

"Tasse!" Rafe hollered.

"You should be dead," Cece shrieked. "You and your ..."

Enraged by the desecration of Bella's sanctuary, Rafe tackled her with a roar. They both fell, the candle rolling under the curtain protecting the portraits.

"Bella," Rafe cried. *This can't be real.* "Cece, why?" He raised his head to the slashed face of his wife and howled, "Why?"

Tasse arrived, eyes wide, hands to his head, not believing the sight before him. "*Mon Dieu, Cece!* Are you insane?"

A flame ignited, lighting the tableau before him.

Rafe used his weight to pin Cece to the floor. He grabbed for the knife, but she bucked and squirmed, her fury aiding her efforts to get free.

Tasse grabbed for the knife, and it scored a gash on his arm. "Non! Cece, Non!" he implored," desperate to stop her lethal intent. Tasse saw a maniacal demon beyond reason.

Rafe grasped her wrist, and the knife dropped. He stood, bringing her off the floor and kicked the weapon away. Cece was shoved into Tasse's arms. Rafe pulled down the curtain and tried to extinguish the fire.

Too late. Flames had leapt across the ceiling and engulfed the drapes. Burning fabric floated onto the bed and set it aflame.

Cece pushed Tasse aside, adrenalin providing unusual strength. She launched herself onto Rafe's back, bringing him to his knees, his head striking the wooden foot board, dazing him.

She scrambled for the knife and raising it screamed, "Die!"

"Non!" Tasse yelled. His balled fist hit Cece under her raised arm.

Motion seemed to slow as she fell, embraced by the burning curtain. Flames consumed her clothing and hair. Her shrill scream of terror paralyzed Tasse. He watched horrified, unbelieving. For a moment, Cece's arms flailed, legs kicked, and her body twisted in torment as the heat intensified. The stench of burning hair and flesh arrested both men. The arm holding the knife was raised, a flaming torch. Sudden silence left them sickened.

Petrified and stunned, Tasse looked around the room, now burning out of control. The ancient woodwork, prime tinder, sparked and ignited.

"Tasse," Rafe called, rising on his hands and knees, trying to use the bed post to stand.

Arms surrounded Rafe and pulled him to his feet. Tasse put Rafe's arm around his shoulder and dragged the larger man to the door yelling, "Fire! Fire!"

Shouts and running feet sounded down the smoke-filled hall.

Minneau arrived and hoisted Rafe over his shoulder.

Roux took the stairs two at a time, meeting Jean-Jacques, Collette, and Rouland, with his arm circling Vanna, coming down, and gasping for air.

"Miss Abby?" Roux asked, his voice frantic.

Rouland looked back, shook his head, "I have not seen her." He kept his arm around his wife as they descended.

"Miss Abby!" Roux shouted and choked on the black smoke clouding his vision.

Abby awoke with a start to raised voices. An acrid smell assailed her nostrils. Someone tried to force open the door, and when the lock held, the person pounded on the door and threw himself against it. "Fire! Fire!" a man shouted. "Wake up, Miss Abby! Fire!"

Roux's voice.

Tendrils of smoke seeped under the door.

Abby scrambled from the bed and raced to grab the handle, which was warm. She fumbled with the key, and the door opened. Black smoke rolled up the stairs, and flames licked the wall and sent a swath of blue flame across the ceiling in front of her. She fell into the hallway, trying to catch her breath and shield her face from the heat.

Strong arms lifted her. "Hurry! We must go." Roux's fear-filled voice urged her to move.

The walls along the steps were aflame, the heat unbearable. Roux ran toward the front of the château, away from the stairs, his hand grasping Abby's arm, forcefully pulling her behind him.

Her senses returned. "Papa, Papa," she screamed, and immediately gagged on the fumes. She fought the hand which imprisoned her.

"Minneau has him," Roux said, coughing and struggling to catch a breath. Thick smoke surrounded them.

The château's on fire. We'll be burned alive. Abby fought the panic racing through her body. Roux fell, pulling her to the ground. "Hold onto me," he said as he began to crawl through another room.

Abby breathed better close to the floor. Visibility was nonexistent, and she clung to Roux's ankle, crawling blindly, as he pulled her along. She dared not let go. Abby heard shoes charging up steps in front of them, someone gasping.

How? Where? Are we turned around, headed the wrong way?

Someone collided with them, and they grappled, trying to stand.

"Abby?" Arms found her.

Jean-Jacques? Her knees buckled.

"We must hurry." he said, holding the front of his nightshirt over his mouth and nose. "The roof could fall at any moment."

Jean-Jacques took the lead down a narrow, winding staircase, Abby between the two men. Roux held her shoulder to keep her upright.

Windows exploded, flying glass raining down.

A loud crash, followed by a whoosh behind, pushed them forward, through an open doorway, flaming debris and ashes falling around them. The open portal sucked in oxygen and fueled the inferno chasing them.

They fell into the courtyard and scrabbled away from the burning building, gulping precious air.

They reached the driveway, and Jean-Jacques turned her around, knocking off bits of glass, ash, and glowing embers from Abby's hair and gown.

Black smoke billowed upward, flames painting the sky an eerie orange glow. The roof caved, its copper tiles glowed red and became lethal weapons which sliced the smoke as they fell. The interior structure crumbled inward into the maw of hell. A screech-like sound of exploding combustion followed, and everyone ducked and moved back.

Abby's body shook as she hugged herself. She looked at the accelerating devastation in disbelief. Sparks flew, and ashes drifted down. *This can't be happening.*

Down the drive, people began arriving on bicycles, running on foot, their shocked faces masked in horror, lit by the blazing annihilation before them. Nothing could be done to put out the fire, which raged beyond what human hands could perform. Questions and comments abounded.

"My God. Oh my God!"

"Is anyone in there?"

"What will happen now?"

"God help us all."

"*Mon Dieu*," Jean-Jacques said, crushing Abby to his chest. "Are you all right?"

"Yes," she blurted. "The others? Did everyone get out?" She looked around frantic to see her father. "Papa," she cried, "Papa?"

She pushed away from Jean-Jacques, her eyes searching the crowd for family members. Collette sat on a low wall, her head down and buried in her hands. She had on the emerald ring.

Jean-Jacques turned to her and knelt at her side, putting his arms around her in comfort.

Not seeing other family members, Abby grabbed her uncle's arm. "Is everyone out?"

"They escaped through the back," he shouted above the roar of flames as it ate through the remaining timbers and contents of the beautiful estate. He stood to watch his home burn, its reflection aglow in his worried eyes.

The pent up energy which zinged through her body and spurred Abby's flight to safety drained quickly. She collapsed on his chest, feeling the aftermath in her quaking body and dry mouth. The sight, smell, and sound of devastation would forever be imprinted on her mind.

She saw Roux, who sat on the paving stones, staring upward, his hands clasped between his knees. Tears made channels through the black soot covering his face, and the light from the fire flickered eerily over him. He had brought her through hell.

A man came forward, took off his shirt, and wrapped it around Abby's shoulders. She looked down, numb. Her gown was torn, her legs, knees, and bare feet scratched, bleeding, and exposed to the elements.

Jean-Jacques thanked the man, helped get her arms into the sleeves, and tackled the buttons.

Abby let him perform the task and then sank to the pavement beside Roux. She touched his arm, and he looked at her, his eyes registering the pain of loss. She understood. This was the only home he remembered.

"Thank you, Roux."

He nodded and looked back at the fire.

Minutes later, she saw Minneau. He skirted the château through the woods, where onlookers pitched in and stamped out small fires as they ignited.

Abby jumped up. "My father?"

"He is fine. They are on the landing." Minneau sat by his brother and put his arm around Roux's shoulder, comforting him.

CHAPTER THIRTY-EIGHT

Abby awoke in a hotel. Her eyes searched and found Gloria outlined by the sun in front of a balcony window. The smell of burned material permeated the room. She looked down. The soot-covered comforter had been pulled off the bed, and Abby lay naked, covered by a sheet. Memories crashed through her, and she sat up, her attention on the woman watching her.

Mouth agape, Abby looked at Gloria who stammered, "You'll ... be okay, honey." She tried to smile, but her lips trembled, so that speech was difficult. "I cleaned you up ... as best I could. I can ... can help you wash up now. The concierge told the family you had asked for me before, so here I am." She leaned toward Abby, her hand out, and looked unsure what to do or say. "I ... I'm so sorry, honey." She looked at the chair. "I brought you some of my things. They're probably too small, but they're clean and loose. Ms. Boucher said she would order you clothing."

The side table held scissors, gauze, tubes of antibiotics and a variety of bandages.

Abby pulled the sheet around her and put her feet on the floor. A pain shot up her leg, and Abby looked down at a bandaged foot.

Her head spun. The nightmare returned. The château burning. The shocked voices, both raised and hushed. The frantic escape. Crawling. An orange glow seared her mind, behind her eyes. She vaguely remembered the aftermath, the confusion, and climbing over blocks of brick and stone which fell and slid down the embankment.

She reached her father, and they held each other on the landing. Her father's shoulders shook as he tried to control his emotion and repeated, "You're alive. Thank God, you're alive."

Rouland and Vanna had joined them, and all four braced together, hugged comfort.

Tasse sat at their feet, hands over his face, sobbing.

Coming back to the present and looking into Gloria's concerned face, Abby stated, "Everyone got out," At least, they had their lives.

The woman hung her head and shook a negative response.

"Who?" Abby asked, and grasped Gloria's arm. "Who?" she demanded appalled.

"The DuMond … from Loire Park."

"Cece?"

Gloria nodded and looked at Abby, her eyes compassionate. "I … I'm so sorry."

Abby couldn't process the answer. "Cece?" she repeated.

"That's what I heard. They removed her remains this morning. The *comte* identified the body to the authorities."

What was Cece doing at Sologne? She shook her head. "I don't understand."

"I'm sure the family will tell you. I'm just the bartender."

Abby took both of Gloria's arms and looked into her face. "Don't say that. You're human. Like me. We're the same in God's eyes. You're so much more than a bartender." She searched for words. "And I appreciate you staying with me. Thank you for the clothes and help."

Abby limped toward the bathroom, and Gloria ran ahead to turn on the water.

"I think I can take it from here. I'll let you know when I'm finished." Abby closed the door and used the facility. She sat on the side of the tub, unwrapped her foot, and stared at the damage. Her arch and heel were cut and cleaned. *Probably glass. How long has it been since I had a Tetnus shot?* Probably seven or eight years ago. While she lived at Gran's. After she cut her hand on a rusty nail in the attic. *I should be okay.*

"I'll call room service and the maid." Gloria's voice sounded through the door.

Abby saw the shirt and tattered remains of her gown stuffed in the wastebasket. She didn't need to look in the mirror to know she looked a fright.

She stood under the pulsing hot water, the uncovered scrapes and cuts on her arms and legs stung as she shampooed her hair. Abby scrubbed her way down, pulling off the adhesive strips and washing until the water ran clear. She would need a nail brush to complete the job. *Why was Cece at Sologne?*

The large, fluffy towel felt luxurious. She wrapped a smaller one around her hair and opened the door a crack to ask for the clothing.

Gloria handed her a big shirt and loose sweat pants which ended mid-calf. No underwear was included, and Abby didn't say anything to embarrass her. "Thank you."

Abby sat on the straight-backed chair and towel-dried her hair. She combed it with her fingers. Some of the cuts had begun to bleed again, and Gloria applied antibiotic ointment and new bandages. She walked to the bathroom and returned with a soapy towel and tried to get blood out of the carpet, without much luck.

They both jumped when someone rapped on the door.

"Room service."

Gloria opened the door and signed the bill for her. The waiter placed a covered tray of food on the desk. His startled glance took in Abby's appearance, and he turned away, embarrassed.

They both thanked him.

Scrambled eggs, sausage, biscuits, orange juice, and coffee were revealed when Gloria uncovered breakfast. The savory aroma and a growling stomach let Abby know she was ravenous. She ate with zeal.

Gloria watched amused. "You sure know how to eat like a hungry human," she said.

Abby looked at her and grinned. "Nothing like a hot shower, a good meal, and a caring person to let you know how great it feels to be alive. You want a biscuit?"

"And get my hand chewed off? Thanks, but no thanks. I can wait."

Abby laughed. It felt good. Felt liberating. *I'm so blessed.* Tears welled, and she looked at Gloria, not comprehending.

"You've had a shock, honey." Gloria picked up the phone. "I'm calling Ms. Boucher."

Vanna arrived five minutes later and rushed to Abby's side.

Gloria backed to the door. "I guess you won't need me anymore. Let me know if I can help in any way."

Abby looked at Gloria. "Thank you. I don't know what I'd have done without your help."

Gloria nodded and disappeared into the hall.

Vanna regarded Abby's appearance. "You look clean and comfortable."

"Are you okay? The baby?" Abby asked, and Vanna nodded, putting her hand protectively over the bump revealed under the sash of the hotel robe.

"We are fine," she replied.

"I know about Cece," Abby said. "What was she doing at Sologne?"

Vanna chewed on her lips. "Trying to kill your father is what I heard."

"What! Where's my father?"

"Rafe is fine. He has a sizable lump on his forehead, but do not worry. He is probably still talking to authorities, or he would be here. Believe me."

A discreet knock sounded on the door. "Maid service."

Vanna opened the door, and revealed a maid outside, folded towels in her arms.

"You called?" the woman asked hesitantly.

Vanna stepped out of the way to let her enter.

The maid looked at the mess around the room and on the bed. Black soot crossed the carpet. She looked at both women. "I think I need help." She backed out of the room.

"Come. My room is made up," Vanna said.

They traversed the hall, arm-in-arm, barefoot.

Vanna made calls, ordering casual clothes for Rouland, Abby, and herself. She included underwear, socks, and sneakers. Local shops were accommodating, bringing their purchases to the hotel. "We will go shopping in a day or two when everything settles down."

"Are you and Rouland moving to the mainland?

"Yes, his mother will want us to stay with her."

"What about your father and Collette?"

"I do not know. They may stay with us, although my father might want to remain on the island with Uncle Rafe because of the construction. You and Collette are welcome.

"The DuMonds have a house on the river in Savannah. We sometimes stay there when business takes more than a day, or we use it for family gatherings with friends."

Abby wondered where the rest of the DuMonds would live. "What will happen now?"

"Rouland told me Cece's estate is cordoned off by the authorities, until their investigation is complete. Her place belongs to the *comte* and will revert to him."

"Why would Cece want to hurt my father?"

"Aunt Cece has not been stable since Uncle Jules was killed. My father blamed himself for sending him away, and he felt obligated to help her. She and *Grand-Maman* were obsessed with family heritage and tradition. They hated each other which made family get-togethers a trial. I guess the changes unhinged what little was left of her sanity. Rafe acknowledging Roux and Minneau probably took her over the edge."

Abby looked for any sign Vanna might blame her for the changes. She and her cousin had become friends, working together in The Project.

The DuMond family conflicts came to a critical point when she arrived on Mast Island to find her father alive. Violence ensued, and *Grand-Maman* died as a result.

Noah's life was jeopardized and his beautiful boat destroyed. Abby held herself responsible.

Now Cece was dead. The woman might have succeeded in killing her father. *What happened last night?*

Vanna caught Abby's expression and said. "Our family is closer knit because you came and spoke accountability. My father agonized over family decisions ... family secrets. We hid our dysfunction behind walls, afraid people would find out. For the first time in years, my father seems more relaxed, even with the prospect of a trial hanging over our heads."

She walked to Abby and clasped her arms, her eyes pleading reason. "And look at the change in your father. Uncle Henri's … Rafe's life has been transformed. He has a daughter, Bella's daughter, someone to live for, to make him proud.

"The changes taking place on Mast Island are beneficial to everyone, especially the DuMonds. Our legacy will be one of using resources to make lives better. We owe you."

Abby bowed her head at this, but she had a hard time believing Vanna's words. Her cousin was young, her youthful idealism piqued, not yet jaded. What about the others in the family? Sologne was destroyed. The portraits, the history, the valuable contents which could never be replaced. Her father's loss pounded in her head. *Bella … gone. Will he recover, or will I lose him again if he retreats into the past?*

"I'll stay at the hotel, until we finish work in The Project," Abby said. "I'll only be using the room to sleep anyway." She limped to the sliding doors overlooking the ocean. Swells rolled along the shore in harmonious sameness, their constancy easing tension in her shoulders. "We need to come up with a better name for the community. Maybe the islanders can choose a name."

Vanna held up her finger for emphasis. "*That* is a great idea. We can put up a sign to make the name official."

They discussed possible names the islanders might choose.

The three men arrived and downsized the room to uncomfortable. They each wore mismatched ensembles, obviously donated. Their unshaven faces and slumped shoulders spoke defeat, sorrow.

"I stopped by your room, and no one opened the door, so I came here," Rafe said to his daughter.

Abby was shaken by his appearance. His color was ashen, his hair falling about his face, sooty and in disarray. Red, gritty eyes looked grim over pouches formed by no sleep. They stared at one another, until Rafe held out his arms, and she walked into them. He drew her to his chest.

Jean-Jacques broke the silence. "We are in need of a shower and rest. I know you are anxious and want answers, but I must get back to my room and Collette. We will talk later."

"You are safe," Rafe said. "You are safe." What sounded like a sob escaped.

Vanna approached them. "I will bring the clothes to your room when they arrive," she told Abby. "We will all get together tomorrow morning for breakfast. Let us say nine o'clock in The Solarium where we can expect privacy. I will make the arrangements. How does that sound?"

They all nodded, glad someone took charge.

Abby went with her father to his room, two doors down from hers. "You need new clothing. If you give me your sizes, I'll see your clothes and shoes are delivered to your room. Have you eaten anything?" She would enlist Gloria's help and not bother Vanna.

He smiled, thanked her, and wrote sizes on the hotel notepad. "Do not worry about me, little one."

"Do you want me to stay with you?" His "little one" threatened a teary departure.

"I will be all right. I just need rest." He handed her a room key.

She took his key to her room and called Room Service first. Maybe they would get to the room before he fell asleep.

A knock sounded on the door.

"Who is it?'

"Daisy, from Daisy's Aromatherapy Emporium. I brought you something."

Abby opened the door, and Daisy held out a bag. "I remembered you liked the lemon scent, so I brought you a few items. I hope they help." Her expression displayed compassion. "Everyone is sorry for your loss. We're praying for you. Please let anyone on the island know if you need anything."

"Thank you, Daisy. We appreciate your thoughtfulness and covet your prayers."

Daisy backed away from the door and gave a nervous little wave.

A few minutes later Gloria arrived with two bags. "One of these is for your father. Betsy's Gift Shop downstairs sent you some useful items from their notions section." Inside her bag were a small hairbrush, tooth brush and tooth paste, disposable razors, and deodorant.

"Thank you, Gloria. We'll take the other bag to my father's room. Hopefully, his meal has arrived." She checked the bedside clock. Twenty-five minutes had passed.

"I'm ordering him some clothing. Will you see that it is delivered to me? I don't want to disturb his sleep." She picked up the keys, and they walked down the hall.

She knocked softly and used the key to enter. Her father sat at the desk, eating a late breakfast. He stood awkwardly when they entered, and she handed him the bag of necessities. "This is Gloria. She will make arrangements for deliveries and anything you need. Just ask the front desk for her."

"Do you want anything else, sir?" Gloria asked.

He looked at her somewhat sheepishly as he sat. "I will need a cane. Maybe the drug store will have an adjustable one. You can charge it to my account."

"Yes sir, I'll get right on it."

Abby hadn't thought about that. "Please bring it to my room, Gloria, and thank you for your help." *Where is Tasse?*

When Gloria left, Rafe said, "I am going to need some prescriptions refilled. Will you contact my doctor and get the medicine delivered?"

"No problem. Do you get refills here?"

"Yes. I'll have the doctor call them in, and you can pick them up."

Abby wrote down the name of the pharmacist. "Do you need the doctor to come here?"

Rafe looked at her, his eyes searching her own. "I am all right, Abby. My mental state is fine. The medicine is for high blood pressure and cholesterol. No, he does not need to come. I had a physical before Christmas."

"Okay. I'll wait until all of the orders arrive and bring them to your room. I'll try not to wake you up."

"Thank you, Abby. Please do not worry. We will have everything worked out in the next few days."

A thought came to Abby. The man who took care of her father was absent. "Where is Tasse?"

Her father shook his head sorrowfully. "He is in custody, being questioned by the authorities. Please let it go for now. We will speak of Tasse in the morning. I really must lie down."

Abby kissed his forehead. "I'll see you then." *Did Tasse start the fire? And where were Roux and Minneau?*

CHAPTER THIRTY-NINE

Abby came downstairs half an hour early. The closed Solarium door had a sign, PRIVATE In use until 2:00. She looked inside, but no one was present, so she walked by the Tiki Hut.

Una greeted her. "Gloria's not in yet. Are you okay? What can I get you? I'm sorry about everything."

Abby nodded. "Thank you, Una. Nothing for now. I have a breakfast meeting. I just need to walk." She headed toward the beach.

"I can sure understand that. Did you know Mast Island made national news?"

Abby turned back at the words. She hadn't given publicity a thought.

"Reporters are swarming the place," Una continued. "Some arrived last night on boats. Most are staying at the Silver Dunes. The fire is big news. The newspapers will carry the story for days."

Noah. He might have heard about the fire. Abby couldn't believe she had not thought about Noah. She turned around and raced inside. He must be told what happened.

When she reached her room, she tried to think of his parents' phone number. *Think. You know the number.* A minute passed. She began punching the area code, and the number came back to her.

Jane Hazzard answered the phone, her voice anxious. "Abby, we've been so worried. We didn't know how to get hold of you. The news said someone died in the fire, but the name was withheld." She continued, her voice shaken. "Noah is frantic. He tried the police station when he couldn't get hold of Kent, but they weren't releasing any information."

"I'm sorry. Everything has been hectic around here. I called to let you know I'm all right. My Aunt Cece is the one who died. I'll have to give you details later. Is Noah there?"

"No, he has rehab in the mornings. He'll want to call you as soon as he returns. Do you have a number where you can be reached?"

Abby gave Jane the hotel room's phone number, and told her she would be in a family meeting until later.

After the meeting, she would try to find the phone numbers for Olga and Mina. Maybe the front desk would use their computers to help.

Abby met Collette at The Solarium's entrance. Collette's face and eyes were puffy from crying. She slid the emerald ring back and forth on her finger, a nervous gesture. "What will we do now?" she asked Abby.

"Whatever needs to be done. We have to be strong for the men, Collette. They need our support more than ever."

She snuffled and stood a little straighter with a refortifying intake of breath. "You're right. Our men have lost the most. We must be strong."

Abby followed her inside.

Two tables had been brought together, and another table had a buffet breakfast. Jean-Jacques, her father, Rouland and Vanna were eating. Roux and Minneau came five minutes later. All of them were outfitted in new casual attire.

Rafe waited until the coffee was poured, and the waiter left the room before standing and giving his account. He spoke of Cece's destruction, her intent to kill him, the fire, and her death. "I do not know if Cece's intention was to burn Sologne, but she did not bring a flashlight. I have been thinking the candle had a purpose. We will never know.

"Tasse is being held for questioning by the authorities. If not for his years of loyalty to me, well, the outcome might have been different. He mourns his sister's death, and I will stand by him and testify on his behalf."

When Rafe finished, all faced him, their shock and varying degrees of horror obvious. Roux and Minneau were the most affected. Roux's cheeks were wet with tears, and Minneau bowed his head, eyes closed, his mouth tight.

Are they worried their status might change because their step-mother was responsible?

Jean-Jacques cleared his throat as Rafe sat, visibly shaken. "Reporters will be here, wanting answers." He looked at every family member. "Refer any questions to Rafe or to myself. 'No comment' is an appropriate response. We can only hope they will not stay long.

"The insurance adjustors should be here today or tomorrow to assess the damage. We are sure Sologne will be listed as a total loss.

"James Toomey will bring more paperwork to sign. Rafe and I will meet our financial advisors in Savannah the day after tomorrow. Our credit is good. We should not have problems in that department."

Everyone sat at their place in silence, knowing the next few days would not be easy.

"Miss DuMond," the desk clerk called as he hurried toward Abby in the lobby. "Miss DuMond," he repeated.

Abby turned, not used to being addressed by the DuMond name. She guessed everyone on the island knew her story by now and about her connection to Rafe, the *comte*, who had returned from the dead. She was sure the DuMond family would be a main topic of conversation on the island well into the future.

She looked around to make sure no reporters were hovering about. "Yes."

The clerk appeared uncomfortable when he caught up to her. "You have a phone call."

Abby looked toward the desk.

"I mean a man called, looking for you, the old you." He colored and shook his head, saying in a deliberate manner, "That's not what I mean. He wanted to know if Abby Parsons was staying here, not Abby DuMond. He said he was an attorney." His words were rushed now, his discomfort noticeable. "We don't give out information about guests. I would never tell anyone, anything about you."

Abby guessed reporters were asking questions, too.

"He left his name and number. He wants you to call him."

What attorney? Abby wondered if lawyers would now be calling, attempting to make her a client. *Maybe it's Mr. Culpepper.* The clerk gestured toward the desk, and she followed him.

He handed her a slip of paper, on which was written, *Mr. Jason Muldoon, Baltimore* and the phone number. *Baltimore? Mina Kresge lives in Baltimore.*

Abby thanked him and rushed to her room to make the call. *Is Mina all right?*

The receptionist put her call through to the attorney.

Mr. Muldoon answered. "Miss Parsons, I'm so glad you called. Ms. Kresge gave me your information, but you haven't been easy to find."

"Is Mina okay," Abby asked anxiously.

"Ms. Kresge passed away on Thursday. She had heart failure. Hospice was called in by her physician, and their loving service kept her comfortable until the end." He let her absorb the information for a few seconds.

"She called me several weeks ago and asked for my help. I have been her attorney for almost thirty years, and I have enjoyed the association. She was eccentric, but she had my utmost respect, a true original, one I greatly admired." His voice conveyed his respect.

"Thank you, Mr. Muldoon. I appreciate your effort to let me know."

Mina was gone from her life before she had an opportunity to explore a meaningful relationship. Abby was glad she took the time to see her.

"Ms. Kresge revealed some of her past to me. She wanted to make amends for her part in the deception which took away your true identity. I have an affidavit concerning fictional information she and your grandmother cooked up to throw murderers off your trail." I must say I found her tale intriguing."

Mr. Muldoon cleared his throat before continuing. "Over the years, she has spoken of you with love. She thought of you as a daughter she never had. Her story took me by surprise.

"I am the executor of her Last Will and Testament. She left the bulk of her estate to you."

Abby was shocked. "Didn't she have other family?"

"I am not aware of any other relationships. In a previous will, she left her estate to your grandmother. After Evelyn Desmond's death, Ms. Kresge updated her will to make you her beneficiary."

"I'm having a hard time believing this, Mr. Muldoon." Indeed, Abby had no idea Mina lead a reclusive life without other relationships. She must have lead a lonely existence.

"I quite understand," the attorney said. "Ms. Kresge's estate is not a large one. She owned the house, its contents, and a ten thousand dollar insurance policy. Her house and grounds are a valuable asset. You should have no trouble if you want to sell the real estate.

"She left her bonds, savings, and checking account monies to a Catholic charity. After notifying the IRS, Social Security, and going through the probate process, the funds will be distributed. I'm guessing there will be a few medical bills her medical insurance did not cover.

"Will you be able to come to Baltimore in the near future? I have papers which need your signature and a house that requires your attention."

"Yes," Abby said. "I'll make the arrangements." She remembered going through her gran's apartment after her death. This would be different. She would be sifting through a stranger's possessions.

CHAPTER FORTY

Abby had been saddened when she learned of the Bohemian artist's death. She was glad she had taken the time to visit Mina that one last time to update the older woman about finding her family. Now, she needed to speak with her father about leaving.

Abby found Rafe in the trailer, which served as an office at the construction site. She told him the situation, and he agreed she needed to schedule an appointment with Mr. Muldoon.

A knock sounded on the door, and Tasse entered.

Tasse lowered his head, avoiding Abby's eyes.

"Have a seat," Rafe told him, and he did as requested.

"I have told Tasse I will help him find a job. He has been my right-hand man for over a quarter century, and I value his loyalty."

Abby nodded. She had mixed feelings about Tasse. He was Cece's eyes and ears at Sologne, but when a hard choice required a response, he had chosen to help her father, not his sister.

"Tasse has some physical therapy training. I am thinking Dr. Noble will have patients who need rehab. Until that time, Tasse, you can help me with the paperwork here at the construction site."

"Yes sir. I can begin work any time you need me."

The family had briefly discussed the desirability of having a doctor on the island. They wanted to start a small clinic. Dr. Noble had been part of a medical group in Savannah, and several local islanders were his patients. He was now retired and visited the island frequently to fish. Jean-Jacques, a friend of James Noble, set aside a room at the Silver Sands for him. They had discussed the possibility of his help, and Dr. Noble liked the idea.

Abby stood and held her hand out to Tasse. "My father believes you will be an asset, and I trust his judgement."

Tasse looked at her hand first and then her face for the first time. He stood and took her hand. Their eyes met, and Abby felt like a covenant of sorts was made.

"Well," she said, "I need to make arrangements to see Mr. Muldoon."

She left the office thinking her father had a forgiving nature. The things she was learning about him, made her proud to be his daughter.

———※———

Abby paced her hotel room. Two weeks had passed since the family meeting in The Solarium. She would see Sologne today for the first time since the fire. She waited until authorities and reporters left the island.

The pencil sketch of Sologne from memory was propped against the desk. The image did not have the perfect lines of symmetry, but enough of the fountain and building were present to bring back her first sight of the estate.

Her car and art supplies were still in a Savannah garage. Would she be allowed to bring the vehicle here?

"Enough," she said to the drawing and the room. "Stop procrastinating. Just get your bag and go."

Abby walked to the back of the resort and chose a bicycle.

She pedaled to Sologne, stopping at the open gate. The elegant arched stone entrance and wrought iron fence were untouched by the fire. She leaned the bike against the empty gatehouse and walked slowly down the drive toward the ravaged remains.

Daphne Du Maurier's famous first line of the novel, *Rebecca*, streamed through her mind. "Last night I dreamt I went to Manderley." The haunting passage to begin a story of death, obsession, and love now gave her a feeling of *déjà vu*. Her gran had given her the book for her sixteenth birthday, and she remembered at the end, hugging the treasure to her chest. A good book was shelved to read again and again. She envied the person reading the story for the first time.

Abby rounded the curve, and the fountain came into view. The tail of one dolphin had been sheared off by something heavy. One side caved inward and allowed the water to drain. The stone-tiled courtyard was intact with smears of black streaked across its surface. Around the pool, the boxwood was singed and brown.

The stark remains of Sologne were outlined against a cerulean backdrop. The Roman-arched stone entrance still stood, along with a few remaining outer walls of varying heights. Most of the debris had been removed and the area swept of loose brick, stone, and glass that might injure a tourist.

Even now, half a dozen people milled around, looking up at the chimneys, and a couple sat on the discolored marble stairs that curved skyward. Jean-Jacques said an iron fence would be placed around the steps to keep people from climbing them. A burnt smell still clung to the ruins.

Her heart ached at the destruction of the historically significant estate. Generations of DuMonds had lived and died here. Would the family blame her for their loss? *How can they not?*

Abby hoped Vanna was right, and the DuMonds would be remembered kindly in the future.

―――――※―――――

The phone rang in the hotel room, and Abby picked up the receiver. "Hello, stranger."

Noah had finally called after two weeks. She held her hand over the mouthpiece, so he wouldn't hear the sound of relief that almost slipped out.

"Hello, yourself," Abby answered, her voice clipped. An uneasy silence followed.

"Are we miffed about something? Your answer sounded a little short."

Abby thought about her reply. She didn't want him to know how much she missed hearing from him. "Actually, I'm feeling sad. I went to Sologne for the first time this morning and saw the devastation left by the fire. A skeleton of chimneys, a few walls, and the marble steps are all that's left. Well, that and piles of sooty stones."

"I can't imagine," Noah said. "I went through hell, until you called to let me know that Cece was the person who died. Now I understand what you felt when I was missing."

No, you don't understand. You didn't have to think I died for several days. It's not the same. Abby left the words unsaid.

"Give me an update on what's happened since the fire."

"Papa and I are still living in hotel rooms. It's not bad. We only use the rooms to sleep. He and I spend our days at the building sites. My father's planning an addition to the Silver Dunes for us."

"Are you going to live on the island?"

Noah sounded surprised, and Abby realized the thought of staying hadn't gelled in her mind. She felt a part of the island now. She belonged here. What had changed? She knew she wouldn't have been comfortable living on the estate. Yet, she looked forward to each new day. Seeing her father physically work and become part of the community made the difference.

"I'm thinking about it."

Noah's response was "Hummm."

"Rouland and Vanna are living on the Boucher estate in Savannah. His mother is still living. She'd been thinking about down-sizing, so she's happy the house will be a home again to family. She's also excited about her first grandchild. They're going to have a boy, and they've chosen the name Andre Devaux Boucher. His mother's maiden name was Devaux."

"With your work in the community and the aftermath of the fire, have you had time to paint?" Noah asked.

"No, I haven't had time. There's still so much to do. Vanna comes several days a week to work with me in The Project. You'll be amazed to see the changes." *You're assuming Noah will return to the island. Maybe he won't want to come back.* Abby sucked in her lips and continued.

"Rouland is going back into law full-time, with the firm his father established years ago. I gather he worked on cases part time while he was at Sologne."

"Does Jean-Jacques still live on the island?" Noah asked.

"Yes, he and Collette have moved into Cece's place. Collette wants to remodel the estate she calls *Belle Vue*. Her mother came to help, and they've enjoyed planning structural changes while Harvey Olsen,

The Project's contractor, is here. Collette has a knack for interior design and choosing new furnishings. Jean-Jacques said he thinks she's missed her calling."

Abby didn't know if Noah had heard the news about what was found in Cece's house. "Cece had the 'bugs' planted. Authorities found a hidden room full of old radio operating equipment that Jules must have used. They found a computer with names and receipts from their illegal activities, and the FBI is tracking that information. They also found tapes of conversations at Sologne, going back several years. They're checking them now."

Noah told her he had been informed by Kent Helms. "Another case is being put together by the Savannah Police Department. Because the main culprit is dead, there may not be a trial. Tasse is being investigated, but authorities are going with unpremeditated manslaughter in self-defense because Rafe's testimony has been taken into account. Tasse probably won't be charged."

Abby thought about Tasse and his part in Cece's death. He had made a choice and saved her father. Rafe told the family, he wouldn't abandon Tasse, and he would try to find him another job if he wanted to stay on the island. He was fulfilling his promise.

"I understand Tasse's feelings over his part in his sister's death."

"He did save lives during the fire," she said, "but knowing he spied for Cece makes me angry. I'm trying to forgive and forget, but it isn't easy. If I let it, his perfidy will eat me up inside."

Noah was silent as if weighing a response. "I've struggled with similar issues, so I can empathize.

"What else is happening?" he asked, changing the subject.

"Gina now works for Collette, and she said she will care for Cece's dog. Collette wants nothing to do with 'the beast.' She and Minneau plan to marry when he finishes his community college courses. He and Roux will live at *Belle Vue* until they build their homes."

Abby updated him about Mr. Muldoon's call and Mina's death. "Mina and my grandmother were extraordinary women. I loved my gran, and I'm so glad for the opportunity I had to meet Mina. They both loved me."

Noah had let Abby talk with only a few interruptions. *What is he thinking?*

"I know you are going through a number of changes now. I'm sorry about Mina. I remember when you spoke of her before, and she sounded like an interesting character. I would have enjoyed meeting her."

Noah continued to ask questions. "I know Minneau said he wants to help with research at the institute. Tell me about Roux. What does he want to do?"

"Roux talked about going to a culinary school, but he's decided to become an elementary teacher and coach. The children love him, and he has a rapport with them." Abby knew he would be a good role model and an unforgettable teacher.

"I'm glad things are working out. I've missed your cards."

"I've missed your calls. I guess you're busy with *The Lady II*."

"Yes. My dad's friends, who work at the boat yard, are phenomenal. They've received most of the materials ordered. Physical work on the boat began two weeks ago. I've been filming their progress to make a time lapse film showing her being built. I go to the yard in the afternoons.

"Does insurance cover your costs?"

Noah told her his insurance company's protection of its legal interest allowed a subrogation action to sue for hospital and medical expenses, replacing *The Lady*, and future court costs.

"Your family didn't challenge the charges." His voice dropped into a lower register. "I've decided not to press for punitive damages."

Abby bowed her head. *Thank you, Lord.* She felt as if a great weight had been lifted. "I don't know what to say. You're a good man, a better man than most." In her heart, she knew he didn't go for the jugular because of her. "Thank you, Noah."

"Don't try to read more into it, sweet cakes. I'm basically a decent fellow."

"I know." *He's distancing himself again. His warning is subtle.* She searched for words to stop her train of thought. "Tell me how you're doing physically."

I still have rehab several mornings a week and I walk every day."

"How's that going?"

"I walk with a cane now, but I've been told if I build up my leg muscles, the stick will be temporary. So, I'm dedicated in the weight room and getting stronger. Healing is a slow process.

"Plastic surgeons have done their best to repair my ugly mug. I don't expect children to run screaming when they see me in public. My parents call my recovery a miracle. I'm blessed."

"Yes, you are. We're both blessed. I've known the love of my gran and her friend Mina, and I've found my family … and a purpose. That's more than many have."

"You're right. One day, I hope to return to the island and see for myself the changes you've described. Take care, sweet cakes."

Abby held the phone to her chest long after he cut short the call. *One day. Maybe. Time changes more things than just the physical. You have to get over him.* The thought hurt.

CHAPTER FORTY-ONE

Abby sat at the desk in her room and wrote her aunt, Olga Pierelli. She updated her on The Project, Noah's recovery, and Mina's death. Her thoughts briefly turned to her Baltimore trip several days before. Mr. Muldoon had been affable, and his handling of Mina's estate, efficient. After signing paperwork, he handed Abby the keys to the house.

She had walked through Mina's life as she leafed through pages of albums stuffed with personal photos, revue programs, playbills, and newspaper clippings of reviews for the *Nonpareil Dance Company*. When she saw pictures of her mother on some of the covers, and her younger gran's photo in a group picture, her eyes welled, and she set the albums in front of the door to take home for closer inspection. *Home.* "I have a home," she said aloud to break the smothering silence. "I have a home." Her voice cracked the second time she spoke.

Although bright with color and Mina's creative touches, the place no longer exuded life. Staleness pervaded the house with its mistress gone, making Abby cut short her stay.

She would have to return at another time to make arrangements for the sale of the house and part of its contents. Many of the items might be used by islanders. Mina's artwork would add more color to community homes. This thought pleased her. Mina would like her decision.

Abby returned to the letter before her.

I'm so sorry the genealogical record you gave me burned in the fire. I found the information interesting, especially the notes in the margins. Would it be possible to get another copy? Words cannot express how much family roots mean to me. Finding family has been a defining moment in my life. With the exception of the emerald ring, my mother's other jewelry left to me, in the box from Mina, was lost. My father and I would also like copies of some of the photos of my mother and your family. Everything was burned in the fire. My father lost the portraits he painted of Bella. Although he tries not to dwell on the past, I know the loss hurt. It's impossible to replace the sentimental treasures and reminders of one's early memories. I'm sorry for the inconvenience, but anything you share will be cherished.

She thought about the DuMond portraits and their destruction. Vanna had told her she took photographs of the portraits before she married, and they, along with copies of genealogical records, were in an album at the Boucher estate. Although not the originals, Abby was glad a remnant of Vanna's past survived. One day, she'd take time to review them.

The institute and lodge are beginning to take shape. I would love for you to visit Mast Island and see the work we are doing. You can stay in the Silver Dunes, where we have taken up residence for the time being. I can give you the Grand Tour.

When Abby ended the letter, she had written five full pages on resort stationery. She was glad her aunt wanted to stay in touch, and she looked forward to the time Olga and Rafe would meet.

The dreaded subpoenas finally arrived.

Abby's chest seized with foreboding when her father called them together to share the news.

They made plans to stay on the mainland while conferring with their attorneys. The impending case was not discussed with Abby. She and Eddie met with a separate attorney. The DuMonds were on the opposing side.

Abby's eyes welled when her father said, "We understand your position, Abby. You have every right to prosecute, and whatever happens, you are still family, still my daughter."

The days which followed stretched emotions to the max. The time passed interminably slow, and somber faces did not improve the mood. Thoughts of prison haunted their days and nights.

Jean-Jacques, Collette, Minneau, and Roux stayed on the Boucher estate.

Abby, her father, and Tasse used the DuMond house on the river. Eddie stayed with friends in Savannah.

The DuMonds met with their defense attorneys, reviewing their testimonies about what happened the night of the explosion, the fatal meeting at the sawmill, and the events of the fire at Sologne.

To save the court time and money, several related cases were brought before the judge for review over a two day period.

Noah, Eddie, and Abby's attorney was a county prosecutor. He had Noah's sworn and signed deposition. Abby and Eddie's accounts were on record along with the testimonies of Detective Sergeant Abel Norris, and Special Agents Mackey and Helms.

Noah, Abby, and Eddie's attorney asked if they would agree to dropping some charges in favor of a plea deal to expedite an otherwise lengthy trial. She and Noah agreed. Eddie balked at first because of his granddaughter's kidnapping and his near death experience. The prosecutor's assistant pointed out that Eddie's position was precarious. Finding out a trial might involve him in the conspiracy, he agreed to the plea deal.

Abby told Eddie a lifetime in prison would not be easy on Marcel, and he agreed.

When the doors to the courtroom closed, the noise abated.

Abby looked around the room

Marcel, Mark, and Paul were brought in dressed in prison jumpsuits. Marcel hobbled on crutches. His eyes connected with Abby's, and she stared down the malevolence she saw in his visage. He was the first to look away. Their attorney was provided by the state as the DuMonds refused to pay for their defense.

The DuMonds sat next to their attorneys, looking stoic and resigned, their eyes on the presiding judge.

Collette and Vanna sat behind them, whispering and dabbing their eyes with tissues.

Tasse sat near but not next to Vanna, his head down, his expression hidden. Rafe had testified Cece's death was accidental. Tasse defended him from death by Cece's hand and helped him escape the fire. The unpremeditated manslaughter charge was dropped and changed to self-defense. Rafe forgave his part in Cece's conspiracy. He provided crucial information, which led to his sister's hidden store of evidence.

Eddie took a seat in the far corner of the room. He mopped his face and looked uncomfortable. He had told Abby he didn't want to be called as a witness.

The attorneys were asked to approach the bench for a consultation.

Abby knew they discussed the plea deal. In Marcel's case, he would get life without parole instead of the death penalty, which had been reinstituted in Georgia in 1973.

Marcel had been a munitions and explosives expert in the Army, so he knew how to use C-4. He was also an undersea salvage diver. Ammonium nitrate and other explosive materials were found in Cece's hidden room along with checks endorsed by Marcel and Mark. Authorities had the evidence and testimonies to send Marcel to death row.

At the sentencing hearing, they each pled guilty.

Mark's sentence was reduced to ten years for involuntary manslaughter involving Noah's Uncle Max and for not reporting the incident. He received an additional five years for displaying a gun during the confrontation in the sawmill. Mark provided information and testified about Cece's operation and Marcel's intent to kill both Abby and Noah.

Paul received ten months in jail, of which he had served six, community service hours, and a year of probation. He knew little about the criminal activity and acted as a liaison between the parties, but he did not participate in the actual crimes.

The two men, whose bodies were found in the family crypt, had been killed approximately twenty-five years before. No evidence was found to connect the murders to Rafe or Jean-Jacques.

Eddie and Abby's written accounts included *Grand-Maman's* revelations at the sawmill. Their testimonies and the corroboration of

Mark under separate questioning of that night pointed to Jules as the probable culprit. Those murders took place before Marcel, Mark, and Paul were hired by Cece, and their testimonies amounted to hearsay.

Tapes of conversations recorded at Solonge and found at Cece's, exonerated Rafe and Jean-Jacques of being part of *Grand-Maman's* scheme. As much as Abby hated being "bugged," the tapes from Sologne were gold for the DuMonds in the hearing.

Jean-Jacques's and Minneau's destruction of the guns and dumping them in the ocean almost two decades before had passed the statute of limitations. Jules's subsequent death in Yeman, and Cece's death at Sologne closed that case.

Although the DuMond family's deception regarding Rafe's identity had also passed the statute of limitations, the judge ruled the Savannah Police Department had used valuable time and man hours to find Rafe. Expenses needed to be repaid. Jean-Jacques was held accountable and fined fifty thousand dollars, which would go into the state's restitution fund. Community service hours were determined, and because of mitigating circumstances, the time could be served working on the upgrades at Mast Island.

Tears of thankfulness were shed as the family filed from the courtroom to hug each other in the hallway and thank their attorneys.

They made plans to meet at The Willows, an exclusive restaurant in uptown Savannah, to celebrate.

Abby was grateful that justice had prevailed, and she looked forward to going home to Mast Island.

CHAPTER FORTY-TWO

Abby watched Noah from the path behind the ruins of Château Sologne. His body was outlined by the setting sun. His hair had grown and looked like a flame halo.

Leaning on a walking stick, he scanned the salt marsh. She shivered at the memory of his pain.

Eleven months had passed since she last saw him in the hospital. Abby walked forward until she stood before him, taking in his appearance. Doctors had performed miracles. His face still had visible scars, but time would only leave fine lines. The damaged eye was a bit larger but not noticeable unless you were looking for change.

His blue-green eyes searched her own, tracking her perusal of his features.

Abby wanted to hug him, but she didn't want Noah to feel obligated to a one-sided romantic crush. She had spent many hours deliberating on this first meeting. "How long have you been on the island?"

"Your father invited me to come. He and your uncle are talking about putting the north end of the island into a conservation easement or land management to prevent further development. They wanted to know my thoughts."

"Yes. They're both excited about the prospect."

"What about you and Vanna? How do you feel about these plans?"

Abby took pleasure in the knowledge he cared what they thought. "We're in agreement if some of the higher areas are left for islanders coming back to the island to build and live. We have plans for the island, plans for opportunities that will put locals to work. We want a library one day and a pre-school, as soon as, we can find an intern with the school system.

"We use an empty storefront is Loire Park as a temporary health clinic. A retired medical doctor helps there several days a week, and a nurse fills in when he's not available. We hope others will get certificates or degrees and return to the island and work."

Noah saw how Abby's hands moved expressively, and her eyes lit with passion for the changes. He wanted to imbibe her animation and energy, the life force motivating her. *Why do I feel she is distancing herself from me?* "Your father met me at the dock yesterday and took me to the construction site. Very impressive. He wanted my help, and I told him I could be bought for the right price."

"What?" Abby couldn't believe her ears. She turned away from him, glad she hadn't rushed into his arms like the silly girl he must think her.

"I have a room at the Silver Dunes," he continued. "Everyone there gave me a rousing welcome, happy I'm alive." His tone changed, lower, more personal. "Are you glad to see me, Abby?"

When Abby nodded and turned back, his eyes searched her own for an answer. She moved beside him at the rail and looked out at the marsh she had begun to love. Abby tried to see the past differently. She had dreamed of a different meeting with a happy ending. She reasoned they shared a traumatic experience which threw them together, obviously awkward for him. Her face flamed. She made more of what happened than he was prepared to accept.

Noah had arrived yesterday, and her father only mentioned the fact an hour ago. He told her she would find Noah at the ruins, and she had rushed to meet him. Had her father taken matters into his own hands and "bought" him to make her happy? *How humiliating!*

"Aren't you going to ask me the price?"

Abby shrugged her shoulders. "What difference does it make? I'm sure you'll be worth every penny." She swallowed the pain.

"How are your parents, and how far along are you on *The Lady II?*" Abby tried to be upbeat because she wanted to know, and because she felt a change of subject was warranted before she fell to pieces.

Noah was not distracted. "Your father was amenable. I didn't ask for money."

"No? Then what?" she answered more than a little annoyed.

"I told him I wanted to continue to see you, get to know you."

"That's it?" she said, looking at his amused face, wanting to wipe off the smile.

Noah laughed. "You are one prickly pear, sweet cakes, but worth the trouble."

Abby leaned in, tracing the zee scar on his cheek. "Dashing. You look better than ever."

He folded her in his arms and then crushed her to his chest, a bear of a man, his head tucked into her neck.

She closed her eyes and enjoyed the sound and feel of his breath in her ear and on her neck. *Noah's alive and breathing. He wants to get to know me. Thank you, God. Thank you for everything.*

Noah stepped back. "I've enjoyed your cards and especially the calls. They gave me hope you cared for me a little."

"That's what you thought?" She blinked back the tears which threatened.

Noah lifted her chin. "What are you trying to tell me?"

"I wanted you to know I thought about you a lot, and I cared more than a little. You're alive after I believed you dead, mourned your loss. You must know how much your life means to me."

"I know you feel responsible," he stated. "You aren't."

She nodded. "So I've been told."

"I knew what was happening, and the signs were there before you arrived on Mast Island.

"I really need to know if you care more about my being alive or if you can care for a slightly damaged scientist. Doctors assure me I can do everything I did before except get through airport security without scrutiny."

Abby rubbed her hand across his stubbly cheek where burn patches existed. She looked into his eyes. "I care for you as a man I would like to know better ... a man who captured my heart on the deck of *The Lady* with a poem and kissed me senseless under a mighty oak."

Noah's face lit with a wicked, piratical grin, his eyes dancing a tango with her own. "My lady wants passionate kisses and can be seduced by poetry. What a find!"

Abby blushed and laid her head on his chest listening to his rapid heartbeat. Yes, her feelings for Noah ran deep, though they had only known one another a short time. She wanted to explore all the facets of the man, and she ached for his kisses.

Noah's hands sifted through her hair, holding her in place. He reviewed his growing feelings for this woman while on the island and in the fantasies he tried to stifle while recuperating.

"The *Lady II* will be ready for her maiden voyage in June or July of next year. Will that give you enough time to get to know the man?" He kissed the top of her head. "She has room for a helpmate on board if you decide to take on another title. I've spoken with your father, and he's given his blessing."

Abby raised her head and smiled. "More than enough …"

Noah captured her lips and the word, *time*, leaving Abby weak in the knees. She imagined a future bright with the promise of adventure.

EPILOGUE

Noah threw his flippers, net, and tickle stick over the side of *The Lady II*.

Abby surfaced with the lobster she caught.

"You did it," he said, taking the crustacean from her gloved hand. He reached up and released the flipping "bug" onto the deck.

Abby took the regulator out of her mouth and grinned. She had tickled the lobster out from under a coral head and caught her first one before they surfaced.

Noah climbed the ladder and dropped his tank before he reached down to help Abby, who had removed her gear and handed it up to him. Noah caught her hand and helped her over the side. "Well, Mrs. Hazzard, today you proved your worth."

"For that, you can cook tonight."

"My pleasure, sweet cakes. I'm all yours." He winked and gave her a heart-stopping, roguish grin.

She wrung out her hair and watched as Noah effortlessly pulled in the buoy, dive flag, and rope with the bag of lobsters on board. She appreciated the efficient way his body moved while completing physical tasks. Rehab had toned his muscles, and the sun had lightened his hair, tanned his skin, and given him a healthier look. He donned his shirt and hat after reapplying sunscreen.

Noah emptied the bag on deck and measured each lobster's carapace. He recounted as he placed the catch in the live well before sorting out the gear.

They had married in the island church a month ago, and Abby marveled at her new life two years after coming to Mast Island. Surrounded by the clear waters of the Caribbean and the tropical islands with white sand beaches, every day brought another discovery, a new adventure.

The coral reefs below teemed with fish and flashed vibrant color as the sun's rays reached them. Abby visualized paintings of undersea landscapes.

She had not taken up Mr. Mobley's generous offer to sell exclusively in his galleries because she received a better deal. Her father wanted to hang her works in the resorts, and maybe add a studio in a year or two where she could mentor visiting artists. Her studio was now the great outdoors.

Abby's father sometimes joined her to paint. Rafe's skin had tanned from working outside. He enjoyed the physical activity, and his health improved. Rafe rarely used the cane now, and he never brought up the past. He had built a suite addition onto the Silver Dunes, where he could be independent with all of the amenities. His accommodations were closer to the institute and the dock where he kept his new fishing boat. Rafe and Jean-Jacques enjoyed fishing and eating their catch, which the hotel kitchen prepared.

The addition had a separate suite for Abby, with a sitting room, kitchen, and patio by the pool. She enjoyed cooking some of their meals, and her father was appreciative of her efforts. To her amazement, Rafe and Jean-Jacques took to the casual life like they had been born to it.

"We need to go ashore and rinse the equipment," Noah said, interrupting her thought.

"Okay. I'll look for a market to get some fresh fruit and supplies." Abby loved exploring the islands, meeting the locals, and taking pleasure in the laid-back culture. Noah seemed to know someone in every port, and she enjoyed listening to their stories.

She slathered on more sunscreen and wrapped a sarong around her hips. Her hair took on gold highlights from the sun, and she combed the strands with her fingers and left it loose to dry naturally. The offensive freckles she was prone to get outdoors had become an asset. Noah kissed them and with reverence had proclaimed they were his personal garden of "beauty marks."

Abby loved Noah's attention to detail. She mused about

scientists and artists, professions which required a devotion to that particular characteristic. Aesthetic beauty was one thing, but who knew a scientist could bestow pleasure in the detail? *Noah's definitely a keeper. Thank, you, Lord.*

She was also grateful he resigned his role as a support professional for the FBI. Noah's work at the institute left little time to take on new cases.

Kent Helms and Jenna Mackey had visited a couple of times. Abby forgave them for allowing her to believe Noah dead, but they made forgiveness easier, since they both supported the family in court. She knew their testimonies kept Jean-Jacques from receiving a prison term.

Abby wondered how everything was going at home. So many changes had happened in the last two years.

The Mast Island Institute and The Blue Heron Lodge would be opened with fanfare by the islanders in the next eight months.

Noah's former employer, The BNRS Corporation, helped the institute stock some of the expensive scientific equipment because their mission in the Southeast, paralleling their own, would be beneficial. And they could still make use of Noah's skills after he left them.

Noah had applied for several grants and believed he stood a good chance of them being awarded.

The locals appreciated the work on their homes and the new jobs that had been created. They talked about selling arts and crafts to visitors who came to *Belle Fleur*, Beautiful Flower, their newly named community. Vacationers biked or used a smaller shuttle service to see and photograph the color.

The atmosphere on the island lightened, and laughter could be heard in Loire Park as families picnicked and children played. Abby's heart swelled at the changes she and Vanna made possible with the support of family, her family.

A small health clinic had been built, and James Noble, the retired doctor, worked there several days a week with the help of a local nurse. So many opportunities had opened up.

"What do you think about Collette having a baby?" Noah asked.

"I'm happy. Jean-Jacques must have changed his mind." She thought about her talk with Jean-Jacques after Collette left him. "Andre is seven months. It's hard to be around a baby and not want one." She looked at her husband. "Are you hinting you're ready to be a father?"

He stood and drew her into his arms. "Maybe we should wait a couple of years. I'm enjoying the getting-to-know-you-part of our relationship too much to share."

Abby laughed, as he unwrapped the sarong. "I like the way you think, Dr. Hazzard."

"That's not all you like," he said, letting his lips speak for him.

CPSIA information can be obtained at www.ICGtesting.com
Printed in the USA
LVOW06s0145311215
468561LV00004B/10/P

9 781614 934042